SHATTERED HEARTS

THE BROKEN SERIES
BOOK 1

SHAE RUBY

Shattered Hearts Copyright © 2022 by Shae Ruby

All rights reserved.

No portion of this book may be reproduced in any form, or stored in a retrieval system, or transmitted in any form or by any means, electronic, mechanical, photocopying, recording or otherwise, without written permission from the publisher. It is illegal to copy this book, post it to a website, or distribute it by any others means without permission, except for the use of brief quotations in a book review.

This novel is entirely a work of fiction. The names, characters, and incidents portrayed in it are the work of the author's imagination. Any resemblance to people, living or dead, and events is entirely coincidental.

ISBN: 979-8-9860000-1-5

Cover Design by: Quirky Circe
Edited by: Lunar Rose Editing Services
Formatted by: Champagne Book Design at champagnebookdesign.com
Published by: Shae Ruby

For all the broken people who keep
fighting for every breath.

PLAYLIST

Love Like Heroin—Hollow City
Animals—Maroon 5
Cry—Parker Jack
All Time Low—Jon Bellion
Look After You—The Fray
Love Chained—Cannons
Ghost Town—Benson Boone
Inferno—Bella Poarch & Sub Urban
Bad Drugs—King Kavalier & ChrisLee
Let Me Down Slowly—Alec Benjamin
Cravin'—Stileto & Kendyle Paige
Hurts So Good—Astrid S
I'll Make You Love Me—Kat Leon

You can find the complete playlist on Spotify.

TRIGGER WARNINGS

Hello reader,

I write dark stories that can be disturbing to some. My books are not for the faint of heart, and my characters, many times, are not redeemable. This book contains dark themes to include graphic sex scenes, choking/breath play, dubious consent, graphic sexual abuse in the form of nightmares and flashbacks, drug use and abuse, mental health disorders, self-harm, suicidal thoughts with a plan, suicide attempt, and physical abuse/domestic violence.

I trust you know your triggers before proceeding, and always remember to take care of your mental health.

For more things Shae Ruby, visit authorshaeruby.com

National Suicide Prevention

If You Know Someone in Crisis:

Call the National Suicide Prevention Lifeline (Lifeline) at **1-800-273-TALK (8255),** or text the Crisis Text Line (**text HELLO to 741741**). Both services are free and available 24 hours a day, seven days a week. All calls are confidential. Contact social media outlets directly if you are concerned about a friend's social media updates or dial 911 in an emergency.

I am terrified by this dark thing
That sleeps in me;
All day I feel its soft, feathery
turnings, its malignity.
-Sylvia Plath-

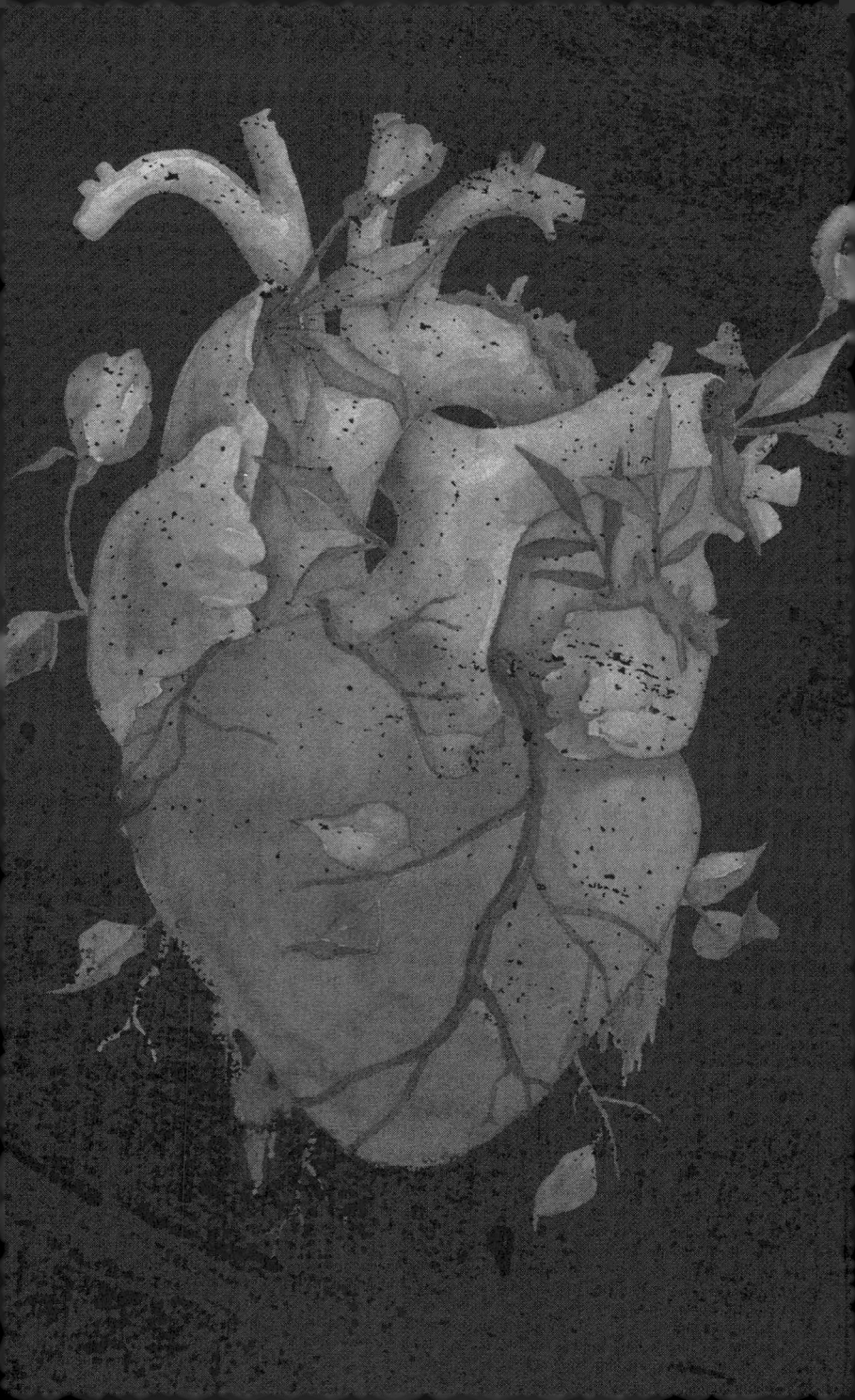

THE
CLIMB

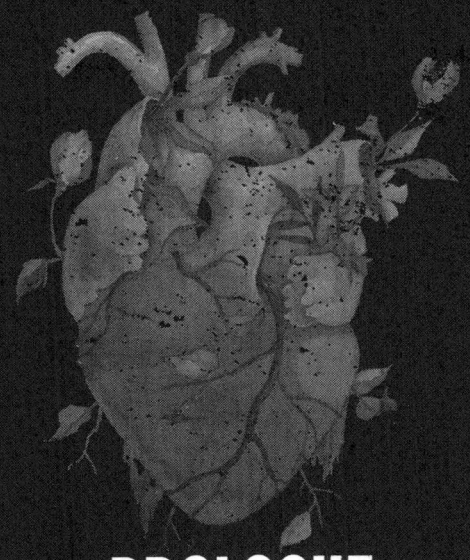

PROLOGUE

"*I loved you the moment I first saw you.*"

My throat gets tight again, and I can't speak but he takes that as his cue to leave. He begins to try to pull out, his knees planting on the mattress, except I reach out and grab his face.

"No. Stay, please. Don't go."

"If that's what you want," he says, and I nod my head.

He lies back down on top of me, bracing himself so he doesn't crush me. I run my fingers through his hair, and he rests his head in the crook of my neck, inhaling me deeply as I stroke him.

"Loving you fucking hurts," I say, not caring that I'm showing him weakness, not caring that my voice is broken.

"I'm sorry, I don't mean for it to ..." he says into my neck, the words muffled. "I don't want you to hurt."

"Sometimes I like the pain," I whisper. "Sometimes it reminds me I'm alive."

And it's not a lie ...

I knew the exact moment of the beginning of my demise. It was the moment I met his chameleon eyes; I saw the ruination flash across my eyes in slow motion. But I couldn't have stopped it if I wanted to, because no matter what, we just couldn't stay away. Even if we knew we were bad for each other.

I learned how to breathe underwater in the ocean that he kept trying to drown me in, until he was the only oxygen I needed. I learned how to swim with the current of the fucking tsunami that he was in my life, but like all tsunamis he destroyed everything in his path.

And he ruined *everything* for me, including multiple eye colors in the process.

But even through it all, he made me feel alive, even if I was fucking depleted.

I guess walking next to the devil will do that to you.

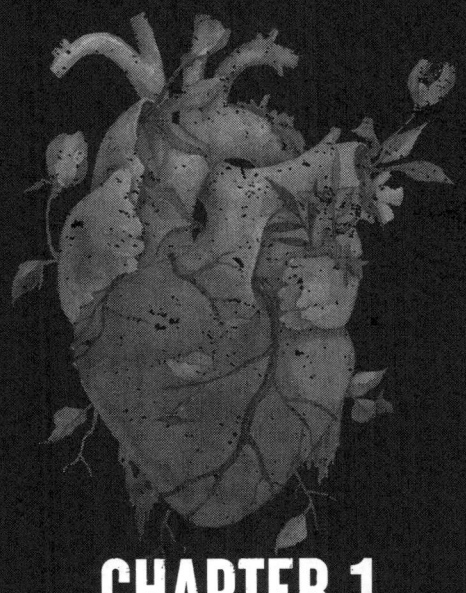

CHAPTER 1

HALLIE

It's the start of the spring semester, my very last one before I graduate from nursing school. Last semester was absolutely brutal, but this is the one when everyone gets lazy. It's okay, though. There's nothing more important to me than graduating.

Except for maybe parties.

I decided long ago that I would live my life to the fullest during this college experience, and I'm proud to say I have. I have been to so many parties I've lost count, drank so much that I forgot momentarily about the demons that haunt my every waking *and* sleeping moment, and I have been under so many people that consent finally felt tangible.

It was right in my.grasp, unlike all those other times.

Even then, I couldn't forget about all the pain, and I've come to accept some things are just imprinted on your soul forever. Dark stains that you can't wash out, no matter what detergent you use.

For me, that detergent was sex.

Sex to make up for everything that wasn't my choice.

And oh boy, did I ever choose.

Brittany and I spent our entire Christmas break going from one party to the next and working shifts at the hospital together. Now we are both ready to settle down and get back in the groove of things.

I met her during orientation during freshman year almost four years ago. She sat behind me at one of the long tables in the classroom, and I looked at her the entire time. There was just something about her that kept pulling me in, as if our souls had been searching for each other. I like to think that my trauma recognized hers, that fucked up people attract each other, even when they don't look to.

I was turned in my seat and distracted the entire time, and I stared at her for so long the professors cleared their throats repeatedly. Even then, I didn't speak to her until the end of the day. I waited until it was over to walk after her.

Ever since then, she has been my best friend, my shoulder to cry on, the one I lean on. She's the one who is always there. We moved in together after freshman year, and my life has never been better. Now instead of my life looking black and white, some faint colors have finally started slipping back in, giving me hope for the first time in so long.

I walk to the tiny kitchen island that only sits two people and plop down with a bowl of cereal cradled gently in my hands. This is dinner tonight, but I guess I'm just lucky it's not ramen again. I love to cook but don't really have the time for it. I'm not as fortunate as Brit, whose family is paying for her living expenses, but I am lucky that she allows me to live here rent-free. I could not afford to live on my own with a part-time CNA salary while also being in school full-time. I don't want to have to choose between the two, especially not when I only have one semester left.

I lift my spoon to my mouth and try to catch the contents

as the milk splashes back down into the bowl, some drops landing on my hand, which I quickly wipe with my shirt.

"Are you seriously eating Cheerios again, Hallie?"

"Beggars can't be choosers, Brit." I sigh as I set my spoon down and look at her. She's wearing a fitted crop top with her perfect, fake tits out on display and the tightest jeans known to humankind. I bet if she bends over, they'll rip right down her ass crack. "Are you going out with Jacob tonight?"

"No," she smirks, "you know I don't do that two-time shit."

Thank God for that.

"Thank the angels… I couldn't bear to hear you fucking that one again."

"Okay, before you moved in, I was very clear that I'm loud during sex. And that's the biggest dick I've ever had."

The smirk on my face only widens when she narrows her eyes at me, and I can't deny that I love the banter we've always had. "So how come you're not hitting it again?"

"Who said I'm not?" Her smoky eyeshadow is a stark contrast to her sea-foam green eyes, which currently sparkle with defiance.

"You just did."

"Well, you should know better than to believe that shit," she chuckles and winks at me. "Don't wait up for me, I'll probably be gone all night."

"All night?" I ask incredulously, trying to calculate how much sleep I can get before I have to wake up in the morning. Probably one hour if I have nightmares. "But school starts back up tomorrow. I was hoping we could ride together since we have the same schedule this semester." My best impression of a pout is pretty pathetic, but it doesn't keep me from trying.

"We can do that, but yes, all night." She heads for the door. "Sleep is for the dead. Especially when I have a dick appointment." She laughs and shuts the door behind her.

She leaves me sitting here asking myself why I don't have a

dick appointment too, and my cereal gets soggy in the milk. I sigh and dump the milk in the sink, then the cereal in the trash.

My hunger left me as quickly as it came.

The silence mocks me in the tiny two-bedroom apartment, but I try my best to ignore it. I've never been particularly good at being alone, always needing to have a boyfriend or a friend to rely on so I don't feel the sadness constantly creeping back in. It's the quiet that gets to me.

I pad over to my room as I feel the panic attack looming in the distance just from thinking about going to school tomorrow. I don't like firsts, they give me anxiety. There's never been any good to come from them. First boyfriends, first kisses, first time having sex… it all makes me cringe. I want to rip off the Band-Aid. Go from zero to the tenth time, skip the beginning and get to the middle.

I go to the bottom drawer of my dresser, where I keep a wooden box of memories; the few that matter to me, the ones I kept through foster care. Pictures of my brothers and my mom staring back at me, taunting my very existence. Even still, I look at them for a short time before grabbing the blunt I've been saving for special moments such as these and snapping the lid of my box shut. My peace stick glows in the dark as I light it and take a hit, not giving a fuck that my bedroom is going to reek for the next week. I just want my troubles to vanish, that's all I care about right now. Usually, I resort to more extreme measures, ones that fill the emptiness even if it's only for a short time. The sluggish feeling I have when I drink myself into oblivion and pop a Xanax is unmatched. Sometimes I just like my world to move in slow motion. It helps me forget everything I need to. I'm pretty sure there's something wrong with my brain, a chemical imbalance, but that's neither here nor there.

The only thing that matters is that I ran out of my little blue pills, so this will have to suffice for now.

This will hold me over.

This won't leave me like everything else does.

The nursing assembly is the most anticipated event at the beginning of the semester. I'm not sure why. It's literally just speaker after speaker, but it gets us out of class, and that's all that matters. Some people skip it, most don't. Technically you're not supposed to. If I'm being honest, I secretly love the prizes, the games, and the competitions. I love the rivalry between students of different semesters. I eat it all up and save some of the energy for later.

Today, I have a poster with pictures of our graduating class encased in glitter and bright colors. We have bubbles, matching shirts, and I came prepared to be the loudest when they tell us to represent our graduation year. They host some competitions, and I win first place in a few. My prizes are a coffee mug that says 'World's Best Nurse' and a clip with a prayer that goes on the visor of my car. Something about the angels I don't believe in.

The rest of the day goes by in a blur of Medical-Surgical and Nursing Management, which are the only two nursing courses I have left aside from the clinical that starts next week. I also have a fine arts course that I have to take to fulfill the degree plan, which I'm not looking forward to. I thought I had fulfilled it already but it turns out French is actually a humanities course.

Who fucking knew? Certainly not me.

Now I'm stuck with an art class I'll probably need to be high to get through. Not that I'm bad at sketching, I'm just awful at vulnerability. I've always believed you need a certain level of emotion to be a good artist; emotions are not my forté. I've been numb for the better part of the last ten years. Partially from drugs and partially from my heart being ripped out of my chest by my traitorous family.

But if there's one place I refuse to end up, it's back in a mental hospital with my shoelaces confiscated and foam trays for my food. My stomach fills with dread just thinking of it, and I shudder. Fake it 'till you make it, right?

So I fake it, I pretend.

I pretend I don't have a heart.

I pretend I can't feel.

I pretend I'm not triggered.

But there's only so much pretending can do when hazel eyes follow you to the depths of your worst nightmares, and they don't let you climb back out. I survived a long time without sleep. Now I take medicine for the nightmares.

Prazosin.

Combine that with Xanax for anxiety and panic attacks, and you have the perfect cocktail to knock you the fuck out, no nightmares attached.

It's bliss, and the closest thing I've known to happiness in over a decade, so I'm clinging to it for dear life. The nights are restful, my sleep seized by a darkness so black, nothing can penetrate it.

Except when it doesn't work.

The car ride home with Brit is silent. I mentally make a list of all the tasks I need to get done. I fully intend to transfer said list to my forgotten planner as soon as we get home. My type A personality, or OCD as my therapist likes to call it, demands that all areas of my life are in order. Which is fucking laughable because my life hasn't been in order since that fateful night when my stepfather knocked on my bedroom door. But here I am, making to-do lists and planning my life by the hour to give myself a semblance of normalcy, a shred of comfort.

We pull into the designated parking spot of our duplex on the outskirts of Austin and head inside. The light gray three-piece sectional with black pillows and white faux fur rug perfectly contrasts the dark brown hardwood floors. The cushions look more inviting than ever as I throw my backpack on the floor and kick off my shoes. Brit heads to her room, where I imagine she also plans on sleeping after never getting to last night.

Just ten minutes. I need a nap so badly.

I lie down on the couch and flip on the TV, searching for my favorite show on Netflix. I lower the volume as *Friends* plays in the background and turn away from the television screen. My eyes start closing of their own accord and my body feels heavy, and I surrender to it. I don't do that too often anymore.

Hazel eyes flecked with gold.

Toss.

My mom punching and screaming at him.

Turn.

I don't believe you.

Toss.

You're a liar.

Turn.

Knock. Knock. Knock.

I sit up abruptly and fall off the couch and onto my ass, my hands hurting from their attempt at cushioning the fall. I force myself to take deep breaths.

In. Out. In. Out. In. Out.

My mouth is dry. My ears are ringing. The only sound I can hear is my pulse beating loudly like a war drum in my head. The dizziness overwhelms me and makes me nauseous.

Deep breaths... fucking steady, Hals.

The steady thumping of my feet is the only sound as I run to the bathroom and dry heave, my stomach absent of any contents since I didn't eat lunch. My knees sting as I lay my cheek on the toilet, the cool porcelain chasing the queasiness away. I really need to get my shit together. *I really need my Xanax.*

I picked up my prescription this morning before school just in case this happened, knowing that my anxiety is crippling and nothing helps it the way my crutch does. The medicine bottle sits on my nightstand, mocking me. However, I still pick it up and pop two blue pills, washing them down with a warm beer left over on my nightstand from a few days ago. Fucking nasty.

My bed dips as I lie down on it, and I yank the covers up to my waist. My eyes hurt as I push the heels of my hands against them, refusing to cry, refusing to feel, refusing to remember. Because remembering never helped anyone, and forgetting is the name of the game.

Like a watercolor painting, I want everything to fade, to blend, and to mix together until the memories disappear and I'm never plagued by them again.

The hallway is bright, the walls white, and the floors have shiny tiles to match. I stop in front of a row of pictures hanging a few feet from me and try to stare at them, but I can't focus when his smile catches me off guard.

I look around, biting my nails, but then suddenly stop when I remember what a disgusting habit it actually is. My nervousness doesn't go unnoticed by him though, and he's staring now as he leans against the opposite wall, his green eyes hooded.

Brit joins me, her own green eyes crinkling at the corners as she speaks to me, and we stare intently at the pictures and point at different ones. At least she's genuine about it, I'm just trying not to stare at him instead.

The feeling of being watched doesn't fade, so when I meet his gaze, I startle, jumping and pushing my friend by accident. A slow grin spreads over my face, and in a sudden rush of bravery, I hold eye contact for a fraction longer than appropriate. He returns my smile slowly, his perfect, straight teeth gleaming white under all the lights. That's all it takes for my stomach to flutter, a stupid fucking smile. I hate that it does, and I remind myself that my heart can't afford to be broken yet again.

That finally breaks the spell, and I force myself to look away, only Brit looks back at him knowingly. We have to go, however. I don't want to be late to class this early in the semester, so we say goodbye to each other. I wave at Brittany until she turns around and saunters to her next class, Art Appreciation. Maybe I should've enrolled in that instead.

My art class is in Room 104, and someone calls out to me as I walk through the open door. "Hey, Hallie!" My friend Anna wraps me up in a tight hug, picking me up off the ground. She's pretty tall for a woman, and she always makes fun of me for being fun-sized. At least, that's what I like to call myself. We say our hellos and part ways quickly. She's probably running late for her class.

I look back towards the door, looking for my green-eyed boy, but he's gone. I walk to the long table, dropping into a chair with just one vacant spot next to me. Perfect. I hate feeling crowded.

As the professor begins to talk to us, I can't help but wonder who he is and if I'll ever see him again. He didn't look like a nice guy, but then again, I've never liked the things that are good for me.

Maybe I need a little chaos in my life after all.

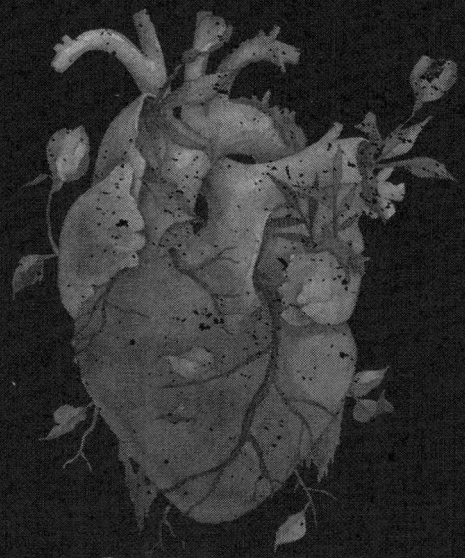

CHAPTER 2

ZAYNE

The registration office is empty, and I count my lucky stars as I stand in line with no one in front of me. I wonder why the fuck I'm feeling so impulsive about her, she barely even looked at me. Maybe it's because she's beautiful, with her dark brown eyes and dark brown hair. Pale skin that begs to be marked, and a cute little upturned nose. What really caught my attention, though were her full, pouty lips that I just wanted my cock sliding through...

I can't figure it out.

That shouldn't be enough to get me to do this. It feels extreme to be enrolling in a class just to be near her, to have her say one word to me.

I just don't know what it is.

My aunt stands behind the tall counter and asks me for my identification card as if she doesn't know who I am. I raise my eyebrow at her and she just smiles at me and shrugs one shoulder. I find it all very amusing, but I came here with a purpose, so I decide to stay focused.

"What brings you here today?" Her voice drips with curiosity, but she's deluded if she thinks I'll tell her the real reason. I've never willingly signed up for a class that I know I'd be shit at, but I'll do it just this once.

"I need your help, a personal favor, if you will."

Now it's her turn to raise her eyebrow, and I chuckle, knowing she's not going to let this one go. My sigh screams of exasperation as I explain to her that I want to enroll in the Art class that Hallie takes, and I give her the exact room number, class time, and class name.

I don't tell her I can tell Hallie will be a victim of my obsessions or that she brings out my possessive side, that I'm already thinking of her as my girl. None of that is important right now.

Surprisingly, she enrolls me without any issues or further questions, and I go on about my life, wondering when I will see Hallie next. It should be interesting to sit next to her until the end of the semester. I wonder how long it will take to snare her in my trap.

Hallie.

A beautiful name for a beautiful girl.

I can still clearly see her bright smile and eyes twinkling in the fluorescent lights, biting her nails and then stopping abruptly. She held eye contact as if in defiance, daring me to come to her.

I *have* to have her.

I leave the registration office and go back to the parking lot to look for my car, the black 370Z shining like obsidian under the sun. The gravel crunches under my shoes as I unlock it and slide my backpack into the passenger side, closing the door carefully.

And then I think of all the ways I'm going to get Hallie to be mine, all the ways I'm going to make her love me, and all the ways I'm going to make her suffer. Because can I even be with her without fucking everything up? Probably not, but I need to find out if she's worth it, even if I ruin everything for us.

Art class is a fucking bust, even as I sit here and try to make sense of what the hell the professor is saying. It goes in one ear and out the other, especially once I notice Hallie sitting a few seats from me.

She looks at her sketchpad intently, shading something that I can't see from this distance, which makes me instantly regret not taking the empty seat next to hers. I mentally will her to look up at me, but it doesn't work, so instead I twirl my pencil in my hands impatiently, wondering how noticeable it would be if I move spots now.

I want to see her eyes again.

The professor stands at the front of the classroom, discussing the syllabus and the different assignments we will have to complete this semester. She rambles about how we are graded and how we can study for tests. I can't remember one fucking word because all I see is *her*.

A dainty hand raises, and the professor asks if she has a question. My heart palpitates in anticipation, and I hold my breath as she nods—

"Hallie," she says quietly, "Hallie Cox." She clears her throat nervously, her neck and face flushing an angry, red color, "I noticed the final exam says to be determined—will it be an art piece or a written exam?" All my breath whooshes out when I hear her husky voice.

"I'm not sure, Ms. Cox, but that's why it says to be determined," the professor says sarcastically.

"Of course," Hallie mumbles, looking back down at her sketchpad.

She tries to make herself smaller, as if folding in on herself would make her disappear. The curtain of hair obscures her face when she tilts her head forward, her brown waves toppling over the desk. I take advantage of this moment and walk over to the chair next to hers, plopping down in it as I give in to my impulses.

Startled, she glances up, staring at me intently, recognition flashing across her features.

Her soft brown eyes widen in surprise. I know she wasn't expecting me to be here, and more than likely, she hadn't even noticed me in the classroom before this moment. A pang of disappointment runs through me, but I shove it down, not wanting to scare her yet. She will be obsessed with me soon too, it's only a matter of time.

I grin at her, showing all my teeth, trying to make her feel more at ease. Like I'm not about to plow through her life and fuck everything up. But rather than disarming her, she looks terrified when she turns forward in her seat to face the professor.

Hallie doesn't look at me one fucking time throughout the lecture, even though she's all I can focus on. It doesn't piss me off like it usually would, instead I feel taunted. Now I have to have her. No matter what happens, I have to taste her. I'm not sure why I get these urges, but once I fixate on someone, it's hard to get me to stop.

Class is over and everyone is rising from their seats, yet I stay firmly planted in mine, waiting for her to get up. I frankly don't give a shit if it's weird. Maybe I want her to know that I am. Which I'm sure by now she's noticed. She glances quickly at me before scooping up her belongings, slinging her backpack over her shoulder, and walking in the opposite direction, so she doesn't have to pass me. But I'm not ready to let her go yet, so I grab her wrist and gently tug. Brown eyes narrow at me suspiciously, and my heart stutters in my chest when she looks me up and down. It's almost like she's assessing me, making mental notes of everything about me. I should be unnerved, although I have this feeling of...excitement more.

"What the fuck are you doing?" Her now wide eyes collide with mine, the brown turning almost entirely black as her pupils dilate. Funny first words, but I'll let it slide this once.

"Hallie, right?" I smirk, which only causes her to stiffen.

"Right."

"Well, aren't you going to ask me what my name is too?"

"No."

Feisty little thing. I love this game even more.

"I'm Zayne." I tighten my grip on her. "I would say nice to meet you, but it seems like I'm the only one who thinks so."

"You're correct, Zayne. I'm not really into bondage," she says, trying to free her wrist from my grasp, but I tighten it even more instead. She looks intently at my hold on her, and I can see how she's trying to figure out the best way to get me to let her go.

"You look like you would be."

"Excuse me?" The look of outrage she gives me is amusing, and a cute wrinkle forms between her eyebrows.

"You could be into bondage if you'd just let me show you."

"Zayne, when I say excuse me, it means don't repeat yourself. That was your out, and you should've taken it." She rolls her eyes, her black lashes almost touching her eyebrows.

"The only out I want is with you, baby." I pause for effect, knowing damn well how corny that just sounded. But it's worked before, so maybe she'll bite. Probably not, though. "Go out with me."

"Wow, you're smooth." I wait with bated breath for her answer. "No, thank you." She yanks her hand out of my grip and struts out of the classroom, leaving me cold from her rejection. I was almost certain she was going to say, no, yet I also knew damn well there was a possibility that she wouldn't. That's because she doesn't know me yet. If she did, she would've never used that word with me. It only riles me up and makes me more determined.

She doesn't understand that she's just made the first move in our game. She thinks she won, but I have plans of my own, and I love a fucking challenge.

Even with anger festering in my veins, I head home, knowing exactly what will make it better. I speed all the way to the house, not bothering with red lights. I'll undoubtedly get a ticket, but ask me if I care. All I want right now is to go to my room and get my fix, and that's precisely what I do after I park in the driveway.

My hands shake slightly as I uncap my prescription bottle

and fish out an Adderall. It's been a habit for a few years now, although I've been taking it for the last ten years of my life. I first began to take more than I should when I was a sophomore in high school, after my parents split up and I needed to take the edge off somehow. I saw people take it during house parties and I knew I had it at home, so why not see what the hype was about? Turns out I fucking loved it.

I have a prescription for two tablets per day, but I probably end up taking three to four. It depends on whether I want an extra bump of energy if I party at night, and once I run out of my prescription early, I call my supplier who I also sell for from time to time, just because I feel like it. He refills my prescription, my own personal pharmacy.

I swallow the pill dry and get ready for work, putting on my black slacks and white dress shirt with the bow tie. The restaurant I work at is the fanciest one in town, and I can make hundreds of dollars on tips on any given Friday or Saturday night, which are the only shifts I usually take.

I don't particularly enjoy being a server, mainly because I'm not exactly a people person. I know how to interact and I can be nice when I want to be, but I don't look forward to it unless it's someone I'm interested in. I also really hate the side work and leaving late in the middle of the night after everything is said and done, but I do what I have to do to get by. Not that I technically have to, my mom is fucking loaded. But I like to feel like I'm independent sometimes.

This job is also very understanding of my mental health *situations*. I can't control when I have to miss work for a week or more, and they quickly find a replacement for me for the time I need off. They work well with the schedule I request since they know I'm a student, and they never pressure me to take on more hours or even shifts on days that they know I can't.

I tie my shoes and prepare to have a long night.

A night without *her*.

A pointless one.

My buddy, Xander, is throwing a party tonight and I heard there will be plenty of alcohol and drugs to go around. Just what I need on my night off from work. In a way, though, I'm not actually off from work, because there will be people looking to score, and I have everything under the sun to offer a quick fix. One backpack full of dope, blow, and fairy dust.

Ice. Molly. Adderall. Xanax. Acid.

You name it, I have it.

I park in the roundabout right across from the front doors, a circular fountain in the center of the Italian-style house. The home is littered with college kids, strobe lights bouncing from the grass and into the sky, but yet it loses none of its charms. One thing is obvious when you look at this house: they're really fucking rich. It must be at least 15,000 square feet, much bigger than my own home, and I thought *we* were rich.

The yard looks disgusting, though. I have to step over people and trash before finally making it inside. There are couples piled onto a huge five-piece leather sectional, said couch barely visible anymore. Some of them are making out, some are grinding on each other, some… well, they're probably fucking. No way to know without looking, and I really don't want to look.

What I want is to find my next target—the one who's going to get my sweet talk and never hear from me again. Sex is just a transaction to me, one in which I don't give much. Some of these girls, however…they don't mind giving.

Like polar opposite sides of a magnet, my eyes are drawn across the room. Drawn to *her*. She's wearing a little black dress that reaches her mid-thigh and sparkles with every turn of her body. It leaves little to the imagination and my eyes wrap around every curve as my cock throbs against my pants.

Fuck.

She's gotta be fucking kidding me. A hundred bucks says she won't give me the time of day, but fuck it. I'll still try.

Hallie's leaning against the wall with her hot friend, only I don't really have a thing for green eyes today. I want the brown ones. The feeling of being possessed takes over my body, and the impulsivity I feel when it comes to her is something I have no control over. And that's exactly what pushes me to walk in her direction until I stop in front of her, and once we're toe to toe, I raise my hands to the wall, caging her in.

Her friend looks back and forth between us in a bit of a panic, but Hallie stays calm within the eye of the storm. And there's a fucking storm, that's for sure.

"Look who's here…" I drawl, "I didn't think a good girl like you would be at a party like this." She snorts at that and laughs, which definitely catches me off guard. Her friend only smiles momentarily before glaring at me again.

"Oh, Zay. There's nothing good about me, honey." I stiffen as she puts a hand on my shoulder, and I look down at it for a second before directing my eyes back to hers. "I'm poisonous…but I can taste very sweet." There's a twinkle in her eye, the only sign her body wants to betray her words.

What. The. Fuck.

Is she flirting with me? Who fucking knows, but I'm going with it.

"And will I get to taste you tonight?" I ask her with a wink, and her breathing picks up slightly. The rise and fall of her chest is hypnotizing, and I have to physically force myself to stop staring.

"No." Hallie smirks, her pouty lips curling slightly, looking like she's fighting a smile.

I grin like a lunatic and reach for a stray lock of her hair, tucking it behind her ear. This feels like a game of cat and mouse, and I have an inkling that she's playing hard to get even though she wants me.

"Will you go out with me? Just once? Just so I can say we did?"

She laughs at that. *Laughs at me.* But for once, it doesn't make me want to rip someone's head off. For once, I feel like I'm part of a joke and not on the outs of one.

"I'll think about it." She pretends to be annoyed as she dramatically huffs, but even I can tell it's an act. "But only because you sound pathetic when you say it like that."

"So you're taking pity on me?"

"Absolutely."

"I've never had anyone pity fuck me before, but I guess I can start today," I chuckle as I watch her eyes widen, the brown of her irises beginning to shrink as her pupils dilate yet again. Isn't that a biological response? Her body is reacting to me, and I watch her intently for more signs of *wanting* me.

She laughs at me yet again, and I can't help but think how beautiful she is. The pink tinge to her cheeks is adorable, and the glassiness of her eyes when she laughs makes me want to find out why they look that way. It's fucking mesmerizing.

She is fucking mesmerizing.

Hallie squirms, searching my face for signs of surrender, or I guess to see if she's free to get back to the party and her friend, but I'm not ready yet. I press closer into her body and bend at the waist to let our foreheads touch lightly. Her minty breath mingles with mine for a few moments, our lips inches from each other. Just when she looks ready to give in though, I abruptly straighten and walk away.

This is a game I'm determined to win, but first, I'll enjoy playing with her a bit. I'll do anything to get my hands on her and probably, more than likely, never let her go. However, it will always be for the wrong reasons because I—

Well, I'm afraid because I destroy everything I touch. I can't help it. It's the way I've always been.

Hallie should've said no.

She should've stayed away.

But now that she didn't...

I can't let her go.

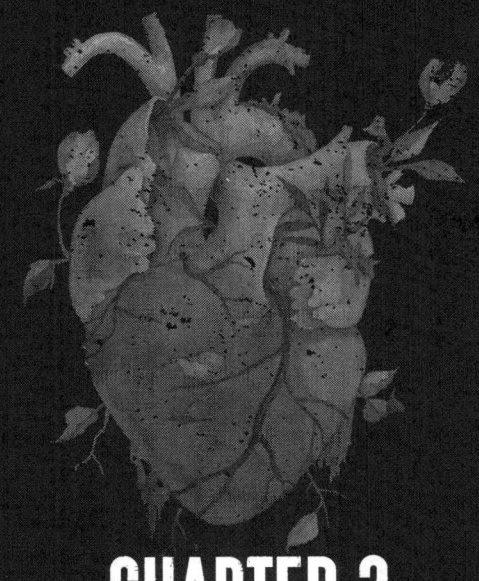

CHAPTER 3

HALLIE

I can almost hear the swoosh of the alcohol and benzos mixing together in my bloodstream, taking me on a ride.

Brittany's hand is clammy as I grab it and pull her as far away from Zayne as possible. Drinking and dancing are my focus tonight, not some bad boy with green eyes. I came here to get fucking wasted, and that's precisely what I'm going to do, even if I just spent the last few minutes flirting with him.

I know he's wrong for me, that much is obvious. That's the reason I rejected him in class, but he just doesn't seem to give up. And when I'm drunk and high…I feel adventurous.

Brittany and I go to the makeshift bartender and ask him to make cherry vodka sours for us—our girly drink of choice before shit gets serious. We'll probably get roofied, but it might be a good time, after all. He smiles and whips up our drinks quickly, but we just shoot them back, not bothering to savor them. We keep going back for more: Jameson, Vodka, Tequila.

One after another until everything becomes a blur.

I haul my friend to the middle of the room where everyone is grinding on each other, stumbling over my own feet, and I take advantage of all the people around me so I can hide from the beautiful man who keeps coming after me. I let myself drown in a sea of bodies as I grind on Brit, my ass to her center as we sway together to the beat of the music. I know it looks sexy, we've been told before, and I close my eyes as I lose myself to the beat of the song, the feel of it.

Focusing is more difficult than I thought, but should I really be surprised when I lose count of the shots?

Some guy with deep blue eyes steps in front of me and offers me his hand; it seems to be an open invitation, except I'm not sure what for. Dancing doesn't come to mind when I take it. He leads me to the couch where everyone was making out earlier, and it's clear that he has set a bar of expectations for how our time is going to go. I would hate to be a disappointment, so I will probably indulge him.

We sit on the couch and I can instantly feel my body becoming heavy, probably the effects of the Xanax and the alcohol. When he pulls out the joint and lights it, I wonder momentarily if this will be the cherry on top to put me into respiratory depression. I wish I could say I let those thoughts lead me to better choices, but that's not what happened, and although I'm a great actress with a generous serving of pathological liar on the side, I'd like to tell the truth about this.

I fucked up again.

The stranger takes a hit and passes the joint to me, my lips drying as they wrap around it. I hold the smoke in my lungs longer than usual to feel the rush in my head, then give it back. We play this game for a few minutes. Puff, puff, pass. It's entertaining at first, and just as I feel my heart slowing down in my chest and my limbs begin to grow heavy, he grabs my head and pulls me in for a kiss. Except it's not really a kiss at all, just trading smoke. I can feel him push it into my lungs with a dizzying effect.

Our shotgunning is abruptly ended by someone roughly yanking me off the couch, making me stumble as I'm set on my feet. I sway in place for a moment before I steady myself, trying to keep my outrage in check for now because I know it will not help the situation. He's fucking *insane*.

"Do not fucking touch her!" Zayne yells as he pushes me behind him, which causes a lot of people to stare. I try to grab his hand, mostly hoping it will get him to calm down, but he quickly shakes me off and climbs on top of the blue-eyed guy who was so kindly sharing his weed with me. The crazed look in his eyes is scary, his face turning red and his neck veins bulging as he throws one, two, three punches that land on the guy's face. On the third punch, my kind stranger is a goner, swiftly knocked out. The psycho who pulled me off the couch just leaves the poor guy there, lying unconscious with blood coming out of his nose in spurts.

"What the fuck, Zayne?!"

"No one fucking touches what's mine!" He's yelling at me, well, more screaming really, and causing a scene. *Of course, this is my life.*

I need more Xanax. I need Zen.

I can barely focus as it is. The fucking ground keeps swaying under me as I make my best attempt at standing. I'm dizzy, and I can feel myself forgetting where I am or how I got here, my thoughts disappearing from my brain like a fog that clears when the sun comes out. Except there's no sun in my life, and this can only end one way—tragedy—just like everything else.

Fuck getting drunk, and fuck Zayne. He's really fucking with my vibe tonight.

There's a pent-up aggression that comes out when I'm wasted. I can feel the emotions beginning to consume me, and all I crave is the bliss of sleep. The oblivion. The dreamless void. I need it like I need air and water. I need to not feel or think or be aware that I'm breathing.

"I need to use the bathroom." I mutter, then look at him expectantly, but he won't let go of my hand. *What the fuck?* "Are you going to let go, or am I peeing in front of you?" My words keep slurring, and I'm sure I couldn't walk a line to save my ass.

"I'll take you. You're wasted." His voice is laced with concern, except after the shit he just pulled with that guy, I don't want to get his hopes up. There's no fucking way I'm going out with him. I have to find a way to let him down easy. I have enough crazy for the both of us, and from the looks of it he will probably make a scene if I tell him this.

"No shit." I laugh loudly, cringing when the sound reaches my ears. "I can go alone. Just wait for me here."

I slip out of his grasp before he can protest and make my way through the crowd, quickly realizing my mistake—I don't have a clue where I'm going. I'm going in circles, and whenever I think I'm heading in the right direction to the bathroom, I forget where I'm going all over again.

Fuck.

I sway on my feet as I stop to try to think, but before I can panic, Zayne is back and leading me toward the bathroom by my elbow. If there was a God, I would thank him right now for this single miracle. Maybe going out on one date wouldn't be such a bad idea, especially if there's a nice side to him. *You're not going on a fucking date with him. Get it together.*

Thankfully, he lets me go to the bathroom *alone,* but he waits for me outside the door. At least he gave me that much, especially since I don't think he's the kind of guy who does what he's asked.

I sit on the toilet for what feels like an eternity. Every time I'm about to get up to leave, I space out all over again. This is all very inconvenient. My high is ruined, and I want to go home and sleep it off. Maybe mixing the Xanax with the alcohol was a very bad idea.

Knock. Knock. Knock.

I get up in a panic and pull my pants up, forgetting where I am. The bathroom disappears, and I'm violently thrust back to my dark bedroom as my stepfather knocks on my door three times—always three times. I pull the blankets over my head and slow my breathing down, pretending to be asleep. But he doesn't buy it, doesn't believe me, doesn't give up as he crosses the room and rips the blankets off my body—

Zayne strides into the bathroom and shakes me lightly by my shoulders, then tangles his hands in my hair and tugs my head up to look at him.

"Hallie," he looks at me with questions in his eyes. "Where did you go?"

"Somewhere no one can follow…"

"Baby, don't you know I will always find you?"

I suck in a sharp breath, feeling like he's moving too fast. Scratch that—he is moving at lightning speed. "I need to get out of here. I'll get Brittany and my keys."

"There's no fucking way you're driving out of here, you could barely get off that toilet. I'll take you home."

"Don't act like you haven't been drinking." I roll my eyes and give him a mocking tone. The drugs and alcohol always make me feel brave. That's a bigger problem than I choose to acknowledge, not that it'll change any time soon.

"I have, but nowhere near as much as you. And it's obvious who has a higher tolerance."

"Is it obvious? Are you calling me a lightweight?"

"No, but you are basically on the verge of alcohol poisoning, so let's get you home."

The drive home is a blur. I don't remember when I got in the car with him or even how I got to the apartment. All I know is that he's tucking me in right now, and I can already feel the beginnings of a headache looming in the distance.

I grab his wrist as he pulls the covers over me and gives me a featherlight kiss on my forehead, so subtle I barely feel it. His lips are the softest that have ever touched me, and they're gone too fast. "One date," I mumble, my lips and tongue numb enough to make my words sound jumbled.

"One," he agrees, and I let go of his wrist.

I feel cold as he leaves my room and closes the door with a soft click, but warmth is a distant memory that I can barely recall anymore. I adjust my head on the pillow as the darkness wraps its claws around me, dragging me down for another round of sour lullabies straight from the devil's lips.

The sun finds its way through my blinds and feels like daggers stabbing my eyes. It takes every remaining bit of my energy to stir in bed. Most of it was deposited into the toilet during my trips to exorcize the alcohol from my body in the middle of the night. It's too bad that the alcohol was the only thing being exorcized, though. It could have been helpful to expel my inner demons too.

My head pounds in tune with my heart, just as I knew it would, but I slowly sit up and notice that my nightstand has a bottle of water and ibuprofen waiting for me.

Zayne.

He was the perfect gentleman last night, bringing me home and tucking me in. He made me feel safe, even if I vaguely remember him pummeling someone's face in for sharing a smoke with me. Damn him and his jealousy. I have enough of that for the both of us, and I refuse to be in a relationship with a mirror image of myself.

He's cocky as fuck and thinks this is going somewhere.

He's wrong.

I don't do bad boys.

Liar, they're just your type.

When our date is over, I'll fuck his friend just to prove my point.

As my mother used to say...

Nothing but a whore, whore, whore.

Well, I'll prove to her I'm a whore again and again.

I did, however, promise him one date, not that I keep my promises.

But just this once, I will.

One date.

It's not like I'm going to fall in love with the guy.

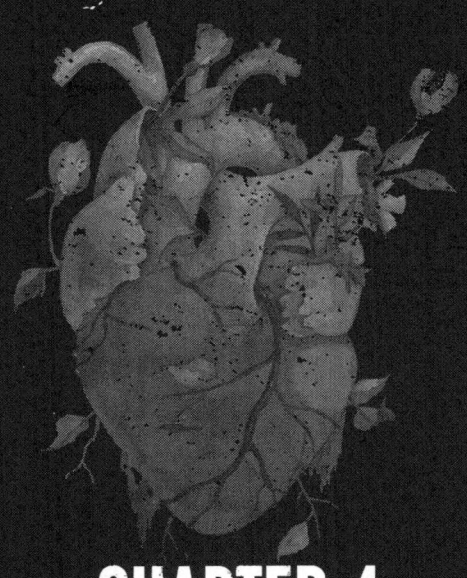

CHAPTER 4

ZAYNE

My room is pitch black as I lie in my bed, listening to the sound of my own breathing. My body feels weak even though I barely drank, and it refuses to function even though I've been in bed for fifteen hours.

I'm exhausted no matter what I do, and I know the darkness has reared its ugly head and settled, ready to keep me company. Lately, I've had a tough time reminding my brain what happiness is, because I haven't felt it in years.

I just don't remember it.

I have abstract memories of events where I know I was happy, but the actual feeling...I haven't felt it in a very long time.

I live in the depths of a darkness I didn't even know existed.

And now I'm fixating on Hallie and where I went wrong. I put my number in her phone and texted myself just to make sure I got her number too, but she hasn't tried to contact me. I'm trying to keep a semblance of self-control, which is not my strong suit. But fuck, I'm really trying. I want to wait for her to text me first, but every minute that goes by plagues me with thoughts I don't want in my head. Every tick of the clock makes me fucking itch, and I need to scratch it badly.

What did I do wrong?

Why doesn't she want me?

Am I not good enough?

Does anyone even love me?

FUCK.

I run my hand through my hair and yank hard, needing some kind of pain to ground me.

I just need to shut off my mind.

I need to make it stop.

I need sleep.

I turn over in bed and let the darkness swallow me whole. I welcome it, embrace it, call out to it.

Hello darkness, my old friend.

Buzzing sounds bounce off the walls of my mind over and over and over again, until I can't drown them out anymore. I squint my eyes open, knowing that it's more than likely the middle of the night and I could sleep until tomorrow. I could welcome the darkness again, but this time I don't. For whatever reason, I am drawn to the little machine with the blasted bright light, and give in, unlocking it.

> **Hallie: Hey, it's me**
>
> **Hallie: I guess that's vague. It's Hallie.**
>
> **Hallie: I noticed you put your name in my phone in typical asshole fashion. Why am I not surprised?**

My heart skips several beats and my palms suddenly feel clammy. I wasn't expecting her to actually text me—let alone at one in the morning. I was definitely hoping for it, nonetheless.

Dread fills my stomach as I think of her being at another party sharing a joint with a stranger again, and I physically shake the thoughts out of my head. What if she's not home right now, and that's why she's texting me so late? I swear, I'm my own worst fucking enemy. My mind controls me when no one else can. I decide to reply after all because there's no way I can sleep anymore.

> **Zayne: It wasn't meant to be a surprise, just another small way of making sure you can't ghost me...**
>
> **Hallie: I couldn't ghost you even if I wanted to. We have a class together.**
>
> **Zayne: Wow... that gives me so much peace of mind. Thank you for that. *laughing emoji***

Somehow this feels natural. The words are flowing effortlessly and I don't even have to put my mask on, which isn't usual. Socializing can be tedious for me, and I don't usually even have to talk to women much at all before they're falling into bed with me. For the most part, I charm them, fuck them, and never speak to them again.

> **Hallie: You're welcome, I'm good at knowing what people need.**
>
> **Zayne: I bet you are. So about that date? How about tomorrow I pick you up at six and I'll take you somewhere for dinner?**
>
> **Hallie: Only if we can go to a movie too...**

I smile for the first time in who knows how long because this girl is something else. She likes me, I can tell, even if she doesn't want to.

Who are you, Hallie Cox?

Do I even want to know?

Or is this how my life ends? With a brief semblance of happiness, just to then be shattered?

Zayne: It's settled then. Whatever my girl wants, my girl gets.

Hallie: Oh, so I'm your girl now?

Zayne: Fuck yes, you are.

Hallie: We will just have to see about that.

Zayne: Oh we will.

I want to pretend that this isn't my impending demise, even though I know that's exactly what it is. And I have no fucking way to escape from it.

"Zayne!" Loud pounding and my mom's screech wake me from a deep slumber.

What the hell?

"I'm coming in!" My mom announces as she opens the door. I don't know what she's expecting to find, because all I've done is sleep my life away.

"What do you want?" I grumble, my voice still thick with sleep and a familiar sadness that threatens to claw my heart right out of my chest.

"I want you to get out of this room." She opens the curtains and blinds, and my eyes hurt from the sudden invasion of my senses. "You've been in here all weekend. It's time to live."

"I'm living right here."

"Your heart may be beating, but this is not life." My groan makes her frown at me, more in annoyance than anything. My mother has a low tolerance for my bullshit nowadays, but I don't push her buttons on purpose. "I made you chocolate chip pancakes. Oh, and you need a shower. You fucking stink." She wrinkles her nose at me in disgust.

"I don't stink." Only I laugh, the sound foreign to my ears, because I do stink. I can smell myself, but if I'm being honest, taking my shower is very low on my to-do list today.

"When was the last time you took your medication?"

Not this again.

"I told you I'm not going to take it anymore."

"Zayne, this is not up for discussion. You know what happens when you don't. Do you truly want to end up in the mental hospital again?"

"No, I hate that place, but the medicine makes me feel like a different person and I don't like it."

"It's supposed to make you feel different," my mother tells me sternly, reminding me of when she would put me in time-out when I was little.

I swear I lived in a corner for at least half of my life, mainly since I've never been one to follow the rules. I may be allergic to them. "You're not meant to live your life drowning in your sorrows or being reckless and endangering yourself…"

"Fine. I'll think about it."

"I'm going to need more than that. I need you to promise."

"I promise." I stare at the ceiling while I tell her my lies, not giving her the satisfaction of even sitting up for our conversation. I don't push my luck by being rude though, I just tell her what she wants to hear. Same as always.

She doesn't buy it, never does. She knows better than anyone that I don't keep my promises, and I certainly don't tell the truth.

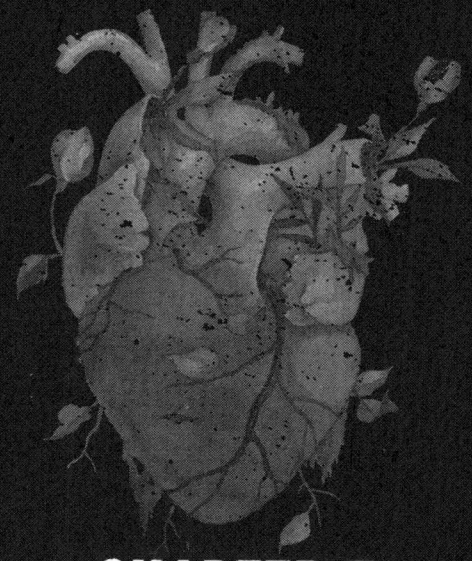

CHAPTER 5

HALLIE

It's almost time for Zayne to pick me up for our date and my hands are sweating, my ears are ringing, and I'm breathing very fast. I don't know why the man makes me so anxious, but there's something about those green eyes that screams at me to run the other way.

Eyes as green as the devil who made me do it.

I'm wearing a burgundy bodycon dress with a corset-style top and spaghetti straps, reaching just above my knees and with a slit detail in the back. I'm not looking for a relationship, but if he's going to take me out to dinner, I'm going to wear something worthy of breaking necks and stealing hearts. Although I highly doubt it would be his, he doesn't look like he has a heart.

I'm pairing it with a light jacket that I can take off when we get to the restaurant since it's only in the sixties today. It may be January, but the weather in Texas has a mind of its own. Chunky, black heels complete the look, and I've curled my dark hair and tousled it to look more like waves. I'm surprised I also did my makeup today, the first time I've attempted a full face in months.

My burgundy lipstick is dark as fuck, and I'm taking the excess off when I hear the doorbell ring. Brittany already told me she's getting the door to give me time to finish getting ready. She suggested earlier for me to make him wait, which I think is funny because I hate being late, so I probably won't purposely do that.

The spritz of my vanilla perfume on my neck and wrists is cold, and I startle when it sprays on my skin. It's quiet in the living room as I walk to the couch where Zayne is waiting, and I realize Brit abandoned him to hang out on his own. She can be a bit of a bitch at times. I still love her, in any case.

He gets up and turns around when he hears the sound of my heels as I stride into the room, and I stop a few feet away from him. His sharp inhale as he looks at me hungrily gives me butterflies, and he continues his perusal as he takes me in all the way from my head to my toes.

"You're so beautiful…" His voice trails off as he walks my way.

"Thank you." I chuckle, "You look handsome yourself." I motion to his body awkwardly and cross my arms over my chest. I've always been shy, and being the center of attention makes me deeply uncomfortable, and right now the way he looks at me makes me feel like I'm the center of his entire world.

Even through my discomfort, I can admit that handsome doesn't even begin to describe him. He might very well be the most beautiful human that I've ever laid eyes on. His black slacks hug his legs like nothing I have ever seen, and his olive green dress shirt matches his eyes perfectly. His straight black hair falls over his left eye, and he brushes it back hastily before reaching for me.

I let him hold my hand during our walk to the car and he opens the door for me. The seats are black leather with red stitching, and as I climb up into them and settle in, I notice that his car smells like a man. Like the woods and citrus; it's intoxicating in the most delicious way.

Like him.

The drive to the restaurant is not long, and when we pull up to Fleming's, my breath catches in my throat. He probably made reservations for this place before I even agreed to go out with him. I almost smile at the thought of him wanting this so badly that he couldn't wait to ask me. Instead, I'm so nervous I can barely breathe. I can't even recall the last time I went on a date, and the thought of making small talk for the next hour suddenly makes my skin feel too tight.

He opts to park himself instead of using the valet, and after he opens my door we walk hand in hand into the restaurant. I can't help but ask myself who the last person who held my hand was. I think it was my high school boyfriend, and suddenly I feel pathetic. I don't know what I'm doing here with this beautiful man who drives a 370Z and pays for my dinner, while I'm literally surviving off student loans and my part-time job at the hospital and eating ramen with beer for dinner every night.

"Earth to Hallie ..." He tugs at my hand gently to bring me back from my thoughts.

"Oh," I laugh softly, "I'm sorry, I spaced out."

"It's okay, but no more of that tonight." He leans in close to my face and stares into my eyes, giving me a good look at the lack of other colors. There are no flecks of gold, no other hues. Just green. "I want your pretty eyes on me."

"Is that all you want on you?" What is wrong with me? I guess I really am the whore my mom believes me to be. I can't help myself though. It's automatic at this point, and as I internally roll my eyes at myself, I promise to not do it again.

"For now." Zayne looks down at me and smirks, his eyes not leaving mine even for a second.

I squirm for a moment but quickly recover, shaking my head at him and smiling. We walk to the hostess stand, and Zayne lets them know we have a reservation. A petite, blonde girl with black slacks and a white button-up shirt leads us to our table, placing menus on it.

The dining room has low lighting and small square tables with white tablecloths draped over them. The leather-back chairs are a soft cream color and Zayne pulls one out for me to sit on. Once I am seated, he walks around to his side, takes the chair across the table from me, and then looks up at the blonde with a smile. I kind of hate that she smiles back with a glint in her eyes, yet I don't fucking understand why jealousy comes over me as my hands tingle, itching to choke her.

"Could we have waters and a bottle of Riesling to start?" he asks her, and she nods her head several times.

"Of course," the girl murmurs, her eyes landing on me like it's the first time she's seen me. Thankfully, she walks away quickly.

The light plays tricks on Zayne's eyes, the forest burning behind his irises as he stares at me like he wants me for dinner instead. I would happily oblige him if he asked, although it's probably too soon for that.

"Hallie." He tips one corner of his mouth into a half smile and looks at me intently. "I love your name. I could say it every minute of every day."

"Do you always talk like this?" I fight not to roll my eyes, but I don't win. He can be a little over the top.

"Only when I want something."

My fingers twist on my lap, hidden under the table. "And what is it that you want?"

"You."

"That's it? That's all you're going to say?" I chuckle, "It's just that easy to get what you want?" It probably is. It doesn't help that he's handsome, clearly has money, and has a very persistent air about him.

"Usually, yes. But nothing about you screams easy."

"That's not what my mom likes to say about me…"

"What?"

"Nothing." I give him a tight-lipped smile that I save for awkward moments when I can't control my mouth. "Never mind."

The night passes by in the blink of an eye as we get into light conversation during dinner and I eat the best steak of my entire life.

We talk about how we both hate steak sauce, enjoy our steaks medium-rare, and I'm not a huge fan of broccoli unless it has cheese on it, even though I'm lactose intolerant. Everyone cheats sometimes, though. We end up sharing sides and dessert, but no one dares to touch the other's steak.

"What do you think, then?" Zayne questions, "Will you let me have another date?" My mind wanders for a moment. This one has been pretty perfect, but do I really want to deal with the kind of things he does? Something tells me what I've seen so far is tame in comparison to his full potential.

Even still, I don't reject him. Maybe I'm stupid, or I just enjoy being hurt. "If you're nice enough," I reply, and his bright smile is so dazzling I have to look away.

When we walk to his car, he holds my hand all the way to the door, opens it, and closes it behind me. I highly doubt that he acts this way all the time, he's probably putting on a show for me, but I'll let him. I want to enjoy myself, and if it were anyone else, I'd go home with him tonight. I probably wouldn't be able to get rid of him if I did that, which is why I don't suggest it.

The silence should make me feel uncomfortable, and even though the stereo is off and the engine is loud, I still feel myself relaxing against the leather seat. I catch him looking at me repeatedly, sometimes with a smile on his face and sometimes with prying eyes that make me feel like he's mentally undressing me. I want to look away, I try not to provoke him, but I can't tear my eyes from his.

Zayne reaches for my hand again, enveloping it in his much larger one. His warmth is so at odds with the temperature in the car that it makes me tense, and when his thumb brushes over my knuckles, the whispered "you're mine" sends shivers down my body.

But he doesn't understand that I can never be his.

Not fully.

Not really.

I'm a walking paradox—I belong to everyone and no one.

Suddenly, rain starts to come down hard, beating on the windshield until even the highest setting can't clear it. We decide to skip the movie and head home instead.

Home.

How ironic that I would ever call any place home. Between my mom leaving me to live with my grandparents for most of my life and only picking me up on the weekends, I never knew what a home or consistency was. I was traded like cards every weekend, and stability was but a figment of my imagination. Before foster care, I only lived with my mom for three years total of my entire life, having lived the previous twelve with my grandparents. Once I was removed from her home, and after waiting to be placed, my grandparents stepped back in to take care of me. That meant I didn't have contact with my brothers however, and they didn't understand the situation at all.

And my dad?

Who even knows where he is.

I last heard from him when I was eighteen, and it consisted of a phone call and a few text messages. Other than that, nothing. I've never met him in person, never even seen pictures of him; I know I've always been awful at relationships due to my abandonment issues.

How can anyone expect any form of healthy attachment from me when it's never been modeled to me before? How can Zayne even want to be with me?

I don't even know how to be with myself.

Escaping my reality is what I do best.

All I know how to do is run. It's nothing personal. Just another fucked up coping mechanism gone wrong. It's a skill that I've honed over the years, crucial for my survival. When I panic, I run.

I'm flighty.

But running ensures that I don't get hurt.

Running protects me.

The rain continues to pour down on us as we pull into the assigned guest parking spot and make a run for the front door of my townhome. Our clothes are soaked, my hair is plastered to my face, and I'm freezing.

I probably look like a damn clown with my makeup running down my face, but I pretend to not feel self-conscious when I open the door and let him come in after me. Once inside, I close it behind me and lean against it, noticing for the first time tonight how badly my shoes are hurting my feet. So I kick them off.

I hear the *drip, drip, drip* on the hardwood floor as the droplets fall from my hair, trailing a path to my room where I go to get changed. Zayne doesn't follow me. Instead, he waits for me to come back to him, standing by the door right where I left him. I take off my dress, which feels stuck to me like a second skin and pull on an oversized t-shirt over my head.

"Zayne," I call out for him, and then I hear the faint footsteps getting closer to my room. "Are you okay?"

"Well, yes, but I should probably get going..." I feel his eyes on me as I pull the rest of the shirt down, covering myself hastily.

"Are you crazy? You can't go out there right now!" There's literally no visibility. The wipers couldn't possibly help him now.

"What do you suggest I do?"

"You can wait out the storm with me." I try to give him a smile, only my face won't work, so I probably look like a crazy person. I don't smile, I'm dead inside. "You can get comfortable and we can watch something. You can sleep on the couch if need be."

"If you're sure, then I can do that, but if you change your mind then it's going to be too late for you." He winks at me, but I know he's serious.

"You can stay. I wouldn't say it if I didn't mean it."

"Okay," he sighs, relieved, and rakes his fingers through his soaked hair. "Where is your bathroom?"

I point him in the right direction, "The towels are in the linen closet behind the door." I go sit on the couch to wait for him, turning on *Friends* and hoping for the best. If he doesn't like my favorite show, he can sleep in his car.

Zayne comes back to the living room shirtless and wearing

only his boxer briefs, and I swear my heart stops beating in my chest. His shoulders are capped, his chest defined, and his abs are deep ridges. The V is even more pronounced due to his underwear being low on his hips, and he has tattoos all over his arms and torso. I realize that I had not seen his arms before now because he's always wearing long sleeve shirts or jackets. My gaze trails down his body again, and I let my eyes linger for a few more seconds before I reel them back in.

How the fuck can one human be so damn near perfect?

There has to be something seriously wrong with him. There's no way he isn't broken; nothing beautiful is ever intact.

He comes to sit next to me on the couch, plopping down on it without a care in the world. From afar, he's beautiful, but up close...

Up close, he's fucking devastating.

Raven black hair frames his face, reaching below his ears. The forest in his eyes burns holes into me as I assess the situation and determine the best course of action.

"Do you like *Friends*?" If we're going to be stuck together, I might as well do something I enjoy.

"I don't want to be your friend."

"I meant the show, you idiot!" I laugh loudly, not caring that I'm not being ladylike.

His eyes narrow at me with the insult, and he looks like he wants to punish me. "I've never seen it..."

"What?" My eyes widen with surprise. "That must be remedied immediately."

"I thought maybe we could talk instead, Hals."

Hals.

I taste the nickname on my tongue and turn it over a few times.

"About what, *Zay?*"

He chuckles and reaches out to me, brushing his knuckles over my left cheekbone, right over my light dusting of freckles.

"You are so perfect," he says as he searches my face, his voice coming out as a groan at the end.

"Far from it…"

"Perfect for me."

"That's cliche."

"It's the truth."

"You'll have to try harder than your recycled lines," I tell him, my cheeks heating from how he's looking at me. "Those don't work on me."

"Oh?" He throws his head back and laughs, the sound echoing off the walls in my living room. "And what works, then?"

"Nothing does. I'm immune to all male charm."

"I doubt that." Zayne purses his lips. "I want you, Hallie. Please give me a chance. Be mine."

"I'm not good for you." My sigh causes his fists to clench, and I'm momentarily stunned. It's like the more I tell him no, the more exasperated he gets. But I'm not speaking lies. I'm not good for anyone.

"So hurt me. Hurt me so fucking bad. I've never had anything good anyway."

Well, shit.

"I think we would destroy each other. We would collide and fuck everything up." I look into his green eyes, a storm raging in his irises. I hate that I don't know what he's thinking. If I could have five minutes inside his head to dig into all of him, I would go directly to thoughts of me.

"Baby, this collision will be so destructive that when the black hole swallows us, we will leave a blaze of glory behind us as we fall to our demise."

"That doesn't sound appealing at all."

Zayne chuckles then scoots closer to me. "I'm beginning to think nothing sounds appealing to you."

"There are a few things that do, but our demise isn't one of them," I say softly.

"And that's where we are different. I welcome that demise. I want you to consume me until there's nothing left."

And I did.

I told him I would hurt him.

I warned him we were no good for each other.

If only I had known he would be the one to hurt *me* instead.

There is nothing more beautiful than a Texas sky during sunset, when it's painted different shades of reds, pinks, and yellows. As I lie on the hard sidewalk and feel the rocks underneath my back, I think of all the sunsets I've ever seen, but somehow none of them compare to this one.

Martin comes around our friends sitting along the sidewalk to sit next to me, looks up at the sky and then back to my face, as if questioning what I'm seeing that he's not.

I'm seeing me.

I'm seeing me in all these colors.

Someone makes a joke, and I laugh. Then, for some reason Martin believes it's the best time to straddle me and begin one of our famous tickle wars. I'm laughing so hard that tears stream down my face and I can't breathe, but then everyone's laughter abruptly ends, and Martin jumps off me in one swift movement.

I slowly sit up and look behind me, seeing my mother speed walking down the sidewalk with a murderous look on her face.

Oh, shit.

She tells me to get in the car, so I do.

She tells me to put on my seatbelt, so I do.

She tells me to shut the fuck up, so I do.

My mother drives us to our apartment and then pulls into our parking space in front of the door. She doesn't turn off the engine and instead adjusts herself in her seat to face me, burning holes into my face as I refuse to look at her.

"Hallie, if you insist on acting like a fucking whore, then I will treat you like the whore that you are."

"I'm sorry, Mom." I look at my hands as I pick at my nails, then set them on my lap. *"It won't happen again."* I lift my eyes to meet hers, and I'm more surprised at myself for not seeing it coming than I am at her for doing it.

The slap echoes in the enclosed space of the vehicle, and I feel the sting go from sharp to dull, duller, dullest. My eyes fill with tears that I didn't summon, and I'm suddenly angry with myself for being so fucking weak.

"Get in the fucking house."

I get out of the car and hurry to the front door, praying it's unlocked so I can run away from her. Except I never have any luck. The universe is always conspiring against me, for it clearly wants me to fail.

I pound on the door, but no one answers, and my mom catches up to me, pushing me out of the way to unlock the door. As we walk into the apartment, I try to get through the kitchen and the dining room so I can make it to the hallway where all the bedrooms are situated—my escape route.

"Oh, no you don't!" She grabs a hold of my hair and yanks hard, bringing fresh tears to my eyes from the sting. *"You're fucking grounded for the rest of the summer!"*

"That's two months! I didn't even do anything!"

"Shut the fuck up!" She still hasn't let go of my hair, but instead of standing and screaming at me, she is now pulling me by my hair down the hallway. I try to loosen her grip, try to get out of her grasp, but she throws a punch that lands on the side of my head and makes me dizzy, then I feel myself falling to the ground.

Marianna continues to pull me toward my bedroom by my hair, and I feel myself reaching up to make the pain stop, but she yanks even harder. I feel some strands come off with more sharp pain, and when I open my eyes, I can see my brother smirking from his place at the dining table.

Fucking asshole.

She throws me in my room, and I land next to my bed on the floor, and then she closes the door, locking me in.

She doesn't love me, so no one does.

She wants to hurt me, so I do too.

She tells me I'm a whore, so now I am.

The razorblade I keep hidden under the mattress calls to me.

So I cut.

I cut until I feel everything.

And then I cut until I feel nothing at all.

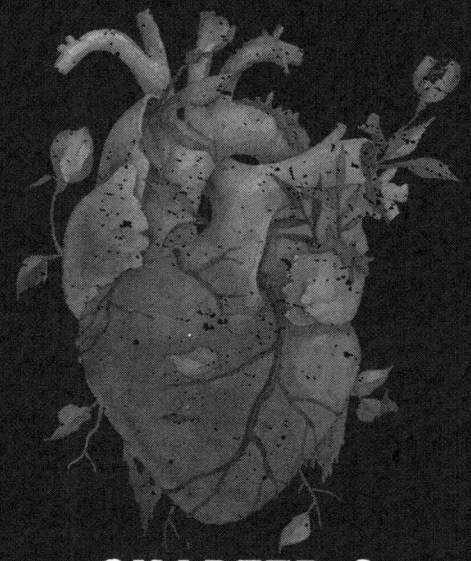

CHAPTER 6

ZAYNE

Friends is playing in the background, but I'm not paying attention. Hallie fell asleep on my shoulder with her lips parted, her deep breaths echoing in my ears.

I stare at her face as she sleeps, which would be creepy with anyone else, but not with her. My soul recognizes hers—like calls to like, and we are two sides of the same rusted coin. Our jagged pieces fit together, even if they don't quite line up and there are cracks in the middle.

Her dark lashes rest on her pale cheeks, lightly kissing the freckles on her face. Her beauty mocks me, reminding me that I'll never have her, not really. My behaviors drive everyone away, and I'm just getting ready for the crash.

In my mind though, once she's mine, it's forever. I don't do relationships, and I've never even been in love. I get obsessed, and I know when I fixate on someone it's hard for me to let go of that.

This is the most peaceful I have seen Hals since meeting her, and it's impossible to look away. I always want to see her like this, but I know deep down in my heart that I will hurt her. As much as I'd love to stare at her all night, I'm beginning to feel bad for how she's lying on me. Her neck is bent at an awkward angle, which she will be hurting from in the morning if I don't move her to the bed.

I gently pick her up bridal-style and cradle her, walking slowly so she doesn't wake up. She stirs in my arms, nuzzling her head against my bare chest, and I can feel a twinge of *something* deep within me.

Surely it's not me feeling anything for her.

Once I lower her onto the bed, my fingers trace her face, and I brush her hair back. It would be so easy to break her, but that thought isn't comforting in the least.

She's so beautiful.

After a few minutes, I practically run out of her room, knowing if I stay any longer, I'll get in bed with her. It takes every ounce of self-control I possess to force myself to go back to the living room and throw myself onto the couch. Before I have the chance to think about anything, sleep welcomes me back into its tight grip.

Faint whimpering noises bring me back from the dead, so they must be louder than my brain is processing. My eyes flutter open as I take in my surroundings, my body refusing to catch up. The television still has *Friends* playing in the background and the brightness hurts my eyes, so I quickly divert my vision. Just when I start to think I imagined the sounds, they happen again, and I realize that they're coming from Hallie's room.

My feet trip over each other as I run to her room, scared that something is wrong, but she's asleep. I hold my breath and wait for the next round of whimpering. Like clockwork, she begins again, her brows furrowing and her bottom lip trembling. She starts to thrash on the bed, tears running down her cheeks.

I can't think, can't breathe, as I throw back the covers and get in the bed with her. My back is cushioned by the tufted headboard, and I pull her up to me, positioning her between my legs for her head to rest on my chest. Hallie startles awake. When she tries to run away from me, I wrap my arms around her chest and rock her back and forth. That makes it worse though, and now she's fully in fight or flight mode as she kicks and screams, limbs flailing as I use a lot of my strength to restrain this feral being.

"Let me go!" she says through gritted teeth, her hair getting in my mouth as I move my face closer to hers and shush her. Her clammy skin feels cold under my embrace.

"Never," I whisper in her ear and keep rocking her slowly. "Breathe with me, baby." She's hyperventilating, sobbing, but she freezes for a split second. Like I just triggered something in her.

"That shit doesn't work on me," she snaps.

"Do it anyway."

I put my hand on her chest and tell her to breathe in deeply, and she obliges, which is surprising, then I tell her to let it out. We do this four more times before I take my hand off her chest and guide her back to lie on mine and relax.

"Breathe like I breathe, Hallie." I take a deep breath and she does the same. "That's it, baby."

Hallie continues to match my breathing, and before I know it our breaths are perfectly in tune with each other. The way she goes limp in my arms makes my heart clench, and I take her hand, drawing circles on it with my thumb.

"Good girl," I say softly in her ear, and I can see the goosebumps breaking out on her arms.

She looks back at me and smiles, a genuine and bright smile, and then it hits me. I had never really seen her smile before, not like this. She smirks all the time but never smiles. Suddenly, I'd do anything for more.

She sits up slowly, as if afraid that I'm going to keep her prisoner, testing the waters. I let her go because I know she'll run away if she feels the pressure, and I want her here with me for the rest of the night. Hallie scoots closer to her nightstand, abandoning my parted legs, then grabs a pill bottle and a glass of water sitting there as if calling her name.

She pops two blue pills and swallows them dry but then takes the glass of water and chugs half of it. Her eyes close briefly, and she makes a tiny little sound like it's the best thing she's ever had. My cock throbs, yet I close my legs and put the blankets over me so she doesn't notice, because this moment is about her and I don't want to ruin it. Hallie lies down facing me, her pillow almost swallowing her head, and she stares at me. I copy her and stare into her eyes.

"Who did this to you, Hals?" I ask her softly, afraid that if I raise my voice, the spell will be broken and she will kick me out of her room for the night. I don't want to leave. I don't ever want to leave her again.

"Someone who was supposed to love me—" She breaks off.

"Is he dead?"

"Sadly, no."

"I'll fucking kill him. Just tell me who he is."

"It doesn't matter, Zay," Hallie pauses. "It won't change anything."

I take a deep breath, feeling like I'm going to lose control as my mind spirals and loses itself in the millions of possibilities of what could have happened to her. Then I realize I know absolutely nothing about this beautiful girl, and that just will not do.

I brush my fingertips over her cheek, memorizing every dip, curve, and freckle as I scoot closer to her. I want my intentions to be clear in case she wants to pull away. I slowly inch closer to her face until my lips hover over hers, but I don't make a move. She comes closer, our lips finally brushing together, and I lightly kiss her. I'm afraid to break her, afraid that she will shatter under me if I kiss her harder. I don't know why I feel this way, because she's clearly not fragile, but I know that everything I touch turns to dust.

I sweep my tongue over her bottom lip, a silent request, and she parts for me, letting me explore her. She deepens the kiss and our tongues clash and stroke each other as her hand wraps around the back of my neck, pulling me closer. My spine tingles with every lick, suck, bite, and I let my fingertips travel from her face to her lower back, digging in until I all but pull her on top of me. We are as close as we can be with clothes on and she seems to grow more needy by the moment.

Hallie's hands find my face as we get lost in each other, searching for something I can't quite put my finger on, and she skates both hands into my hair, burying them while she tugs my head back and breaks the kiss. We are both breathing hard as we stare into each other's eyes, and she surprises me by coming back for another taste.

She pauses over my mouth and does something completely unexpected as her tongue darts out and slowly licks my lips.

She smiles.

My vision goes black as I grab the back of her head and claim her mouth again, but this time when I go for her lower lip, I suck it into my mouth hard and bite down on it.

She moans.

I groan.

The metallic taste fills my senses, and I draw her lip back into my mouth, sucking softly on it, hoping she will give me more but praying for her soul that she'll give me less.

I break the kiss and turn over onto my back, ensuring the covers are on me so she doesn't see my cock jutting straight up. She watches me take deep breaths and steady myself, and when she deems me ready she turns over onto her side, giving me her back.

"Will you stay with me tonight?" Her voice is small, as if afraid to ask, and I can tell that rejection is as expected as the breath in her lungs.

"Always, just say the word."

"Can you rub my back?" I smile and nod my head but then realize that she can't see me.

Hallie's breath starts getting heavy as I slowly drag my

fingertips over her back. Up and down and in circles until I'm sure she's fast asleep. I get close enough to smell her hair and wrap my arm around her waist. The light from her bathroom hurts my eyes, but if she needs it to sleep, I will deal with it. I can bury my face in her hair if I need darkness, and I do, so I let her vanilla and berries smell consume me until sleep claims me again.

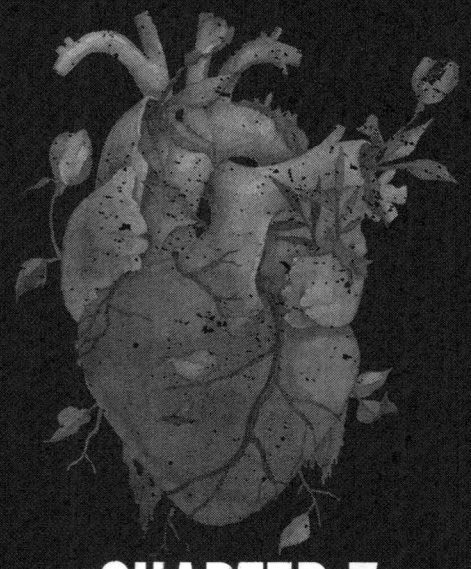

CHAPTER 7

HALLIE

My body is on fire, and I can feel my hair sticking to my face as my alarm goes off in the background. What the—

Fuck.

Zayne's body is threaded with mine. His left leg is between my legs while his right leg is draped over the top, keeping me trapped with no way to escape. His forearm tattoo almost shimmers in the sunlight streaming in through my windows, the pine trees and howling wolf staring at me from how close his arm is to my face.

I mentally sift through ways to untangle myself while my alarm continues to scream at me and then decide to just get up and turn it off. As soon as the bed dips from my movement, Zayne's eyes fly open and his hand catches my wrist.

"I just need to turn off my alarm. I can't stand it anymore."

"Okay," he breathes, rubbing the sleep from his eyes after he releases me.

Mondays are not my longest day of the week but they are still busy enough that I only have one hour left before I have to head out of the house. I turn off the alarm and walk into the bathroom to brush my teeth, shower, and start getting ready. When I come out, he is sitting on my bed texting someone. He looks up at me with a genuine smile, the kind that reaches his eyes.

"Come sit with me for a minute." He pats the spot on the bed where he wants me to go.

"Okay, but only for one minute. I really need to get going."

"Alright, I'll make this quick." Zayne grabs my hand between his and looks into my eyes. I squirm a little under so much attention, but I manage to not look away. "Will you meet me for lunch tomorrow?"

"Where?"

He looks like he has to think about this one, and I smile at the effort he's making. I haven't given anyone a second date in years. "How about Carrabba's? Do you like Italian food?"

"I do," I smile. "But you're paying, and I'll meet you there."

He chuckles. "Of course, I'm fucking paying. What kind of man do you think I am?"

A bad one.

"I'm not sure yet." I shrug my right shoulder, my shirt lifting slightly, and I see him follow the movement.

"Can I ask you something else?"

"Do I have a choice?" I roll my eyes, smile, and feel my dimple deepening.

"You always have a choice."

I sigh and look up at the ceiling, "What do you want to know?"

"How often do you have nightmares?"

My heart stops in my chest, knowing exactly where this conversation is headed. I never speak of him. I don't enjoy it, but above all, it triggers me. Saying his name is like calling out to the devil. Nothing good can come from it.

I debate how this could possibly benefit me, telling him about my nightmares, but the cons are more powerful than the pros in this situation. Maybe it's the way he's looking at me with such anticipation that makes me cave, but the way his eyes flash at the realization that I'm going to give him an answer makes me question myself for a brief second.

"Often. I take medication for it, but it doesn't always work." My lip kicks up into a half smile. "I'm used to them," I lie, and it tastes bitter on my tongue; the pills never seem to work anymore.

"No one can get used to that." Zayne scoffs, then tilts his head at me. "What happened? Why do you have nightmares?"

"I don't really want to talk about it right now, Zay."

"Okay. I can respect that, but I'm here for you. I want to know you. I want to know the *real* you."

No one knows the real me. "That's very sweet, but you should cut your losses and move on before one of us gets hurt."

"It's too late for all that, Hallie. I want you, and when I want something," he pauses, "I fucking take it."

"I'm too fucked up to be good for someone else."

"I don't want you to be good for me, just let me be here for you." We search each other's eyes. However, I'm not looking for answers. Maybe I'm looking for his soul, though I don't think his eyes are the window to it after all. "Be mine."

I take a deep breath, slowly letting it out like a deflating balloon. He's really not giving up, is he? I don't think he will be leaving me alone any time soon. What do I get out of this situation, though? More trauma?

"No. I don't want to put a label on anything yet. I have no reason to trust you, and as I said before, I am not the relationship type. You don't look like it either, in all honesty."

"You don't have a choice. I'm not letting you go." Zayne shrugs his shoulders and walks out of my room, leaving me with more questions than answers.

The entire day was a blur after he left, if I'm being honest. Between Nursing Management and Med-Surg classes, I didn't have a moment to breathe, except once I got home each minute felt like an hour. I haven't texted Zayne nor has he texted me either, and for some reason I feel dread in the pit of my stomach as I pull into the Carrabba's parking lot.

I don't see his car, but I still go in and let the hostess seat me at a table for two. I know this is a bad idea as I'm scanning the menu and then order myself some water. When the waitress asks me if I need more time, I give her my tight-lipped smile and tell her yes. I have an awful fucking feeling about this.

The minutes tick by, feeling like hours all over again, until it's been ten minutes past the agreed-upon meeting time and I give in. I didn't want to have to text him first, but maybe he's stuck in traffic or running late for another reason, and I have to go to clinical rotations in two hours.

> **Hallie: Hey, I'm at the restaurant waiting for you. Are you coming?**

Ten minutes after the first message...

> **Hallie: Are you on the way yet? I have clinical today.**

Five minutes after the second message...

> **Hallie: Zayne... I swear to god I will never fucking talk to you again. Answer the fucking phone!!!**

I order myself the ravioli to go and leave the restaurant. I can't believe I was stupid enough to think this would ever work. He screamed flaky from the beginning and I took the bait anyway. It's hard to put myself out there, to be vulnerable, but I tried. I was willing to give him a chance, and he didn't let a bitch down easy. He just stood me up. He could have at least texted me.

Fuck him. There's no way in hell he's getting another chance.

And when he comes back for me, I'll be the one not to let him down easy.

Mark my fucking words.

Brittany is on the couch working on a care plan as I enter our cozy home. I smell food baking in the oven, she loves to do that, unlike me, and the kitchen is sparkly clean.

God, I love her.

Her green eyes meet mine, narrowing at me as I walk toward her, and she closes her book with a loud thud. "What crawled up your ass and died?"

Bitch.

"What the fuck kind of expression is that?" I huff, but she just rolls her eyes at me. "And why would anything want to crawl up my ass?"

"Beats me. Your ass makes for uninhabitable conditions, too cold if you ask me." She smirks and I want to wipe it off her face, but I refrain.

"No one asked you."

"Spill it already, I'm getting bored." Brittany tends to do that a lot, so when she says that, I believe her. I just also don't give a shit right now. Zayne has put me in the worst mood.

"You're getting bored? I live bored," I reply.

"I need wine already." She gets up from the couch and walks to the kitchen, "I can tell."

The couch dips as I sit on it, and I grab one of the throw pillows to get comfortable. "Remember Zayne? The bad boy with the green eyes?"

She nods quickly as she brings the bottle of wine to the couch and takes a pull straight from it, then hands it over so I can do the same.

"We had a lunch date today." I pause and look at her.

"And?"

"And he didn't fucking show, Brit." My eyes fill with tears, and I pity myself for letting it affect me this way. "He stood me up."

"*No!* That motherfucker did NOT stand you up," she yells, outraged, her eyes almost popping out of their sockets.

"Oh, but he did." I chuckle, not missing the irony of the situation. He begged me to give him a chance, and now look what he did. I will probably never have the courage to put myself out there again. "And he didn't reply to any of my text messages asking when he was getting there. It was humiliating, and I never want to see him again."

"Do you think he was with someone else?"

I scrunch my nose, beating myself up for not thinking of that. "Like a girl?"

"Well, I would hope it's not a guy, but, yes, that's what I mean."

He better not fucking have been with someone else. That would just be the cherry on top of my humiliation. This is getting embarrassing. "I don't know. I guess anything is possible…"

"Well, you know what this calls for!"

Brittany laughs at my groan, but this is not amusing, even if sometimes she is helpful. I'll never tell her that, though. "Do not fucking say it."

"Detective Brittany at your service. I'm going to need a last name."

"I think it's Wolfe. I saw it on his license when he was carded for our date the other night."

Her eyes light up as she unlocks her phone and begins to search for his information. "Zayne Wolfe? That's hot."

"Not fucking helping. We hate him, remember?"

"We don't have to like him to acknowledge his beauty."

"Would you like to date him instead?" My tone has a bite that doesn't go unnoticed by her. Even to me it sounds like jealousy, which couldn't possibly be what's happening here. I don't feel that emotion. Right?

"Are you kidding? He clearly only has eyes for you." She smirks and clears her throat, but her giggle escapes regardless. I narrow my eyes at her and debate on whether I should strangle her before or after her research.

"Yeah, that's why he stood me up. Anyway, just do your stupid research so we can move on."

An entire bottle of wine later, we are sitting on the couch with a notebook full of Zayne trivia between us, courtesy of Brittany. He's twenty-three years old, lives with his mom, his parents are divorced, and he is an only child. He's also a sophomore in college because he took a break for a few years, and he is still undecided on his major. Oh, and he works as a server and bartender at a restaurant downtown.

We stalk his Facebook and Instagram accounts and ogle him, which admittedly is not my proudest moment. But the multiple shirtless pictures and the way his olive skin makes his abs look even more defined make me forget all about it.

The body of this man.

"He's fucking delicious, Hallie. If he comes back—when—you should just forgive him and keep him forever."

Wow, she's funny today. "I don't keep anyone for any amount of time, but forever is a hard no."

"Fine, for the semester then?"

I smile, knowing I have to give her something or she won't stop. "Now we're talking."

"You need good dick in your life."

"Yes, I do." I agree. "But Zayne is not the one who will be giving it to me. He already stood me up, I'm not putting myself in that position again."

"Fine. Enough talk about him." Thank the stars, the universe, and God, if there is one. I can't spend one more minute talking about this man, or I might just cave and forgive him the second he apologizes. He seems to cloud my judgment. "How about we do face masks instead?"

"Yes, please!"

We put on white face masks that make us look like ghosts and open a bottle of wine, which we drink surprisingly fast, making over half of it disappear within minutes. I'm swaying on my feet, but she has a way of making me feel better about everything, so I don't think about the impending alcohol poisoning for the second time in a week. I take a few more sips of wine, wash off the mask's residue from my face, and then moisturize.

Brit plays a Beyoncé song I can't remember the name of, and we get up and start dancing around the living room. When she starts to twerk—fucking *twerk*—I laugh so hard I literally pee myself and run to the bathroom to change. She just follows me and laughs the entire way.

"Hallie, are you drunk?" She asks me while I change into clean underwear and pants, giggling the entire time.

"I'm so fucked up!" I laugh hard enough that I almost pee myself again, and decide to jump in bed, ready to take advantage of the wine in my system and use it for sleep instead. Brittany joins me, and we cuddle with each other to sleep, which happens more often than I'd like to admit.

I swear Brit has been present for most of my embarrassing moments but also my good ones. Probably the bad ones too. She's been there through it all.

She's my rock.

She may be the only person who truly gets me, who has seen all of my sides, all of my personalities. And she has never run away from it, and she will never leave me, because she's also suffered from abandonment and a terrible childhood. Her rich girl facade is only a front for a significantly damaged heart. Yes, her grandparents take care of her financially because they are rich as fuck, but her parents are just as shitty as mine, and that connects us on a deeper level because—

At the end of it all, she's just as fucked up as me.

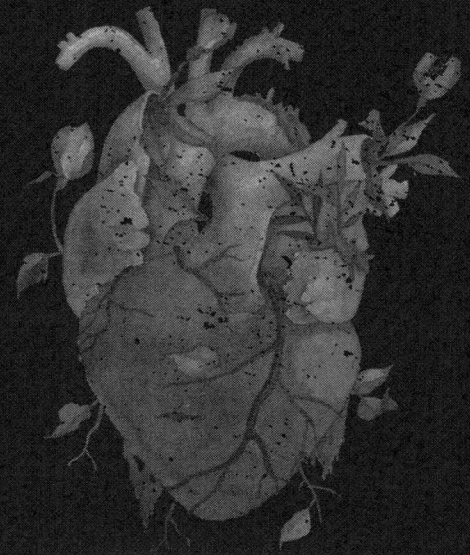

CHAPTER 8

ZAYNE

I have been depressed for months now.
    I could feel it in my bones. Numbness seeped from my pores, and the weight of an elephant sat on my chest, constantly making it hard to breathe. It was like a smudge I could not get out, a darkness that I could not shake.

And that darkness had me by the throat.

However for the past three days, I've been feeling different. There's a rush of energy flowing through my veins, like I could work out and never have to rest or clean the house all night and never have to sleep. And I *haven't* slept. I haven't slept at all since the weekend. I also don't remember the last time I showered. Which I probably should do, but I won't.

    I call my friend Toby, and we talk for three hours. I clean my room and fold my laundry and eat endless amounts of food. The dishes pile up in different areas of my room until I have to start moving shit around to sit on the bed, but I begin to clean them up because my room only gets this messy when the darkness drags me under.

Sirens blare in the background again, which is weird because no one should be able to get on this property. I live in the middle of nowhere, and our nearest neighbors are about a half mile down the road. I look out the windows, searching for the blue lights in the darkness, but see none. Someone's there though, I know it.

You get that prickly sensation when someone has been staring at you for too long, I have that right now and can't shake it. I pick up my phone and text my mom.

> **Zayne: Are you home?**
>
> **Mom: No. I'm driving from the airport.**
>
> **Zayne: I think the cops are here but I can't see them.**
>
> **Mom: What do you mean?**
>
> **Zayne: I hear someone. I think they're here for me mom...**
>
> **Mom: Why would they be there for you? I will be home in an hour. When was the last time you slept?**
>
> **Zayne: I don't have an hour mom! I hear someone out there and they want to kill me. They've been watching me for days!**
>
> **Mom: Zayne do not fucking leave your room. No one is there to kill you and there's no cops there. I'm looking at the feed on the cameras right now. Stay put. It's just in your head.**
>
> **Zayne: It's not in my fucking head I HEAR them!**
>
> **Mom: I know you believe you do, which is why I'm saying to stay in your room until I get there. If there's someone there I will talk to them.**

I hide in my closet and close the door, only I'm freaking out as I sit in the dark, cramped space. It's hard for me to sit still for long periods of time on a regular day, but right now it's fucking impossible. I hear a crashing sound in the house, and I cover my ears and rock back and forth, willing my breathing to slow down. I hear people running; I know they're in here.

My palms are clammy, and the perspiration coats my skin, making my shirt stick to my body. There's no ventilation in the closet, and it feels like I'm slowly suffocating. The footsteps get closer to the closet door, yet I refuse to open my eyes. Instead I hold my breath until I can be sure they left. I strain my ears to hear the footsteps again, but it's more difficult when they are ringing. I slowly let the air out of my lungs and hear the footsteps recede again, my heart thumping painfully in my chest.

I try to distract myself by texting a friend but instead land on Hallie's messages.

Oh, fuck.

Hallie.

Shit! I was supposed to meet her for lunch three days ago, and I didn't. She's probably never going to talk to me again. Oh my God, what am I going to do? I think flowers will help, but that probably won't be enough. I need to come up with something, anything. She can't leave me—

"Zayne!" My mom bursts through the door, searching for me in the dark.

"I'm here," I mumble, opening the door as she turns on the light. I stand and walk out of the closet, carefully stepping around the mess in front of it. She looks at me carefully as if assessing how dangerous I am at the moment, which she should probably be doing, given my history.

"How old are you?" she questions in the same way as always. This trying to assess how oriented I am, that's what they call it at the mental hospital, is getting fucking old. But I answer anyway, because if I don't she will admit me again. It's not that bad. I'm fine.

"Twenty-three."

"What is today's date?" Alyssa arches an eyebrow.

Shit. She always gets me somehow.

"Uhhh. I don't know?"

"Put your fucking shoes on." She sighs, probably exhausted from doing this for years now. I can't hold it against her, I'm exhausted too. Sometimes I just want to put myself and her out of our misery. "We're going to the hospital."

"Fuck no!" I scream, backing away from her.

"We are going, Zayne, so put your fucking shoes on!"

"I'm not fucking going anywhere, Mom. I'd rather fucking die than go back to a hospital!" I feel myself blacking out as we walk to the kitchen, and I start throwing dishes against the wall, furniture flying around the room as well. It's fucking irrational. I'm acting insane.

I'm so fucked.

My mom takes her phone out and dials 911. She starts speaking a hundred miles an hour and it freaks me out.

Fuck. Fuck. *Fuck!*

I tear the picture frames off the walls and they go flying in every direction. I pace again, running my hands through my hair. My mom tries to touch my shoulder, and I—

I look down and my hands are wrapped around her throat, and I'm squeezing, squeezing, squeezing.

Shit.

I step away from her and she falls hard to the floor. I tell her I'm sorry repeatedly but she's not hearing me as she crawls out of the room toward the front door. She opens the door and the paramedics and the police both run into the house, and I know this is the end of my fight. Nevertheless, I always go down swinging.

I kick my legs and throw punches as the police try to restrain me. I grab a hold of a side chair and swing it away from me, and it doesn't go far, but I do hear it crash against other furniture. The police get me on my stomach and hold me down, and I feel an injection in my left glute. Probably Haloperidol.

"I'll kill myself!" I try to turn my body away as they inject me, pain radiating up my back. "I'll fucking kill myself!"

My body begins to grow heavy from the injection, my limbs

limp, and my brain is not working properly. It's as if a fog has settled in, and it won't clear.

Not again.

The darkness gives me a sinister smile and welcomes me back.

There's shuffling at my side, but it's as if my eyes won't function, they don't want to obey my commands. My eyelids are heavy, my mind feels groggy, and my limbs aren't working. Loud beeping hurts my ears and my eyes fly open, which brings me face to face with the IV pump sitting next to my bed. I reach up to—

Oh, not this again…

My wrists are tied to the bed on either side of me with restraints. I move my feet, testing for the ankle restraints I already know are there. Great.

"Hi, my name is Liz. I'm going to be your nurse during this shift. Amy will be your sitter, and she will be watching you when I can't be in the room." It's not the first time I've had someone sit with me on suicide watch, and I'm sure it won't be the last, either. Even still, I hope this hospital stay is uneventful. I want to go home as soon as possible.

"Okay." I take a deep breath. "How long will I be here?"

"You're on a seventy-two-hour hold for homicidal behavior."

"Homicidal?" I ask incredulously.

"You tried to kill your mom."

"I didn't try to—" I breathe in deeply, attempting to control my rage. "I didn't mean to," I say through gritted teeth.

"Are you feeling suicidal?" Liz asks me, wholly unfazed and overlooking my attempt at an explanation.

"Fuck no!" I deny, although a tiny voice that sometimes shows up during these times whispers that I should do it.

Kill yourself. Do it. You won't. You should. End it. End it all.
Shut the fuck up!

I can tell Liz is watching me closely and if I act even a bit weird, there will be another cocktail going in my IV or shoved into my ass cheek, so I'd better get in line.

"We've already started you on antipsychotics and your next dose is in three hours." Of course, they did. They think pumping me full of drugs is going to help me, but newsflash, it never does. "I will be back to check on you before then, but is there anything you need right now?"

"My mom. Is she here?"

"She is in the waiting room, and we wanted to ask you for permission to talk to her about your situation. But unfortunately, you can't have visitors during your three-day hold. It's against hospital policy."

I nod, closing my eyes. I'm so tired of dealing with this kind of shit. "That's fine, just tell her whatever she wants to know."

Liz nods and makes a beeline out of the room. Amy sits in the corner as far as possible from me, staring at me intently. She has a paper I'm sure she's using to take notes about my behaviors and other unimportant information. I feel like a damn guinea pig, always being observed, prodded, and messed with.

The hours drag by as I stare at the white walls surrounding me. Is it possible to die of boredom? I still have that nagging sensation like someone is staring at me, but it feels more justified at this moment. I talk to Amy about the weather, my favorite movies, and even about my family. I talk about how I want to see snow, and want a new car, and how I like a girl who probably hates me now. I talk and talk and talk and—

Liz walks back into the room with a medicine cup and her portable computer. She clicks a few times and begins to scan the medications, then my armband. Just like all the other nurses, she asks for my full name and date of birth and begins to put my pills in the little plastic cup. The gloves taste funny as she places the medicine on my tongue, and she gives me water after I've already swallowed them dry.

Each day looks like the one before. I'm not sure how long I have left to stay here until Liz walks in and tells me I can go home.

I see my mom standing anxiously behind her. Liz tells me she needs to withdraw my IV before I leave and I tell her to do it now.

My Hallie is going to be a nurse soon, she's in her last semester. Not that she has told me anything. I found out her schedule through other means that I will take to my grave, but that's a conversation for another day. I really need to start thinking about how I'm going to get her to talk to me again. It's one thing to stand her up, but it's another to go a week without talking to her, especially without any explanation. I'm sure she must have texted me at some point and I just look like an asshole.

What am I supposed to say, in any case?

Hi, I'm Zayne Wolfe, and I have Bipolar 1 disorder. Nice to meet you. I hope you stick around even though I destroy everything around me, and I'll probably choke you, just like I did my mom. She's going to run away as fast as she can, and I honestly can't even blame her for it. I want to run away from me too, but I can't do that.

Instead, I want to run to her.

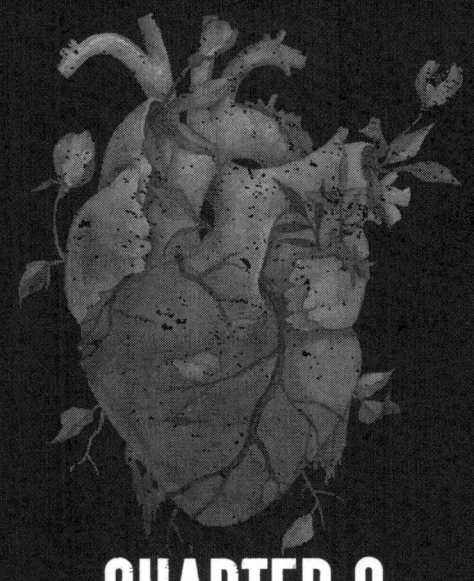

CHAPTER 9

HALLIE

It's been a week since I spoke to Zayne, and I'm angry with myself for even caring at all. I can't help it, though. There's something about him that makes me want to keep going back for more, even though I know he's bad for me.

I need a distraction.

Someone to get under so I can get over him.

I know just the person who would prescribe me that.

I smile deviously as Brit sits on the couch next to me with a pile of books and a notebook. We are studying for our Med-Surg test, and we know it's going to be brutal. Nonetheless, it is Friday, and today, I want to party more than I want to pass my test. I need it even more after going to Art class today and feeling empty without his green eyes to stare into.

"Why are you smiling like that?"

"You know why." I do my signature eye roll and her eyes light up in return.

"You got laid?"

"Sadly no, but I need to."

"I was joking. I know exactly what you look like when you get laid. You've been too mopey for that to have happened, unless it was bad dick, then I'm sorry you had to go through it." She smiles at me. She's always smiling, but she's probably the only person who doesn't annoy me when she does.

"Gosh, sometimes you need to be quiet, Brit Brat. It's like you have diarrhea of the mouth."

"Bitch, do not call me that! You know better!" She throws some couch pillows at me while she laughs.

"Fine, but only if we go to a party tonight."

"Is that what this was about? Of course, we can go to a party. But I'll be on a mission tonight. My one objective will be to get you laid, and it won't be with Zayne."

"If it makes you feel better, go for it."

"Oh, you have no idea what you have unleashed."

"I might have a clue."

"Okay, maybe one." She winks. "Let's start getting ready. Go shower. We need that pussy fresh in case someone wants to feast."

"Oh my fucking God, don't ever say that again!" I screech.

"Oh, please. I think it's my turn to hear you scream." Brit takes the pile of books and opens her bedroom door. "I've done enough of that for the both of us."

"Amen, sister."

I shower, get dressed, do my makeup in record time, and wait for Brittany. My phone buzzes in my back pocket and when I look, Zayne's name is on my screen.

Of course it is.

Zayne: Hey baby. Can I come over? We need to talk.

Is he fucking kidding me? This motherfucker must be insane if he thinks I'm going to let him come over now. He probably just wants to get laid ... Well, not today.

> **Hallie:** There's nothing to talk about. Your silence said everything I needed to know.
>
> **Zayne:** It's not what it looks like. I've been sick.

I hate excuses.

> **Hallie:** I hope you're better. I still don't want to talk to you.
>
> **Zayne:** Is this really how you're going to be?
>
> **Hallie:** Me? Are you fucking kidding me right now? You ghosted me for a week! You could've texted me and said you were sick.
>
> **Zayne:** No I really couldn't have. I was in the hospital.
>
> **Hallie:** Can you just stop texting me? I hope you're better but we are done.
>
> **Zayne:** Fine, whatever. Okay.

And somehow, even though I told him to, a fucked up part of me is angry and hurt that he would agree to leave me alone.

The fucking nerve of him.

How dare he do what I ask him to do?

Fuck, I sound insane.

Maybe I am.

Brittany and I get in the car, and before I know it we are pulling up to the house. It's a modern home with glass walls, and you can see everything happening in there. I'm surprised the police haven't been called, and I figure it's only a matter of time. I hope I'm not high when it happens. We park and go inside. The entrance has a large, white credenza with a cement vase on top and a lamp in the corner. The mirror propped against the wall is ornate and antique-looking, the gold color bouncing from the strobe lights in the house.

I check myself out in the mirror and make sure everything looks in order, and Brit does the same. The hardwood floors feel like they're vibrating under my feet from the bass, and as we make our way through the house, I see some people moving to the beat with each other while others are partaking in activities that aren't suited for the public eye. I cringe internally as I see a girl dry-humping some guy on the couch. Alright, move along Hallie. Nothing to see here.

We find the alcohol and take four shots each. I savor the burning in my chest, wanting to save some for later. The guy with the deep blue eyes from the last party finds his way to me once again, and this time I notice he's tall, blond, and really fit. Just my type. Good fucking job Hals.

This is who I'm taking home tonight.

"Well, you look much better." I wink at him.

"Is your boyfriend with you tonight? I think you're bad for my health." He cringes, fidgeting with his fingers.

Pussy.

"I don't have a boyfriend, but I was really hoping you could pretend to be mine for the night." I smile sweetly, my fakest smile of them all. But he doesn't know, doesn't even catch on at all.

Zayne would know.

"That can be arranged. I'm Daniel." His voice lowers an octave, and it sounds sexy, even if I can barely hear him over the music.

"Daniel," I taste his name on my tongue, the same way I hope he'll be tasting me later. "Let's go have fun!" I pull him to the center of the room with the crowd of people. We sway to the music at first, until the alcohol kicks in and we're dancing together. I feel eyes on me, but I can't tell where they are coming from. I try to look around, but Daniel grabs my hand and pulls me toward the bathroom.

"Do you like Adderall?" he asks me as he closes the door behind us, pulling out something I can't quite see from his back pocket.

"Never tried it."

"Well, tonight is your lucky night," Daniel says as his hand reaches into his back pocket. "We're going to stay up and party, fuck, and party some more."

I laugh at that, "And what makes you think we're going to fuck?"

"Come on, babe. We wouldn't be here if you weren't willing to." He has a point, he really does, but his cockiness is not as attractive as he believes. I'll let it slide this one time since I'm here on a mission.

He pulls out two little baggies full of a pale powder and dumps one on the bathroom counter. He takes his debit card out of his wallet and gathers the powder until it forms a line.

"Have you ever snorted anything before?"

"No." My voice sounds small, and I can't tell if the flips my stomach is doing are from fear or excitement.

"Watch and learn, baby girl."

He rolls up a dollar bill, puts it to his nose, then snorts the entire line and breathes in hard repeatedly. He dumps the other baggie onto the countertop and repeats the process.

I grab the rolled-up dollar bill and imitate him, snorting the white powder. It burns like hell and I can taste the bitterness on my tongue. The post-nasal drip is fucking intense. I repeat the snorting a few times to try to clear my passages and hopefully get the disgusting taste out of my mouth. My heart rate picks up to a gallop and I know my respirations would be up to forty breaths per minute if I cared about counting them.

He hoists me up onto the countertop and I part my legs for him, giving him easy access. His mouth comes down on mine hard, but I can barely focus on the kiss when it feels like my heart might stop at any moment. My chest almost hurts from the intensity, and I don't think I can drink any more than I already have.

Our tongues collide, and I can taste the bitterness on his tongue too. My face scrunches up at the nastiness of it, but I keep kissing him. He yanks my crop top up to expose my breasts, and I immediately feel my nipples pucker, because I didn't wear a bra today. Easy access was the point, but as I kiss him, there's only one thought circling in my brain.

He's not Zayne.

Fuck my life and his too.

I deepen the kiss because I want to feel some spark, some fire, anything. I'll take any feelings as long as they're not about Zayne, but instead, all I can focus on is the bitter taste of the Addie.

The door bursts wide open and before I can process what is happening, Zayne has Daniel pinned against the wall by his throat.

No fucking way.

"What the fuck didn't you understand last time when I said 'that's my girl?'" he growls at Daniel, their faces so close together it's a little weird.

"She said she's not."

"Did she now?" He looks at me with daggers in his eyes. If looks could kill, I'd be six feet under right now. "Well, she lied."

I laugh loudly at that, full-on giggles. I try to cover my mouth as my body shakes from them, but it does nothing to stifle them.

"What the fuck is so funny? You *are* mine."

"Oh, get over it." I snort and roll my eyes. "We were together for five fucking minutes." My giggles continue, and... fuck, is it the Adderall?

"We *are* together, Hallie."

"I don't fucking think so," I cut in. "I broke up with you."

"You don't break up with me, Hallie. That's not how it works." He releases Daniel, and the guy slumps down the wall and to the ground.

"I do what I want, Zayne. This is done. You and I," I motion between us with my hand, "it's not fucking happening, so just let it be."

"I'll decide when this is over, Hallie, and we are far from it. We're just getting started."

With that, he grabs my hand and tries to pull me out of the bathroom, but when I look down I realize my shirt is still above my breasts and they're completely out. I take my hand out of his grasp and fix my shirt while Zayne makes a sound disturbingly close to a growl low in his throat. Daniel must have gotten up in the middle of our argument, because when I look behind me he is shifting on his feet, seeming unsure of his next move. He should run away as fast as possible, only he seems to be waiting for me, and I couldn't be more thankful for it right now.

"I thought you were better than this..." Zayne tells me, his voice low and for my ears only.

Another time, another place, another voice.

Nothing but a whore.

Slap.

Doors slamming.

Belts hitting my legs.

Mom.

"Don't you know? I'm nothing but a whore. So go ahead and lower your expectations of me, because you're about to be so fucking disappointed."

"What the fuck just happened? How do you get that from what I just said?" Zayne visibly shakes, "I'm disappointed that you would give up on us this quickly."

"Oh, honey. There was nothing to give up in the first place." I pat his chest condescendingly, and he looks at me like he might break my hand. "There was nothing here."

"Fuck you, Hallie. That's fucked up."

"Welcome to my life."

I grab Daniel's hand and pull him out of the bathroom. We go to sit on a couch on the other side of the house, and I grab two more drinks on the way there. Once seated, I hand a drink to Daniel and shoot mine back. His eyes flash with something close to lust and he stares at my lips as I run my tongue over them, savoring the vodka.

My eyes find Zayne across the room, pulling a brunette I recognize from some of my past classes toward the staircase.

Catherine.

Well, fuck them both, because I will be doing the same damn

thing tonight. I grab Daniel's face and kiss him again, then wait until Zayne is out of sight to whisper in his ear that we should get a room. We walk up the stairs together, but when he tries to hold my hand I pretend I need to steady myself on the rail, then use it the rest of the way up.

I don't bother knocking on doors before trying to open them, if they're not locked then these people want to be joined or seen. Or maybe they were too drunk to remember to lock it, which is a valid possibility. I walk to the end of the hallway and go for the door straight ahead, then open it.

The room is dark, except once my eyes adjust, I can see a naked ass facing the door. A woman is straddling someone fully clothed, yet she's completely naked. She looks over her shoulder and as the light washes over her, I see it's Catherine. I begin to take steps backward to leave the room, but I run into Daniel.

"Let's get the fuck out of here," I mutter. I'm fucking outraged and want to rip her off my fucking man, but I did this to myself. So I force myself to retreat.

Zayne sits up on the bed, but he's not smug that I caught him. He just looks guilty as he shoves Catherine off him and begins to get off the bed. I turn on my heel and run out of the room, passing even Daniel in the process. Surprisingly, he catches up to me at the bottom of the stairs and grabs my hand.

"Let's go," I say through gritted teeth. "Now." I pull him towards the front door, his hand sweaty in mine. I want to wipe it off on my pants, but I force myself not to.

"Okay."

Before I can process what is going on, I'm in his car, my seatbelt on, and my head spinning. I'm drunk and high, and now that my adrenaline left me, I only see blurs for lights as he drives toward what I'm assuming is his house. I'm wondering how he can drive when I can't even think straight, but that's a question for another time. I don't care where he takes me as long as we make it there in one piece. I also want to get laid, so I'll be making that clear.

I need to forget.

Forget about him.

Forget about *Zayne*.

The problem is that Zayne is not someone who's easy to forget. In fact, it might be fucking impossible. There's no way in hell those green eyes will ever be erased from my mind, which makes me hate him even more, because I can't afford to feel anything for him. I can't afford to be vulnerable. I can, however, afford to erase him from my brain with different hands, different lips, and a different name.

Even if it's only for one night.

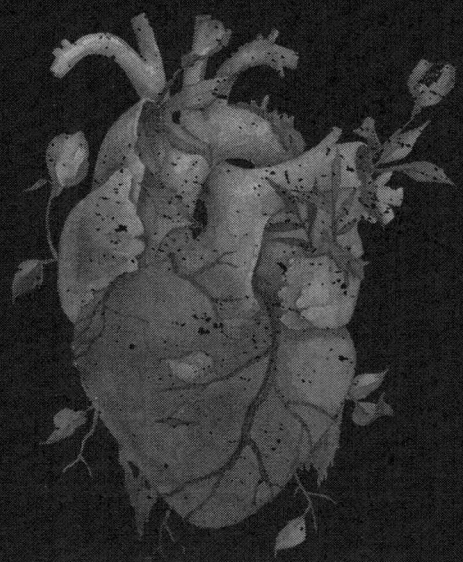

CHAPTER 10

HALLIE

Last night was not what I needed at all. Some might say it was the opposite of a productive night, between the sloppy kissing and the anticlimactic finger-fucking. Turns out Daniel was too high to get *it* to work.

That's what I get for wanting revenge. Karma is a sloppy bitch.

At least he paid for my Uber.

There is a God.

My headache is killing me this morning, so I chug my water bottle until it's empty and throw it against the wall just because I can. I'm in a horrid mood and I don't want to get out of my bed, but I can hear Brit making a smoothie—it's really fucking loud.

There's a moment of silence and then she starts the blender again, but for some reason I don't understand, I hear heavy footsteps outside my door. I see the doorknob twisting—I guess she's not going to bother to knock. Good thing I didn't bring Daniel here. However, when the door opens, Zayne is stepping into my room instead of her.

Is she fucking kidding me right now?

That little *bitch*.

"What the fuck are you doing here?"

"Good morning to you too, baby," he says with more cheer than I could ever muster at eight in the morning. He walks to the front of my bed and stands there, watching me intently as if willing me to get out of bed.

I am not in the mood for this shit.

"Don't call me that. We aren't together, remember?" I snap, remembering Catherine naked on top of him.

"How could I forget?" He chuckles. "You won't stop reminding me. You all but rubbed it in with your tits last night and not in the way I care for."

"I'm glad you enjoyed the show." I give him a sarcastic smile. "Serves you right for walking in where you weren't wanted."

"You really know how to kick someone when they're down, you know that?"

"You're down?" He's got some fucking nerve. Did I say that already? "It didn't look like it when you had Catherine on top of you last night," I say with as much venom as I can muster.

"Are you jealous?" The smirk on his face and the lift of his brow, both piss me off even more. "You left with that guy, and don't even try to tell me you only kissed him." Zayne doesn't dare to come closer but he's also not far away. Even now, it feels like his heated stare licks flames across my face.

I will my facial expression to tell him that I did so much more, but I still don't admit to anything. "How do you know I left with Daniel? You didn't even go after me."

"I have eyes everywhere, baby girl."

"Great. So you're a fucking stalker, too."

"Only when I don't get what I want." Zayne crosses his arms over his chest, making his biceps bulge and his corded forearms flex. I close my eyes so I don't have to look at so much perfection.

I don't think I can resist him for much longer. "I'm not sure why you aren't giving in because I know you want me, too."

"I don't want you." I don't believe it, and he most definitely doesn't believe it, but if he thinks I'm going to forgive him as soon as he asks me to, he's got another thing coming. "I said I would give you a chance and you fucked it all up."

"Why? Because I stood you up? I'm fucking sorry. I was sick."

"You weren't sick enough to not be able to pick up your phone and text me."

"Oh, yeah?" He laughs. "And how would you know? Were you there with me?"

"So tell me what was wrong with you."

Zayne leans toward the bed, grabbing the footboard. "No."

"NO?"

"That is what I just said."

"So, that's it? You're not going to explain yourself?"

"I'm not. There's no point, Hallie." His green eyes burn into mine, and he looks determined. I don't like it. I want to know what the fuck is going on. "I was sick, and I missed school for a week. Do you think I would do that for fun?"

"I don't know? I don't know anything about you." Lies, but he doesn't need to know that. "Why can't you just tell me the truth? Why is that so hard for you?"

"Trust me, Hallie. You don't want my truths."

"Trust you? That's rich." I'm getting really fed up with him. "You want me to trust you, and yet you're telling me you will lie?"

"Have you always told the truth?"

No.

"Yes."

He throws his head back and laughs, and I know how it sounds after it flies out of my mouth. No one has ever been entirely truthful every day of their lives.

"Oh, Hallie." He sighs. "Who's the liar now?"

Well, damn. I guess I am, but that's nothing new.

"I don't want to deal with this anymore, quite honestly. I need a shower and to brush my teeth. You can just see yourself out."

He still won't move, even after I practically just kicked him out, so I get out of my bed and walk around him to my bathroom. As I shut the door, I see him walking out.

I take my sweet time between washing my hair, shaving my legs, and exfoliating. Basically, everything important in one long shower. When I come out though, he's sitting on my bed instead of leaving like I asked him to. But should I even have expected any less?

I completely ignore him and start digging for underwear in my drawer, my body only wrapped in a towel. I find an old t-shirt and a pair of leggings to wear and don't bother to find a bra, since he isn't staying anyway.

"I'm not trying to be rude, but did you not catch the part where I kicked you out?" I ask without even looking at him. "Or are you confused? Do you need directions back to your car?"

"I'm not lost or confused, Hals." I can almost hear the smile in his voice and it irritates me to no end. "But I'm not going anywhere until we are back together."

"You are persistent, I'll give you that. I don't really want to get back together. Besides, I don't even think we can call it that. I don't think we were ever together. We kissed one fucking time, Zay."

I turn around to see Zayne get up from the bed and walk my way, and that's when I notice the door is closed *and* locked. Every single instinct screams at me to get out of this room, that if I stay I will never be able to break his hold on me again, but instead I stay rooted to the spot.

"And yet that was the most perfect kiss I've ever had." Zayne pauses, searching my face. "Everything about us feels right."

His steps are slow and steady as he approaches me, as if he is trying not to spook me, even though right now I'm a deer in headlights. I still don't move, even as my body screams at me to fucking bolt.

My body has always betrayed me since that fateful night when

I was twelve years old, and now when I'm in a dangerous situation, I just... freeze.

My feet finally start working and I back away from him, but that gets me closer to the bed and I have to maneuver around him. Once Zayne notices I'm running away, he's quick on his feet and relentless in his approach. He's in front of me again in no time and gets close enough that there is barely any space between us. I have to tilt my chin up to look at him, and at this angle he looks even more beautiful. How is that even possible?

Zayne's thumb brushes over my bottom lip, and his touch trails across my jaw and neck until his fingers get lost in my hair. He tilts my head back and kisses me, his tongue slipping into my mouth. My body, unfortunately, betrays me and I open for him. It's as if he knows all the right things to say, all the right things to do, and exactly what I need. He knows how to snare me in his trap every time, and I'm easy prey now—because as much as I like to play hard to get, I know I want him. I want him more than I've ever wanted anyone before.

But I also know he enjoys the chase.

So I'm going to make him run for me.

He throws me onto the bed and I land on my back, but before I can process what is happening, he pushes my knees apart and folds my legs against my chest as he climbs on top of me. His mouth collides with mine again and he deepens the kiss, tongues gliding with each other. It's a bit sloppy, but it's making me so hot I feel like I might catch on fire any moment.

My towel is open and I can feel my bare pussy rubbing against his jeans, although any friction will do now. I grab his ass and begin to gently rock against him, making him groan into my mouth. The vibration from his throat sends a chill down my spine and I grip him harder. Why is this so fucking hot? I've never cared to do much of this before. Usually, I just fuck people and move on, even foreplay isn't my thing.

Zayne begins to rock back against me until I'm sure I'm soaking his pants, which he should mind but obviously does not. If he has me more worked up than I have ever been with just some kissing and dry humping; I can't even imagine what sex with him would be like.

I break the kiss, breathing hard, and scoot up in the bed, seeking some distance between us so I can think clearly. I make sure my towel is wrapped around my body and that nothing is visible, and I feel his eyes on me. He clearly has different plans as he crawls back up to me with a predatory smile and sits in front of me, crossing his legs, as if waiting for me to say what's next.

Doesn't he know I won't fold?

I raise my right eyebrow at him and let my towel drop, watching his reaction as it pools around my hips. His eyes widen slightly, but then he slowly looks down my body, as if memorizing every square inch of me. Oddly, it doesn't make me self-conscious like it would with anyone else. I feel confident, beautiful even, so I spread my legs and give him a generous view of my sex.

He reaches for my ankles and yanks me across the bed, the towel falling away completely and exposing me to him more than before. His thumb presses against my clit and he lowers himself onto his elbows, licking his lips. His breath is warm against my skin, and I squirm when he blows on me.

"I'm not usually into this… I might not be able to come." It typically feels like it tickles or it hurts, which can't be right.

Zayne grabs my thighs, pulling me up to his face rather than coming down to me, and the way he smiles makes me want to clench my thighs, but he's currently holding them. His hot breath on my most intimate part sends tingles down my spine. He's driving me fucking crazy and he knows it as I buck my hips toward his face, seeking friction, anything that will make this ache go away. When he cups my ass and gives my clit a kiss, I groan.

He begins to lick slowly, tasting me, then licks me from center to clit a few times. When he takes the bundle of nerves into his mouth, sucking with slight pressure, my eyes roll to the back of my head. It feels… fucking *amazing*.

Nothing should feel this good from the first contact, but it's like every nerve ending in my clit has come alive and I have never felt anything so intense. I might finish in under one minute, I can already feel it. How fucking embarrassing.

His tongue swirls over my clit over and over until I feel the heat blooming inside of me, scorching and low. I can hear myself gasping and moaning, and it's like I'm outside of my body. I don't sound like me.

"I should probably stop since you don't like it." he rasps and begins to pull away, except I grab his hair and hold him in place. I feel him smiling over me as I rock my hips against his tongue, but he pulls slightly away and asks, "Is this what you want?"

"Yes!" I close my legs around his head. "*Please.*"

Zayne begins to lick me again and I put the pillow over my face and groan as I feel the orgasm building. His tongue has a steady rhythm exactly where I need it, and I meet each flick of it. My right hand is lightly pulling at his hair while the left one has a death grip on the sheets, and he doesn't seem to mind that I'm probably choking him with my legs. He reaches up and threads his fingers through mine with one hand, the other still gripping one of my hips.

This lasts only a second though, because he reaches up to each of my nipples and squeezes them lightly once, and then again with more pressure.

I see fucking stars.

I'm so close to finishing I can almost taste the orgasm, but he raises me higher and begins to lick my ass instead. I squirm under him, but the longer he does it, the better it feels. He stops pinching my nipples and begins to rub circles on my clit while he licks me, but it's driving me so crazy that I pull on his hair, directing him back to where I want him again, which he actually lets me do.

He sucks my clit between his lips and begins to move his head from side to side, and I literally lose track of what is happening, except for what is building inside of me.

"*Zayne.*" I sound needy, and I must admit it's foreign to my ears. Men don't get me worked up like this. I don't beg anyone to let me come.

He gives me just the right amount of pressure and I feel the orgasm tear through me like a category-five hurricane, the force of it knocking me off center. My legs are shaking and I swear I see white spots behind my eyes, even as I squeeze them shut. The dizziness I feel even though I'm lying on my back is concerning. What the fuck did he do to me?

Never in my fucking life have I come this hard.

I realize he has something I want. I'm the queen of using sex as a crutch, but no one has ever made me feel quite like this before, and I want more... I think I'd do just about anything to get it.

"What the fuck..." I whisper, completely forgetting he's even in the room with me still as he gets up from between my legs.

Zayne smirks when I look his way, wiping his mouth with the back of his hand. "I almost came in my pants from listening to you, Hallie."

"Your turn." I smile shyly, but he shakes his head.

"I don't want this to be about me today."

"So that's it then? What happened to all this talk about getting back together?"

He stands from the bed and adjusts himself in his jeans, shoving his hand in his pants to get it done. I want him to take them off and finish this. "Do you want to?"

"I don't know."

"Then call me when you figure it out. You have my number."

Oh hell no, he's not walking away from me right now.

"Zayne, wait." I raise my voice, trying to get his attention before he leaves me naked on the bed. "Let me get dressed and we can talk."

"I thought you wanted nothing to do with me."

"Are you serious right now? What game are you playing? Either you want this, or you don't. Just say it now, so I don't talk to you again and this whole thing can be fucking done."

"I'll say when this is over, Hals." My body tenses as he comes to the edge of the bed once more, leaning over it to get close again. "Remember?"

The heaving of my chest draws his attention, and his eyes once more focus on my puckered nipples. "You're not in control here."

"Oh, Hallie."

"What?" I search his face, "'Oh, Hallie' what?"

"Tell yourself whatever you need to."

"I will. Now leave." I'm not sure what's going on. How does he go from giving me the best orgasm of my life to... this? I literally cannot keep up.

"No."

"I thought you wanted to. You change your mind too much, and you're giving me whiplash."

"Get used to it."

"No thank you, not into it."

"What *are* you into?" He smiles, "Wait, don't tell me. I really think you liked it when I sucked on your clit."

"Zayne, don't talk about that!" I can feel my face turning redder than a tomato, and he smirks at me.

"Why?" His fingers trail a path from my belly and down to my pussy again. "Are you embarrassed?"

"I don't like talking like that."

"Oh baby, I didn't think you were a prude." I almost groan at how good it feels when he dips his fingers in my wetness and rubs them up my slit. Although I refuse to give him the satisfaction. "You don't look like one."

"Wouldn't you like to know?"

"Oh, I think I just found out when you let me lick your ass."

"Out." I sit up abruptly, "Get out."

"I'm staying." He chuckles, "I won't say anything else about it for now." I don't believe a word he says, but I sigh in defeat as I search for my towel on the bed, trying to shield my body from his view as much as possible.

"Are you stepping out while I get dressed?" I get up from the bed and search for the scattered clothes. I can't remember where I put them, but then again, he seems to make me forget everything around me. The only thing I can focus on is him.

"What's the point? I've already seen it all, and I loved every second of it." He licks his lips suggestively, his teeth scraping his bottom lip when he's done. It makes me hot all over again, but I tell myself I will not have sex with him yet.

I roll my eyes for the millionth time today and put on a t-shirt first so he can no longer see my body, then pull the pair of leggings on, altogether foregoing the underwear. I climb back in my bed and push the covers away toward the foot of it.

"Are you staying?"

"Didn't think you were a cuddler."

I narrow my eyes at him, "What did you think I was then?"

"Well… the kind who would probably kill me if I got too comfortable?"

I laugh so hard that my stomach hurts and I shake the bed. It's probably the first time a guy has made me laugh this hard in years. *Wow, I can still laugh. Who knew?* "Damn. Those are the vibes you're getting from me?" I wipe my eyes. "I like that a lot."

"I like *you* a lot," Zayne tells me under his breath as he climbs in bed and lines up his body behind mine.

His face is in my hair and his body is flush against mine down to the tip of my toes. My feet are slightly between his legs and his arm is draped over me as his breathing slows down, taking deep breaths. I can feel him smelling my hair, his inhalations so deep I'm almost afraid he's going to breathe me in instead.

"I just want one chance, Hallie. One chance to make it right. One shot at making you fall in love with me."

"I don't fall in love."

"Everyone falls in love, and I want you to love me." His draped arm moves from my waist and begins to trail fingertips up my arm, giving me goosebumps.

"I can give you my body, but I will never give you my heart."

"Why?"

I scoff, knowing damn well this can't end well between us. He screams of trouble. One look at him, and you can see the cloud of chaos hanging right over his head. "Because I know how this plays out, and I've been hurt enough for this lifetime and the next."

"Hallie…"

"What?"

"Baby, yours is the only heart I'll never break." I taste his lies on my tongue, but the problem is that even those taste sweet right now.

Zayne smiles against my hair and tightens his arm around me, and I settle into him as I feel my body getting heavy with sleep. I probably shouldn't be getting this comfortable with him, or any other guy, but I quickly forget that when I feel him twitching. I decide to let sleep claim me as well, even if only for a short amount of time.

As I begin to fall, I wonder how long it will be before I land on my face. How long will it be before my heart is shattered beyond repair? How long will it be before I don't recognize the person in the mirror?

My alter ego reminds me again, as if I could forget: I've never liked the things that are good for me.

CHAPTER 11

ZAYNE

I know I can't tell Hallie about my diagnosis, because she will run as far from me as she can. Everyone always does. Honestly, who can even blame them? But it would be nice for someone to have my back once in a while, to just know what I'm going through and love me regardless.

My dad wasn't one of those people. He left when everything was the heaviest, when I was at my lowest. I was fifteen years old, and he told my mother that I wouldn't ever get better and that he didn't want to keep doing this.

He left us because of *me*.

He left us because of my mental illness.

And someone loving me regardless of it, well… I don't think it's in the cards for me.

I hate lying to Hallie, but it's second nature at this point. I can't tell her the truth, I'm too far in. I'm feeling too deeply, and I can already feel myself wanting more and more.

Hallie twitches under me, the sound of her breathing pulling me in and out of a deep slumber. I bury my face in her long, straight hair and inhale. I love the smell of her hair, it grounds me. It's addicting, just like her. Her hair smells like the rest of her, but even better. The vanilla and flowery smell are more potent, but there's something else, something fruity like berries.

She stirs in her sleep and tries to turn to face me, but I tighten my grip around her waist to keep her in place. Her breathing is no longer slow and sleepy, and I'm sure she's ready to kick me out again right about now. Maybe she realized this was all a mistake and she doesn't actually want me the way I want her.

"Hallie, baby." My voice is deep from not talking for so long, and I clear my throat and let her turn around to face me.

"Hmm?"

"Do you want some coffee?" I ask her, and she opens one eye to peer at me. She's fucking adorable. "Donuts?"

"I love donuts." Hallie's hopeful face makes my chest hurt. It's like she's not used to people being nice to her, which is weird because she's a nice person overall. Unlike me. "Blueberry, please."

"Anything for you." I get up from the bed and go to the bathroom to take care of business, then go in search of my clothes around her room since I removed my shirt and pants in my sleep.

Her back is to me, as her oversized t-shirt rides up to show me her underwear and perfectly round ass. I put my clothes back on slower than I should, definitely distracted by what I'm leaving in bed, and head out in search of donuts. I regret it the entire time, however. I should've fucked her instead. I undoubtedly had a good chance. I try to remind myself that I'm doing something nice for her though, and she will appreciate this way more than my dick. This shows her that I care about her for more than just sex. Or maybe that's what I tell myself to make me feel better.

The bakery is one block away, so I don't bother to drive. I get a dozen donuts, a few blueberry and an assortment of other flavors as well. I figure I might as well get some extras in case her friend wants a few, I should probably stay on her good side since she did let me in without Hallie's permission.

I go back to the apartment and I'm greeted excitedly at the door. I guess next time, I might as well just buy her donuts when I ask her to get back together, or maybe eating her out will do the trick.

I walk to the kitchen and turn around in front of the island, smiling at her while admiring how quickly she cleans up. "Here you go, baby girl." I hand her the box, and she gets on her tiptoes and grabs it from my hand while simultaneously giving me a kiss—the ultimate distraction.

"Thank you!"

"You're so fucking beautiful." I reach out to grab her free hand, bringing her wrist to my lips and planting a soft kiss on it. "So perfect. Everything I need in my life." The words I'm saying are true, but even now I'm trying to hold back and not spook her. I can tell she gets scared easily and I don't want to push her away again.

"I'm sorry I don't respond well to compliments." Hallie's smile is weak, barely there. "It's not personal."

"Why?"

"Because people usually don't say nice things about me. I destroy everything good."

"Maybe we have that in common."

"I don't think it's a good thing."

"Never said it was." I gently tilt her chin up and stare into her eyes. It's like she's looking straight into my soul with the way she searches my gaze. As if she's hoping to find something within me, but I know she won't be able to. "Who said mean things about you?"

"It doesn't matter, Zay."

"It does. I want to know you. I want it so badly." I brush her hair away from her face and tuck it behind her left ear. "What will it take to get you to talk to me?"

"I'm not sure. I don't really trust you." I search her eyes, " You don't feel like my people."

"And what do your people feel like?"

"They feel like the kind that stay." She whispers, maybe hoping I don't hear her answer.

And I understand what she means, even if I don't like it. I understand that maybe, more than likely, I will never be her person, because I slip through everyone's fingers like smoke in the wind.

But then why do I want her to catch me?

Fishermen's Park might just be one of my favorite places, and I take in the view as I sit on one of the benches in front of the riverwalk area. I light my blunt and take a hit, savoring the taste and holding the smoke in my lungs until it makes me violently cough.

I ponder what I should do about Hallie. She said she would give me a chance, but is that really the right thing to do? Should I be letting her go?

Oh, who the fuck am I even kidding?

I've never done the right thing, and I'm not starting now, especially not when it comes to her. I have to have her.

Zayne: Can I come over?

Hallie: For what?

Zayne: Do I even need to say it?

Hallie: Yes.

Zayne: I want more of you. I want to taste you again.

Hallie: *typing*

Zayne: I tasted your sweet, sweet pussy and now I need more. I NEED MORE.

Hallie: What do you have in mind?

Zayne: I want to make you scream my name.

Hallie: Really, now? How about you come over and we play some games and drink then?

Zayne: Yes, I'm in.

Hallie: Come over at eight?

Zayne: I'll be there.

I look up from my phone to see my friend Jeremy walking my way, and I scoot over to make some space for him on the bench, offering him my blunt when he sits down. He takes a hit and hands it back to me, and we pass the next few minutes doing this. I can't help but think about how much peace this place brings me.

"What's up, man?" Jeremy asks after he exhales the smoke.

"Not much." I shrug, then take back the blunt. "Just keeping to myself lately."

"Really?" He chuckles, "Because last time I saw you, I couldn't figure out if you were with Catherine or the other brunette."

"I will never be with Catherine." I try not to feel insulted, but fuck, is this what people think? Fuck that. "I don't like her enough for a relationship. In fact, her very breathing annoys the hell out of me."

Jeremy laughs and slaps his leg, his head thrown back as his shoulders shake. I'm not lying though, I didn't say it to be funny. I really can't stand a hair on her fucking head. I mostly just want an easy lay, and that's her all the way. Someone I don't have to put in any effort for. She's not work, and sometimes it's appealing.

"Well damn, bro. At least you're honest." Jeremy shakes his head, and I offer him the blunt again. He takes a hit and hands it back to me, then I take another hit.

"Only when I want to be."

We spend some time in silence and I get lost in my thoughts. It's a chilly night, and all I can think of is how I want to bring Hallie here next, I know she will love it. She has that girl next-door vibe that I love. I'm not sure what I like about the good girl facade, because there's unmistakably nothing sweet about her. You can tell she has a good heart, but she will chew you up and spit you back out without thinking twice. I *want* her to chew me up, though. I want her to ruin my fucking life if that's what she wants, as long as she's in it.

Have you ever needed someone more than the air in your lungs?

That's what she feels like.

Like I'm coming up for air.

She's my oxygen.

And it's scary as hell that I feel this way already.

But I do.

Somehow.

I just hope she doesn't cut me off and suffocate me.

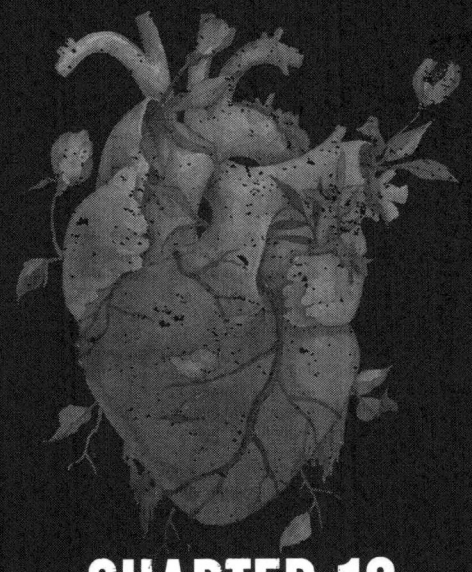

CHAPTER 12

HALLIE

Eight o'clock rolls around and Zayne is not here. I hate tardiness, I really fucking hate it. Maybe it's because I'm used to people not showing up in my life, and it triggers my anxiety.

Brittany has gone to someone else's house for the night and has promised to give me some space to let whatever needs to happen with Zayne… happen. I'm not sure I'm ready for a relationship, but it doesn't seem like there's any going back when it comes to him. Even if I wanted to, he's the type of guy who wouldn't let me. He's intense, and I can tell he's overly jealous and controlling from the encounters with Daniel. I don't like that about him, but it seems to be a package deal, and I already know Zayne has my heart in a chokehold. Even if I never agreed to let myself feel for him.

I pace my living room until I'm sure the hardwood is worn and my feet hurt. My phone begins to ring and I answer it before looking at who it is, thinking it's Zayne. My mother's voice comes from the receiver, and my heart stops dead in its tracks.

"Hallie. How are you?" My mom has always been one to pretend everything is okay. I don't talk to her often, in fact I rarely ever do. Out of all the people I hate, she's definitely the second on my list.

"Is something wrong with my brothers?"

"Can't a mom call her daughter without there being something wrong?"

"Not when it comes to us, no."

"I just wanted to see how you were doing."

"Really? Did you want to see how I was doing when I was taken from your house, and you ran away with Michael?"

"Hallie, it's been seven years since that happened. I think it's time to move on."

I laugh darkly at that, the irony of the situation is not lost on me, but somehow she always manages to get under my skin, no matter how hard I try to dig her out. Sometimes I think I try so hard that it transfers physically. I pick at myself until I draw blood, and it doesn't even hurt. It feels like relief. It feels like I'm clawing my demons out.

And I really fucking want them out.

"Yes, sure. Let's pretend like nothing ever happened. Is that what you want, *Mommy*?" I ask her sarcastically. "You want me to sweep it all under the rug like you always do?" I dig my nails into my arm until I feel pain, which apparently takes a lot because I see the blood pooling where the half-moon marks appear.

"Nothing even happened. You're just a fucking liar."

"I learned from the best, didn't I?"

"This is going nowhere, Hallie. It's no wonder we have no relationship. You can't get your shit together enough to have a civilized conversation with your own mother."

She can't be serious. But then again, it's her. Of course, she's fucking serious. "My mother died the day that she took Michael's side. As far as I'm concerned, she doesn't exist. You should stop calling, especially if you're going to call me a liar. It's never going to end well."

I hang up the phone and toss it on the couch, then watch it bounce and fall to the floor. Tears prick my eyes, and I feel the frustration bubbling to the surface as I think about how Zayne stood me up again. How could he do this shit to me *again*? There's no way he's sick now, he looked fine this morning.

Knock, knock, knock.

My heart stutters in my chest at the familiar sound, and about ten different memories flash through my mind in slow motion. The knocks come again, louder this time, pulling me out of my waking nightmares.

I open the door and find a smiling Zayne holding something behind his back, but as he looks me over the smile turns into a frown. "What happened?" he asks, the concern evident on his face.

"I thought you weren't going to show up."

"Did I make you cry?" He searches my eyes for answers, "Fuck, Hallie, I'm sorry, baby. I swear I wasn't going to stand you up, I just wanted to do something nice for you."

"What?" I ask, confused, "No. I was crying about something else."

"Is that supposed to make me feel better?"

"Yes?" I wipe my face and smile at him. "I'm all better. Now show me what's behind your back."

He grins at me and hands me a bouquet of red roses—a dozen of them. They're beautiful and smell incredible. I let him in and walk to the kitchen to find one of Brittany's vases to put my new flowers in while he makes himself comfortable on one of the barstools at the kitchen island.

He looks cozy today, wearing a black V-neck shirt and gray sweatpants that make his ass look amazing and give me a good view of the bulge in the front.

God have mercy on my soul, I'm so fucked.

Hopefully, literally.

"Thank you, Zay. This was so nice of you." They really are

beautiful, and I continue to admire them as I set them on the kitchen island. "No one's ever gotten me flowers before."

"You're kidding, right?"

"No? Why would I joke about that?" I say, chuckling awkwardly. The fact of the matter is that I've always hated flowers. They die and remind me that nothing sticks around, but I don't tell him that.

"All your other boyfriends sucked then."

"Boyfriend? Is that what you are?"

"Obviously. I don't get anyone flowers." I can see that. He doesn't look like the type of guy who would get flowers on the regular.

"Well, now I feel special," I say, rolling my eyes at him, but nothing could wipe the grin from my face, even if I can't look him in the eyes. He gets up from the barstool and walks around the island until he's standing next to me, and I turn to look up at him. His pupils dilate until the storm behind his irises begins to rage harder, faster, stronger.

There's something unique about his eyes. I thought they were olive green, but I was wrong. They're similar to a mood ring; I see them change colors based on how he feels and the color of his clothes. Today they are a gray-blue, the color of the ocean on an overcast day, and they are so beautiful I want to drown in them.

"You're the most special person in my life." My stomach drops at his statement because I know it's much too soon for these kinds of comments, but I feel it in my soul that they're true. I feel it in my bones that this is right.

"You can't say things like that yet, Zay." I grip the edge of the island. "It's too soon…"

"Too soon for what?" He walks closer to me until we're toe to toe. "When you know, you know." He smiles at me and brushes his thumb over my lip, which seems to be something he loves to do, then grabs my chin roughly and tilts my head back. "And I fucking know."

He leans in for a kiss, and I grab the back of his neck to pull him down further. Our mouths collide, and we kiss each other as if the world is ending right at this very moment. My hands tangle in his hair and I yank hard, pulling his head back, which only makes him moan into my mouth. He seeks me out hungrily, ready to devour me.

I break away from the kiss and he looks confused for a second before a mask of indifference settles over his face. I'm assuming this is his defense mechanism to cover up the hurt of rejection. However I'm not actually rejecting him. Quite the opposite, truly. He just doesn't know that yet. He can't see it.

"Why don't we play a game?" I ask him.

"What kind of game?"

"Oh, I know!" I already texted him this, so I'm surprised he doesn't remember. "Let's play a drinking game."

"Only if I can ask you questions." He looks thoughtful for a second and then his eyes light up. "I want to play 20 questions, but if you refuse to answer, you take a drink instead. We alternate, so a question for a question."

"That sounds fair. So, a shot for each skipped question?"

"Yes, that could work."

"I'm going to be wasted!" I laugh, even though I've been wasted more times than I care to admit in the last week. What's one more time?

"You better answer all my questions then." He laughs, and I feel my stomach flip at the sound of it.

"Let me grab that bottle, then let's go to my room." Zayne smirks at that. "We can just play on the bed."

"If I go to your bed, I'll be playing with something else ..."

"Fine, the floor it is." I go to the freezer and grab the Crown Royal Peach Whiskey which always tastes better freezing cold. "Guess you're going to have to be uncomfortable since you can't keep it in your pants." I can almost feel the delicious burn and fruity aftertaste, making me want to skip questions on purpose. When I turn around, Zayne is already in my room so I make my way to him and shut the door behind me, locking it just in case

Brit comes home unexpectedly. We sit on the plush white rug on the side of my bed and I arrange our shot glasses and the whiskey, ready to get hurt.

"I ask the first question," he says with twinkling eyes, reaching for the shot glasses.

"Okay, shoot."

"What's your favorite color?"

"Are you serious right now?"

Zayne chuckles, the sound vibrating through my body. "We have to start small with you, baby. Don't want to spook you yet."

"Blue," I sigh. "What's your favorite ice cream flavor?"

"Cookies and cream."

Mine's Rocky Road, see? Not meant to be.

He thinks hard before asking the next question, "Do you believe in love at first sight?"

"No. Do you?" I ask, skeptical.

"Yes, but *no* I will not elaborate," he says, and I chuckle at him. "What was your first impression of me?"

"Honestly, I thought you had the most beautiful eyes I had ever seen," I answer quietly. It's hard giving him my thoughts. I don't often share them willingly with a man. "I thought you were just… intense."

"Intense?" He scoffs. "That's one way to put it."

"What was your first impression of me, Zayne?" I ask him, getting more curious by the moment.

"Skip." He grins down at me. "Pour me a shot, baby."

"That was quick," I laugh. "Already chickening out?"

"Gotta keep it interesting."

"Yes, of course."

The shot skips his turn and now he can ask his next question.

"How many people have you said 'I love you' to?"

"No one." I hold my breath for a second and release it. If we are on the topic of love, then I'm going to just ask the questions I'm genuinely curious about. I want to dig into the deepest levels of his soul. "Would you rather love someone and lose them, or never love at all?"

"Love and lose." He stares into my eyes as if he knows all my deepest darkest secrets. "I'd rather lose you than never love you."

I grab the whiskey, pour myself a shot, and then throw it back. He smiles although it quickly turns into a laugh that has him doubled over on the floor. "What is so funny?" I narrow my eyes, trying to think of whatever I did that has him reacting this way. "I don't understand."

"You, baby." He straightens up, looking at me with curiosity. "You're scared of me."

"Terrified."

Zayne tilts his head, "Why?"

"Because you're the first person who has affected me in a long time."

"I don't think it's a bad thing."

Not necessarily for him, but for me, it's fucking tragic. "I think it's inconvenient to feel all of this right now, especially since I've been trying to block everything out."

He reaches for my hair and tucks a strand behind my right ear. I feel myself relaxing, my body betraying me at every turn when it comes to him.

"Let me in, Hallie. I want all of you."

"No one can have that." I breathe out slowly, and he gets closer.

"My turn again…" He looks up at the ceiling as if praying to someone. "What are your nightmares about?"

"Skip," I say, pouring myself a drink. "I may never answer that question."

"Why? What could be so bad that you can't share it with me?"

"It was something that never should've happened, Zayne." I take the shot, grimacing as it burns my esophagus. I still love the taste of it, in any case. "Now, please drop it."

"No, I want to know. I *need* to know."

"I said no." Point blank. This is not a topic I want to discuss now, possibly ever. "I won't change my mind."

"Hallie, please. I'll beg if I have to."

"Save yourself the humiliation. It's not happening."

"Fine." He looks irritated, but I honestly couldn't care less. This is where I draw the line. Talking about Michael is not happening. My mind conjures him up enough in my sleeping moments. I also don't want to think of him in my waking moments.

As much as I want to act like none of this matters, a part of me is happy he cares at all. I have never had anyone press me about my nightmares the way he has, and I think that's why I'm uncomfortable. No one has ever cared. Instead, everyone has pointed out how the incident was somehow my fault. That I let it happen for too long, or simply that I was just a liar.

It feels good to be acknowledged this way, even if he has no idea he is doing it. I can slowly feel the puzzle coming together, our pieces being arranged to fit awkwardly.

I just hope none of them are missing as I let him into my heart, bit by bit.

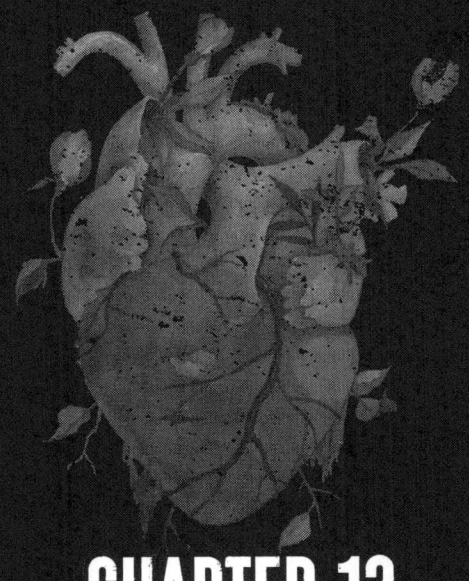

CHAPTER 13

HALLIE

I pace back and forth in my bathroom as I contemplate my choices. I either let Zayne stay over tonight and we have sex, or I tell him to go home before everything escalates.

Memories of the last time he stayed flash through my mind in quick succession, and I wipe a hand down my face. I feel like a horny teenager who can't think straight when he's near, and right now my body is screaming at me to just give in. The lingerie bodysuit that I'm wearing under my clothes seems to make the decision for me; I'd hate to let such a pretty thing go unseen.

I take off my clothes and leave them on the floor next to my bathtub. Taking one last look in the mirror, I ensure everything is in order before opening the door with as much confidence as I can muster and walking across the room to my bed. The lights are already off and a small bedside lamp dimly illuminates the room.

How did he know?

I push the covers back as I climb on the bed and crawl to

the headboard slowly, giving him a full view of my ass. The few shots of whiskey I took make me brave, and he stares at me for a second before taking off his shirt and his pants at the side of my bed. He lets them fall to the floor and just stands there, waiting for my next move.

I turn around and kneel on the bed, lifting my hands to my hair and tangling them in the dark mass of curls I styled just for him, and then I sweep them off my shoulders. In a light caress, I slide my hands down my chest and over my breasts, lightly pinching the rose buds through the lace. His eyes stray down to witness what I'm doing, and he holds them there, all but pinning me in place.

Zayne groans as I make my way lower, his eyes becoming a wildfire, threatening to burn me alive. It's as if my body belongs to someone else, someone unfamiliar, so willing to put her body on display, confident and determined.

"Come here," I say, motioning with my finger.

He stands his ground, but I crawl back to the edge of the bed and offer him my hand. He raises one perfect eyebrow at me and walks closer, taking my hand. He gently lowers me to the bed, and I feel the mattress dip with his weight as he joins me, kneeling between my legs.

Zayne runs his hands over my legs and I close my eyes, losing myself in the feeling. His warm hands roam up until they cup my ass, and he gives it a firm squeeze. He moves his hands back to the inside of my thighs which has me screwing my eyes shut even harder, and I almost stop breathing when his fingers meet the edge of my bodysuit, trailing over my center with light pressure.

When I open my eyes and see his face, my breath hitches in my throat. I'm privileged to be looked upon with so much desire. His eyes keep blazing that emerald fire, burning me to an incredibly dangerous temperature, and I feel as if I could be incinerated to ash.

The lines of his abs stand out against his tan skin and I can't take my eyes off him as he sits back on his haunches in front of me.

"So beautiful," his voice is husky and goes straight to my pussy as I spread my legs wider for him in invitation.

He leans over me, getting closer, bodies barely touching as he reaches for my face. His lips part and he closes his eyes as he leans in for a kiss, gripping my jaw painfully.

"Hals..." His need is evident in the reverent way he says my name. I tremble, a storm of desire ravaging my insides. When his eyes open again, they glow even brighter, the emerald looking like it's melting.

I close the distance between us, taking a hold of the nape of his neck and all but dragging him down to my lips. As soon as they touch, a jolt of electricity runs through me. The touch of our lips is a soft caress, barely there.

I need more.

I deepen the kiss, gliding my tongue against his lips, and he grips me harder as his mouth opens for me. A soft moan escapes me, and he matches it with his own.

Zayne's hand curves around my hip, straying lower to cup my ass again, kneading my softness. His touch makes my body go tight, my nipples hardening to near-painful peaks, and his hand drifts over my abdomen as he begins to trail light kisses along my jaw, his warm hardness pressed against my leg.

His hand slips below my navel as he moves south until his mouth is over my left breast and pauses there, licking it once and moving on to the other. His mouth replaces his hands and he moves even lower, and I feel my body tensing, screaming at me, begging for contact, for anything.

Anything he will give.

"Let me worship you, baby girl." My answering groan is all he needs to grab my hips and lift me off the bed toward his face.

Zayne drops between my legs and moves my bodysuit to the side to taste me, his breath dancing over the bundle of nerves between my legs for a split second, and then he lowers his mouth onto me. The first lick is long and slow, as if he's licking an ice cream cone, entrance to clit, and my back arches off the bed. He knows exactly what he is doing as he closes his mouth around my clit and sucks, pinching the bud lightly between his teeth as he pulls away.

Shock splashes through me as I feel the cool air on the most sensitive part of me as he pulls back, lifting his head to look at me. I grab hold of his head and push him down onto me again, until his mouth is brushing against me, only he doesn't move.

"Please," I whisper, begging for more. I can't breathe, can't think. My body shudders as his breath caresses me, and I am desperate for him, would give my soul for him to take me now.

Oh, God.

He dips his head, and the air leaves my lungs in a forced exhalation as his tongue slices over the center of me, over and over. His wet, open-mouth kisses and light sucks turn more desperate as I buck my hips and grip his hair, and he knows I'm getting closer to the edge. My moans are loud in the small space of my room, and I can't control them anymore. It feels way too fucking good. I prop myself onto my elbows to peer down at him, his hand splayed on my lower belly holding me down, and he grows frantic, nipping, biting, and licking. I cry out louder as my head falls back onto the bed again and my body trembles slightly.

His skin looks golden against the soft lighting in my room, the dying rays of the sun kissing it; he reminds me of an angel for a split second, despite the devilish things his tongue is doing. I close my eyes, almost tasting my orgasm, and I know it's heavy on his tongue. He grips my hips tighter and closes his mouth over my clit, threatening to make me come undone. The heat is building, the tightening sensation low in my belly making me grip the sheets and hold his head closer to me, fisting his hair. My legs wrap around his head, and I shake violently under him, shattering as I ride the waves of pleasure until my body is limp and weightless.

"I want you inside me, I can't wait any longer." I pull his hair so he can look up at me from his position, and he nods slowly, straightening out. "I can't wait any longer."

He lifts up from the bed and kneels between my legs, his cock springing up, jutting up toward his abdomen. He somehow managed to take off his underwear while pleasuring me.

Holy fuck.

I reach out to trace the bulging veins over his shaft, his cock jumping at my touch, and he inhales sharply. I itch to touch him. When I wrap a hand around him, he gasps at my touch. I take that as my cue to squeeze tighter. His moan is so low I can barely hear it, but he grips my shoulders as he attempts to catch his breath. I let go of him abruptly, smiling as I unclasp my bodysuit in the back and begin to lower the straps over my shoulders. He helps me pull it down, exposing my tits for him. I let myself fall back, and as my head meets the pillow, I scrunch my eyes closed and say a quick prayer that I don't see Michael in my head right now.

Zayne's cock brushes against my entrance, and the first press is gentle as he goes in an inch, but he doesn't try to go any further. I hear him sharply inhale, the ragged exhale that comes after turning into a whimper. The sound borders on desperation and physical pain.

The hot wetness dripping down to my ass is distracting until he gives me a gentle kiss on the cheek, "Hold on tight." He tells me, then jerks forward, hard.

Sharp pain slices through my center, and I hiss into his neck as he stills over me for a moment, waiting for my permission. I nod my head and he begins to move again, the pain lessening with every stroke. Pressure and pleasure ripple through me with each stroke, and I look at him, his eyes flashing at me as he begins to roll his hips, slow and easy. He is the poster child of control, even as I know it's just a facade, and I want to make him lose it. I want him to hand over everything.

I demand it.

"Fuck me, Zay," I cry, "harder," as I lift my hips to him in the next stroke, voluntarily clenching his cock in a silent demand.

His eyes roll into the back of his head as he grips my hips, lifting them a few inches off the bed. I'm getting the best view of his muscles, hard chest and capped shoulders, as he slowly rolls his hips against me, creating more friction than I have ever felt in my entire life. His black hair is shining against the lights, an onyx halo, and his eyes threaten to devour me whole. He is determined to keep eye contact with me throughout the entire ordeal, and I am more than happy to oblige as he reaches for my face and holds it with one hand. He picks up his pace and frowns slightly, the angle he creates taking some concentration. The rolling thrusts are doing something to my body, and the sounds we're making only serve to turn me on even more.

Sweat begins to mist my skin and my hands scramble on the sheets, as if looking for something, but all I can do is fist them. I press my shoulders against the mattress and lift my hips higher towards him, trying to fuck him back, growing desperate as the sensations coil low in me again.

"Oh my God!" I nearly yell, and his laugh is husky but I can tell he isn't amused as he picks up his pace even further and all but lifts me completely off the mattress, my shoulders barely on the bed at this point.

He's losing himself to the feelings, his head tilted back and eyes skyward, praying to anything, anyone. His moans are urgent, matching my own as he reaches down and begins to rub circles on my clit. His thrusts turn frantic and we lose rhythm for a brief moment, but I find his legs and grip him, nails digging in, drawing blood.

Something violent sweeps over me as I find my release, my mouth clenching shut as I make desperate sounds, shaking under him for the second time tonight. My body twists and squeezes and falls, and when I open my eyes I can see his are squeezed shut as he slams into me over and over. His lips part with a gasp and he smiles softly, his cock pulsing deep inside me. He is fucking entrancing, and I can't find the will to tear my eyes away when he groans and grips my face tighter, even though it hurts. When he's finished, he collapses on top of me, burying his face in the crook of my neck. His tattoos shimmer in the dying light and I vow to memorize them all, I vow to memorize *him* completely.

"What are you doing to me?" I ask, my voice hoarse from being crushed underneath him. "I don't know if I like this…"

"What don't you like?" He whispers in my ear, sending chills down my spine as my heart clenches in my chest and he makes me feel everything I don't want to.

"Feeling like I'm falling."

"I'll always catch you," he promises, but it sounds empty just the way every other promise has been for me.

"Will you?" I can feel the tears threatening to fall, but I blink rapidly, willing them to stay in my eyes.

"Please catch me too, Hallie." He lifts off me, putting his weight on his forearms on either side of me, and looking into my eyes. The low light plays tricks on his irises, and it's as if I'm seeing paint blended in real-time, the colors shifting right before my eyes.

"Only if you catch me first," I whisper as he kisses the inside of my wrist, his lips lingering longer than usual, as if he's trying to cover his lies with them.

I don't miss the way he deflects, his lie bouncing around in my chest, and as I said it I knew in my heart he would never catch me, but I want to live the lie just a little while longer.

I've always been destined to fall on my face.

Completely and utterly alone.

Always.

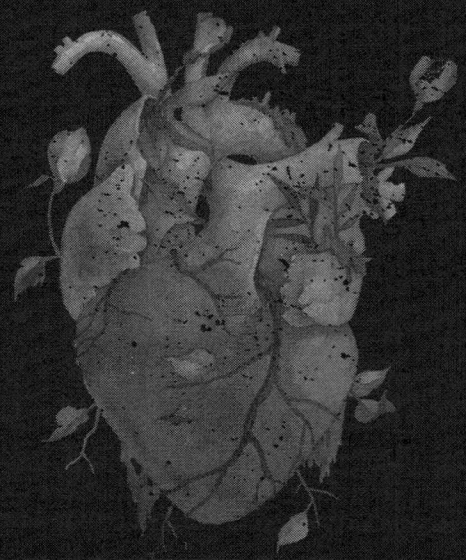

CHAPTER 14

ZAYNE

Hallie's chest rises and falls in a steady rhythm that always soothes me to sleep better than any lullaby my mom used to sing to me when I was a kid. I'm in a hazy place between sleep and waking, but I don't mind it because it means I get to wake up next to her again. This is the second—scratch that—third time that I'm spending the night with her, and my body is getting too used to hers. I seek out her warmth even in my own bed now, which is highly inconvenient.

My fingertips caress her arm, trailing our initials on her skin.

Her skin is the softest I've ever touched, and it drives me insane. How can someone's skin be this soft? It's like she was made for me…

It's mind-blowing.

Hallie stirs in her sleep, pulling me from my thoughts, and I watch the morning sunlight caress her face. Right now, she looks like an angel; all she's missing is the halo. She settles back into her pillow, nuzzling it, and then goes back into a deep slumber.

Last night was amazing. Hands down the best sex of my life.

How am I supposed to quit her now?

I'm not a good guy, I know I won't do it willingly.

I quietly get up from the bed and slip into the bathroom to shower, feeling a pang in my chest at the thought of having to wash her smell off me. Hopefully, she won't wake up, so I can make her breakfast and surprise her. I know I don't have the best track record, and I have been awful at being in a relationship with her, but I really want to show her how much I care. I want to show her what it means to be mine. I will treat her like a princess and worship the ground she walks on, as long as I'm the center of her universe.

I want to be the sun she orbits and gravitates to.

I want to be the oxygen she needs to survive.

I want to consume all her thoughts, dreams, and nightmares.

I want her to be obsessed with me, the way I am with her.

I shower and dry myself off in record time and quietly slip into the kitchen, undetected. The pantry is small but filled to the brim and I have no issues finding the pancake mix. I turn on the gas stove and place the pan on it to heat, then add milk and an egg to the mix and work on it for a minute before pouring two circles onto the pan with a ladle.

As the first two pancakes cook, I have a prickly sensation in the back of my neck. When I look back, I see Hallie leaning on the island, resting her chin on her hands. A smile lights up her face, reaching all the way to her eyes, and they sparkle in the morning light.

"You're making me breakfast?" she breaks the silence, sounding surprised. She's wearing a bubble gum pink silk night tank top and shorts that look fucking amazing on her. The strappy little top has her tits spilling out and I have to adjust myself in my pants. What happened to the t-shirt?

"I had to thank you somehow." I give her a pointed look and she blushes, remembering last night, I'm sure.

"For what?" Her voice is hoarse, but it doesn't get any better after she clears her throat.

"Letting me have the most beautiful pu—"

"Don't finish that sentence," she groans and scrunches her face up in embarrassment.

"Why can't you hear me say the word 'pussy'?" I smirk. I think it's adorable how embarrassed she gets over it. Her cheeks are flaming red, and she won't meet my eyes.

"It's indecent..." She looks flustered. "I just don't like the way it sounds."

"Well, I *love* the way it looks," I drag out the love on purpose just to press her.

Hallie groans again and covers her face, and the sound travels directly to my cock.

Deep breaths. I'm not fucking her again right now.

I turn around and flip the pancakes to keep myself from doing just that on the kitchen island. I feel her continue to watch me as I put her food on a plate and get her silverware and maple syrup.

"Would you like some coffee?"

"I'd love some, thank you."

I pour coffee into a cup that says 'Best Nurse Ever' and mix it with the almond milk creamer and sugar that I hope she will like, since it's in her fridge, after all. I hand it over to her and our fingers graze, setting my skin on fire. I inhale sharply and she cocks her head to the side, watching me with curious eyes. Brown eyes that look black right now.

Black like my soul.

Black like my demons.

Maybe she belongs with them, but it's too soon to tell.

I clear my throat and look away, going to the other side of the island to eat my own food. I need space between us right now because I don't know what will happen if we're next to each other again.

Might just bend her over the couch.

"Why are you so surprised I made you breakfast?" I ask, breaking the silence.

"Well... no one has made me breakfast before."

Her previous boyfriends sound like a waste of time, but then again, technically, so am I. "You're my girlfriend, isn't that what I'm supposed to do?"

"I'm not sure. I've only had one boyfriend before, and it was in high school." She pours more syrup on her pancakes and begins to eat them. She acts like she hasn't eaten in a week, but I suppress the laugh that threatens to escape me.

"Interesting." *Very* Interesting.

"What is?" Hallie tucks her hair behind her ear and leans in to take a bite of her pancake again, stuffing her face until she can't anymore.

"With a face like that, I don't see how it's possible." I gesture to her face, trying to make my point. She's fucking perfect.

"Because I don't give people a chance." Her voice is small, as if she doesn't want me to know these things about her. I've noticed she's a very private person and it's very difficult for her to trust, and even though I know I'm the last one she should trust it only makes me want to try harder.

"So, I'm special?"

"You could say that. But you won't be if you continue to push your luck with me." She rolls her eyes.

"And how am I pushing my luck?"

"By disappearing on me, for starters."

"It won't happen again. I promise, baby." I walk around the island and stand at her side, my shoulder brushing hers.

"It better not. I won't take you back again."

Sure you won't. I try my hardest to suppress an eye roll.

"Let's go on a date. I'll pick you up this evening?" I ask Hallie, reaching for her hand. She doesn't pull it away as I grab it, and my chest tightens when she wraps her fingers around mine. We fit so perfectly together, and last night proved it.

"What are we doing?"

"Dinner, but you can dress casually." I tell her with a smile, "I'm taking you to a little hole in the wall on Main Street." A place I freaking love. It's the best in town, at least I think so. The best part is we don't have to drive to Austin for it.

"And then?"

"Then I will make you love me."

"Good luck with that." Hallie scoffs, but I catch the corners of her mouth twitching, and at this moment I would give up everything I own just to have her love. I *will* make her love me. It's just a matter of time.

My lips curve into a grin that makes my face hurt. I don't even remember the last time I smiled in earnest, and it makes me itch. Is it her? What is she doing to me? Is this what happiness feels like? Do I even deserve it?

I should tell her the truth.

I should let her run while she can.

Except I can't. I won't. I feel her becoming imprinted in my soul, ingrained into every cell in my body. I'm officially fucked, because I know exactly what this means, exactly what to call this.

Obsession.

And at the end of the day, it means I'm going to ruin her completely.

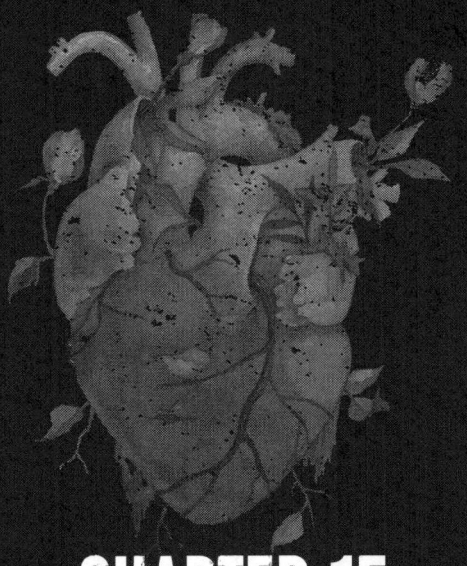

CHAPTER 15

HALLIE

Main Street in Bastrop, Texas is exactly as you'd imagine. Historic buildings line the entire street and there's everything from homes to restaurants and even a pharmacy. The boutiques have display windows and the antique shops are beautiful. The small town has a certain charm that is difficult to recreate, and I know I will miss it as soon as I leave. I've lived here for a very long time, and I don't do well with change. Most people left after high school, and even I left for a while. Now I commute to school since Brit didn't mind moving out here instead of being closer to campus.

Zayne parks at Fisherman's Park, which is within walking distance of my apartment, so we can walk down the street to PawPaws Catfish House. I've never eaten there before, even though I've walked past it for years. It's a shame because I've heard it's fucking amazing. I'm kind of excited for this meal.

The walk from Fisherman's Park is short, and the weather

is lovely today. It feels like it's about sixty-five degrees outside and the sky is splashed in reds, oranges, and pinks. Finally, some color slips into my life and now I'll never forget my favorite sunsets being next to *him*.

There's wrought iron patio furniture with blue umbrellas in the front, and we promptly snag the first empty table we come to before someone else can. The hostess comes out to greet us and tells us our server will be on the way shortly, handing us menus.

A girl with curly brown hair and hazel eyes that looks to be our age walks in our direction, holding two waters in her hands. She sets them on the table and pulls out a notepad.

"What can I get for you today?" she asks with a heavy Texas accent, her eyes searching my face as if she might guess what I would pick from the menu.

"We'll take two of the combo platters, darling," Zayne says without looking at her. "With... beans, coleslaw and fries, please." I watch her face closely and she just tilts her head to the side, watching me back. I nod once and she writes it down on her notepad.

"Right away. Let me know if you need anything else." She doesn't take one look at him the entire time, and I feel as if I'm missing something. Did he fuck her too? Does she know something I don't?

"Did you need to order for me? I wasn't sure what I wanted."

"The combo platter has everything they sell here. I just wanted you to try it all." It sounds thoughtful, but the more I think about it, the more I know there's something very wrong. It feels like a red flag, but I'm currently color-blind so I can't tell.

Bullshit.

Ignoring the voice in my head, I pick at something on my arm until I feel the scab give way. Zayne's eyes go to my hand and he looks curious but doesn't say anything, but I still let my hand drop.

I wouldn't call it self-harm, but I do pick at my skin when I'm anxious. I pick at bites or any imperfections until they bleed, and then when they scab over... I pick again. It's part of my anxiety and obsessive-compulsive disorder, although I would never tell a soul I have it. They could probably figure it out by looking at my closet, which is organized by season and the length of the sleeves of the shirt. The dresses and pants have their own section, and the shoes are neatly arranged by color and season as well. Not to mention, my pantry has its own code that only myself can decipher, so Brit just lets me put the groceries away, so I don't feel like I'm itching. It's more than an itch though, and I'm not even sure how to describe it, but my body will not let me physically move on from a task until it feels *right*.

And only I know when that is.

The volume on the television can't be set to odd numbers, only even ones. Mostly 12, 14, 16, 18, and 20 are my most used. Sixteen might be my happy medium but switch it to nineteen and I might have an aneurysm.

I also need to do everything equally on both sides of the body. Let's say someone kisses my right cheek, they also have to kiss my left cheek. It's a need for symmetry, balance, and stability. Everything must be equal. It helps me breathe easier. I know I sound insane, but I don't make the rules. I live by some sort of crazy code that only my body understands, and my mind doesn't agree with. I'm still trying to come to terms with it, but I don't know if I ever will.

Most importantly of all, the one thing you need to remember is that when I like someone, really like them, I become neurotic.

Obsessive.

Jealous.

Crazy.

It's in my nature. I truly can't help it. I am who I am.

"Penny for your thoughts?"

"You're going to need a lot more than a penny." I force my lips into a smile that I know he can tell is as fake as the purse I brought with me today.

"What's happening in that crazy brain of yours?" I know he doesn't mean it that way, but I flinch like I've been slapped, and his features go from smooth to panicked. "I'm sorry, it was just a—"

"It's fine. Nothing is going on in my brain, other than the fact that I'm hungry as heck, and I want to find out if the food is as good as you promised."

"Oh, it's good." He chuckles, trying to move on from the awkwardness, "You're going to want to eat this every day."

I don't say anything after that, mostly because I don't feel like I have the energy for small talk or even to pretend I'm okay. I hate when people call me crazy. It's something I've been called more times than I care to hear. I try to relax though, and it's not that difficult with the delicious smells around me.

We settle into a comfortable silence and the waitress brings our food to the table. The catfish and shrimp make my mouth water, and all the smells mixing make my stomach growl loudly. Zayne smiles at me from across the table and nods at the food, as if giving me the green light to eat. It kind of makes me angry, and I narrow my eyes at him but he's too busy looking at the food in front of him to notice.

"Would you like anything else?" the waitress asks, watching me, as she hands us both napkins. When I look up at mine, I notice she wrote, 'order water if you need help'. I feel myself pale, but I ball up the napkin and drop it before Zayne can see it.

"What drink would you recommend?" I ask her, not looking at the napkin so I don't draw attention to it.

"Alcohol?"

"Yes, anything sweet," I waggle my eyebrows, "or with tequila."

"We have an amazing frozen strawberry margarita," Hailey, according to the name tag, says with a knowing look in her eyes.

"I would love one, please!" My enthusiasm makes Zayne's eyes narrow at me, but I ignore him.

"Coming right up, girl."

"Why are you getting alcohol?" Zayne lifts an eyebrow, and I can't tell if this is him questioning me or if he's annoyed that I am.

"Because I want to. Besides, tequila makes my clothes fall off." I wink at him, and he rolls his eyes but smiles when he looks away.

"You should've led with that," he mumbles, but I can still hear him.

We both savor every bite of the meal. It really is amazing, and the weather and the sunset only add to the experience. Hailey sets my drink in front of me and Zayne watches me with interest as I take the first sip. I moan and settle back in my chair, taking the mason jar with me. The sweet taste of the mixed drink explodes on my tongue, and this might just be the new spot to get alcohol from now on.

"That good?" He smirks.

"Better than sex."

"Well damn, I will have to fix that then."

"I don't think you can." I say as I take gulps of my drink, feeling the brain freeze building up in my temples.

"I've always loved a challenge."

"Is that why you're with me?" I'm hoping he answers honestly, but I have a feeling I wouldn't like his answer anyway. He seems like the type of guy who *would* do that. I don't know how to feel about it. "Because I'm a challenge?"

"No. I'm with you because I can't stop thinking about you, even when I want to."

Relatable.

It's nice to know I'm not the only one with strong feelings, even when it seems a bit over the top. I think he can come off very strong though, so my reactions may not scare him as much as they scare other people.

Lucky me. Lucky him.

Zayne pays for the food, and we head back to our parking spot, but instead of going to the car, he directs me to a bench overlooking the Colorado River. There's a wooden walkway in front of us, similar to a dock, and it has sections that have their own private areas where you can hang out. It looks like a balcony on a dock, almost.

I stride toward one with purpose and hoist myself up to sit on the ledge, my legs hanging off the side that faces the river below us.

Zayne comes up behind me slowly and wraps his hands around my waist, pressing his face to my side and inhaling my shirt.

"Your smell is like a drug to me now, I fucking need it."

Chills run down my spine and my stomach flips at his words. I know I shouldn't be excited because it feels too soon, but words of affirmation are my love language, and he seems to be in tune with me.

"Do you need another hit?" I ask him with a smile, I guess the margarita made me brave after all.

"I need a hit every day, forever."

I stay quiet and try to not let that sink in. When I don't answer, he starts digging in his pockets for a joint. Zayne lights it and takes a long drag, doing tricks with the smoke coming out of his lips and directing it back into his nose. He inhales deeply again and his eyes light up. I shouldn't let that affect me, but somehow my insides liquify and turn to molten lava.

He puts the joint between my lips and I take a drag too, keeping my face neutral, but when it hits me I don't feel the way that weed usually makes me feel. A wave of tiredness takes over my body and I feel heavy. I lean back into Zayne and say a quick prayer that I don't fall into the river and drown.

"Can you help me get down? I don't feel right," I say, feeling slightly nauseous. What the fuck?

"What's wrong?" He seems concerned as he helps me get off the ledge, but surely he must know his weed is fucking dirty. He doesn't seem one bit affected by it though, and it makes me want to punch him.

"Your weed is dirty as fuck, that's what's wrong," I spit, not even trying to keep the venom from my voice.

"It's not dirty, it's laced with fentanyl."

"What the fuck, Zay? You couldn't say that before I took a hit?"

"I thought you would like it." He shrugs his shoulders but puts it out and helps me walk back.

The day has given in to night now, and there is no moon

shining down on us to direct our steps. Everything is a blur of lights, and nothing makes sense. My body feels like it's floating away and away and away.

Once we're in the car, I let myself close my eyes.

I feel myself drift.

Down.

Down.

Down.

Into nothingness.

Into the same thing I've always been:

No one.

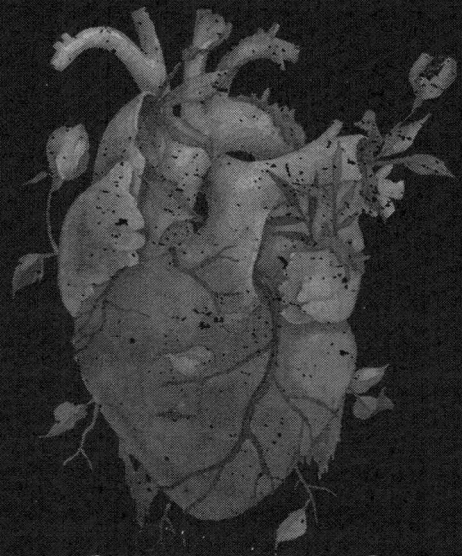

CHAPTER 16

HALLIE

We pull up in front of a building lit up with a name that's still too blurry to read. I can feel myself coming down from the high—or should I say coming up from the low? Who fucking knows? But I never want to do that again. I can understand liking downers, but that was another level of fucked up.

Zayne adjusts himself in his pants and looks at me with narrowed eyes, as if he thinks I'm faking this. Or maybe I'm too messed up and reading everything wrong.

"What?"

"Are you okay to go in and dance, or do you need more time?"

"I don't think I can dance, but we could sit at the bar. I need something to perk me up." I need Adderall again, I think.

"I know just the thing," he says with a glint in his eyes.

He turns off the engine and gets out of the car, walking to my side to open the door for me.

How nice.

I make sure I have my phone and get out of the car, following after him. Zayne is walking faster than me, probably because he has longer legs, and I have to do a little shuffle to catch up. Once I do, I grab his arm so he can't get ahead again.

The dancehall is playing some honky-tonk music, and people are two-stepping everywhere my eyes roam, which I will admit is not usually my vibe. I don't like clubs, or even dancing establishments much, but here we are. The bar is mostly full but there are a couple of empty stools waiting for us. Zayne walks with purpose and pulls out my chair, but I shake my head.

"I need to use the bathroom," I announce, "I'll be right back."

"I'll take you."

"I can go by myself." My hand lands on his chest, keeping him away. Geez, he needs boundaries, for fuck's sake. "I'm a big girl, you know."

"Fine but make it fast. If you're not done in five minutes, I'm coming for you."

"Fair enough."

I find the bathroom sign and head in, do my business and go to wash my hands. I stand in front of the mirror and take in my reflection. I look rough. Gone is the girl with the pretty makeup and the flawless hair. My mascara is smeared under my eyes and my hair is frizzy. How the fuck did he let me leave the car?

Making quick work of it, I fix my makeup by removing the smears and smoothing my hair down with my hands. Much better. My jeans still make my ass look fantastic, and this top compliments my skin tone, even if it's not fit for this almost March weather.

As I head back out, my thoughts drift to the exams coming up, mid-terms, which is weird in itself because I should be enjoying myself. Only when I part through the crowd do I stop dead in my tracks. Even as people bump into me from all sides, I still can't move.

Catherine is sitting with her barstool flush with Zayne's, draping her legs over his lap, looking into his eyes and laughing. Her light brown hair shines under the ugly lights and it makes her look almost green. He's looking back at her in the way I thought he only looked at *me*.

What the fuck is going on?

My breath catches in my throat when she grabs the back of his neck and brings his face to hers, and then *kisses* him.

And he fucking *lets* her.

Tears prick the back of my eyes and I'm tempted to walk up to him and make a scene, or at the very least stare until he realizes I saw everything. But my feet drag me away of their own volition, and I don't even know where I'm walking as I turn around quickly. I want to be anywhere except here.

People get out of the way for me as I run through the crowd and someone kindly opens the door so I can step outside. I must look insane because no one tries to stop me as I run for the side of the building and dry heave. My forehead touches the cool wall and I can feel the urge to throw up receding, although I still hyperventilate.

How could he do this shit to me?

Is he fucking kidding me?

No, he's not.

I knew he was going to fuck me over, I just never thought it would be with someone else and this soon.

Delusional.

Stupid.

Whore.

I run through the list of words my mom would call me, and somehow it brings me comfort in this unfamiliar situation. I have never experienced anything like this because I usually don't play the relationship game.

Someone places a hand on my shoulder, and for a moment I think it's Zayne, so I jump out of my skin.

"It's okay, Hallie." The hand squeezes me slightly, "Deep breaths."

Daniel's familiar voice soothes the ringing in my ears, and I turn around to face him. He looks handsome in Wrangler jeans and a button-down shirt. His cowboy boots peek from under the hem of his pants, and I look at his face, trying to figure out what he wants.

"I don't have anywhere to be. Do you need a ride home?"

I nod my head, because I think that my voice would betray me. I know Zayne would flip out if he saw me get in a car with him. I'm a bit afraid for Daniel's life, if I'm being honest. However, I can see the colors slipping from my world again, and I decide I need to get away from this place.

Away from Zayne.

Away from Catherine.

Away from the pain.

He scribbles something once we're in his car, and hands me a small piece of paper with his phone number. I put it in the back pocket of my jeans and close my eyes.

Even after we drive away from the dance hall and I begin to drift off into sleep, I can still feel my chest caving in. I can feel the cracks of my heart growing wider apart.

Stretching.

Fracturing.

Shattering.

I don't know how I'll ever recover from this. I never planned to hand my heart over to him. I don't even know how it happened. All I know is that I'll never fall for his bullshit again. At least that's what I tell myself, but when I become obsessed with something, it can be really difficult for me to disconnect. Difficult to move on from.

And he's become my new religion, a cult even.

He's the devil… and I just want to worship at his altar.

The sun comes into the kitchen through the blinds that I have raised halfway so I can look outside while I do the dishes. The soap bubbles coat the dishes on the dirty side as I rinse the plate I just scrubbed, and

I hear faint footsteps headed in my direction but I continue my task, not looking at the person coming my way.

Michael stops walking, and when I look back, I see him leaning against the stove watching me. He appraises me in a way I'm all too familiar with, his neutral expression betraying the hunger in his eyes, and I do my best not to cringe at the attention he's giving me right now.

Something isn't right.

Mom isn't here. She took David with her to the dollar store, leaving me alone with my four-year-old brother Matt and my stepfather. She assured me she would be back in less than an hour though, so at least I don't have to put up with Michael's shit for too long.

"Hallie, I know how I can get you ungrounded," Michael says softly, and all the hairs on my arms stand on end. Something tells me that I should get out of here. Every instinct in my body is telling me to fucking run.

I whip my head back to him instead and we make eye contact for one brief moment before I respond, "How?"

"Are you a virgin?" My blood turns to ice in my veins at the question, and I desperately want my mother to get home.

"Yes," I breathe, but I'm not sure if he can even hear it over the running water since my voice is barely a whisper.

He moves to stand next to me now, his shoulder brushing the side of my head as I do my best to ignore him and continue washing the dishes, but I can barely even focus on my breathing.

"Do you know how to suck cock?"

"No," I say with a neutral face, the hammering of my heart betraying my body language.

"You will learn. That is how you get ungrounded."

Is he serious right now?

"No." It's the only word coming out of my mouth right now.

"Have it your way then, Hallie. I couldn't care less."

My frozen blood cracks as he walks away, leaving me wondering if he even meant any of it. He couldn't have, right? But then why would he ask those questions?

My mom returns shortly after that, and I go back to my room like the prisoner that I am. I pace back and forth, convinced I'm wearing holes into the carpet while my mind races hundreds of miles an hour. I force it not to stray from its course, yet the harder I try not to think about the conversation with Michael, the more I do.

Did he mean it? If he did, would I really be able to get out of here?
No. No. No.
I'm not that desperate.
Right?
It's just two months.
I'm only twelve. He can't do that. He won't do that to me.

The hours crawl by and I end up falling asleep on the bed, not even bothering to brush my teeth, shower, or put on pajamas. When I sit up on the bed again, it's almost midnight, and I decide to at least take off my jeans so I can go back to sleep comfortably.

Knock. Knock. Kock.
My heart ceases to beat in my chest.
I stop breathing.
Surely I imagined it?
But just as I'm convinced it was all a figment of my imagination, I see the doorknob turning.

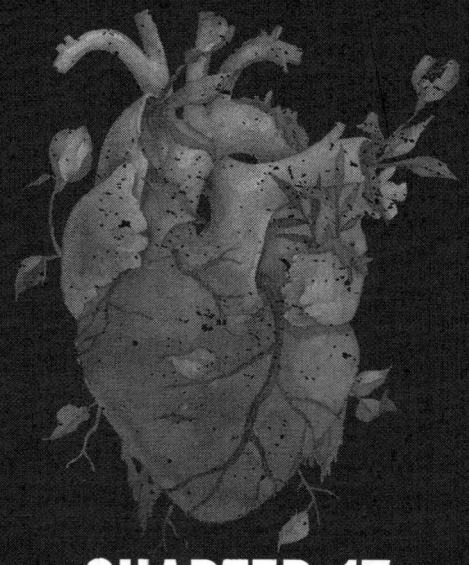

CHAPTER 17

ZAYNE

"What the fuck, CC?" I push her away, "I'm with Hallie now!" She tastes like the nasty beer she's been drinking, and I want to wash her out of my mouth. I still think she's hot, and I'd probably fuck her if I wasn't with Hallie, but definitely not while I'm with her.

"Who?" She looks confused and thinks for a second, "Oh, that weird bitch."

"She's not weird, and don't call her a bitch." I get more irritated by the second. Someone needs to teach this slut a lesson or two. "Respect my relationship. It would be a whole different ball game if I were single, but I'm not."

"I think you might be, and you just don't know it," Catherine smirks, her long lashes fanning her cheeks. I want to fucking throttle her. How can someone so repulsive be so pretty? Suddenly her small nose and blue eyes look ugly to me, even though I know she's not.

"What's that supposed to mean?"

"Nothing." CC shrugs, but I don't believe a word coming out of her mouth. She knows something I don't, and that really bothers me. "Do you want Tina or not?"

"Yes, but I need to check on Hallie first. She's in the bathroom."

"Hurry. I don't have all night." She rolls her eyes, and I walk to the ladies' room at a brisk pace.

I shouldn't have talked to Catherine this long. I have a bad feeling Hallie is throwing up or asleep in a stall. I wait for her outside the bathroom door for three minutes before I gather the courage to go in, praying there are no other women in there. It's empty when I enter, and there's no sign of her.

Where the fuck is Hallie?

I call her cell phone and it goes straight to voicemail. I look for her through the crowd, outside, everywhere, but I don't find her. Completely pissed off and without an ounce of patience left, I walk back to Catherine. She senses my rage and cringes away from me.

"What the fuck happened to you?" She looks scared. She should be.

"She left me." I snap, not in the mood to talk about the way my skin is crawling just thinking of the reason she did. Why would she leave? Is she even sober enough to know where she's going? How to get home? But no, fuck that. She shouldn't have done it. "She fucking left me."

"Let's just go then…"

"Gladly." But I'm not glad. It's not *her* I want.

We head out to my car and she swings her hips side to side as she walks in front of me, giving me a full view of what she wants me to sample tonight. I start to think of Hallie again, about why she'd do this to me. I don't want this bitch, I want *her*, but she evidently doesn't feel the same if she left me here.

I'll take what I can fucking get.

The drive to Catherine's place is a blur and I don't know how I even got here in one piece. The weed and fentanyl are still lingering in my system, hanging on by a thread, and I need to bring myself back up. I need a better high. A higher high.

I want to soar.

Climb.

Rise.

Ascend.

I want to forget about *her*.

She's ruining my life. Why do I even fucking care that she left me? I've never cared about anyone before, and I don't want to start now. However, she's like an itch I can't scratch, and I need a hit of her. Just one more time. Just so I can move on.

But since I can't have her, Tina and CC will have to do.

I park in Catherine's driveway and take a deep breath, considering the weight of what I'm about to do. I asked her for Adderall and she said she had none left, and that this was the closest thing to it. Surely that means it's not as scary as people make it sound. People always tell horror stories about this drug and how it's the best high of their life but comes with the worst crash. That it destroys you. That won't be me though. This is the only time so I can get a fix until my regular dealer has Adderall tomorrow.

I'm lost in my thoughts as we enter her place and I don't notice anything except that it's dark and there's not much furniture in the townhome. I plop down on the small, green velvet loveseat, the sole piece of furniture, and she leaves me to get the supplies we need.

My heart beats erratically already and I'm a mix of nerves, anticipation, excitement, and something else I can't quite put my finger on. *Fear*. It's subtle, but it's there. It's screaming at me to get the fuck out of here, that this is a mistake. Little do I know right now, it's the most monumental mistake of my life.

CC returns to the living room wearing nothing but her pink thong and a tank top without a bra. She's holding a lighter, a glass pipe, and a baggie with blue-white crystals in it. She asks me to take off my pants and I oblige. If I'm going to fuck up tonight, I'm fucking up all the way.

Hallie and I are clearly done, so no hard feelings.

Right?

Catherine kneels on the ground between my spread thighs and lights up the pipe. She hovers the flame under it for a few breaths, then takes a long hit. Moaning, she pushes her thighs together and repeats this process one more time. The look on her face says it all, and I take the pipe she's offering with unsteady hands. I mimic what I watched her do and hover the flame under it, watching it bubble with the heat.

Her hands go to the waistband of my boxer briefs and she pulls down, attempting to remove them. I lift my ass off the couch and she pulls them down my legs, leaving them pooled around my ankles.

I take one hit and feel the rush of heat spread quickly throughout my body, unlike anything I've ever felt before in my entire fucking life, almost like a lightning strike in slow motion. Holy fucking shit.

What the fuck.

My heart races, pounding wildly in my chest, and I'm suddenly breathing very fast. The heat travels down my spine to my asshole and my balls. My balls tighten almost painfully, rising higher toward my body, and Catherine's mouth is on my cock at that same moment. I'm almost sure she timed it in her head. One suck is all it takes and I'm coming down her throat harder than I ever have. My body shakes and my chest heaves, and she looks up at me with horny blue eyes while my dick is still in her mouth.

I still hate her, probably always will, but at this moment she's a goddess.

At this moment, I'm a god.

I *am* God.

Forget Hallie, all I need is Tina.

So what if Hallie wants to play?

I'm better at this fucking game, anyway.

And I *always* win.

My body fucking hurts, my skin is crawling, and my mouth feels like I'm swallowing glass shards every time I move my tongue.

This is definitely the last time I will do this.

Fuck.

This.

Shit.

I crash and burn and light myself on fire again as I come down from the high, and I don't even know how long I've been trapped in Catherine's place, but she's nowhere to be found.

I need water, food, sleep, and probably Adderall. I need to go back to normal and pretend this night never happened. I definitely need to pretend I didn't fuck her face multiple times. I shudder at the thought because I fucking hate her and everything that she is, although Tina made me forget. Tina made *everything* better, and I'm starting to believe nothing and no one will ever measure up to her anymore.

My phone is on five percent, and I know I at least have a car charger so I can call Hallie and beg for her forgiveness. Even if I don't know what the fuck I did last night. Even if she left me there. She left me, like everyone else does.

But when I look at my phone it says it's Monday, meaning it's been two whole days since I went chicken flippin'. How the hell does that even happen? It's almost evening, and I call Hallie as I head out to my car.

Ring, ring, ring—voicemail.

She rejects my call, but she doesn't realize that I can do this all day and all night. I leave a voicemail and repeat the process twenty more times.

Call.

Reject.

Voicemail.

Repeat.

I pull up to my mother's house and say a quick thanks to the heavens that my mother isn't home, since the last thing I need is for her to see me in this state. I rush inside the house so she can't see me on the security cameras then plug in the code to the alarm and lock the front door.

I take the best shower of my life and I let the hot water beat on my back to soothe my muscles. I brush my teeth, comb my hair, drink water, and eat. By the time I look presentable enough to leave my house, it's already eight. I don't care, though, and I head to Hallie's house anyway.

I won't lie, I'm fucking nervous about showing up right now. I just have a feeling I'll probably get rejected, which I deserve, even if I don't know what the fuck happened. It's somehow always my fault. Everything is. I hold my breath as I pound on her door, fully expecting not to be able to see or talk to her, so when her roommate opens it for me, I am stunned as my fist freezes mid-pound.

Brittany rolls her eyes and steps aside, muttering "fucking dumbass" as she walks away. She knocks on Hallie's door and peeks her head in, and I can hear her tell Hallie she has a visitor. When she questions Brittany, she doesn't answer and just goes to her room and slams the door.

I sit on the couch and wait for her to approach, yet I don't hear footsteps. Looking back, I see her staring at me from the doorway.

"What the fuck are you doing here?" she shouts at me, her face scrunching up with anger and tinged in pink.

"How could you leave me like that?" I raise my voice back at her, standing in front of the couch and turning to face her. Two can play this fucking game.

"Me?" She laughs, but it hurts my ears this time. "You were the one with your tongue down someone else's throat at the bar. I got the feeling I was just inconveniencing you."

"She kissed *me*! I pushed her away..." I take a deep breath. "And what do you mean inconveniencing me?"

"I made it easier for you to go home with her. I wasn't in your way anymore, so you should really just be thanking me."

A chill runs down my spine and guilt punches me in the gut.

Did she see me leave with Catherine? Was she still there, and I left her behind? Was she stranded? *Who took her home?* I narrow my eyes at her and slowly, as if weighing my words on my tongue, ask her, "Who took you home?"

"Wouldn't you like to know..." she mutters under her breath and turns to go into her room. I walk after her and go inside before she can think of shutting me out.

"Who. Fucking. Took. You. Home?" I walk forward in front of her, and she walks backward until she hits her dresser. She might want to start talking now before I lose my damn patience. There's only so much of that left in me. I'm not known for self-control. Obviously.

"Daniel." The thump is loud as the dresser digs into her back, but I don't care if she's in pain as I close in on her.

One word. That's all it takes. All it takes for my heart to bottom out and for my vision to turn red. I'm going to kill that motherfucker. "Are you fucking kidding me, Hallie?"

Her face changes, going from scared to angry in less than a second. Well, I'm fucking pissed too, baby girl. "You were kissing someone else!"

"It wasn't like that! She was kissing *me*; I didn't kiss her back at all. I was looking everywhere for you!" I think I might really cry. Why doesn't anyone ever believe me? This is getting ridiculous. I know I have a bad track record but holy fuck. "You rejected my calls..."

"Why didn't you call again until today?"

"I wanted to give you some time," I lie, looking her in the eyes while I do it. I know how to lie and make a person believe me, it's one of my specialties, and I almost feel bad while I do it to her. *Almost.*

"I don't believe you."

Wait... *what?* "What do you mean?" I ask her slowly, "I'm serious."

"You're fucking crazy, you would never give me time."

She's not wrong, and my frustration makes me run a hand

down my face. She doesn't miss a single beat. I hate that she can catch me in a lie this easily. How can she see right through me? It's fucking annoying.

"Why are you lying to me?"

"I got high." My sigh makes her face relax slightly, almost like she's relieved that's what I was doing. If only she knew with who, she wouldn't be this calm. "Are you happy? I got high after you left me. I was upset. I was so fucking upset that I got so high I didn't come down until today." There, a half-truth.

"What the hell did you use?"

"Hallie, I'm sorry you had to see Catherine doing that," I swerve away from her question. "But I swear she's repulsive, and I only want you." I close my eyes and drop to my knees, hugging her waist. "Please, baby, please don't leave me. I don't want us to break up. Nothing like that will ever happen again. I won't talk to her anymore."

"I don't know if I can trust you," she whispers, her voice breaking, and I hate that it does.

"You can. You can!" I beg with my eyes too, as I look up at her, and she stares right back at me. Am I trustworthy? Probably not.

"Swear?"

"On everything. I can't lose you. I won't lose you," I plead.

"You keep playing these fucking games with me." Her hand comes to my hair and she grips it tightly in her fist, summoning tears to my eyes from the sharp pain. "On and off, hot and cold. It's not my style. I need you to make up your fucking mind."

"I thought you broke up with me, and I couldn't fucking stand it. I need you in my life." I stand up and press my front to hers, but I don't get closer. She averts her eyes, she can't meet my gaze anymore.

"I guess that was a breakup."

"Let me back in, baby." I still haven't let up at all. My body is pressed to hers, front to front, our breaths mingling, and her anger tickling my skin. She thinks it's a wildfire, yet I can barely feel the heat. I need more.

"NO."

My hands drop to my sides and I take a deep breath, but then just as quickly wrap a hand around her throat and squeeze lightly. "Don't tell me no, baby girl." I lean in and take her bottom lip between my teeth, biting until I draw blood. She winces but stays still for the most part, letting me injure her. "I don't fucking like that word."

I lick the blood from her lip and then kiss her deeply, my tongue sweeping her mouth and hers meeting mine on the way back in. I grab the back of her thighs and hoist her up, walking her to the bed and dropping her on the edge. She's only wearing a t-shirt and nothing underneath, it seems to be her favorite attire.

Perfect.

I kneel in front of her and have her pussy right at the level I need it. I pull back her shirt and she stares at me, leaning back on her elbows to watch what I'm about to do. "Open for me, baby." She does what I say, and I lean in, the scent of her driving me fucking insane. "Good girl."

I lick her slowly, entrance to clit, and then I focus on what I know she loves. I need to make this fast. I need her to want me back. I need to remind her who she fucking belongs to. My hands splay on her lower belly as I work her clit, licking in circles and spelling my name on her. I feel her heat intensify the longer I lick her, and as I add two fingers inside of her, her hips buck off the bed. Hallie whimpers when I suck her clit into my mouth, and she fists my hair and falls back, no longer leaning on her elbows or watching me.

I twist my fingers inside of her in a come-hither motion, massaging her g-spot while I continue to suck on her clit. Hallie moans under me, her sounds growing louder and more frantic the faster I go. It's fucking addicting, the way she sounds, tastes, smells. It's my new goal in life to make her melt for me every day.

When I suck harder, I can feel her walls flutter around my fingers, and I know she's close. It's instinctual at this point, the way I can tell that she's almost ready to give me everything. I reach up with my free hand and pinch her right nipple hard while I bite on her clit simultaneously, and I almost feel bad. I would if her knees weren't squeezing the hell out of my head in a vice grip while she shakes. Only I don't care. If this is how I'm meant to go, let her fucking end me. I can't think of a better death than drowning in her pussy.

She continues to spasm and shake under me, her knees giving way enough that I can finally draw breath again. Although, instead of being grateful, I just want her to do it again for longer. "Take me back," I say breathlessly, as if I just ran a marathon. I might have.

"I hate feeling this way." Her voice is not a whisper, but it is soft. Like she's telling me a secret, something for my ears only.

"What way?" I wipe the back of my hand across my mouth, her wetness dripping from my chin.

"Jealous. Irrational." Hallie clears her throat, as if it could clear her feelings too. Or maybe she's embarrassed I just did that.

"Hallie, I love your jealousy. I *need* it." I emphasize the word, so she knows I'm just as fucking crazy as she is. Nothing she does will ever scare me.

"It's because you're crazy." She has no fucking clue.

"So let's be crazy *together*."

And we were.

Fucking crazy.

Together.

For each other.

Until it destroyed us both.

Hours later, after I've left her place, I sit in my car and call my dealer, except he tells me he still has no Adderall. I contact someone else, and they say they have it, so I head to pick it up. *Fucking finally.*

I dump a line onto the middle console and snort it. However, it doesn't make me feel anymore. It doesn't make me focus anymore. Not like Tina. *Nothing is like Tina.*

Disappointed, I head home. Driving is almost impossible when all I can focus on is the crawling of my skin, the intense fucking itch I feel that I can't scratch. I park in the driveway, and when I engage my emergency brake my car jostles a bit, making a plastic bag fall from the passenger side to the floor. A few baggies full of pills and rocks and a glass pipe fall out of the bag and twinkle in the moonlight.

I grab one of the baggies, the pipe, and a lighter. Reclining my seat, I open the zipper of my pants, ready for another orgasmic rush. I don't even care that I'm in perfect view of my mom's security cameras, or that she will know exactly what I'm doing. I just want to smoke.

The problem with Tina is that she gives you a dopamine rush four times stronger than cocaine. Seven times stronger than sex. And an orgasm after a hit? You could never forget that experience. I get ready to soar, but I promise myself just one hit this time. I need to go to school this week, because sitting at home to tweak is not an option. My cock is hard in anticipation as I light the pipe and hover the flame, watching the bubbles come to life. I fist my cock and hold the pipe with my other hand, taking a long hit.

And then I blast the fuck off.

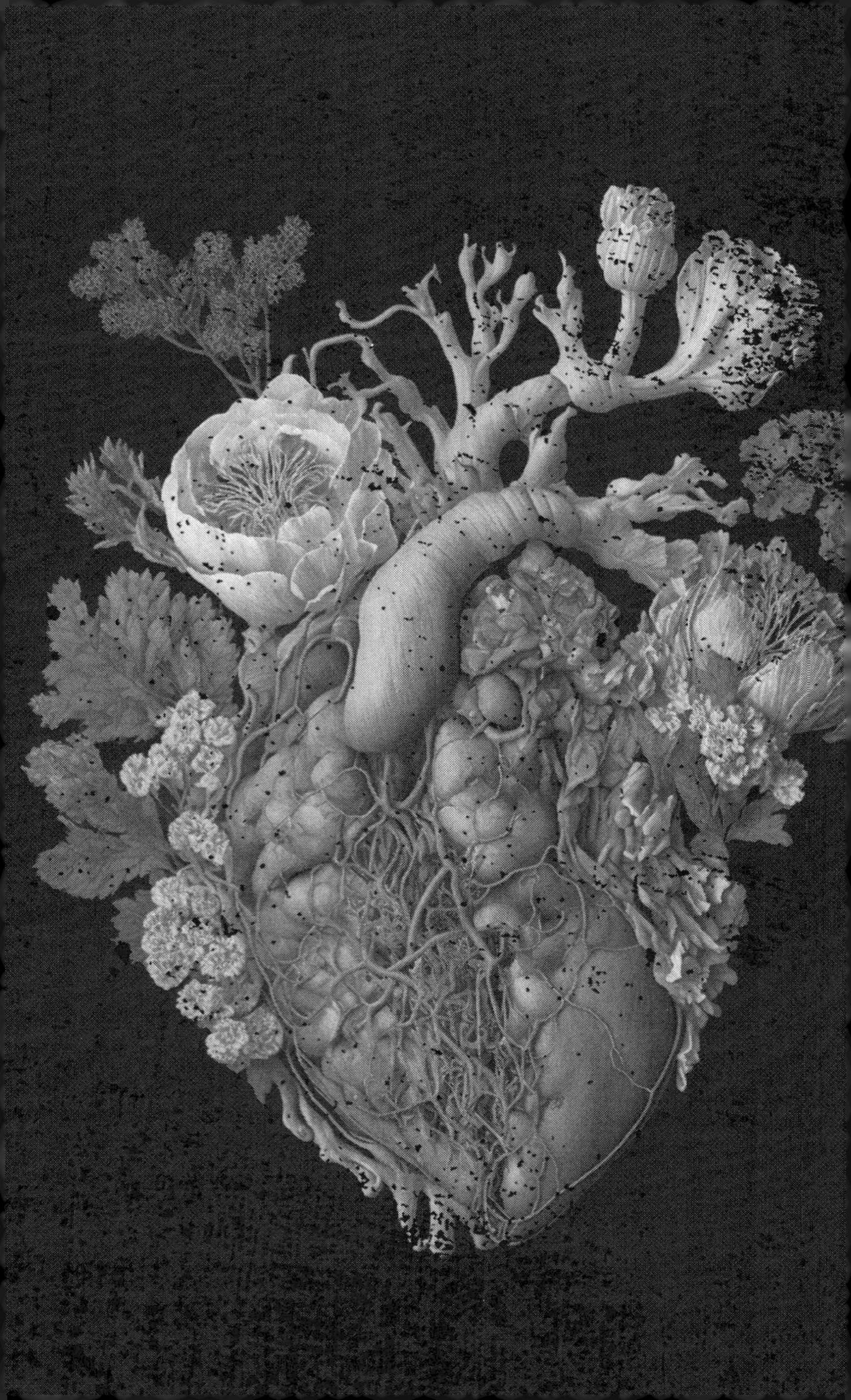

THE
PLUNGE

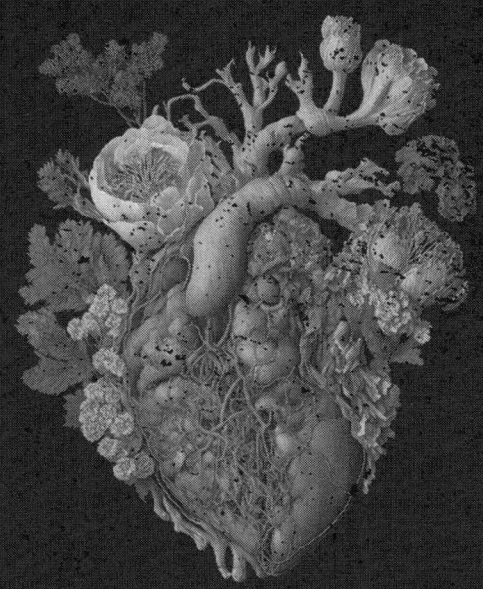

CHAPTER 18

ZAYNE

My mother comes into my room without knocking, even though she knows I hate that shit. I could be doing anything—such as, I don't know, smoking meth—and I don't want her to find out. Maybe that's the only reason I'm so paranoid right now.

And that's why I'm fucking snappy, "Mom, what the hell? I've asked you to knock before coming in." But she looks pissed off as it is.

"Your dad is here to see you. I don't have time for pleasantries."

My face heats from the anger blooming inside of me, my chest tight as I strain to catch my breath. Why is he here? *He left me.* He doesn't get to fucking come back. "I don't want to see him."

"But you will."

I scoff, leveling her with a look that could kill. "The fuck I will. I'm a grown-ass man, and I refuse."

"You live under my roof, and you will get your ass off this bed and talk to him."

Why the fuck is she even defending him? Trying to force me to interact with the fucking traitor? Doesn't she remember what he did to us? How he left us and didn't love us? "No. He can come here if he wants. Give me ten minutes."

I go to the bathroom and lock my door, turning on the vent so it can swallow the smoke. There's no way I'm doing this sober. I prepare the pipe and Tina, sit on top of the toilet lid, and take a few hits. Enough to clear my head, but not enough to fuck me up anymore. I need to be less stressed, except not too high where I can't focus on a conversation.

I hear footsteps outside of my door and then their voices. I spiral down into—

"I'm fucking done! I'm packing my shit, and I'll be out of here in the morning!"

"No, if you're done, you need to leave right fucking now. Stop prolonging this, you're only going to hurt him more."

I hold my breath as I hide in their closet, since wanting to borrow my dad's favorite jacket now has me trapped in here.

"Hurt him more? How about the way he hurts us*?"*

"He's just a child—"

"He's not a fucking child. He's almost sixteen years old. I can't keep doing this."

I see my dad packing his stuff, digging in his drawers, and stuffing everything into a large black suitcase that looks as beat up as he does. Maybe I am screwing everything up, but I don't know how to stop. It's all I've ever known how to do.

"You don't love him anymore, huh?"

"Maybe I fucking don't."

The tears well in my eyes, and I close them, not bothering to keep them in. As I open them back up though, my dad is standing in the doorway to the closet, staring at me with a guarded expression. I bolt out of the room and don't look back, but I will never forget the way my mother gasped when she saw my face or how her wails followed me all the way to my room.

"How fucking dare you?!"

"He knows the truth now."

"Get the fuck out of my house!"

"I thought you'd never ask."

I snap out of the memory, my hands shaking slightly, and it only makes me want to take another hit of the meth. Instead, I put it out and brush my teeth. Maybe mint will disguise the smell of my doom.

I change my clothes quickly and fix my hair, noticing the circles under my eyes getting darker and darker. I guess that's what drugs do; no way to hide it now. My parents probably won't be the only ones to notice, so I have to be more careful about my appearance.

I open the door and do a sweep of my room. Everything looks the same as always, which is what I want. As I exit my room, I notice no one is in the basement, and I go up the stairs to see my father for the first time in eight years.

The house looks exactly the same as it did yesterday, yet it feels different. Is my mom trying harder for it to be clean? Or is this all in my head?

I hear their hushed whispers coming from the kitchen, and even though my curiosity makes me itch, I sit on the couch in the living room. They shouldn't be talking this way, it's suspicious as fuck. Why are they even having a conversation after everything that happened? And when did they become this civil? Last time we saw him, my mom screamed him out of the house. I clear my throat loudly in announcement and my father appears from around the corner.

He's wearing a suit with a deep green shirt that makes his green eyes stand out. He fiddles with his cufflinks as I stare at him from across the room, daring him with my eyes to come closer. I've been waiting for this moment, and it's taking all my effort to not beat his ass right now.

"Z, how are you?" His voice is small, and it's laced with regret. But I don't give a fuck about regret. I didn't have a father who cared about me. *He didn't love me.*

"Zayne," I reply, "We aren't friends, and we aren't family. You can call me Zayne." Fuck him and his familiarity. He looks as if I've already hit him as my mom interjects.

"Zayne—stop."

"It's okay, Alyssa." My father sighs, "I deserve that." Yes, you fucking do, asshole. It pisses me off that he's even acting like a victim. Why the fuck should I stop anyway? He didn't stop. He still fucking left me. Us.

"What do you want?" Straight to the point. I don't have time to play games with him; those are reserved for Hallie only. "Did you forget to say goodbye and you're here to fix it? It's too late."

"I'm here because I want a second chance. I want to be part of your life."

I start laughing, a hysterical sound even to my own ears. If I don't stop, my mother will probably drive me to the mental hospital, and I can't have that. Tina can't come in with me. "Dad—you're not getting a second chance." I smile, but I can tell he knows it's fake. "Now get the fuck out."

He looks momentarily hurt but then straightens his suit as if there was a crease to begin with and makes his way to the door. "Your mother has my phone number if you want to reach out to me." Hell will freeze over before that happens.

"I won't."

"Goodbye, Z." He opens the front door and steps out, shutting it quietly. The door clicks behind him and it feels final. It feels conclusive. It feels like the closure I didn't get when I was fifteen.

Fuck him.

I don't need him.

I never had him to begin with.

As I scatter the pieces of teenage me, I realize… I don't want to put them back together.

I'm fine just the way I am.

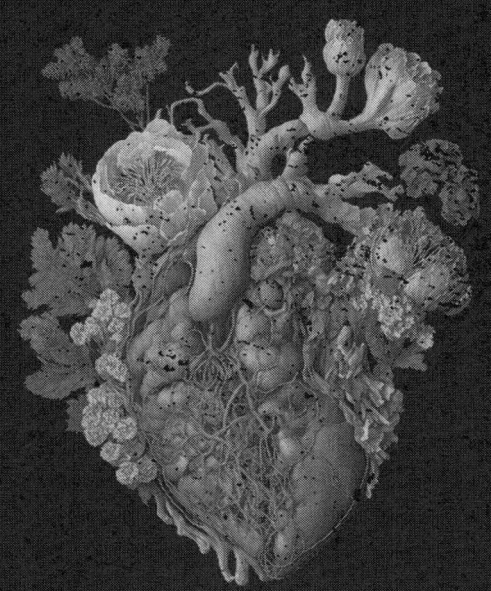

CHAPTER 19

HALLIE

I can't believe I fell for it again.
    It.
    Him.
His words.
His lies.

I know that it's just a matter of time before he crushes my soul again, I'm starting to recognize the pattern, but no matter how hard I try I just can't bring myself to stop. I can't bring myself to end it. I can't bring myself to not *feel*. When did I even start feeling? When did I start needing him more than the air in my lungs?

I don't remember the shift; I don't remember the moment it happened. It may have been a series of moments leading up to this big moment, but I was too lost in him to realize what was happening. I should be able to point out when my life was ruined forever, but I can't even do that much. Now I can never go back to how it was before *him*.

I know in my heart this will always be my life from now on. If my life were a movie, the title would read *Waiting For The Other Shoe To Drop*. Pathetic. Why can't I forget the way he twirls his fingers in my hair? The way he always smells me. The way he buries his face in my neck. The way he always takes my hand and kisses the inside of my wrist in the same exact spot, invisibly branding my skin forever. The way his eyes see straight into my soul and rob the air from my lungs.

I have it bad.

I know he's not good for me.

I should run away as fast as I can, but my feet won't move.

I want him.

I *need* him.

I'm keeping him.

I'll take whatever he will let me have.

I worked a mid-shift today, since they needed more people here than on the night shift. Hospitals are short-staffed, always. It makes me nervous for when I'm a nurse, because I already know I will be picking up slack and drowning in my patient assignment.

It's 11:00 pm on a Saturday, and anyone else my age would be going out to a party or on a date, yet here I am feeling the most exhausted I have in a long time, ready to go home and sleep my life away.

It starts to drizzle as I get on the highway, but it quickly turns into a downpour that has my wipers going at maximum speed, and I can barely see the lines on the road anymore. Suddenly, I begin to feel my car slowing down even though I'm not pumping the brakes. I manage to pull my steering wheel to the right to get on the shoulder before my car comes to a complete halt. What now?

Fuck.

Jesus, I know I said I don't believe in you… but if you're up there, please make this all stop. I don't know what I did to make you hate me. I don't know why you gave me this shitty life, but please make it stop now.

Please, I'm begging you.

I pull out my phone and dial Brit, but she doesn't answer and I know she is either sleeping at home or having sex with her newest plaything. I run down a list of people in my head. But what do you know? I have no one.

Dad? Never met him.

Mom? We don't talk. She lives in another state.

Brothers? Same story.

That leaves me one person: Zayne.

He picks up the phone on the second ring. Thank God.

"Hallie?"

"Baby, I'm stuck on the highway." All the air deflates from my lungs, defeat weighing down my limbs. I can't believe this is happening after a shift. Or that I even have to call him in the first place. "My car broke down on me, and I have no one else to call."

"I'm on my way. Send me a pin."

My eyes burn from unshed tears, and I feel pathetic. Someone doing me a simple favor should not be this significant. It sure as fuck shouldn't make me this emotional. "Thank you, thank you, thank you."

"Anything for you, my love."

My love.

Two words.

How can two words put me back together so quickly?

I hang up the phone and close my eyes, deciding to take a nap while I wait for Zayne to pick me up. After what feels like five minutes, a knock on my window startles me awake. I lower it and he pokes his head in the car, stealing a kiss and my breath. The rain soaks me in just a few seconds, the cold droplets beating down on my face and hair.

"Let me see what's wrong with it." I pop the hood for him and put my window back up. He looks at the car for a few minutes, then walks back in my direction, his head down to shield his eyes from the rain. I lower my window again as he gets closer.

"It's not the oil or your fluids, and your car isn't overheated, so you should probably call a tow truck since you can't move it."

"Okay," I sigh in annoyance, but not at him, just at my life in general. I can't seem to catch a damn break.

I phone the tow truck and they give me a two-hour timeframe for them to come pick up my car. Holy shit, I just wanted some sleep. Why can't anything go my way for once?

I tell Zayne all about the tow truck and he says he will wait with me until they retrieve my car and then take me home. I could kiss him right now. I put my window back up as he walks around to the passenger side and sits in the car with me, and his unique scent fills every crack and hole and gap inside of me until there's no room left for doubts. No room left for suspicions. No room left for anything but *him*.

I breathe him in again, filling my lungs to the point of bursting until it literally hurts from how much air is in them. He tilts his head to the side and smiles, but it's not a kind smile, not a cute smile, not a gentle smile. It's animalistic, a predator stalking its prey—a shark scenting blood in the water or a lion going straight for the neck.

"Hallie, why do you feel so close but so far away?"

"What do you mean?"

"I want to know you. I want to know *more* of you." He leans back in the seat until it's reclined all the way and avoids eye contact with me. "I need some simple truths from you, no avoidance, no lies. I just want answers to my questions and then we never have to talk about it again."

"I don't really know what I'm agreeing to."

"You're agreeing to let me love you," Zayne replies, like it's that simple. "You're agreeing to loving me and trusting me. Please. Just this once."

"Three questions is all you get tonight."

"I'll take it." He all but jumps out of his seat, suddenly full of energy and very interested in what I have to say. He returns the chair to its original position and faces me.

"There's a lot I don't want to talk about, so choose wisely. I may never talk about it again." I recline my seat now and close my eyes, ready for him to destroy me with his questions. I'd rather not look at him while I answer them; I don't want him to see how fucking traumatized I am.

"What was your childhood like?" Zayne asks quietly, barely above a whisper.

"Which part?"

"All of it." He reaches across the middle console and grabs my hand, squeezing it lightly. "I guess start from the beginning."

Fucking hell, it's going to be a long night.

"We're going to be here all night on one question."

"I have time."

I take a few steadying breaths and will my heart to slow down, but it doesn't help. Nothing helps. Nothing ever will. This is the first time I've shared details with anyone. But for whatever reason, here I am about to bare myself for him.

"My childhood was sad. I guess that's the best way to describe it. My dad left us after my brother, David, was born… my mom was very young, twenty years old, and couldn't take care of us financially. She left us with our grandparents and picked us up on the weekends. She met a guy when I was five years old, and I still vividly remember that part of my life. I was confused about why she was with him. Only before we could get used to the idea, he was already living with her. I couldn't adapt. I've always been rebellious…" I smile at this, taking a deep breath again. I don't want to talk about this, but so far, it's not as bad as it could be or as I thought it would be. "Before long, she wanted us to call him 'Dad'. Even pretend that he was," I scoff at this. "And when I refused… it was never pretty for me."

Zayne tenses, his hand tightening around my own. "What did she do?"

"Is that your second official question?"

"No," he replies. "Please finish answering this one."

"I lived most of my life that way—with my grandparents, while my mom lived with him instead. I'm not ungrateful for my grandparents taking me in, but I do resent my mom for not loving me enough to want me with her. When I turned nine years old, they had a child together, and David and I still stayed with my grandparents... she never came for us, Zay." I can feel the tears building; this is why I never talk about this. I hate how weak this makes me feel. Even still, it's as if I can't stop talking. Everything just pours out of me. "We ended up moving with her when I was in middle school, and it all just went downhill from there." I despise how my voice cracks on the last word, making me feel fragile as if I were made of glass, and one slip will shatter me to pieces.

Zayne is staring at me intently, still seemingly afraid to say a word so I don't stop talking. He doesn't say he's sorry. He doesn't look at me with pity. He doesn't judge me. He simply turns my hand over, bringing my wrist to his full lips. They're as soft as silk and feel like a whisper on my skin. My chest is flooded with sudden warmth and it's so scary I want to pull away, but he senses it and grips my hand tighter. "Why do you have nightmares?" Well, he's very direct. Wastes no time.

"Because I've lived through unspeakable things."

He groans, "Elaborate."

"Why?"

"This isn't a good enough answer for my second question."

"You won't be getting one for this question." It's fucking annoying that he keeps asking. When I trust him enough, if I ever do, I will probably tell him. But probably not, still.

Zayne's eyes flash, and he grips my hand to a painful degree, but I don't flinch away. His expression evens out quickly, though; it's as if it never even happened. I get whiplash when he proceeds to kiss me softly, so soft I barely feel his lips brush against mine, and he looks deep into my eyes with his mouth hovering above mine. "What are you most afraid of?"

"You. Love." I pause. "Everything," I whisper.

"I'm afraid of you, too," he whispers back and kisses me again, but this time more urgently. He sucks my lip into his mouth and lets go. He brushes his tongue over my top lip, and my bottom lip and then sweeps it in my mouth. Our tongues collide, our hearts collide, our souls collide.

But even as I know he will break me again, I let him tape me back together.

I let him rearrange my broken pieces and fit them with his own.

Two pieces of the same puzzle.

I pull away, and his eyes flash with anger. I know he doesn't like it, and maybe I taunt him on purpose to see how far he'll go, which is probably a terrible idea. Something tells me this man has no limits when it comes to me.

The rain is falling harder, so I look at the car insurance tracker on my phone for the tow truck. It still says they are over an hour away. That means we still have another hour to wait alone in this car together. It's not that I'm scared of that, but I know he's not going to give up until I give him what he wants. Although now that I look at him, he seems to want something entirely different.

Zayne reclines his seat all the way back yet again, and he takes off his shirt, tossing it in the back seat. He then unbuttons his jeans and unzips them, his light, happy trail taunting me in the darkness.

A subtle glow settles over his skin, the faint moonlight peeking through the storm, and he looks as if he's carved from stone. His body is all clean lines and hard angles, and his abs flex under my stare.

"Come here." Zayne grabs my hand and tugs, pulling me toward him so I can jump over the center console and onto his lap.

I straddle his lap and his hands roam down my back and over my ass, cupping it. My hands slide up his torso in return, until I reach his face and grip it. "I've never done this before." I hear myself talk, but this low husky voice doesn't sound like me.

"I like that I'll be your first with this, even though no one existed before me." Zayne's hands tighten on me. "Those people are forgotten, erased from your memory, never to be thought of again."

He pushes the backrest all the way back and scoots the seat back to give me more space, showing me exactly how we're about to spend our time before the tow truck shows up. I can feel his hard cock under me, his pants doing nothing to mask his erection. His hands slip into my scrub pants and he cups my ass again, pulling toward him and slowly rocking me against him. A gasp passes my lips, quickly followed by a moan, and I can see the smile on his lips in the dim light.

I lean in and kiss him hard, showing him how much I want him with one single gesture, and he matches me stroke for stroke. His hands knead my ass harder and continue to push me onto him at a torturous pace, causing heat to spread low in my belly until *want* is all I feel.

I begin to take off my scrub top and lift up a bit so he can slide his jeans down, but they stick to his skin from the rain and cause him to struggle a bit. As I kneel in front of him, he begins to tug on my pants as well until he slides them down to my knees and I have to shimmy them down awkwardly, my underwear tangled up on them and coming off as well, landing between his feet.

Zayne's hands slide up my back and unclasp my bra, throwing it to the other side of the vehicle carelessly. It lands with a thud that I can barely hear over the thundering of my heartbeat and the rain beating against the car.

He gently pulls me up to sit on him again and wraps his arms around my body, pulling me in for an embrace. My breath hitches in anticipation and I notice his chest rising and falling much quicker than a few moments ago. I kiss my way down his neck, and he tastes a little salty, yet I love the way he always explodes on my tastebuds.

"Fucking goddess," he groans. "You're ruining me for the rest of the world. No one will ever compare to you." His right hand palms my breast, kneading it softly and tweaking the nipple between his fingers.

"I want to ruin you," I reply, but I almost cringe when I say it. I'm not sure why. It's obvious we're dating now, but I don't think I'm ready for whatever comes attached to that fact. It is, however, overshadowed by everything he's making me feel physically, and I push the worries away for a different time.

Zayne reaches down between us and rubs circles on my clit until I gasp, and then he grabs his cock, making me lift off of him. My hands land on his shoulders as he pumps himself a few times before directing it to my entrance.

I look into his eyes and slowly ease myself onto him, knowing he doesn't like when I look away. It's a war between us, who can keep their eyes open the longest, and I want to win this battle. We gasp simultaneously, and one of his hands grips my right hip while the other slides up my back to tug my hair, exposing my throat to him. I take a moment to adjust to him and then rock my hips slowly back and forth, the only sound in the car being our gasps.

He licks my neck and sucks on it lightly, making sure not to leave marks. That makes me angry though, I want him to fucking mark me; I want everyone to know I'm *his*. My hands on his shoulders tighten, and I dig my nails until he hisses in pain, meeting my gaze with narrowed eyes. I arch my eyebrow at him in a silent challenge and he dips his head and bites my neck *hard*. I gasp and begin to pick up my pace, this time shifting my hips to go in circles. He lets my hair go and we make eye contact again, his eyes looking the most alive I've ever seen them.

My hand finds his throat and I push his chin up, leaning in to lick his lips but not kissing him. I stay leaned into him, our lips brushing while I go faster, and both his hands meet my hips now, pulling me closer to him as the friction against my clit begins to make my head spin and moans slip from my mouth.

I dig my fingers under his jaw while I stare into his eyes and give myself over to the pleasure, our lips still brushing against each other but not quite kissing. I dart my tongue out to lick his bottom lip again and then take it into my mouth, biting hard as I let go. The taste of his blood fills my mouth when I lick my lips, and it only adds to the tension building in my body.

Zayne stiffens for a split second, then shifts down a bit on the seat, lifting his hips to thrust into me. His fingers dig into my hips until I'm sure bruises will be present tomorrow, although the intensity of this is enough to make me forget about temporary pain.

Our bodies begin to crash into each other, moving together seamlessly toward the same goal. Our pace continues to escalate until I'm sure it's impossible for him to fuck me any harder, or he'll break me. We meet for a frantic kiss, tongues stroking, teeth crashing, and our moans muffled by it.

He pulls away from me and scoots back in the seat, pulling me up as I grind on him again, rubbing my clit as I circle my hips quickly, picking up the pace even more. He reaches down between us and begins to circle my clit slowly at first until his hand comes to rest against my throat.

With every hitch of my breath, he picks up the pace of his rubbing and tightens his grip on my neck. Soon enough, I can't take a breath, and it's a race toward orgasm or asphyxiation. I know it's right there, I can feel myself being so fucking close. My chest begins to tighten with the need to take a breath, my lungs burning as if on cue, and I try to calm myself enough to focus on the orgasm. If I panic now, I know I won't get there, and I also know he won't let go until I do.

"Come with me, baby girl."

My fingers dig harder into his shoulders, nails drawing blood all over again. My mouth is open on a silent gasp, and I know I would be so fucking loud if he let go. Spots explode behind my eyes and the interior of the car begins to spin in my vision, blurring with tears now as well.

A wave of warmth pulls me under, and as my body trembles on top of him, he lets go of my neck slowly, as if trying to prolong it so I can feel everything more intensely. I feel him tense under me and he pulls me tight against him, coming inside of me as his fingers dig into my hips again and he thrusts into me without rhythm.

Our bodies slow down and then go limp against the seat of the car, our quiet breaths the only sound now save for the rain. He buries his face in the crook of my neck and kisses me sweetly. I sag against him, bringing my face to rest on his shoulder, until I notice the streaks of blood from my nails. I lick the blood off him, savoring his taste in my mouth and treasuring the groan I elicit from him. I'm addicted to him: his smell, his taste, his feel.

He's my kryptonite, yet I've never wanted anything to wreck my life this way. I consciously open myself up to the hurt, welcoming it if it means keeping him too.

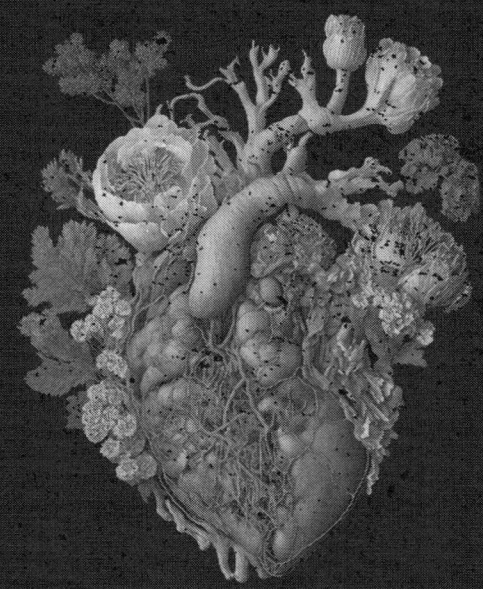

CHAPTER 20

```
HALLIE
```

The older man who works for the tow truck company is fast and efficient and loads my car in record time. I ask Zayne to take me home and settle in for the drive but close my eyes, because I worked twelve hours and then waited for two more. So now that we are on the way home, it's almost three in the morning. When I open my eyes, we are parking in an unfamiliar driveway, and I narrow them to slits, but Zayne doesn't even notice or glance in my direction.

"Where are we?"

"Oh, Sleeping Beauty wakes." His chuckle turns my insides. "We're home."

"This isn't my home…"

"It's mine." He looks at me now, his eyes tender. "I wanted you to see where I live. I want you to stay here tonight."

"Fine, but no sex. I feel disgusting and I don't want to shower this late. I just want to sleep."

"Deal." He smiles as I extend my hand. "What are you doing?"

"Shaking on it."

"We don't shake on deals and promises," Zayne says with a low voice. "We kiss." My stomach clenches as he leans over to kiss me. His tongue brushes my lips once before I open wide for him, letting him devour me.

He breaks the kiss and gets out of the car to open the door for me as he always does, and he uses his jacket to shield me from the rain. Right now, I fucking love him for this. Probably because no one is ever nice to me, and I'll take whatever scraps someone throws my way.

The house is a ranch-style home with a white stone exterior and a metal roof. It has a wrap-around porch with beautiful rocking chairs and other furniture, but I can't really take a good look as we rush into the house, attempting to escape the storm.

The house is tastefully decorated with rustic and modern touches and as I try to look around, Zayne drags me to one single door at the other end of the house. The door leads down a flight of stairs—a basement. Strange, since I've never seen a Texas home with a basement before.

"This is my side of the house," Zayne says proudly. "No one comes down here."

I'm not sure what I was expecting the basement to look like, but it definitely was not this. It's almost as big as my entire apartment, and it's even divided into rooms. There's a main area that could be a living room but there's only a pool table in the middle of the room, along with a small kitchenette in one corner. There's an open door with a desktop, a huge television, and a gaming center across from a comfortable-looking leather couch. The next door is his bedroom, which is pitch black, so I can't see much except for a king bed in the center of the room. There's a bathroom door next to his room, but it's only a half bath, I'm assuming for guests.

"Wow, Zayne. This is incredible." I can hear the awe in my voice, and I hate myself for it. I had never seen such a nice home. His family undoubtedly comes from money. And then there's me.

Dirt poor with no family. I'm not sure why he's with me, and I can feel myself having doubts about everything. Am I pretty enough? Good enough? Nice enough? Does he even like me enough?

"I know you said you weren't showering tonight, but there's a bathroom in my room and the shower is yours if you want it."

"Thank you, I actually might take a shower right now." He came inside me, and I'm leaking. Fuck that.

"I'll be in bed waiting for you."

I go into his bathroom and there's a walk-in shower with no doors and multiple shower heads. There's a fucking bench in the shower. Just how rich are you, Zay?

I make quick work of the shower, even though the hot water feels amazing on my skin, I'm so exhausted I might fall over. I dry myself and head over to his closet, which is part of the massive bathroom, and pull a soft crew neck shirt over my head. I brush my teeth with his toothbrush, I use his comb for my hair, I break all the rules.

When I come to bed, he's already asleep. I hear the light snores and deep breaths as I pull the covers back and settle in. As I lie here, I remember I don't have my Xanax or my Prazosin and my chest begins to feel really tight. My mouth is dry, my ears are ringing, and I'm panting.

I can't go to sleep. I can't go to sleep. I can't go to sleep.

"What's wrong?" Zayne reaches over and grabs my sweaty palm. Are we connected? Why can he always sense this?

"I don't have my meds," I whisper.

"I'm here, baby, it will be okay." He squeezes my hand and my breath stutters. "I won't let anything hurt you, not even your nightmares. Go to sleep, I'll rub your back."

I don't believe him, but I also don't argue as I lie on my side facing the opposite way so he can make good on his offer. His fingertips are whispers on my skin, unspoken promises thrown to the wind. I relax slightly as he rubs circles on my back, then up and down, then letters.

I-L-O-V-E...

I suck in a sharp breath and he stills his hand, scooting so close that we're now flush together, my back to his front, his face in the crook of my neck. His fingers dancing down my arm, and his lips on my earlobe. His rhythmic breaths rock me to sleep, the sweetest lullaby that even my mother couldn't beat.

I'm drifting, drifting, drifting.

I'm suddenly a raft drifting away in the open ocean, the waves dragging me toward the current, floating toward him.

Always *him.*

The one who made me do it.

And, as always, he's the one who drowns me.

"It's okay, honey. Shhhhhh. It's okay … it will get better in just a minute," he whispers in my ear, his breath sending spiders crawling down my back as the shiver rakes through my body.

The ring of fire makes me hold my breath, but then I realize this won't be like the other times. This won't be over before I know it. This pain, I can't ignore.

A sob escapes me and he clamps his hand over my mouth until I can't draw a breath in, and I taste the saltiness of his skin as bile rises in my throat. I force myself to swallow it down, just like I force the tears to stay away.

Stop being so fucking weak.

He'll hate you, too.

Michael pushes himself in slowly, and I feel like he's dragging this out on purpose.

What do you get out of my pain?

I need to know.

I need to get something out of my pain too.

Indulge me.

But I don't say it. I force myself to stay quiet.

I don't even make a sound as he pushes in the rest of the way, making me feel like I have to bear down. I don't even make a sound when I feel like he's tearing me wide open, ripping me in half, exposing parts of me that no one has ever seen before and no one is supposed to. I don't even make a sound as the slaps echo in the dark room, the only light from the antique streetlamp right outside my window. I don't even make a sound when he pulls out and his semen is coming out of me, shame setting my skin on fire. I don't even make a sound when I use the bathroom and there's blood when I wipe, making me wonder about the extent of the damage. I don't even make a sound as I fall to the floor and cry, the sobs so strangled that no noise can escape my throat. I don't even make a sound when I cut myself again and then again, again, and again.

Because good girls don't make sounds, and tonight I'm a good girl.

I slowly open my eyes and glance at the clock sitting on the nightstand next to my side of the bed—it reads one in the afternoon.

Oh, shit.

It's been a long time since I slept in, and I have a test I need to study for today. Zayne is still sleeping and doesn't so much as twitch when I get out of bed. After making myself presentable enough, I go to the kitchenette to grab a water bottle, but he's fresh out.

I don't want to be rude, but I'm really thirsty, so I go upstairs to hunt down some water. As I open the fridge and spot the waters, a woman's voice comes from behind me.

"Good afternoon," She sounds curious, and it makes me tense. Does he do this a lot? Is she used to it by now? "I didn't know Zayne had company today."

"Good afternoon," I choke out, spinning quickly to face her with my hand over my chest as if she scared me half to death, which she did. "I'm so sorry to just open your fridge, but he didn't have any water bottles left downstairs…"

"It's okay. Please help yourself." She smiles warmly at me, and it makes me feel right at home. "My name is Alyssa."

"Hallie," I walk in her direction and extend my hand. Her grip is firm but not painful as she shakes it, and her warmth brings me comfort. "It's so nice to meet you."

"Are you his…?" Her expression is puzzled, as if she doesn't even know I existed until this very moment.

"Girlfriend." I clear my throat, almost surprised he didn't mention me.

"Oh, he—"

"Hey, Mom," Zayne appears out of nowhere like he always does. "I see you've met Hallie."

"Did you sleep alright?" Alyssa asks him with a look of concern on her face. But why is she so concerned? Does he not sleep?

"Better than ever." He smirks and she rolls her eyes.

"Keep it to yourself."

This time I clear my throat instead, and I can feel my face burning with embarrassment. My most annoying trait is my fair skin, and how I look like a tomato when I blush. Zayne laughs and offers me breakfast while I go sit at the kitchen island.

"I have to run a few errands, but I will be back later." Alyssa grabs her purse from the chair next to mine. "Hallie, you should come over for dinner tonight."

"Yes, ma'am, I would love to."

"None of that proper talk. Call me Alyssa."

"Yes, Alyssa." I smile.

Alyssa kisses Zayne on the cheek and heads out, leaving me all alone with him as he goes back to make me breakfast again. I could get used to this. This time he makes scrambled eggs with bacon and toast. He sets a glass of orange juice and a mug of coffee in front of me, then hands me everything I need. We sit in silence as we eat, but it's not uncomfortable. It feels normal. I've never known normal, which suddenly makes me self-conscious.

"Is there any way you could take me home after this?" I hate not having a car. Now I need to figure out when I'm getting it back. "I would like a change of clothes, and I need to study for a few hours before coming over for dinner."

"That's fine, Hals."

"Thank you, baby."

He reaches for my hand and squeezes it once, then lets it drop. I wonder if he can tell I had nightmares last night. I wonder if he can tell I really like his mom. I wonder if he can tell I'm falling in love with him.

He's becoming a habit, even though I don't want him to.

Habits are predictable.

Habits are routine.

Habits bring you comfort.

But Zayne... he's none of those things.

Many hours later, as I sit at the dinner table across from Alyssa, I wonder if my apple pie was the right choice to bring as dessert. I should've asked Zayne what she would have preferred instead of picking it myself. The dinner has actually flowed pleasantly up to this point.

He squeezes my hand under the table and our eyes connect for a breath before I continue to eat some more of my food. Alyssa is an amazing cook, and I don't remember the last time I had a home-cooked meal like this one, if ever. She made a pot roast with mashed potatoes, coating them both with a delicious gravy. The vegetables from the pot roast are tender and the perfect balance for the meal.

"So, Hallie," Alyssa begins, "what are you going to school for?"

"My Bachelor of Science in Nursing. I actually have a job interview coming up for my residency."

"Wow, that's incredible. Congratulations..." She trails off and looks across the table at Zayne. "Are you going to get your life together and choose a major now that you have a successful girlfriend?"

I feel her jab in my chest, almost as if someone punctured my lung and it is now quickly deflating. I look at him, but the way his jaw is ticking tells me that this is going to turn into a disaster, and I better get out of the way.

"I still don't know what I want to study and choosing

something specific makes it feel very final." He sets down his utensils and shoves his plate away, clasping his hands in front of him as he sets them on the table.

"It *should* feel final, that's the fucking point." I know she doesn't mean to cuss when she shoots me an apologetic look, yet her words still make me flinch. Or maybe her apology was for saying this in front of me? I can't be sure.

I don't think I want to know.

"Nothing should ever feel final. I don't want finality in my life. I want to let it ebb and flow… I want to live right here, right now. I don't want to live in the future. Just let me live, Mom."

Alyssa laughs loudly at this. She doubles over and clutches her stomach while tears run down her face. I'm not entirely sure why it's so funny. I thought there was something poetic about what he said, and I could even relate to it in a way.

"There's no way for you to not think about the future, Zayne," Alyssa replies, wiping tears from her face. "Everything you do right now affects it. Every decision you make has a consequence. Can you honestly say you're prepared to face the consequences of your most recent actions?" She looks him dead in the face. "Do you think Hallie can deal with them? Don't think for one fucking second I don't know what you're up to. I checked the cameras. Does she know?"

"Do I know what?" I ask, but my voice is barely a whisper, entirely inaudible for their ears as they square off against each other.

"This conversation is fucking over, Mom," Zayne tells her through gritted teeth. His face is red, and if I'm being honest, he looks fucking scary right now. On the verge of snapping. "Whatever you have to say, you can say it after I take her home."

"Hallie, you seem like an amazing woman." She levels me with a serious face, "You clearly have your head on your shoulders and you know what you want out of life. You may think you want him, you may think you love him, but this is not what you need. *He* is not what you need. You should break up with him. Move on. Have a good life without all the troubles he brings. Because if you don't, you will soon be drowning in his empty promises and painful regrets."

I feel anger at first, but I try to push it down. She sounds a lot like my mother, and it fucking pisses me off. Then, unexpectedly, I only have one burning question in my mind.

What the fuck did Zayne do to her?

Before I can think about what to say, Zayne grabs my hand and hauls me out of the dining room, making me stumble when my foot hits the edge of my chair, and heading straight for the front door. I pause and look back at his mother; she appears regretful, sad, but also determined.

"It was nice meeting you, Alyssa," I whisper as my eyes fill with tears. The embarrassment and humiliation I feel right now are enough to send them spilling over. I hate that we are parting this way, that he's dragging me out. Is this what life with him is like? An endless downward spiral?

"Take care of yourself, Hallie. Don't close your eyes for too long when you're with him, because then you can't see the truth of what is actually happening around you." What the fuck does that even mean? What is he lying about now?

Clearly something.

As we get in the car, I think of asking him about all the things his mother said. I think about demanding he tells me his truths. I think about accusing him of not actually loving me. But instead, I'm quiet. I bottle up my pain, my questions, and my insecurities.

I look out the window and try to erase the last hour of my life, because at least that gives me a little more time with *him*. A little more time before I have to face the inevitable.

Everybody leaves.

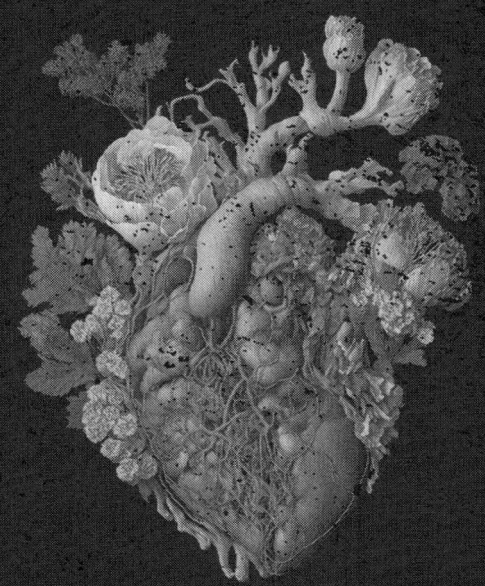

CHAPTER 21

ZAYNE

It's been a week since that dinner with my fucking mom. I hate her sometimes. She doesn't seem to realize that every bit of her is constantly sabotaging everything I work for in my life.

I'm never good enough.

Always the fuck up.

Never the achiever.

Well, fuck her. I don't want to be an achiever, anyway. I don't want to make her proud. I just want to live my life chasing the tiny glimpses of happiness I'm allowed to see.

The sunrises and the sunsets.

Hallie's smiles.

Just Hallie.

She's everything.

And now?

Now she will know.

She will know I'm nothing.

Nothing at all.
And she will leave me.
She always does.
I only know one girl who can numb this pain.
Her name is Tina.
So I get my glass pipe ready.
I get my heart ready.
I get my soul ready.
Ready for mass destruction.
Because I know that's what I'm doing.
I just don't want to acknowledge it yet.
I want to pretend, pretend, pretend.

Pretend that this will all get better and I won't have to think about how Tina is my new obsession now, and absolutely vital for my survival.

Pretend that Hallie will stay with me when she sees how deep I'm in.

Pretend I'm still taking my medications as I should.
Pretend I'm passing my classes as expected.
Pretend I won't be doing this more often.
But instead of pretending…
I light the glass pipe and watch Tina bubble.
And then…
I let her make me forget.
I let Tina make everything better.

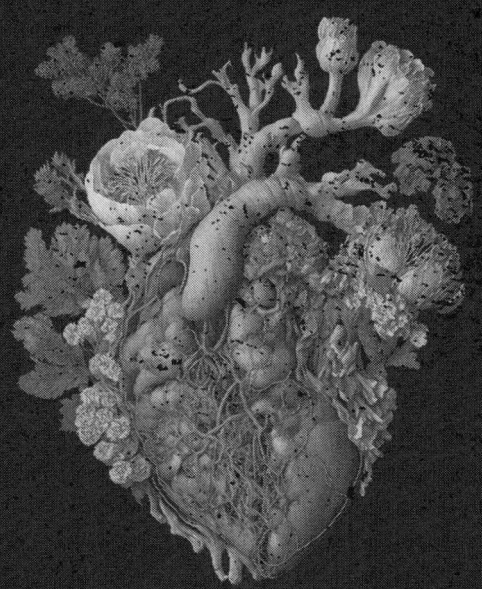

CHAPTER 22

HALLIE

Brit is singing along to some country song I don't know as I drive to Zayne's house. He invited us both for a get-together with his friends, and it's a sunny day but unfortunately still cold. Other than drinking and possibly a movie, I'm not entirely sure what we will be doing.

I pull up to his house and park in the driveway, noticing three other cars parked in front of and beside me, none of them being his mom's. I'm thankful for that, and I make sure to tell the universe as I get out of the car. I hug my jacket to myself as we walk toward the door, the wind making my hair tangle across my face.

Zayne lets us in, and I'm surprised I came back this quickly after having the worst dinner with his mother. But now that I'm here, I'm ready to have fun. Brit and I walk into the house, the surroundings familiar to me as we head to the sectional couch in the open floor-plan living room where everyone is sitting. Three guys are talking and laughing, agreeing on a movie. It smells like popcorn, the butter invading my senses and making my stomach growl.

"Hallie, Brit—" The guys all look at us at the same time, and my hands itch from all the attention. "These are my friends. Jeremy, Xander, Tim." Zayne introduces us, his eyes flashing between Brit and Xander as if trying to relay something. Xander is dark-haired with brown eyes, tall and has tan skin. Exactly Brit's type.

"Nice to meet you," I say to all three, and Brit quickly follows with her own. We walk across the living room and sit on the side of the couch that is not occupied, and as I sit down I notice Brit and Xander making eyes at each other from across the room.

"You could be more subtle." I give her a crooked smirk, and she laughs. She's never been subtle about anything in her entire life, and she knows I know that. When she wants something, she fucking takes it.

"Sorry, I'm not sure about the meaning of that word," Brit says while keeping eye contact with Xander, who is now openly smiling at her. "He's sexy, dude. I just want to lick him."

"Please, please refrain from doing that in front of me."

"No promises will be made." She rolls her eyes and then looks at my man. "Hey, Zayne, do you have any candy?"

"Yes, it's in the pantry."

"Xander, be a darling and help me get the candy, please." Brit winks at me as she gets up from the couch and heads to the kitchen, her new toy obediently following after her.

Zayne sits next to me on the couch, and it dips from his weight, making me almost topple over. He laughs and it makes me smile. I notice I smile a lot more when I'm around him.

"What are we watching today?" I ask him, glancing over at the seventy-inch television gracing the room. Sometimes I forget he comes from money, but when I'm here, it's so obvious.

"We're watching the Wonder Woman movie. The guys picked it."

"Of course, of course." I chuckle as I think about how typical these men are.

"Come, baby girl. I want cuddles," Zayne tells me as he scoops me up into his arms, as if I weigh nothing at all. He sets me on his lap, then opens his legs so I'm sitting between them as he wraps them around me. I lean back on his chest, my head resting perfectly under his chin while he grabs my hand and interlaces our fingers. We fit so perfectly together.

Brit and Xander sit on the other side of the couch while the other guys seem confused. I'm not though. She probably was making out with him the entire time in the kitchen. Xander throws Zayne a chocolate bar, and he splits it in half with me.

The movie is played and I can't help but keep looking back at Brit, wondering if she really likes this one or if he's a game just like all the others. I know her reasoning, she's lonely. She always has been. There's a void she desperately wants to fill, no—*needs* to fill.

In some ways she's just like me, even if her trauma is different. Her mother is a drug addict and in prison for possession and distribution of drugs, while her dad wiped his hands of her as soon as he could. Her grandparents stepped in, just the way mine did, to raise her and try to patch her up. But nothing could ever erase the pain from the most important people not wanting you, not caring about you. That's why she jumps from one guy to the next. She needs to feel wanted, important, needed.

Loved.

Nevertheless, she doesn't realize those things don't come from temporary people. Those things come from people who stay, and even I don't know what that's like. There's no advice I could give her to make everything better, so I just don't say anything. I let her live her fantasies, and I'm always there to pick up the pieces when someone doesn't pan out.

Lately I think she's tired of the heartbreak. She hasn't gone out on a date in months. It's just been casual sex and the occasional booty call, but nothing is ever serious enough that she feels sad when it ends. It's as if she's building a wedge between her and the outside world, afraid to let anyone in.

I can't say I blame her when I constantly drive a wedge

between myself and Zayne. He wants this to be serious, a relationship, but I don't even know how to be with myself. I still haven't learned how to deal with other people.

Brit is not someone I have to try hard with, she doesn't know how to be with other people either. We both just exist in the same house, and our weirdness interacts well with each other.

Zayne is different. He's intense, demanding, possessive, and ready to spit fire in every direction if someone dares come near his treasure. He wants me and I want him, but I still don't know how to have a healthy obsession. Is there even such a thing?

He shifts behind me and I can feel his erection press against my back, my breath stuttering in my chest as I attempt to not flush in front of everyone in plain daylight. I clear my throat lightly and Zayne squeezes my hand, reassuring me. "Don't worry," he whispers in my ear, making a shiver crawl down my spine when his lips ghost against the shell of it. "I won't act on it."

I wish he would. I wish he would bend me right over this couch, but I know it's obviously not happening today as I roll my eyes and answer, "I know."

The next two hours fly by, and then Brit and I are leaving. I'm surprised she didn't fight me harder to stay with Xander. I think she can tell I don't want to be here, which might be noticeable at this point, but I want to leave this house before his mom comes home. The dinner was awkward and I have no intention of showing my face for at least a few weeks. So she lets me drag her out and take her away from her new boy toy.

Brit plays music on her phone, "Your Love is My Drug" by Kesha blasting in my speakers. I lower the volume a few notches and listen to the song. It's fitting for Zayne and I, but I don't mention anything. I think of all the reasons why we're good for each other, all the reasons why we should be together, instead of all the obvious reasons why we shouldn't.

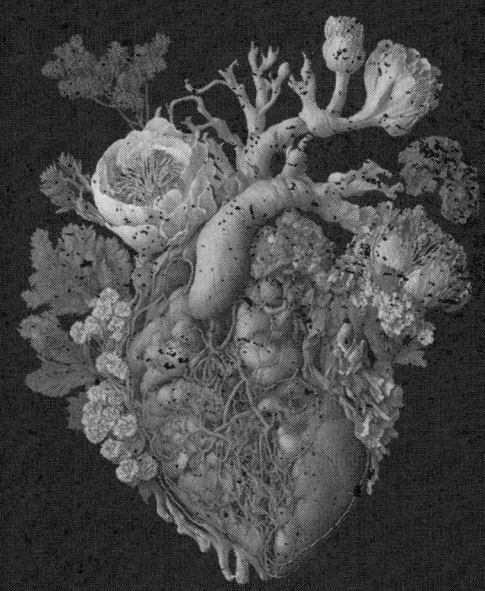

CHAPTER 23

HALLIE

Zayne texts me to tell me his mom wants me over for dinner again, but I lie and say I have to study for an exam tomorrow. He believes me, or maybe he wanted me to say no. I didn't miss the way he got me out of his house as quickly as possible after she started talking about him. It's clear that Alyssa doesn't want me with her son. I think maybe he did something really fucked up and she doesn't want me to get hurt. I'm just not sure what could be so bad. My heart probably can't take knowing the reasons, in any case. It probably can't handle the pain, and I don't think I can watch myself break.

Not yet.
I need more time.
More time with *him*.
More time as us.
I haven't even scratched the surface.
I haven't put my dent in his heart.

But even as I beg for more time, I already know that it will never be enough.

Never.

I want him to eat me alive.

Gobble me up.

Swallow me whole.

I just never expected him to spit me back out.

Technically, I should be studying, even though I lied about it. It's April now, which means it's crunch time for me when it comes to my nursing courses. I'm working on my big care plan for my critical care clinical and I'm barely scraping by with a B for my Med-Surg course. I finished my management course, thankfully, but I still have Art to worry about, which isn't much of a worry for me, except that Zayne has been more distracting than usual.

He's been acting strange lately, but I can't put my finger on it exactly. It's as if he's still himself but with more energy. But also, wants to go to more parties than usual and he's sleeping less, which means he's staying over less. There's been many times he goes to parties without me now, since I have to work. He's making me feel like I'm on the outs.

The outs of him, if that makes sense.

He's hiding something, I can feel it in my bones. I don't think he's cheating, but he's not being truthful. I didn't go back to his mother's house after dinner that night, but I can still hear her words playing in my mind like a broken record.

You should break up with him…

You should move on…

Because if you don't…

You will be drowning…

Empty promises…

Painful regrets…

Repeat. Repeat. Repeat.

I've considered going back, but I can't handle our bubble bursting. I don't want to find a reason to leave him. He doesn't want to tell me his truths, and somehow I've been okay with that. Because if he tells me his truths, it means I have to let him go.

My phone vibrates on the table and I snatch it before my Med-Surg professor can see me on it so I don't get kicked out. He has a no-cell phone policy in class. He says it has to do with distractions and learning. Who even knows? But I'm always distracted by Brit. It's a miracle we're even passing the course in the first place.

"Zayne keeps texting you," Brit whispers, although I still haven't looked at my phone. It's just on my lap with the screen facing her.

I look down at my screen discreetly and try my best not to blush.

> **Zayne: Baby I need to taste you!!**
>
> **Zayne: Come to the PAC.**
>
> **Zayne: I'll wait for you in the men's bathroom…**
>
> **Zayne: Meet me in thirty minutes.**

My class ends in ten minutes, so that's actually perfect. There's one thing I haven't told anyone, but it's that Zayne loves to have sex in public places. The riskier, the better. So far, we've had sex at the park, in the car, in the restroom of the clubhouse in my apartment complex, a pool. He loves it, I love it. We chase the thrill together. We chase the excitement. It's better than weed, better than pills.

Nothing compares to him.

The anticipation has my thighs clenching together and my brain counting down the minutes, seconds, milliseconds until I can run out of this classroom and straight into his arms.

Class is over before I know it, and Brit stares at me as I gather my things in a rush. She tilts her head and raises one perfectly drawn eyebrow. "Where are you going in such a rush?"

"To get some dick."

She throws her head back and laughs while she shakes her head and gathers her own belongings. We are two peas in a pod, and she knows me so well that she didn't even need an answer to that question, but she asked it for her own amusement.

"I love what Zayne has done to you." Brit smirks as she swings her backpack around and hoists it over one shoulder. "I mean, you were dirty before, but now you're a little slut. When you're done with him, I call dibs."

I roll my eyes and smirk, as if she hasn't been calling dibs for years. "Yes, daddy," I reply with amusement. "You know you're next in line."

"As long as we're clear. I don't want to have to get in the middle of the next fling."

We walk out of the classroom together but then go in opposite directions. Brittany walks to the parking lot and I walk to the Performing Arts Center, heading for the bathroom.

I look around to ensure no one is watching and hope for the best as I open the doors to the men's restroom. There are urinals lining almost all of the visible walls except for one line of stalls and one wall of sinks. It's actually clean, which I'm thankful for.

Zayne is leaning against the furthest stall from the door, wearing a black pair of skinny jeans and a long sleeve deep green V-neck shirt that brings out his eyes even from this distance. He pushes off the door and opens it, stepping into the stall with his back to me. I follow after him then close and lock the door, then wrap my arms around his waist and squeeze him tightly.

He takes my hand and spins around to face me, then pins me against the door as he leans into me. I strain my neck to look up at him; his eyes are oddly more dilated than I've ever seen them. It's no question that he's high, it's just a matter of what he took.

My heart is thunder that echoes in my chest as he kisses the corner of my mouth, my jaw, and then trails open-mouth kisses down my neck while he unbuttons my jeans. I pull them down while Zayne gets his unbuttoned and pulled down as well, throwing mine on the ground as I try to focus on slowing my heart down, but it doesn't want to cooperate.

Zayne lifts me up and I wrap my legs tightly around his waist while he pushes against my opening. He slams into me in one quick thrust that steals all the air from my lungs, bringing tears to my eyes, and then... then he *fucks* me.

There's nothing sweet or gentle about how he pushes me against the door and uses it as leverage as he slams into me over and over. Luckily, the friction has him rubbing against my clit exactly as I need it, and soon enough I'm coming apart under him, but he seems insatiable. He's usually done by now, and I'm wondering how much longer until he comes. This never happens. I'm usually never waiting around for him to finish, and this fact is reiterated by the sweat dripping from his forehead onto my face. What the fuck is going on?

I glance at my watch on my wrist, and it says we've been fucking for an hour. I'm starting to get dry, this is no longer fun, and I want down. I'm beginning to wonder how much longer he will be able to hold me up, surely not much longer. He continues to thrust into me, my back slick with sweat slipping against the stall door. My stomach tumbles in a panic that I really am going to fall on my face any moment, and I decide I'm fucking done.

"Enough, Zayne," I groan, pushing him away and trying desperately to get down, but he won't let me go. "Put me down."

"I'm not done yet..." His fingers tighten around my legs painfully, and I start to shove him away.

"No, but *I'm* done." Zayne stops abruptly, cocking his head to the side. It looks like he's trying to decide how serious I am, so I reiterate, "*Now.*" He finally puts me down and I don't make eye contact as I put my underwear and pants back on. He still doesn't bother with his own clothes, and somehow his cock is still hard as a rock, which he begins to fist and stroke right in front of me. I narrow my eyes at him in confusion and irritation except he doesn't seem to notice.

Zayne doesn't seem to be aware of my emotions at the moment, or possibly even the situation. His high is compromising his decisions, and I don't think I've seen him like this in all the months we've been dating. This doesn't feel fun or adventurous or spontaneous anymore.

This feels like a problem.

This feels like he's in trouble.

"What are you doing?" I ask, trying to keep my voice from shaking as I start putting my shoes on.

"Finishing." He looks like he's in pain, but it doesn't bother me right now. I want him to feel a fraction of what he's making me feel.

"How come it's taking so long?" I ask him, thoroughly confused.

"I don't know, but I don't want blue balls."

"I'm just going to go..." I open the stall door and start to step out.

"Suit yourself." His voice is hoarse as he continues to beat his cock, and I glance over my shoulder at him, narrowing my eyes into thin slits.

Suit myself?

Fuck.

Him.

Zayne can be a very sweet person when he wants to be, but whatever he's on right now, makes him the opposite of sweet. When he wants to, he can become poison, infecting everything and everyone around him to their death.

I don't want to be around him anymore, so I leave.

I leave him behind, proving his claim that I always do.

But as always, he won't take responsibility for his actions.

And I'm here to bring the consequences.

I haven't talked to Zayne since I walked out of the men's restroom a few days ago. He hasn't called or texted, and I just have a terrible feeling that it's because he's been high this entire time. What could be this fucking strong? I almost don't want to find out, but I also know that I need to help him.

I'm late to Art class and, somehow, the only empty seat is next to him, even though I know we generally sit together. I just wanted to be early to find a different seat. The class drags on as I try to hear the lecture over the pounding of my heart. My breathing is quick as Zayne stares at me the entire time and I don't glance in his direction once. If looks could burn, my entire face would be roasted.

I bend down to pick up my backpack once the class is over, and Zayne does the same, but he didn't zip his and everything falls out. I drop my backpack on the table and begin to help him pick up everything from the ground, until I find a tiny little bag with blue-white rocks in it. These are the drugs. I know it. I just don't know what they are.

"Zayne." I suck in my breath. "What the fuck is this?"

"Oh, I'm just holding that for a friend."

"Don't do that." I laugh without humor. Is he fucking kidding me right now? "Don't fucking lie to my face."

"Why would you think I'm lying?"

"You've been acting strange for a while now. Your eyes are always dilated, you're horny but can't finish, and you don't sleep anymore. You're losing weight…"

"I'm fine, Hallie." *The fuck you are.*

"You're losing me."

Zayne chuckles, which kind of pisses me off, if I'm being honest. "I'll never lose you."

"You will if you don't get your shit together." I take a deep breath and lower my voice so no one around us can hear what I'm saying next. "Tell me what it is. Now."

"Meth."

Can one single word destroy your life? Flip it upside down? Crush your soul? Shatter your heart?

Flashes of my mother telling me about my father's drug addictions play like a broken record in my mind. "No," I whisper as I feel one tear roll down my cheek. He wipes his thumb under my eye as more follow. Of all the drugs he could've picked, why did it have to be this one?

"I'm so sorry, baby," he tells me, and he does sound like he means it for once. "I didn't mean for this to happen, I swear. I swear on everything this was never my intention."

"I can't do this." I clutch at my chest as if it will keep my heart from continuing to break, and his face crumples when he watches me fall to pieces in front of him. "I can't be with you if you're going to get high on this shit." I point at the little baggie and a tear slides down his cheek. He wipes it away furiously, not liking to show weakness.

"Come with me, please."

He pulls me out of the classroom into the restroom and takes the little bag and dumps all the contents in the toilet. I watch him as he flushes and then we walk out, still holding my hand. "I'm done, Hals." Zayne holds up his hands in surrender. "I swear I don't want this. I will be done for you." His shoes touch the front of my own, and he tilts my chin up with his finger. "I will be worthy of you. I won't let you down again."

"Promise?" I look him in the eyes, and I see sincerity. I see a broken man. I see someone who wants to change. Maybe it's all in my fucking head though, and I just imagine what I want from him.

"Swear."

"Let's kiss on it then." I grab his hand and squeeze, a silent reassurance that I believe him as he leans down to kiss me.

It doesn't matter how many times we kiss on it, I can still taste all his lies as he slips his tongue into my mouth. I can still feel it that this isn't the last time we will have this conversation. But I pretend and let myself have one more day, one more hour, one more second by his side.

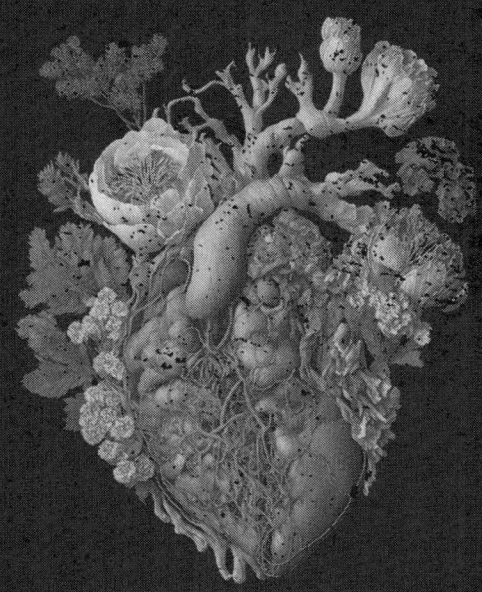

CHAPTER 24

ZAYNE

*F*UCK.

Why the fuck did I flush it all?

I don't have any more left, and now I have to score a teener to ration for the next week, so Hallie doesn't suspect I'm still using.

I slipped up. I've *been* slipping up.

What started out as a subtle craving has now turned into me needing it more than food or water. And by it, I mean *her*.

Tina.

I thought I loved her, but now she's ruining a lot of things for me. I can no longer act normal because I keep smoking more and more. A teener used to last me a week. Now an eight-ball doesn't even last me a week.

I have to cut back. I'll still take a hit because it's necessary for my survival now, but I won't do it to chase the rush. I won't do it for the high itself. At least, that's what I keep telling myself as I try to cut back for Hallie.

I'm not a junkie. I'm not a junkie. I'm not a junkie.

I don't need to get high, I just like to.

I don't need Tina, I just love her.

Right?

The problem is that as much as I want to, I don't know how to stop. The withdrawals are going to be so strong that I don't know how I'll ever be able to hide it from my mom. Though I don't think that's necessary anymore with the way she spoke to Hallie. She alluded to seeing me in the car doing drugs, but nothing was ever mentioned again after I took my girl home. My mother probably doesn't think it's necessary to have a conversation about it; maybe she believes that her bringing it up at the dinner table was warning enough. I guess she doesn't know me that well, after all. I've never cared about her blackmail. If she wants to tell Hallie, fucking let her. I already took care of that for us. And Hallie is still here, even if she talks about leaving me. I know she could never truly go through with it.

As I lie back in my bed, I feel something else trying to grab onto me.

The darkness.

Welcome back, she teases.

I've missed you, she taunts.

You can't escape me, she goads.

Ever.

What she doesn't know is that I have Tina already, and she protects me. Tina holds me when I need her.

Tina keeps all her promises.

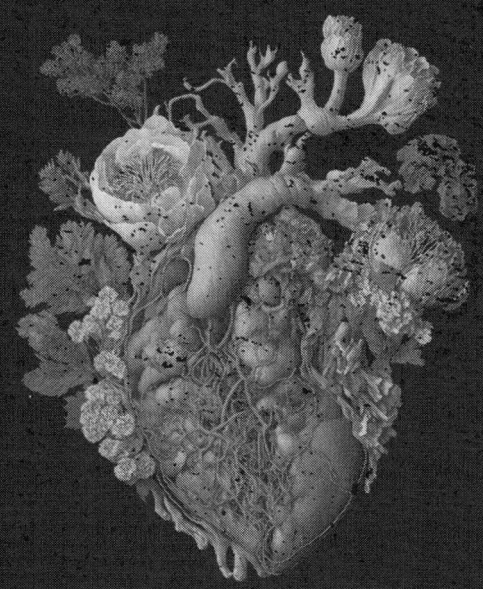

CHAPTER 25

HALLIE

It's been a few weeks since I caught Zayne with the meth in Art class. He has been acting less erratic, less crazy, and more like himself, finally. I believed him when he said he would stop, but I secretly expected to be let down yet again. He seems to have done it though, and he even detoxed for about a week right in front of me.

He has been more present and even sleeping at night now. He stopped going to parties, and is answering his phone again. He's acting normal, if you could call an obsessive, possessive, and jealous man normal.

So why do I keep waiting for the shit to hit the fan?

Because it will.

My thoughts continue to spiral as I get ready for our date tonight. I'm wearing a black linen maxi dress with strappy, black wedges that give me about four more inches of height. My dark brown hair falls in soft waves down my back and my eyes have subtle eyeshadow with winged, black eyeliner and mascara. Everything is understated, yet I have learned that Zayne likes me best that way, with fewer eyes on me.

We were supposed to go out to dinner but got Chinese takeout instead and are now on the way to a secluded campsite at the state park to do my favorite thing in the world: look at the stars.

The night sky brings me a semblance of peace that I never get to experience. It makes me forget about my past, my present, my future. It's hard for any of it to matter when I feel insignificant under so much beauty and looking at the stars makes me rethink my spiritual beliefs. Can something so beautiful exist without a God?

But would God let my stepfather rape me over and over?

I always wonder who I would've been without the trauma. I believe I would be nicer, softer, more loving, more patient, more optimistic, more forgiving.

I would just be... *more*.

It's frustrating when you're trying to be a new person, but the old person is right there, struggling right below the surface, clawing herself back to where she belongs, refusing to fucking drown.

I fought and pushed for this one chance at a new life, to give it everything I have, but I've noticed that I don't have anything left to give. How do you leave a life behind? How do you become a new person when your circumstances have turned you into the one you are? How do you become someone new when you don't even know who you are in the first place?

I've tried to stop remembering my past and not let it define me, but it's easier said than done. My past doesn't let me forget it, and doesn't want me to let go. So I'm stuck going in circles over and over, because I don't have any direction. I don't have a why.

I've always known I haven't been significant to anyone or mattered to anyone in my life, and that knowledge never gets easier to carry. The weight never gets lighter. I didn't ever quite figure out how to deal with the pain and anger. Instead, I decided to run. I ran past the dark fields of emptiness that were my life, and

I pushed. I tried to push through the pain because pain is temporary, but no one ever told me that memories are engraved into your brain forever.

The details might fade over time.

The paint might blend.

The colors might bleed.

But sometimes, you get one vivid memory that knocks the breath out of your lungs and renews the pain.

So is the pain truly temporary?

No.

The pain is as cyclical as the abuse itself.

Zayne parks in front of a lake and I grab a blanket and my phone as he reaches for our bag of food and our drinks. We sit down to eat in the dark with the headlights in the background. It's not cold enough that I need a jacket, but it's also not warm enough for the bugs to be out—perfect weather.

We share our food and then lie back on the blanket after he turns off the headlights. The sky is beautiful tonight since there are no clouds present, and it's a new moon. The stars are shining brighter than I've ever seen them.

Zayne props himself on his side to look at me as I continue to look at the sky and lie down, pulling out my phone to play with a stargazing app that helps me find constellations.

The lake flows and I can hear the water lapping in the background. I close my eyes and hear Zayne move closer to me until I can feel his breath caress my left cheek. I don't have to open my eyes to know his eyes look hungry. I've gotten to know him so well that I can tell his moods as if they belong to me. And they do, because he's fucking *mine.*

He climbs on top of me and settles between my legs, pulling up my dress above my waist to reveal that I'm wearing no underwear. I can see his face darken and his eyes light on fire, threatening to destroy everything in his path.

His nostrils flare with the effort of keeping himself in check, and one of his hands grips my hip while the other travels across my stomach, over my left breast, and then grabs my neck. Zayne squeezes. Squeezes. And squeezes.

His fingers continue to dig into my throat, and it's getting harder to breathe. I see white spots dancing around in my vision as the edges begin to turn dark, and tears are streaming down my face now. I want to tap out, I want to tell him to stop, but I refuse. If this is how he wants me to go, then let him take me out.

Zayne takes my bottom lip between his teeth and bites hard enough that I taste blood, and I'm quickly reminded that I am on the edge of fainting. He licks my blood and sucks my lip back into his mouth and I feel myself fast fading at this point, but I barely register his grunts as he savors me and grinds into me over and over, his hand never loosening up on my neck.

He suddenly lets go of my neck and I suck in big gulps of air and cough violently, which he allows me to do as he undresses. As I lie on the blanket and watch him, I notice my skin is tingling from my arousal and I'm so wet I can feel it on the inside of my thighs.

Fuck.

Zayne grabs my ankle and spreads my legs, sitting back on his haunches naked from the waist down to stare at me. I wonder what would happen if someone saw us. How would he even get dressed? But no, I think that would just excite him, get him even more turned on. He loves danger.

He slips his hand up until he reaches my pussy and rubs my clit, going slowly the way he knows I like. When he settles between my legs and enters me in one quick thrust, I cry out and throw my head back, but he pulls my face back to him and withdraws to the tip. He slams back in and repeats the process, but he does it with so much force that I scoot up and off the blanket, and my brain doesn't even register where I am anymore.

Zayne grabs my hips and pulls me back to him, also yanking down the front of my dress to expose my breasts. His lips meet my right nipple and he sucks it into his mouth, taking a long pull that has my pussy clenching around his length. I scoot my ass down even closer to him and plant my heels on the ground, rising up to meet him thrust for thrust, and gyrating my hips as I do it. My eyes roll back with the impending orgasm, and I try to breathe through it so I don't come so fast, but it's not working.

"Oh no you don't." He grips my neck again, but much lighter this time, "You will look into my eyes as you come." With one arm, my hips are lifted, forcing me even closer, and he rubs against my clit in a way that has never felt this intense before.

When his finger begins to circle over my puckered hole, my toes begin curling, and my stomach bottoms out. Holy shit, why does that feel so fucking good? He strokes harder and faster, and the sensations of my clit and my ass, along with him hitting a sweet spot inside me, make me squeeze my eyes so hard that I see white spots behind my eyelids. I momentarily stop breathing, and I scream so loud he puts his hand over my mouth.

Zayne buries his face in my neck and breathes me in as his thrusts become erratic, and I feel his cock pulsing, spilling inside me. He groans and whimpers, his body shaking with the strength of his orgasm, and then he collapses on top of me, knocking the wind out of me. After a minute, he kisses my neck and pulls back to look at me; this time, his eyes seem more blue than green. The outer rim of his irises is dark blue, while the inside looks like a cloudy sky right before a thunderstorm.

I want to get lost in his eyes.

I want to get lost in him.

I would crawl under his skin and stay there if I could.

I would bury myself in his chest and live next to his heart for the rest of my days.

I give him the last few cells of my body that don't already belong to him.

I just hand them over.

He can fucking keep them.

Zayne hasn't brought me back to his house since we had dinner with his mom together months ago, but he says Alyssa is out of town for a week and that now is the perfect time to stay here without interruptions or judgments.

He takes me into one of the rooms down in his basement—an office, or at least it should be an office. There's a television and a couch along with a desktop computer, but what I didn't see from the outside last time was the piano hidden just out of view in the corner of the room.

The LED lights make the room glow blue and red, and it's so dark it's barely visible until I light a lamp on the side table next to the couch. There are sketchbooks and charcoal pencils next to me on the couch, and I thumb through the pages, but they're all empty.

"Do you not use these?" I ask, waving the sketchbook in front of me so he understands what I'm referring to. I sit on the couch and get comfortable, waiting for him to join me.

"Not those." His face is cast in shadows and neon lights, making him look like he doesn't belong in this world. Which he probably doesn't. "I just got them."

Zayne walks over to the piano and sits on the bench in front of it. He closes his eyes, feeling the keys by sheer muscle memory. "Fur Elise" plays softly as his fingers seem to never touch the keys, and he only opens his eyes for me.

He smiles for me.
He plays for me.
He breathes for me.
Everything is for *me*.

I tilt my head back and let it rest on the couch as I soak in the music and attempt to commit it to memory. I want this moment burned into my brain for the rest of my life.

Walking over to him, I comb my fingers through his hair as he continues to play, then trail them down his neck and onto his shoulders, my touch soft as I memorize his very essence. Zayne visibly shivers when I bring my mouth to the side of his neck and kiss him gently; he stops playing momentarily but then regains his composure.

The sofa calls my name again and I oblige, picking up one of the sketchpads. The pencil strokes lines as he starts to play a different song, and another, and another. I remember him hovering over me. His brow furrowed in concentration as he thrust into me, his hands gripping my hips to the point of pain. His moans, sighs, grunts, and whimpers are engraved into my memory forever.

Once I've finished, his face is unmistakably the one staring back at me from the page. I sign and date it at the bottom and write down that I love him, and before I realize what I've done he starts playing a brand new song, making me close the sketchpad with a soft thump and getting it far away from me before I do something stupid again like tell him instead.

Zayne begins to Play "Look After You" by The Fray, which is ironically one of my favorite songs ever. I say ironically because no one has ever actually given a shit about me in my entire life, much less taken care of me. The melody almost lulls me to sleep, but I can hear myself humming the song softly until it turns to my favorite part, the bridge, which I then sing out loud softly at first, but then my voice grows more confident.

"It's always have and never hold
You've begun to feel like home, yeah
What's mine is yours to leave or take
What's mine is yours to make your own"

I didn't miss the look he gave me after that second line or how we made eye contact by the end of the bridge. My heart is beating so fast I can barely hear myself sing the rest of the song; it feels like Zayne is staring deeply into my soul. He somehow sees me—the real me—and I'm terrified, because I've never shown anyone all my colors before, and I'm afraid he won't like the palette.

"Hallie, that was beautiful..." Zayne trails off, then repositions his hands on the keyboard. "Can we do that again?"

"The same song?"

"Maybe a different one? Do you know 'You Found Me'?"
"Yes, I do."
"Perfect, baby."

He begins to play that song and I sing it for him, loving that we can have a simple moment like this together. We look into each other's eyes the entire time, and I begin to question everything.

Why does it feel like I love him? I don't think I've ever loved anyone before, but as I sit here and stare at him, I know I do. Or at least that's what I think right now. However, deep down, I know there's a different word for what I'm feeling. *Obsession.*

And I know there's nothing simple about it.

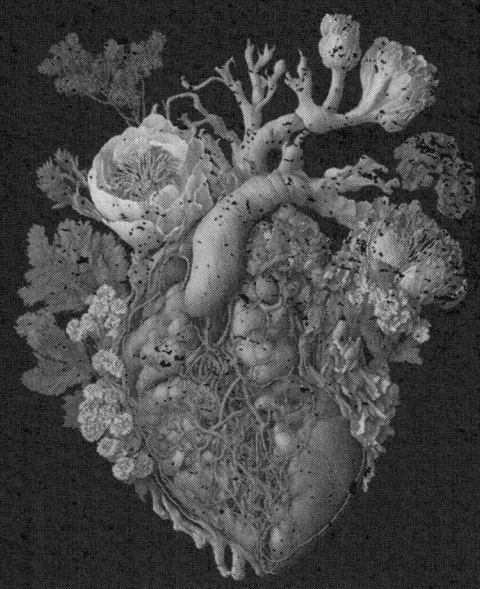

CHAPTER 26

ZAYNE

I'm in English class, ignoring Catherine, who decided to sit next to me at the long table. She keeps moving her chair closer to mine and it's annoying as fuck. Her smell is intoxicating me in the worst way, and I keep having to divert my head to keep from inhaling it. She smells like flowers, but probably really ugly ones. Or maybe I just hate flowers.

"I have something for you," she leans in to whisper in my ear, her hair tickling my cheek.

"There's nothing you can give me that I don't already have." I don't bother whispering back. Let everyone fucking hear.

"Are you sure?" When I turn to look at her, she has a smirk on her face and one eyebrow raised. She digs into her cardigan's pocket and retrieves a small bag with a white powder, which looks very similar to cocaine.

"What the hell is that?'

Catherine's smirk hasn't dropped, and she dangles the little baggie in a taunting motion. "This is meth, babe, but this is a whole other monster."

"What do you mean?"

"You don't smoke it, obviously. You slam it." She tucks her hair behind her ear and digs in her backpack, trying to be inconspicuous about it so she doesn't get caught by the professor.

Catherine hands me the meth and a few needles and tucks them into my hand, closing my fingers over it. I gasp, only because I didn't think before taking it, and even though I know that's a whole different side to addiction, I can't give it back now.

I put the paraphernalia in my backpack and face forward again, hoping she will leave me the fuck alone. She just ruined my life even more and knows it, but instead of feeling even a smidge of guilt, she looks ready to throw a party. *Fuck her.*

"Fuck you, Catherine," I tell her through gritted teeth, my fists tightening until it feels like my fingers might snap. "Fuck you for this, and fuck you for getting me in this fucking mess."

"You already did, and it was really good, I have to say."

"I'm not a fucking junkie. I don't fuck with needles."

"So give it back, then." She stretches out her hand, waiting for me to hand it back over even though she knows I won't and *can't*. "That's what I thought. This will make it all better, Zayne. Help you escape whatever you're running from."

"Nothing could ever do that."

What the fuck am I going to tell Hallie?

I promised I wouldn't keep doing meth, and now look at me, about to shoot it up instead.

One step forward, three steps back.

I guess she should be used to this.

I'm nothing but a fuck up.

"This shit is pure, Zayne." Catherine faces forward again, speaking softly enough that only I can hear. Even still, it now feels like eyes are on us. Maybe my paranoia is back. "Don't use the whole thing, you'll OD. Learn to walk before you run, little daddy."

"Don't fucking call me that," I growl, turning in my chair to face her, and look into her eyes. "You're a bitch, you know? You prey on the weak and take advantage. There's not one nice bone in your body, and I never want to talk to you again."

"If you say so, but when you want to shoot up together and fuck me again, you know how to reach me." She's a fucking snake. I should've never fucked around with her. "And when that bitch doesn't want you anymore, I'll be here waiting."

"Hell will freeze over before that happens."

I'm not an addict, I just like getting high.

I'm in control.

"I really fucking hate you, Catherine."

"Trust me, you don't know real hate yet," she winks, then smirks, "But the monster will show you."

A few hours later, as I'm sitting in my driveway, I grip the steering wheel and contemplate how I'm about to ruin my life. I try to feel something, anything, but I'm numb. I can't even bring myself to give a shit about the impending chaos I'm walking into with open eyes, because I don't feel like it matters anymore.

I believe in fate, and I have to believe that I was destined to live this moment all along and that I will come out on top. If not, I wouldn't be able to find the will to play the shitty hand I was dealt. I'm a pessimist by nature, and it's hard to see any positives in my life, which at times quickly leads me into a downward spiral when the darkness beckons me again. Just like it's doing right now.

The darkness keeps calling my name. It was merely a whisper at first, but now it's screaming at me, and I can't help but want to succumb to it. If I give myself over, she will comfort me. She'll make it all better, but not better than Tina.

My choice has been made long before this, and I practically run into the house, looking for a spoon and a lighter as well as something to use as a tourniquet. I go into the bathroom hastily and grab a cotton ball. I make sure the door to the basement is locked and then do the same to my bedroom door before going to bed, not wanting my mother to walk in on me and realize what a fucking disgrace I've become.

I don't want her to realize there's no saving me.

Let her have the shred of hope that I can't have.

I sit on the bed and stare at the baggie in my hands. The angel on my shoulder tells me this is wrong, that I shouldn't do this, that I'm making the biggest mistake of my life. Then there's the devil's voice that tells me to pull the trigger, rip off the Band-Aid and get it over with.

The glass pipe sits on my nightstand, screaming at me to grab her rather than to take this path because once it's done, there's no going back. There's no high that would compare to this one. I grab the water bottle right next to it instead of the glass pipe and quickly twist the lid off before opening the packaged needle and setting it on my lap. I dump some white powder onto the spoon without measuring and add water until my shaking hands make some of it slosh all over me and my bed. Deep breaths don't make the shaking any better though. I don't think anything will. My body knows I'm fucking up.

Ignoring the soaking bed sheets, I flick my lighter under the spoon and watch the flame come to life. I stare in awe while the meth cooks, and I feel in my gut that this is the end of the road for me.

I'm so fucked.

I drop the cotton ball into the liquid on the spoon and then get the syringe ready to draw my liquid poison into it. Once my syringe is ready, I grab a tourniquet I stole and wrap it around my upper arm, then start to look for a vein.

Once I find a suitable vein, I slap it a few times to bring it to the surface the same way the nurses do at the hospital. The blue vein stares back at me as I hold the skin taut, putting the needle against my arm at a ten-degree angle, or at least I think it is. The sharp pain of the needle brings me back to reality and I exhale forcefully as I push it all the way in.

I'm so sorry, Hallie.

I'm *so* fucking sorry.

I push down the plunger and my life literally flashes before my eyes. Hallie spinning in circles, her beautiful brown hair glowing almost red in the sunlight. My mom smiling at me from across the dining table, thinking I'm going to get better even though I still see the pain in her eyes. My dad leaving us because I was too much work for him and he wanted an easier life.

It feels like a climax.

It feels like the beginning of the end.

I pull out the needle and loosen the tourniquet, falling back onto the pillows. Heat rapidly fills my body and I can somehow feel it spreading over every surface. It travels down my spine in the familiar way that I was used to, but this is someway a million times more intense. Once the heat makes it to my balls, I literally feel myself come in my pants from the intensity of it, making me shake.

It's fucking blissful.

My heartbeat picks up and so does my breathing until my chest hurts and I feel almost nauseous. Only I don't fucking care because this rush is unlike anything I've ever experienced. I smile, lost in the euphoria, and think of everything I've been missing out on since I decided to smoke instead of slam.

Tina, I'm home.

I'm here, baby.

But it's not Tina this time. Not really, not anymore. The monster just laughs as he sinks his claws into my heart, whispering sweet promises of never letting me go.

I ride out the wave like it's my last, because from now on, every slam might very well be.

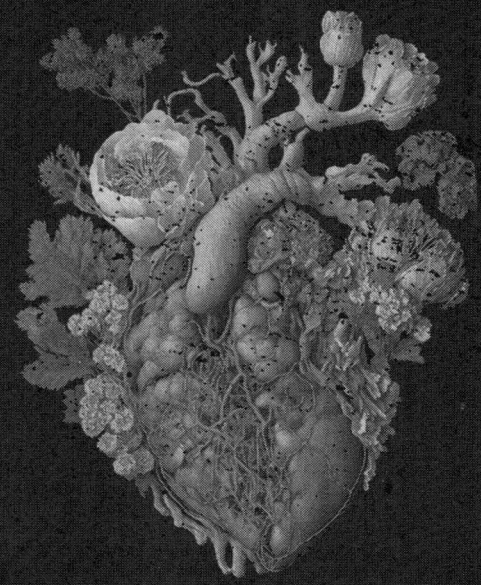

CHAPTER 27

HALLIE

Today is a very special day for me: Graduation day.

In my twenty-three years of life, never did I think I would actually accomplish this goal. Yes, I dreamed of it, but I never considered it would become a reality. I always thought I was too weak, too stupid, too damaged to amount to anything. Now that I think of it, it probably just had to do with how my family made me feel. Nursing is my way to nurture others the way I wasn't. I've always enjoyed caring for people, and it's even more special to think of it as healing from my past.

As I sit on my bed and contemplate the past four years of my life, I realize I'm actually a strong woman. I've overcome so much and I have also accomplished every goal I've put my mind to. This has probably been one of the most challenging endeavors I've ever set out to do, and the pride I feel right now is indescribable.

I fucking did it.

I *really* did.

I graduated nursing school with fucking honors, and now I have only the NCLEX standing between me and my career.

Brit knocks on my door and comes in before I can respond, as she always does, and catches me bouncing on the bed with excitement. One of these days, I'll be in the middle of getting fucked and she will barge in here; I can just feel it.

"Are you sure you don't want to go with me?"

"I'm sure, babe, but thank you for caring enough to ask me again. I just don't think I can stand there and not have anyone cheering for me as I walk the stage."

"Zayne and I will cheer for you."

"You know what I mean," I say with an eye roll. "Although I'm grateful for the support. I just can't bring myself to see everyone with their perfect families."

"I can respect that."

"Thank you. You know I love you, and I'm so fucking proud of you, Brit…" I inhale sharply and try to keep the tears at bay. "Thank you for never leaving my side. You're my person."

"I thought *I* was your person, Hallie," Zayne says from the doorway, smiling widely as his eyes twinkle from it.

Brit makes a sound that sounds very much like *tsk, tsk*, and laughs softly, knowing that he could never be my person in the way she is. "Well, I have to get going before I'm late. I love you," she tells me, standing up and straightening out her red dress.

"I love you, too."

As she walks out of the room, I watch Zay sauntering in my direction. He looks so damn handsome it hurts. He's wearing a navy blue t-shirt with black sweatpants, and his eyes can't decide if they want to be blue or green today. They look like a Caribbean beach and I long to swim in them.

"You're staring." His lips twitch and kick into a half smile.

"You're perfect."

I pat the bed so he can come lay down with me, and he obliges, kicking back the covers so he doesn't overheat. That man has more body heat than anyone I've ever met and constantly feels like a furnace. My cold body is always a nice contrast against him, and I wonder if he craves the coolness of me to counteract his fire.

He snuggles me in the way only he has ever done, like every part of us was made for each other, fitting perfectly together. I want him to hold me and take all my pain away, all the pain I don't want to feel. I probably will never admit it to him or anyone out loud, but my family not being here for me today may be one of the hardest things I've had to go through since being estranged. Zayne's steady breath against my neck is soothing, and I don't know when I even started trusting him, but I decide that now is as good a time as ever to just let the tears fall.

My shoulders begin to shake with the force of my sobs, and I bite my knuckles to keep myself from making a sound. He rubs circles on my back and kisses the back of my neck, bringing me comfort. "Let it out, baby."

He continues to soothe me, and I decide I never want to leave his arms again. I want to stay tucked into him forever, forgetting about life, responsibilities, and decisions. Forgetting about trauma and sadness and lost hope. Forgetting about bad dreams and battered souls and shattered hearts.

But also remembering.

Remembering that he found me when no one else could.

I don't know how he does it, but just ten minutes later, Zayne somehow convinces me to leave the house after watching me cry it out in bed the entire day. I can't believe I broke down in front of him, that I let myself be that vulnerable. However, I'm starting to think it's going to happen a lot. I can't seem to keep the lid on my emotions around him.

The summer heat of Texas is another level of evil in the world, so I told him I would leave the house as long as we stayed in the car tonight. I have no intention of being even more miserable today because I *really* hate hot weather. I'm getting out of Texas as soon as I get the chance. Nevertheless, I can't deny that I would stay anywhere just for him.

Stop, Hallie. This is temporary. He's *not* forever.

I sit in the passenger side of his car, my sweaty thighs sticking to the leather seats, and the heat burning the backs of my legs, but I ignore it. The sun is setting, kissing Zayne's face and bathing him in a golden hue.

Angel.

God.

Devil.

I can't decide which one he is, but he embodies all of them right now. He conceals the worst parts of him well. That's why he's so easy to love. You don't realize how deep you're in until you can't come back up for air in time, slowly drowning in all that he is, and all that he isn't.

His eyes shine the palest green against the sun, with no hint of any other colors in there, making them look as if they don't belong on his face. The thing about him is that he takes everything that doesn't belong to him, regardless; he takes everything he wants.

Zayne lets the windows down, my hair whipping around my face against the force of the wind, and I relish the feel of it and the smell of the pine trees as we drive through the neighborhood close to the golf course.

"So what comes after this?" He asks me, glancing in my general direction for the briefest of moments.

"After what?"

"Now that you graduated, what will you do? Where will you work? Are you staying? Are you moving?" he rattles on, not waiting for an answer to any of his questions before he asks the next one. He finally pulls up in front of a lake and parks the car, and we sit in silence for a few minutes while I contemplate what answers to give, and thankfully he doesn't pressure me.

"I already applied at the hospital in Round Rock which will probably be about a forty-five-minute commute. If I move, it'll just be closer to that hospital, but as of right now Brit and I have no plans of moving."

"If you move, I'll be going with you."

"You would do that for me?" I ask him in awe, but I'm clearly delusional if I ever thought he'd let me go anywhere without him. "Would you move in with me If I leave this town?"

"I'd do anything for you, and I would expect to move in together if I moved to a new town for you."

"Would you ever get married and have kids? I can't picture you doing that for some reason." I'm trying to soften the blow, even though I genuinely can't imagine him doing that.

"Only with you. I would only do that for you."

My heart bursts in my chest with his words, and my body feels lighter, happier, as if nothing could be wrong with the world right now. "If we ever break up and we're still single when we're thirty, we will get married," I say, just to see how he reacts. His face goes dark, but then he gives me a half smile.

"We will never break up, but if we did, I can agree to that."

"Promise?"

Zayne makes eye contact with me, then reaches for my face, pulling me in for a kiss. "I promise."

And for some reason, I'm content with the promises he makes that I know he will never keep. I'm content with letting him deceive me forever if that's what it takes, as long as he lies to my face while he stays by my side.

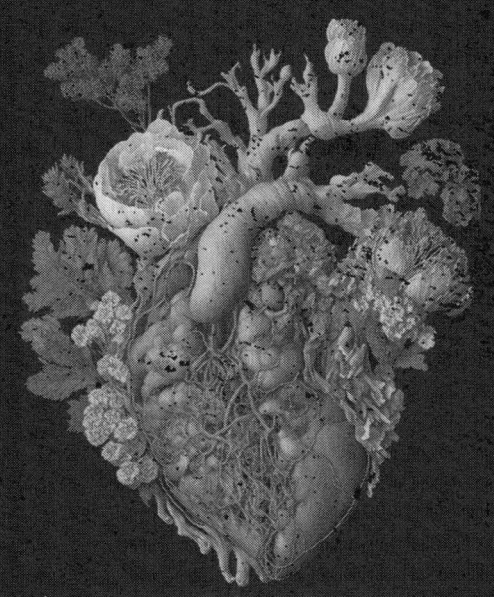

CHAPTER 28

ZAYNE

Golden hour has always held a special place in my heart, and I always thought there was nothing more beautiful than a sunset. But now, as the sunlight reflects off Hallie's pale skin, I realize there's nothing more beautiful than *her*.

It's as if all the colors have blended together, the oranges, reds, and pinks shining on her skin, making her look like a painting. I hold my breath as she sticks her right arm out the window and holds it up, letting the wind caress her fingertips. Her head is out of the car now too, her hair whipping around her face, the sunshine bouncing off her skin, her eyes closed as she gets lost in the feel of it all.

She's fucking mesmerizing.

And me?

I'm a goner.

"Dandelions" by Ruth B. plays in the background, and I notice the curve of her lips as I turn the music up, and when I grab her left hand and squeeze, her mouth rewards me with a grin.

Now I know I've never seen anything more beautiful than her.

She steals the breath from my lungs.

She's fucking art.

Stardust and magic.

"And I've heard of a love that comes once in a lifetime, and I'm pretty sure that you are that love of mine." I sing the song for her, and she whips her head around to face me, her throat bobbing as I look at her from my peripheral vision, but I keep my eyes trained on the road. I squeeze her hand harder and let a smile take over my face as I keep singing the song for her, and I know she returns the smile even though I don't look at her.

We drive down one of the back roads by the golf course, and she surprises me by taking off her seatbelt and sliding up to sit on the edge of her open window, holding on by just the grab handle as the rest of her body dangles and she relaxes against the wind.

She's fucking crazy.

I love it.

Her laugh is intoxicating and I see her body shaking from it. It's like she's high on her own recklessness and she hasn't even touched drugs today.

She turned the gas on and lit the match, and now I can't take my eyes off her.

If you light yourself on fire, the world will come watch you burn.

And Hallie …

She's fucking *breathtaking* when she burns for me—and she always does.

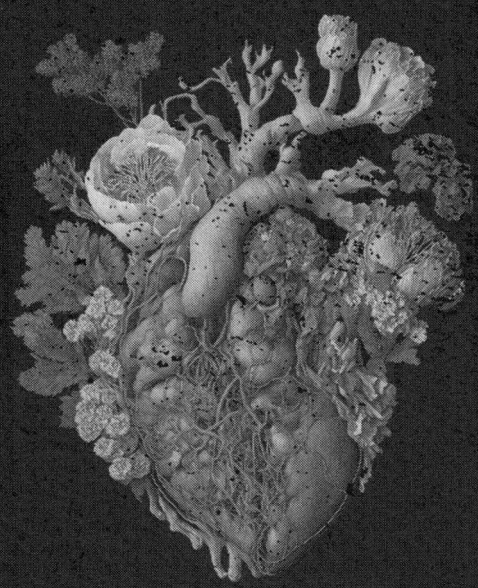

CHAPTER 29

HALLIE

The last few days since graduation have been bliss. Zayne has been the sweetest to me, even more so than at the beginning of our relationship. It doesn't feel like a switch was flipped, though. It feels almost like he's falling in love with me, like he cares, like *intimacy*.

It's weird to feel wanted. It's foreign to me in every aspect of my life, and sometimes I don't even know how to act, knowing that he gives a damn about me. Even while I care about him, and that scares me, I can also handle my feelings for him much better than I can accept his feelings for me.

I wonder how long it'll last: the bliss, the ignorance, the supposed love, because I know nothing lasts forever. I'm not naive enough to believe this will, but who is lying to who? Or are we both just lying to ourselves? Where is this going? Is this a dead end? A road with no destination? It sure feels that way as I stare at his pictures on my phone.

But I'm not ready to let go yet.

I know it's coming, but I can only stand back and watch, waiting for it to happen. It's as if I'm watching two trains on the same track, knowing the collision is coming, unable to do anything to stop it.

Fated.

Destined.

Cursed.

Thanks to him, I have so many questions about my future, and I don't even know what to do with myself now. All I know is that I had planned to move to a new town, work at a new hospital, and have a new life; that life never included him, only now I can't see myself without him.

Although he's the one who has been persistent in labeling us, I still see no future, except is that more my own insecurity or a realistic view of the relationship? It's difficult to tell when what we have feels real, but our highs and lows are extreme.

When we're high, we're up in the clouds and it's bliss, but when we're low, he drags me to the lowest pits of hell and doesn't let me come back up until he deems me worthy. Loving him is painful and amazing and confusing and just right. However, I have to figure out where it's going and if he's actually going to change.

If *I* am.

Thankfully, the tube rental business has a short line, and we are in and out quickly. They provide us with two tubes, a cooler, and ice, and I'm even more grateful that it's right across from the river because the one-hundred-degree temperature is making me sweat even with my lack of clothes.

My white bikini shows most of my ass, and Zayne has not been able to keep his eyes off me as we walk toward the river. I brought the sunscreen, and he brought the beer, which works perfectly for me. The river will be packed today, from the look of all the cars parked across from us.

I throw my tube in the water, and it makes a small splash that lights up every centimeter of skin it touches. It's fucking freezing, but it feels refreshing and awful and fantastic all at the same time. I hop on the tube, my short legs barely even dangling, and he comes to my side and does the same, grabbing my handle so we don't get separated. He pulls out a rope and ties it between the handles of both our tubes before he brings the cooler around to float alongside us, tied to our rafts as well.

I cross the distance between us, offering him my hand as we float side by side down the river, the hordes of high school and college students passing us by, a frenzy of horny boys and underage drinking.

Move along. Nothing to see here.

They all stare as they float by, and I glance down at my chest to make sure I'm not flashing a nipple. All good, nothing is showing. When I look over at Zayne, he has a smirk on his face. "What?"

"You're fucking hot, that's what." I can't tell if my face heating is due to his compliment or the sun beating on my skin. "Everyone can see it, and no one can have you because you're *mine*." His possessiveness lights a fire low in my belly, and realistically I know he can't take me here, but can't we find a new spot?

"What if we get out of here?"

"For what?" he asks in confusion, "We just started…"

I raise my eyebrow at him, and his lips stretch into a knowing grin, all questions dying on his tongue. "I'm sure you know a place. You know all the places, right?" I ask with a wink, knowing he will get us out of here as fast as possible.

Zayne looks around for an escape route, but the riverbanks are tall and muddy—not worth the trouble or the snakes. It's about ten more minutes until we find a shallow area and make a quick exit, dragging our tubes behind us deep into the woods while he carries our cooler full of beer.

We're in the middle of the forest now, surrounded by pine

trees and no civilization. No one can reach this neck of the woods unless they walk miles from the parking lot. The river isn't even visible anymore, so unless someone follows us in here, they won't know we've taken up temporary residence.

Zayne drops the tubes on the ground, the grass dry in the way that only Texas can accomplish, and there's dirt and rocks and even sticks underneath my bare feet, but I don't care about any of it as I hurriedly strip. I'm not sure if he'll be taking me over the tube or if I'll end up with cuts all over my body from being fucked on the ground.

Frankly, I couldn't care less.

I just want him to make me feel something.

I drop my top on the tube, my swimsuit bottoms swiftly following, and the air is cold on my wet skin, causing goosebumps to break out across my body. As I stand bare in front of him, I see his pupils dilate, the black devouring the blue-green, an oil spill on a Caribbean beach.

Zayne closes the distance between us, and I palm his erection, rubbing him up and down over his wet swim trunks as he takes steps forward, forcing me to retreat until a tree meets my back. The trunk is rough against me, scraping my entire backside, and I swallow a whimper as he presses into me. For a moment he just looks at my body, and I keep my eyes on his face, watching him take me in.

He runs his hand down my belly, making me gasp, and wastes no time gliding his fingers between my lips, circling me slowly. I spread my legs wider, planting my feet on the ground to avoid slipping on the pine needles, and he looks at me like I'm a goddess he wants to worship. As if on cue, he drops to his knees in front of me and I squirm a bit, feeling uncomfortable as he parts me, exposing me to him and the open air completely.

"Such a pretty pussy." Zayne's eyes are so heated I have a brief hysterical thought of him starting a forest fire, until he looks at me and licks his lips. I can feel myself dripping down my thighs. He grabs my right leg and squeezes it as I grip the tree behind me, holding on for dear life. "Put this leg over my shoulder." He taps me, and as I obey his command, he rewards me with his tongue.

I buck my hips into his face, tightening my leg around his shoulders as he licks me from center to clit. He pulls back slightly. "Just like that, baby." Every word is murmured against me, and the feel of his lips brushing against me shoots a jolt of desire down my spine.

He spreads me wider with his thumbs and continues to lick me, his tongue warm against me, unlike his thumbs against my skin. His hands drop from me as he sucks lightly on my clit and pushes two fingers inside me, up to the knuckles.

I grab his hair, yanking hard until he looks up at me with tears in his eyes, and I feel a strange satisfaction at his suffering. He's rough with his fingers, and I yank him closer as he circles his tongue over me, forcing him to put more pressure on my clit. The way he licks and sucks and bites and twirls his tongue drives me absolutely crazy.

I want him. I need him. I love him.

Pleasure spreads like wildfire through my veins, my skin, my entire body, and I feel the orgasm within reach. He just needs to—

Zayne curls his fingers and bites my clit and I see fucking stars, my body shaking as I ride the waves and his hand, his name on my lips. "Zay..." A prayer, a plea, a declaration of love with a single word.

I let go of his hair and he stands slowly, holding on to my leg that was over his shoulder and crushing his body to mine against the tree. I'm still panting, and my body feels like a live wire, ready for him all over again. He kisses me deeply, his tongue in my mouth, until all I taste is myself on his lips.

He spins me around and I grab onto the tree bark, my fingers digging into it until they hurt, but I don't make him stop. I can't. His fingers trail a path from the back of my thighs and up over my ass, stopping at my hips and digging in before he drops his hands.

The wet slap of his swim trunks hitting the ground breaks the silence like a starting gun. I arch for him as his hand comes to my lower back, fingers splayed over me, and spread my legs wider in anticipation, ready for him to do his worst.

He nudges my entrance with his cock, his hand shifting over to my hip, and pushes into me gradually as if any sudden movement would break me, and I'm grateful for his gentleness for once.

For once, he fucks me slowly, taking his time, worshipping me as he promised. My nipples are painfully hard, the tree bark scratching them, and I reach down to rub my clit as he buries his face in the crook of my neck, lightly sucking and biting.

My scalp stings as he wraps my wet hair around his fist once, twice, three times, and speeds up his thrusts until the sounds of his hips driving into me are loud in my ears. Zayne uses his grip on my hips to pull me back onto his cock in time with his thrusts, hitting a new and impossibly deep angle, pressing my face deeper against the tree.

I keep circling my clit, feeling the pleasure coiling low in my belly as I clench around him. His groans echo in the desolate woods as he pounds into me, his thrusts growing uncoordinated as he finds his release and I follow closely. I shiver as he bites my neck, feeling him come inside me, and my knees buckle when he moans. My fingers hurt from the bark biting into them, but as he slowly wraps his arms around me, holding me close to his chest and nuzzling his face against my hair, it doesn't even matter. I've always wanted someone to love me this way, without inhibitions, and I think I finally got it.

We stay here for a while, forgetting about the world around us, our problems, and even our solutions. Forgetting about everything except the feel of each other's skin and the rocks and sticks underneath us.

The lasagna in the oven smells amazing, and I revel in it. My body feels wrecked from our little escapade, it turns out the tree trunk did more damage than I initially felt. I watch the food and massage my arms while Brit sits at the kitchen island. Her green eyes twinkle as she looks at her phone, a crooked grin on her face. Her hair is down, the light brown of it catching the light in a way that makes her look angelic. She looks... happy.

She's talking to Xander.

"I can't believe you're making me your famous lasagna. It's about damn time!" She squeals, joy pouring out of her. I wish I could be a happy person again.

"Well, it's about time we take a girl's day." I give her a pointed look, even though I know I've been far up Zayne's ass and that's why I'm not spending time with her. Not that she has time for me either lately. "I want pedis and a movie after this." I'm trying so fucking hard to act normal, to act like my life doesn't feel like it's in shambles.

"Only if I can make margaritas."

"Duh, but I want a mango or a strawberry one, please." She knows mango is my favorite, and I know she won't disappoint. She's always made me the best margaritas.

"You got it!" Brit gets up and walks across the room to the pantry, grabbing the cocktail shaker along with all the ingredients she needs. She mixes everything together, looks up at me, then at her phone, and smiles.

"So, Xander?" I smile knowingly and wag my eyebrows.

"It's not serious, obviously, but he's nice and wants to date me. I might be considering it short-term. Just for free food."

"You don't need free food," I point out, twirling my hair for something to do.

"A free steak never hurt anyone."

I mean, she has a point, but I know that's not her reason. We both know she could go on dates with anyone. "So, have you fucked yet? How was it?" Her face twists in a grimace, and I'm caught off guard. "No! That bad?" Oh shit, I know she's dropping him.

"We haven't done anything. He says he wants to wait because he likes me."

"I thought it was the other way around?" I know she's not going to wait. She likes sex; it's non-negotiable.

"Tell me about it," Brit mutters under her breath. "So what about Zayne?"

"What about him?" I feign ignorance, not wanting to talk about him. There's genuinely nothing nice to say.

"What's the game plan?"

"There is none. We don't have any plans." We don't. We talked about the future, but there's no concrete plan.

"No plans at all?" She sounds outraged.

"It's only been a few months."

"Surely he wants to keep seeing you."

"I'm sure he does," I reply, "He probably would tie me to his side if he could. I just don't think there's a future in this." I chuckle, trying to lighten the mood. But it's not funny.

"Why not?"

I think of the parties, the drugs, the alcohol, the withdrawals. "He doesn't make me a better person."

"We both know you don't give a shit about that." She motions with her hand at me to hurry up. "Spill."

"He's on drugs."

"Aren't we all?"

I want to laugh because she has a point, but this shit isn't funny. Everything about Zayne is complicated. "But he's an addict."

"That sure does complicate everything." She looks pensive, and I realize I've never confided in anyone about this before. It feels oddly like a betrayal, so I don't say what drugs he's using.

"I love him, but I can't see it being permanent."

"Nothing has to be." Brittany shrugs, like it's that easy. Maybe for her, it is. "You're twenty-three years old."

"I know. Anyway, let's go get our toes done in the living room while the lasagna bakes." I'm dodging her and she knows it but lets it slide. She lets me gather our nail polish and everything we need, allowing me to pretend I'm okay.

We sit on the hardwood floor, careful not to get close to the rug so we don't stain it. The evening passes in a blur after I take my Xanax and drink my margarita, and I catch a worried glimpse from Brit, but she doesn't say anything. And it doesn't affect me anymore.

Because I—

I can't feel anything.

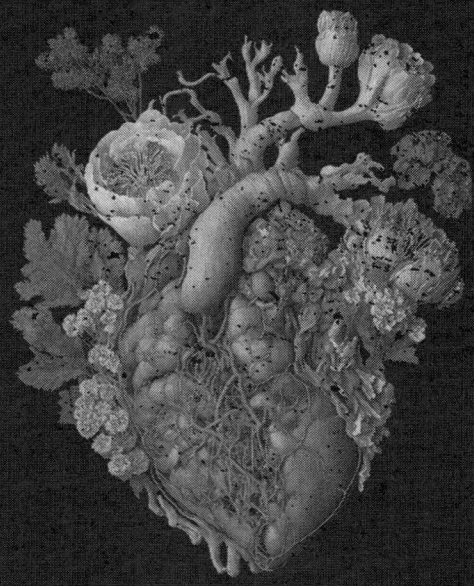

CHAPTER 30

HALLIE

My room is dark, no moonlight shining past the blinds as I sit on my bed in my underwear and try to catch my breath. My nap turned into a nightmare about Michael, and now my chest is tight, my ears are ringing, and my body is covered in sweat. As I sit here trying not to turn to Xanax, I remember my little friend who has never disappointed me.

I walk across the room to the bottom dresser drawer where I keep a little box and pull out my razorblade, then go back to bed and sit on it cross-legged, baring my thighs to myself so I can pick a spot to cut.

It's been a long time since I resorted to this, but it feels like a full-circle moment as I consider doing it again. I guess I'll always be the fucking same, no matter how hard I try to run away from myself.

I rest my hand on my thigh and dig the razorblade in lightly, a pinprick of blood welling up in the single tiny cut. I flick my wrist and slash a shallow line.

Baby steps.

It's not enough though; I barely feel a sting. I need it deeper. I need to feel *something* again. I cut again, in a different spot above the previous one, and this time I go deeper. I watch the blood run down to the inside of my thighs, the pain fresh, finally clearing my mind.

I poise my wrist to go again, when suddenly my door opens without warning. I look back and find Zayne shutting it and strolling toward me. He seems to be letting his eyes adjust to the light, yet when he sees my leg and the razor blade between my fingers, he seems confused.

Zayne looks back and forth between the razor blade and my thigh, as if not understanding the situation. I clear my throat and begin to get up from the bed. I need to clean up, I need to pretend this never happened. "What are you doing?" he whispers, his voice barely audible over the pounding of my heart.

"Feeling something."

"Give me." He extends his hand to me, motioning for me to lie down. I hold my breath as he spreads my legs and settles between them. He leans over me and gives me a chaste kiss on my lips and then withdraws, as if he doesn't want to make this about him. He runs his fingers through the blood, mesmerized, but then snaps out of it and traces the inside of my thigh where I was going to cut next. He presses the blade against my skin, and I don't make a sound. "Hallie, tell me how deep to go."

He begins to press into my skin, going and going until I hiss. "Like that." I feel the sting, I feel the sharpness of the blade, and I just want one more dose.

He cuts three times, the pain clearing my head for a moment, and I let myself savor it. He helps me sit up and I stare down at my thigh where he cut a 'Z' into it. My breath catches in my throat at his possessive act, but something else stirs as well, something hot and sinful.

Zayne stares at me with fire in his gaze, then suddenly turns around and gets me a pair of sweatpants. I go to the bathroom and clean up, putting my pants on more carefully than usual so I don't rub against the cuts. The healing is worse than the cutting.

When I leave the bathroom, Zayne is sitting on my bed waiting for me. He extends his hand, waiting for me to walk across the room and take it. "Come home with me, baby girl."

I nod once, and we head out of my place and go to his.

I try to leave my pain behind a bit longer.

I try to live in the now for once.

The drive is a blur as I close my eyes and lean my head back on the seat, not paying attention to anything until we park in the driveway. He basically pulls me all the way down to his room, which is cold as fuck, by the way. The shivers coursing down my spine and the goosebumps on my skin are just a reminder of the darkness and frost that have enveloped my life, holding on tightly without leaving room for anything else.

Zayne brought this darkness into my life, but he also brought colors. He's a marching oxymoron. He stomps all over me, picks me up from the ground and puts my pieces back together after trampling me.

"What do you want, Hallie?" He asks me as we lie down in bed and he glues himself to my body, my back to his front, no gaps between us. So much body heat. So much *him*.

"I don't want to feel alone anymore," I reply, taking a slow breath. "I want to love someone who will accept the darkest parts of me and not see me as broken."

"Why do you have nightmares?"

My mouth twists into a grimace as I think about how to put the betrayal into words. I don't want to fucking talk about this, I've told him repeatedly, but it seems like he's not giving up anyway. I might as well just make him stop. "When I was a kid, my stepfather started coming to my room every night." I swallow audibly, willing my voice not to waver. "He would wait until my mother was asleep before he knocked on my door three times—always three times. But he wouldn't wait for an answer. He would come in uninvited and take advantage of me."

"Take advantage of you, how?" There's a cold rage simmering just below the surface of him, his hold on me tightening as he asks the question.

"First, my mouth. It was like that for a while, but then that didn't seem to be enough anymore. It seemed that he wanted more. He always wanted more. He's not the type of person who is satisfied with anything, ever."

"What happened, Hals?" he whispers, maybe afraid that his voice will break me if it's any louder.

"He *raped* me." My voice cracks on the word, and I hate how I can't get over how it makes me feel. I hate that the word makes me feel like a victim.

His hold on me suddenly threatens to break my bones, and I hold my breath as his heat envelops me tighter. "You don't have to be alone, Hallie," he whispers against my ear, kissing it as his hand comes up to my throat. "You're so fucking strong, except you don't have to do it alone." His hand wraps around my throat possessively and I lean into his touch, my skin searing from his body heat.

"I can't." I shake my head against his hold. "I can't break again. If I break, I won't be able to put myself back together. I can't use you as a crutch for it. It's not right."

"Use me," he rasps against my ear. "Fucking use me."

He tries to kiss me, but I jerk away, and the look of determination that crosses his face is scary. "I can take care of myself. No one deserves that. I have taken care of myself all this time."

"You don't fucking have to." He turns my body his way and captures my chin between his fingers, tilting my head back so I can look into his eyes. "I'm alone too. Keep me company."

I grip his shoulder to steady myself, to ground myself, to remind myself to be strong. "I don't think it's very smart—"

My objection falls on deaf ears as he swallows it up, capturing my face in both hands and kissing me hard. I kiss him back, clinging to him as his tongue sweeps into my mouth. Our tongues dance and tangle with each other until I feel the heat of his body pooling to my core, and I'm desperate. Desperate to feel him, desperate for him. I want him on top of my body, in me, whispering against my skin. I open my eyes, and we make eye contact as we continue to kiss, and my fingertips coast along his cheekbone, light as a feather. I slow the kiss down, savoring him, memorizing how his eyes shift colors even in the room's low lighting.

He's fire, and I want to get burned.

My fingers slide into his hair and I tug, loving the way he hisses against my lips. He gets on top of me and I spread my legs eagerly, only a t-shirt separating my body from his. He takes off his clothes and returns to his place between my legs, spreading me, rubbing a finger up and down my slit. My hand follows the curve of his jaw and then glides over his shoulders, noticing the way his bones feel. He's thinner, much thinner than when I first met him.

He kisses my temple, my jaw, my neck. He licks over my pulse point. He kisses every inch of my torso, lingering over my breasts to capture one in his mouth. He kisses down to my pelvis until I'm gasping for air, and the heat of his touch makes me catch on fire.

I tug on him, "No, I want you now."

Zayne comes back up and spreads my legs wide, the tip of his cock brushing my entrance. He pushes slowly inside of me, gasping at the feel of it. His forearms frame my head, and his fingers twist in my hair. This doesn't feel the same as all the other times. This feels intimate.

When he starts to move, he presses his forehead against mine and captures my lower lip between his own. He sucks on it as his pace quickens, and his moans vibrate against my mouth. I clench around him as he continues to moan, and my stomach flips as he gets louder.

I grab his face between my hands and deepen the kiss, my moans now mixing with his. His thrusts create friction against my clit, and I can feel myself coiling tight. Zayne is the only thing that matters. Nothing exists outside of him and the way he's making me come apart under him.

Everything he's been making me feel keeps growing into something akin to an explosion, and as he kisses me and touches me, I come apart under him. My muscles grow taut, and the fire inside me grows even hotter, threatening to burn everything down. I can feel my expression contorting and my body arching to meet him. His pace doesn't falter as I hiss and moan, and I rake my fingernails down his shoulders.

"Oh my fucking God!"

"*I* am your God," he says through clenched teeth and then groans as he finishes inside me.

I pant and gasp and try to catch my breath, and he buries his face in the crook of my neck. "Do you believe in fate?"

"Zayne…" I sigh. "I don't believe in fate, no. I don't believe in a higher power either, if that's your next question." I tell him while picking at my nails as I look up and meet his gaze. "I don't believe in anything."

"I believe in us," he says as I suck in dry air into my lungs, feeling like I might faint. "All the stars in the sky aligned for us to meet. So I believe in *us*."

"What exactly do you want from me?"

"I already told you. But if I'm being honest, what we want doesn't matter. We are as inevitable as the changing of the seasons. There's no choice here, and there never will be." He takes my hand in his and softly says, "You're mine, Hallie."

"I—"

"Mine," he repeats, just before he kisses where my neck meets my shoulder. Just like that, I know the pinks are coming back into my life.

"Yours," I whisper back. "Promise me forever."

"Baby, you don't need to make me promise. Nothing is going to keep me from you." His tone has a finality to it that brings me peace, but at the same time I know nothing about him brings peace to my life.

We're destined to decimate each other.

But will we rise from the ashes?

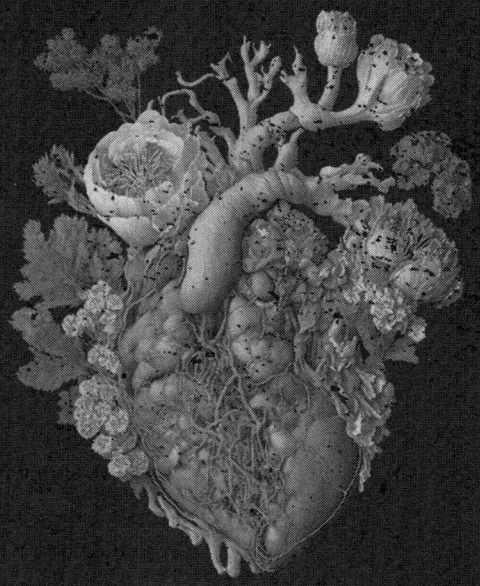

CHAPTER 31

HALLIE

The quiet is loud against my ears and the hairs on the back of my neck are standing on end as I open my eyes. Zayne is lying beside me in bed with the covers thrown over his head and wrapped in the blankets like a burrito. The curtains are drawn and the room somehow is even colder than the rest of the basement, making me shiver in my nakedness.

Bad choice.

"Zayne?" I ask, grabbing my phone from the nightstand and turning on the flashlight. He stirs and pushes the covers away from his face, wincing as the bright light blinds him. I flip the phone over to face the ceiling and look him over. Something is very wrong. His hair is plastered to his face and his eyes are sunken in with dark circles underneath. "Zayne, you need to get out of this bed. Let's go."

I throw on some clothes, then help him out of bed and open the door to his bathroom, turning on the light. He flinches and looks away again, shielding his eyes. He looks even worse than he did a second ago. Why is he so sensitive right now, anyway? He's never acted this way before. "Brush your teeth, babe. I'm going to take care of a few things." He looks pained as I start walking away. "Can you get the shower ready for us, please?"

I go upstairs and fix him a plate of fruits, nuts, cheese, and crackers and get him some milk. He looks like he hasn't had food in a few days, but I don't want him to throw it up, so I get him finger foods to snack on, praying he will eat even a few bites for me.

I turn the thermostat up and hope the room warms up enough for us because I don't want to be cold after the shower. When I return to the bathroom, Zayne is rinsing his mouth and the shower is running. He has stripped for me, and even though he looks a bit leaner, he still looks amazing. His abs are more defined and the V-shape of his waist leading to his cock is more pronounced. I can feel my mouth watering, and I have to remind myself that I'm here for him. To comfort him, to make him feel better.

"Get in the shower, baby." I tell him as I begin to strip my own clothes. I watch him as he dips his head under the water and relaxes, looking up at the ceiling and letting the hot water soak his hair. He washes his hair with his eyes closed, and I can't help but admire his biceps as he works, the curve of his ass, and the oblique muscles rippling with his movements. In the span of the few minutes I was getting everything for him, he somehow looks better. More relaxed, less sickly. Not sure how he managed that, but I feel better about ogling him now that he doesn't look like he should be bed bound.

Zayne rinses his hair as I step into the shower and move to grab the bar of soap, but I take it from him, stepping under the opposite shower head. He stands under the water across from me and watches me lather myself up slowly, his eyes hooded and his pupils dilating until there's almost no green left, swallowed by the darkness.

Once my body is rinsed, I walk over to him, stopping when

his erection prevents me from getting closer. He tries to pry the soap from my hands so he can get clean, but I shake my head at him. I soap my hands up and begin to lather him up instead. I work my way down from his neck to his shoulders, armpits, then his arms. I notice a couple of scabs on the inside of his left upper arm, but I don't mention them to him, even as my brain analyzes what could have caused that.

I continue to work my way down his body until every surface is clean except his cock, and then I put more soap on my hands and stroke them along his length, making him twitch. The slippery sensation elicits a moan from him, and I work him faster until he's panting and throwing his head back, then I stop abruptly and rinse him off. He groans in protest and grabs the back of my head as I put the shower head right over his cock, and when he notices that he's thoroughly rinsed, he pushes me down to my knees in front of him, the shower head hitting the wall with a clank.

The penny-round tiles dig painfully into my knees and the water from the showerhead behind me is beating on my back and soaking my hair. Zayne walks even closer to me, stopping when the head of his cock rests on my bottom lip, and I grip the base of him and pump him a few times, making pre-cum leak from his slit. I lick him clean, tasting the saltiness on my tongue and craving more.

I lick the length of him, and he sucks in a sharp breath; the taste of the soap overpowering my taste buds does nothing to deter me. Zayne squeezes his eyes shut, grabbing onto my hair with both hands and gripping tightly. The pain brings tears to my eyes, but I ignore it as I take his cock into my mouth and swirl my tongue repeatedly over the head, noticing the whimpers escaping him and growing bolder by the second. I grip him again and pull him out of my mouth to talk for a moment, stroking and twisting him in the process.

"Yes, Zay, be loud for me." I make eye contact as I get ready to take him back into my mouth, and his green eyes become heated pools of desire.

I open wide for him, taking his cock as far as it will go. My mouth salivates as I gag, drool dripping out of the corners of my mouth and down my chin as I keep working him. We hold eye contact as I take him deep into my throat over and over, reaching my hand up to his balls and gently squeezing and tugging on them.

"Fucking hell," he hisses, closing his eyes and gripping my hair even harder, bringing fresh tears to my eyes.

Zayne seems to be losing control as he grabs onto my hair like reins and forcefully pushes his cock down my throat, my nose grazing his pelvis with every thrust. I begin to gag around him and try to swallow, but I feel the acidic burn in the back of my throat when he doesn't give me any time to recover. I swallow it down and try to breathe in while keeping eye contact with him, but he is relentless and makes me cough and drool all over him as he continues to thrust into my mouth. I should make him stop and be gentle with me. I should refuse to be treated this way, but I can't help it if I want to please him in any way he wants it. I want to give him whatever he wants. I want to make him come harder than anyone ever has.

He somehow gets rougher the longer he shoves his cock down my throat, trying to get further back with each thrust. His assault on my mouth is brutal, and I feel my lips splitting open as I surrender to him with tears streaming down my face. I keep playing with his balls and make my way farther up, seeking his tight hole. He spreads his legs wider for me, grunting as I rub him slowly while his thrusts become erratic.

"So perfect, baby, yes… just like that."

Zayne slaps the wall as I press my finger further into him, and I don't stop until he is visibly panting, his chest heaving as I drive him over the edge. He grunts and whimpers as he gives me a few more furious pumps and comes down my throat, one hand gripping my hair while he uses the other to brace himself on the tiled wall. "Good girl," he says in a low, husky voice that has my pussy clenching with need. "Look how pretty you are swallowing it all for me."

The praise fills holes in my mind, body, and soul that I didn't even know I had, and I would do *anything* to have those words directed at me again. I don't think I've ever felt so loved in my life. As I swallow every last drop he gives me, I know in my heart that no one will ever make me feel the way he does.

Not ever.

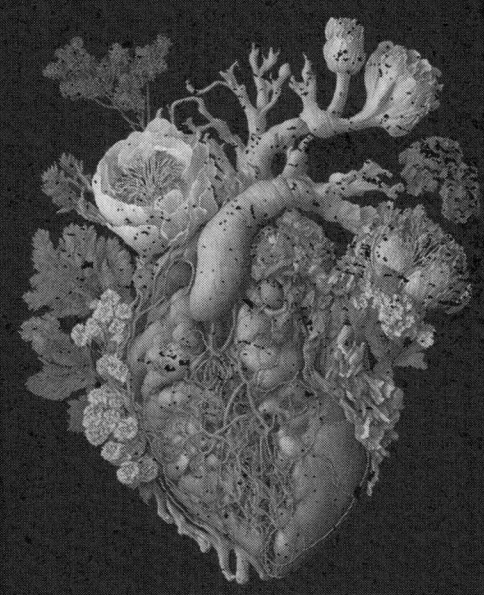

CHAPTER 32

ZAYNE

Hallie and I cuddle in bed after the most amazing head of my entire life. She makes me feel things that I didn't even know were possible, and I'm starting to get scared that it's going to be the same as always and it'll end with her leaving me. She's too good for me.

She's like an angel.

Or a drug.

My drug of choice.

Don't lie to yourself, the monster whispers.

I look over at Hallie and even in the dim light I can see the dry blood coating her lips. I almost feel bad for being so rough, except she took it so fucking well that all I feel is pride. She did that for me, she wanted to please me more than she wanted the pain to stop, and that tugged at something in my chest.

"You took it so well, baby girl," I whisper in her ear, watching her arms break out in goosebumps. "Let me clean you up, and I'll go get the first aid kit."

"No. Stay, I'll get it." She smiles softly at me, a corner of her lip splitting back open all over again. Fuck, ouch. "Rest for now."

Hallie goes to the bathroom, where I have directed her to find the first aid kit. When she gets there, she makes a loud banging noise and I hear her gasp. Realization zaps me like a lightning strike at what she just found: my stash, but not just any, no, of course not.

She found my rig.

I brace myself as she walks out of the bathroom with my spoon, a syringe and needle, and a teener of meth all wrapped in her slender hand. Also, her fucking tourniquet.

Shit.

"What the fuck is this?"

"What do you think it is?" I inhale slowly, trying to calm my heart, which is currently attempting to claw its way out of my chest. I never wanted this to happen. If I could be stronger, I would do it. For her. I'd do anything for her. Except stop using drugs, I don't think I can do that for anyone. Not even myself at this point.

"You promised me." Hallie points at me, her hand shaking. I don't know if it's from anger or fear. "You fucking promised you would stop, and now you're shooting it up instead?" She shakes her head with tears in her eyes. "And you stole my tourniquet?" Her voice rises an octave, "Why would you do this to me?"

"Hallie, I didn't do it to you. I did it to me!" I can feel the tears threatening as I feel her slip through my fingers. "I'm sorry, baby, I really couldn't stop. I haven't been able to stop." She laughs at that, and I know now that she doesn't understand how this works. I'm not in control. I haven't been for a long fucking time. "Please don't go…"

She's already dropped the rig on the bed and is putting her clothes on in a hurry, trying to get away from me as fast as possible. All I want for her is to stay a few more minutes, maybe let me try to explain to her this fucking demon inside of me who possesses me. But she doesn't want to, doesn't want *me*.

"Why the fuck do I always believe you? You're nothing but a fucking liar." Even though I know she's right and I deserve that, her words hit me like a blow to the chest, stealing my breath away and making me double over from the physical pain I feel from her rejection. I get up from the bed and chase after her as she takes the stairs two at a time. As I grab her hand, she turns around and swats me away. "Leave me alone!"

"Fuck off with that. I'm never going to leave you alone," I growl and reach for her again, only she's faster this time and already at the top of the stairs. I stop and stare up at her.

"Fuck *you*!" Hallie yells at me with unrestrained anger. "I need space, and you *will* leave me alone. I need to be away from you." With that, she turns back around, not bothering to wait for a response.

"Fine. Have it your fucking way!" I yell after her, throwing my hands up in the air as I let out my frustration—a scream of rage builds in my throat, but she walks away from me. She leaves me behind, and I leave her alone, just like she asks.

I know I can't truly bring myself to do that, ever, but I let her walk away when perhaps it's the only time I should not have. I can't help but think that she might be done with me for good this time. Our relationship is a fucking rollercoaster, the one that takes you all the way to the top and drops you out of fucking nowhere, making your stomach bottom out. It doesn't feel good half the time, but the rush you get from it keeps you coming back for more. And goddamnit, it feels so good until it doesn't.

I yank on my hair and scream at the top of my lungs until my voice is hoarse and my body is exhausted, later I lower the thermostat again and prepare to hibernate. If Hallie hates me, then there's no reason to keep my shit together. There's no reason to love myself and not let the darkness consume me until there's nothing left.

I walk to the office and turn on my computer, needing a distraction from everything. I search for my baggie on the desk, the one I left there a few days ago, but instead find something else. Something completely unexpected.

A sketch of me.

By Hallie.

And it says, 'I love you'.

FUCK!

I really have to just go and fuck everything up, don't I? It's all I know how to do, but as I sit and stare at my perfect likeness, I'm beginning to think it's not a good excuse anymore.

I need to change.

Truly this time.

I can see myself through her eyes, looking at this portrait of me, and now I'm wondering if I've crushed everything good she's ever believed about me.

And suddenly, I don't want to know how she would sketch me now.

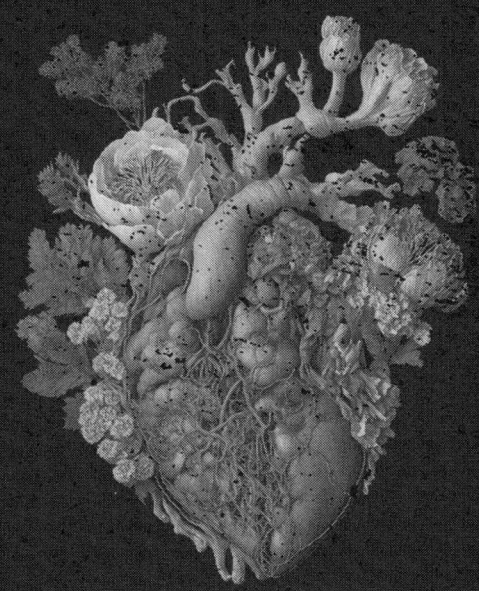

CHAPTER 33

HALLIE

Saturday nights are always the worst at the emergency room, and sadly I was floating here today—my unit didn't need me, and I have a per diem position, which means I'm the first to go. It doesn't bother me, since I take it all as a learning opportunity before I start my new position as a nurse in the step-down ICU within the next three weeks.

I'm excited to learn new skills and be able to do more than I do on the unit I work in currently, so I don't complain when the nurses give me more and more tasks. My work phone keeps going off every few minutes, and between vital signs, finger sticks, and cleaning people up, I barely have a moment to catch my breath. I'm thankful for that though, because I want the shift to go by quickly. I want to get back home to my bed where I can forget all about him.

My phone goes off for the hundredth time in the last thirty minutes, and I answer it quickly, looking forward to the next task. "Hallie, we need you in A pod, room 6."

"Be right there. Do you need me to bring anything with me?"

"Soft wrist restraints, please!" the nurse yells, and I can hear things crashing against the wall in the background.

I grab the restraints for her and take a deep breath before pushing the door open, but that could never have been enough to prepare me for the shock I'm feeling as I step into the room.

My green-eyed devil stares back at me, a snarl on his face as he thrashes on the bed while two nurses attempt to gain enough control of him to restrain him, and they expect me to do the fucking honors. What the fuck is going on? Why the fuck are you here, Zayne?

I try to show him what I'm thinking through my eyes, but he's not seeing me. It's as if he's seeing right through me. His eyes are glazed over as he fights us all. I close the restraints over his wrists and move to the side of the bed to tie them, ensuring they don't have much slack. Considering his aggressive behavior, I would be surprised if he wasn't on a psych hold, but I'll ask his nurse shortly.

After making sure we can fit two fingers between the restraint and his wrist, we move on to checking for other biological needs. He seems to not want to talk to us, especially me, but I will be back for him. I need to know why he's here. I need to hear it from his lips.

Crystal comes into the room, assigned to sit with Zayne, and as I get ready to leave, I ask her if she'd like to trade spots. I use the excuse that I could use the experience of having a patient in this particular situation, one I don't even know about, but that seems to appease her and she agrees to take the floor.

I let his nurse know that we switched, and I will now be his sitter, taking advantage of the circumstances to ask for details about why he's here. She tells me he's here for a manic episode and withdrawals, and that I need to be careful around him. *Manic episode?*

"As in bipolar disorder?" I ask her, trying to keep the surprise out of my voice. How the fuck is that even possible? He has shown no signs for months, I think. Have I missed something? Did he actually show me, and I just missed it?

"Yes."

"Are you sure?"

She points at Zayne. "This is his fifth time here for this in the last year, so, yes, I'm sure. He's awful at taking his medication. He's one of the most self-destructive frequent flyers we have."

"Okay." I nod slowly, trying to take in the information. This is a lot to process in such little time. I don't even know what to do right now. "Is there anything else I should know?"

"He chokes people when he's manic, so stay away until it's not an option. Do *not* trust him."

My stomach drops at her suggestion to not trust him, and my heart clenches in my chest. I hate that she speaks my fears out loud because I want more than anything to be able to trust him, but drugs and now this? What else hasn't he told me? Why does he feel like he can't trust *me*? What did I do to deserve to be treated like this?

The nurse leaves the room and I'm left alone with Zayne in the most uncomfortable silence I have ever experienced. He doesn't even look at me as I settle in the chair on the opposite side of the room. My computer cart is pulled up in front of me as I peer into his chart. I can't deny that there's a conflict of interest, yet I keep my mouth shut because this might be my one and only chance at learning what I want to about him.

As I look in the chart, I notice he has already been given Lorazepam and Haloperidol since he arrived here, and they have him scheduled for a few doses of Abilify per day. It says he's supposed to take 7.5 milligrams twice per day, but he is noncompliant, clearly. He is waiting for a bed on a different floor of the hospital, but sadly there are many sick people and not many beds left. He is here for suicidal ideation with a plan, so he is on an involuntary three-day hold, and his mania is making him aggressive toward the hospital staff.

"You're not even going to talk to me now?" His voice sounds pained, and it makes my heart break down the middle. It's hard enough that I left him without a second thought and haven't answered the phone in days, but now I traded places with another tech just to be in this room with him. Why am I such a masochist?

I look up from my computer once at Zayne, then quickly divert my eyes and purse my lips. His face is pale and sweaty, and his hands visibly shake even from this far away. He's clearly withdrawing and asks me to bring the emesis bag to him. I cringe as I bring it to his mouth and he hurls in it.

I get up and walk to the sink, soaking a washcloth in cold water and wringing it out. Zayne's forehead is cold and clammy as I touch his face, wiping the cloth softly across his skin. I place it on the back of his neck, and he leans back against his pillow and closes his eyes, taking deep breaths and refusing to look at me.

"Why didn't you tell me?" I whisper, the tears falling down my cheeks before I can stop myself. I'm so hurt and I want him to know it, although do I even have a right to be upset when I left him behind?

"I was scared you wouldn't want me. You keep leaving me behind, Hallie." He's not wrong, it's what I do best. I fear abandonment, so I want to control every situation, which means choosing when to leave. It's easier to deal with my feelings that way, because being abandoned makes me feel and act crazy. "You left me behind when you realized I couldn't stop. I can't help it, Hallie. I can't stop now. I'm not strong enough. I'm sorry I didn't tell you that I'm sick, I didn't think it mattered. I figured you weren't sticking around, and I wanted every second of you that I could get." His eyes search mine, but I'm not sure what for, and just like that my control completely evaporates.

The dam breaks, and I can no longer keep my composure, falling to my knees at his bedside and covering my face as my body is wracked with sobs. I can hear his voice in the distance, except I can't snap out of it.

"Hallie, baby, *please* come back... look at me!"

I'm lost in my emotions but I can feel myself understanding the need to pull back out of them, I just can't seem to accomplish it. I dig my fingernails into my arm until I feel a bit of pain, and then continue until the pain is so much I have no choice but to look down at my arm. There are crescent marks in my skin and fresh blood pouring freely from each wound.

These are definitely leaving scars.

Perfect.

I watch the bloody trails on the skin of my arm and I can hear the little splats of the droplets hitting the tiled floor. Zayne looks close to tears himself and is fighting the restraints now, not even caring about his own wrists as he yanks and yanks.

"I'm so sorry, baby..." I say as I get up from the ground at the side of the hospital bed and take his face in my hands, kissing the top of his sweaty head. The saltiness of his sweat grounds me and his smell makes me dizzy, yet I still manage to stay on my feet and wrap him up in a tight hug. His face fits perfectly as he buries his nose against my neck and kisses me there, making me forget about all our problems. "We're going to get through this, okay? You're going to take your medication and we will get through this."

"I need you to promise me something," he whispers as he pulls away from me. His eyes are filled with unshed tears, a sight that makes my breath catch in my throat.

"What?"

"That one day you'll be fully mine." He begs with his eyes, the tears finally spilling over his black lashes and tracking down his cheeks.

"I promise." I avert my gaze, and I can't tell if he understands what it means. "One day until forever." I have always been a liar. Even as I utter the words, I know they will never be true.

"Please don't leave me, Hallie," Zayne chokes out, finally relaxing on the bed.

"I never left you. I just needed some time to process everything, but I didn't actually break up with you." *Yet.*

"Please. Please don't."

"I won't... shhh..." I stroke his hair, trying to get him to calm down. *Liar.*

I soothe him as best as I can before his nurse comes back to medicate him yet again, and then I clean up my arm and say a prayer that it doesn't get infected from this nasty hospital. I spend the rest of the shift trying to make him comfortable through his psychosis, and then when my shift is done, I still stay with him. I stay with him until he feels reassured, is no longer crying, and doesn't think I'm going to leave him.

Even if it's all a lie.

We're living a fucking lie.

Nobody makes it through this in one piece.

It sure as fuck won't be us.

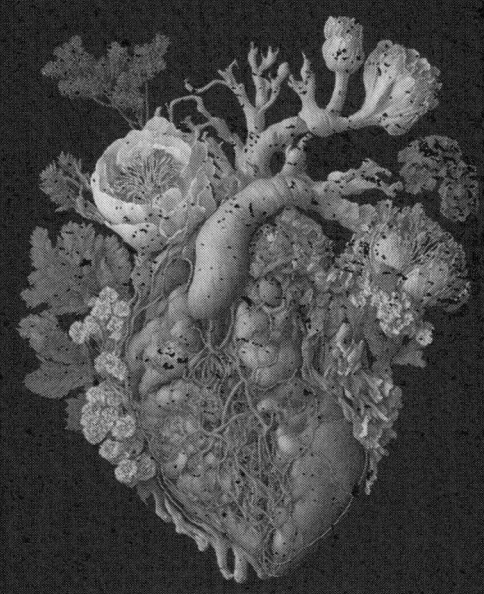

CHAPTER 34

HALLIE

"Daddy loves his little girl."

He pulls my hair and pounds into me. The shriek that leaves my mouth is unbidden; he must be angry about something because it's worse than usual. He wraps his hand over my nose and mouth and I can't breathe. I try desperately to, and I want to tell him that I can't, but he won't let me go as I scratch his arm and try to pry him off.

Try to get him off me.

I scoot up in the bed, trying to run away from him, but his fingers dig into my hip and I flinch, that pain making me forget about the other ones momentarily. My vision begins to fade at the edges, going black, and bright orbs float around the room as I attempt to draw breaths, but my desperation makes me burn through my reserve even faster.

My world tilts on its axis and then goes black.

I'm not sure how much time has passed, but when I wake, I do *so in the darkness. I open my eyes ever so slowly, straining to hear, but there's no one here with me. No ragged breaths, no whimpers or groans.*

No devil.

Nothing except for a world of pain.

My tears soak the pillow, cold under my cheek. I'm still on my stomach, positioned at an awkward angle, when I feel it, and I freeze.

Something isn't right.

I pull a shirt on and run to the bathroom, locking the door behind me. When I look down, there's blood running down my right leg, warm and sticky and dirty with him. I do my best to clean up, the warm water not inflicting the pain I need to feel.

I want to forget, forget, forget.

I return to my room and find the razor blade, my confidant, and I return it to the inside of my thighs, where no one will bear witness to my desecration.

But even that doesn't relieve it anymore.

There's no outlet for my pain to depart through.

And now... now I just want to die, die, die.

I sit up in bed abruptly, dragging the covers with me. I glance over at the clock on my nightstand, which reads three in the morning. Zayne turns over to me and grabs my hand, sitting up as well.

"Baby?" His voice is thick with sleep, and as I peer over at him I can see his hair sticking up in different directions, the soft glow of the moonlight making him appear ethereal.

"Just a nightmare," I mumble, wishing they would stop. They've been worse than ever lately. I've been having them every night, even when I take my medications, and I can't quite figure out the connection.

Zayne hasn't moved in, even though it's almost as if he has. He's been sleeping with me for the past three weeks, only leaving my place to go to work or see his mother. I convinced him to stay with me temporarily so I could take care of him. I've been making sure he takes his antipsychotic medications, forcing him out of bed, and making sure he eats when he needs to eat. Essentially, I've become his second mother, or a wife. Or both.

Not busting him with drugs has been the highlight of the last few weeks, and his emotional regulation has been the cherry on top of our accomplishments.

"Okay, baby, let's go back to sleep…" Zayne brings me back into his embrace and snuggles me in the way that always makes my heart flutter, burying his face in my hair like he can't get enough of me in his lungs.

I close my eyes, and when I open them again, I can see the morning sun struggling to make it past my blackout curtains. The faint glow is soothing rather than blinding, and I find myself in a much better mood, even though I'm not usually a morning person.

Zayne still has his arm draped over me, and I can feel his warm breath on the back of my neck, steady inhales and exhales. I also take a deep breath and smell his unique scent in the air—forest and citrus, my favorite smell in the world. I want to bathe myself in it, live, and bury myself in it.

I attempt to roll over to face him, and he breathes into my hair as he stirs in his sleep, but I manage to turn over and look at his face. He is so peaceful when he sleeps. His brows are no longer furrowed, the wrinkle between them smooths out, and his eyes are peaceful for once instead of scrunched or intense.

At some point in our sleep, Zayne took off his clothes and is now lying next to me, completely naked, with the most beautiful morning wood I have ever witnessed. I stare at him for so long that I'm afraid he can sense my eyes on his cock, and as if summoned he opens his own and stares right into mine.

His irises are at war with themselves as they fight for what color to be today, the blues and the greens mixing until you can't tell where they begin or end. He is utterly breathtaking, and I want him to ruin my life forever, as long as he's in it.

"Touch me, Hallie."

"No, *you* touch me," I say with a shaky breath.

He flips me over and pulls my hips back to his cock, grinding into my ass until I'm wet and needy. I don't even recognize the sounds coming out of me as he pulls down my underwear and rubs his finger between my lips, seeking my clit.

With his other hand, he pushes my face into the mattress as he lifts my ass high into the air and starts to lick me from pussy to ass, getting me ready even though I distinctly don't need it. I'm fucking aching for him.

He presses the tip of his cock to my opening and slowly slips into me, filling me to the brim with every inch of him. I spread my legs wider and arch my back for him, keeping my upper body on the mattress, and he groans when I back my ass up on him.

"Fuck, yes, Hallie," Zayne hisses, as he grips my hips so hard that I'm sure I'll have bruises by the time he's done with me.

"I want you to use me, baby," I tell him as I fist the covers. "Make yourself feel good."

He slowly pulls out of me to the tip and drags his hand up from my ass all the way to the back of my neck, gripping me there to hold me in place. With one thrust, he slams his cock back into me roughly, making me want to run away, but he keeps a tight grip on me. He keeps his thrusts violent, everything on the edge of pain, just as I want it.

I need to feel. I need to feel. I need to feel.

I swear I can feel his cock in my stomach as he pounds into me repeatedly, and when he hits my cervix, I push away from him, trying to escape the intense pain. Zayne grips my hips hard as he picks up the pace even more, preventing my escape.

He begins to slow down, pushing my body onto the mattress until I'm lying on my stomach and he's on top of me, almost crushing me. His chest meets my back, not an inch of skin separated, and he pushes his hand between me and the mattress to touch me. His fingers connect with my clit, rubbing circles as he starts a languid pace, his gasps in my ear making me shiver.

He goes slow, as if savoring every thrust, and his moans echo in my fucking soul. I've never heard a more beautiful sound. My stomach flips when his groan turns into another moan, and I clench around him as the heat in my lower belly begins to spread down and I start to ride his hand, seeking more, more, more pleasure.

My breaths come in pants as I get closer to my orgasm, and as I feel it tearing through me like a hurricane, he pushes my head into the pillow. His hand slides up to my neck again, holding me in place and not letting me breathe. I shake under him, trying to catch my breath but unable to, which makes it all feel even better, as always.

Zayne's other arm snakes around my waist and pulls me closer toward him, and he hits a deeper spot. His pace increases, but he keeps his thrusts shallow this time. As he gets closer to his climax, the hand holding down my face into the pillow wraps around my hair and yanks hard, pulling my head back roughly and bringing fresh tears to my eyes. He comes with a whimper and falls to his side, bringing me close to him as he wraps his arms around me and buries his face in the crook of my neck again, his favorite spot.

I relish this moment like it may be our last, because it may very well be, and somehow it makes everything more beautiful.

Knowing we're doomed.

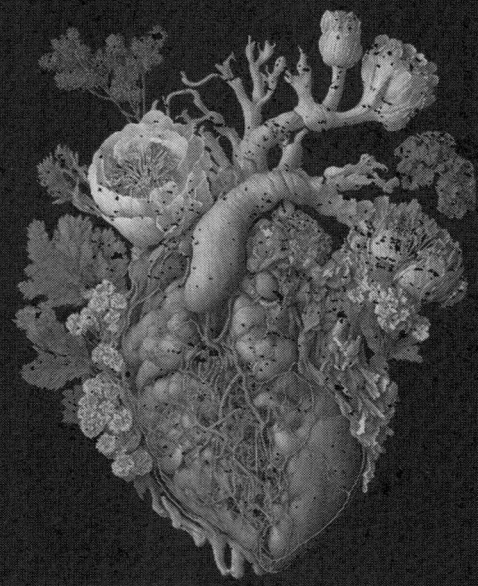

CHAPTER 35

ZAYNE

My hands are shaking slightly as I tear the sticky bed sheets from my skin, the sweat making the air conditioner in the room feel about ten degrees colder than it actually is. I go to the bathroom to shower, but I sneak a look at Hallie's naked form, arms stretched above her head and hair pooling on her pillow like a halo. Her exposed nipples are pebbled and the comforter rests against the skin around her hips. I want to be that comforter so badly.

She's a fucking angel.

I shouldn't be this horny after everything we did just a few hours ago, but somehow I can't seem to get enough of her. She's no longer a habit for me, not even a simple addiction. She's become my *favorite* obsession.

I can't get enough of her.

I can't say no to her.

I have to have *more*.

The way she screams as I make her come. My name on her

lips. The way she claws my back. It's all fuel for the obsession, and I want her to light me on fire. I want her to consume me until there's nothing left.

I know Hallie only feels bad for me, and that's why she stuck around after the hospital. I've always been a selfish asshole, but if her pity for me is enough to keep her with me, then I'll take anything she gives.

I'm greedy.

I'll bleed her fucking dry.

It's obvious she cares about me. I can see it in the way that she looks at me, no matter how tough she likes to act. Hell, maybe she does even love me, however will she falter if I'm not by her side? I'm really not sure. On the other hand, I know my world will cease to exist without her.

But my world will also cease to exist without the monster.

I know I said I would stop, but I haven't. My doses have been low enough to keep myself from having withdrawals but also not high enough that I'm really high. I don't feel anything special right now when I shoot up, I just do it to feel normal. I do it to live.

I want nothing more than to feel the pure ecstasy of the monster climbing on my back, shooting down my spine, and racing in my veins. I don't do it though, because I want to keep Hallie, but I also know I'm not strong enough to hold off for very long.

I always promise Hallie it's the last time.

Every time is the last time.

I say it to myself too, as if trying to convince my brain, but all it wants is the dopamine rush, and the monster can give that to me. He's seductive, alluring, and whispers lies in my fucking ear. And even though I don't believe him when he says it's not that bad, I convince myself that I'm still in control and not in a dark place, that I'm not a fucking junkie. But those are all lies. I'm in the darkest place of them all, with the monster riding on my back, its claws sunk so deep I'm not sure I'll ever get them out.

I almost feel guilty for the lies I feed Hallie, but she always eats them up so greedily, and who am I to deny her?

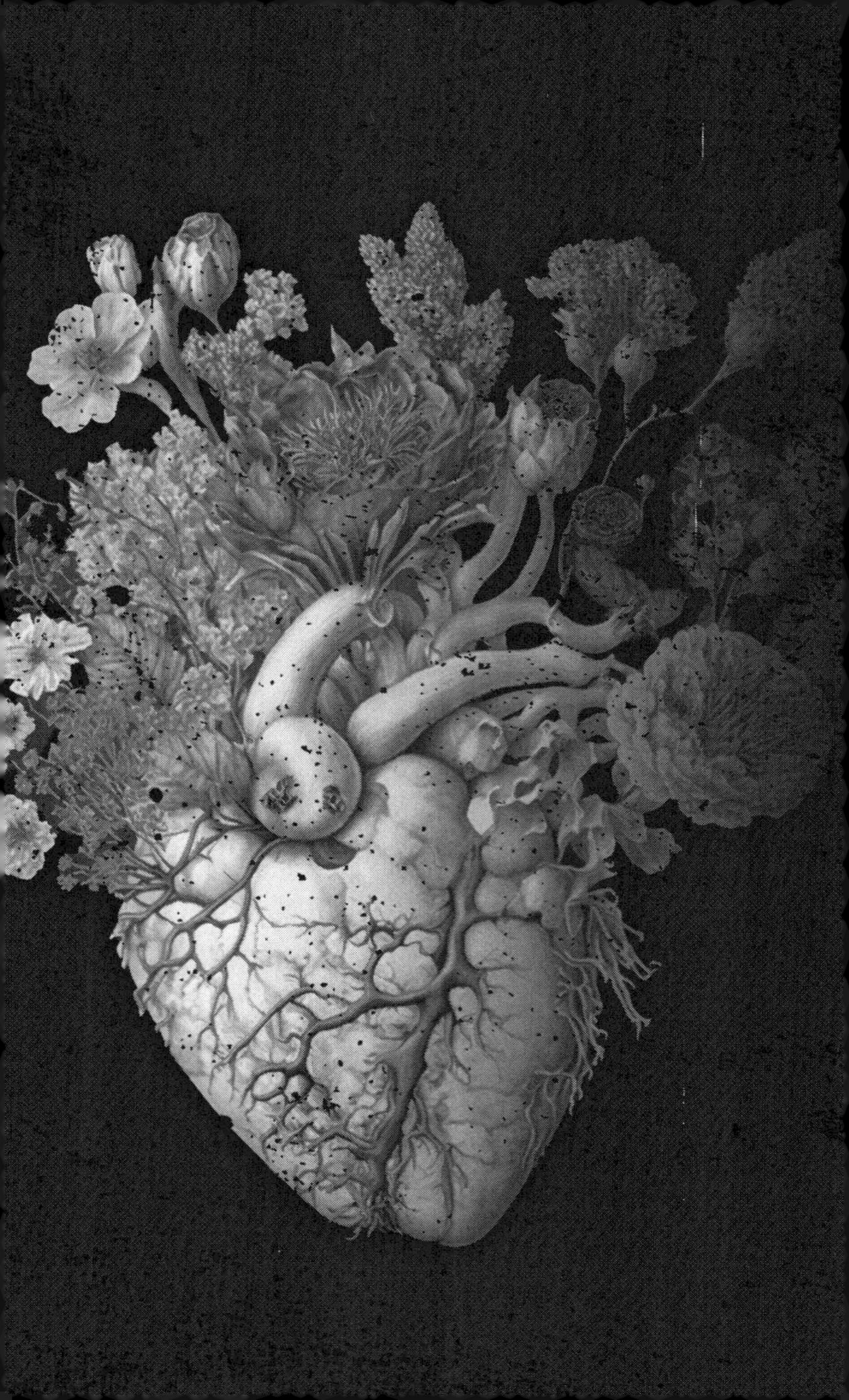

THE CRASH

CHAPTER 36

HALLIE

I had the mid-shift at the hospital today, and I'm fucking exhausted. We had so many admissions and discharges that I'm sure my brain is no longer properly functioning. I don't want to do anything else except order some takeout and take a long bath, then maybe have a glass of wine before bed.

I walk up to my front door and have the prickly sensation of someone watching me, but as I look around, I don't see anyone at all. My keys jangle as I unlock my door and open it, the sound slightly comforting. I kick my door shut with my foot and then turn around and lock it, trying to juggle my work bag as I take my dirty shoes off before stepping all the way into the apartment.

I take all my stuff and strip in the laundry room as I always do, then go put on a pair of sweats and a t-shirt with no bra, ready to be comfortable and relax for the rest of the day. A knock sounds at the door, and I hurry to the door, wondering if Zayne or Brit forgot their keys. Just as I open it, I come face to face with someone who I never thought I'd see again.

My mother.

I drop my phone on the ground and gasp while my mother just smiles at me on the other side of the door. I don't understand what she's doing here, how she got my address, what she could possibly even want. I suppose now that she's here, I need to look for a new residence.

She tilts her head to the side, "Won't you let your mother in?"

"What the fuck are you doing here?" I spit. She has some fucking nerve in showing up at my house uninvited. I hadn't seen her in almost a decade, and I could've lived my entire life without doing it again.

"I'm here to see you, of course."

I laugh. Wow, she's funny. Or delusional. "You're not coming in."

"The fuck I'm not. I didn't come all this way for you to slam the door in my face." She shoves past me, leaving me to stare after her as she walks through my home.

"Get out, Marianna. I don't want you here." I try to move, to force her out, but my feet are rooted to the spot. Please don't have a panic attack right now. Do *not* give her the satisfaction. "You need to leave right now."

"You have no respect, do you?" She smiles, but it doesn't reach her eyes, "It's time we talked."

I finally walk over to her and attempt to lead her to the door by her arm. Only she turns around and takes hold of my hair instead, gripping it until I feel tears in my eyes, but this time I just laugh.

I laugh hysterically until she looks puzzled and doesn't know what to do with herself. This is the last thing she expected from me, to find this amusing. Nevertheless, she doesn't understand that I don't see this as amusing at all, just ironic. Ironic that she is coming to my house uninvited and treating me the same fucking way she used to when I was a child. People never change, as she used to tell me all the time.

Don't trust anyone; I guess she didn't expect to be included on the blacklist.

My hair is still under her vice grip, and she shakes me as she moves toward the couch, breaking my heart all over again in the process.

I won't cry. I won't cry. I won't cry.

She throws me on the couch and stands across from me, and as my head bounces off the cushion, I see Zayne walking quickly toward her. Oh shit.

Time slows down and I see him grab her arm and yank hard, pulling her toward the front door. Marianna is quick though, and she pulls something out of her purse before he can see what she's doing. The zap of her taser echoes in the small living room, making him jump back a few feet.

"Much better." Marianna smiles, holding the taser pointed at Zayne. He looks slightly uncomfortable, but I also know he's not scared of her. He would get her out of here if I asked. He would do whatever it takes. "I'm just here to talk to my daughter."

"You need to get the fuck out of here. You lost your daughter the day you chose your husband."

"I will decide when I lose my daughter."

"She doesn't want you in her life. Let's do this the easy way, there's the door. Please leave." Zayne looks rapidly between the two of us, as if expecting me to contradict him. He should know better, I never want her to be a part of my life again.

"Stay out of this, you fucking junkie!" my mom yells, and Zayne visibly flinches as if he's been slapped. "Oh, did I hit a nerve? I know a drug addict when I see one." She looks over at me and makes eye contact, letting pity show on her face. "Oh, honey. You're just like me. Always falling in love with the wrong guys. He's going to end up just like your dad."

"Get the fuck out of here before you leave in a goddamn body bag," Zayne says through gritted teeth, my arms covering in goosebumps as his voice drops an octave. I've never seen him look scarier than now, and I'm grateful that he's here defending me.

My mom throws her head back and laughs, her eyes wide as she makes eye contact with me and grins. She looks more unhinged than ever.

"I will call the police right now if you don't leave." I've had enough of her shit, and I don't want to hear one more word out of her mouth. I hold up my phone for her to see so she knows I'm not playing with her anymore.

"Fine, I'll leave." She turns on her heel to walk out of the apartment, and Zayne follows to close the door behind her. But, at the last minute, she turns around and shoves the taser into his ribs and zaps him, holding it for a few seconds, long enough that he flops to the ground and grabs his side, grunting through his pain.

"You fucking bitch!" I scream, running to the door to get her out of my house.

"I will fucking shoot you!" Zayne says, knowing damn well he doesn't even have a gun on his person, but she smiles at us both as she walks out of the apartment, leaving a dark cloud hanging over us.

I run to Zayne and lift his shirt to look at his ribs, and I can already see the bruise forming on his skin. I can't believe she actually fucking tased him. "Are you okay?" I ask him as I try to help him up, but he's heavier than I gave him credit for.

"I'm fine," he grunts with effort as he gets up, clutching his side. He stretches his body and cracks his knuckles, looking scary in his anger. "What was she here for?"

"She said she wanted to talk."

"She wasn't talking though." He brushes a thumb under my eye and wipes a traitorous tear away. "I literally saw her pulling your fucking hair."

"That's because I refused to talk to her."

"Good. You don't need her in your life." He notices the expression on my face and pulls me into a hug, resting his chin on the top of my head and rubbing circles on my back.

His phone begins to buzz and he takes a step back to answer it, then walks away to the kitchen, leaving me in the living room to stare after him. Who the fuck is that? He mumbles into the phone, and then I catch him saying he will be right there.

"I have to go, baby. I'm sorry." At least he does look apologetic. Kind of. "I'll be back in a few hours."

"Where are you going?"

"My mom said she needs me." I don't believe him. But why? He's been clean. He hasn't given me a reason to doubt him. "I'm just going to go see her for a few hours."

"Okay, baby. Call me when you're headed back."

He gives me a kiss and heads out, leaving me to question our entire conversation. I don't believe that he's going to see his mother, and it makes me feel crazy. Before I can analyze it any further, I wait until he's in his car and pulling out of the parking area to run for my keys and follow after him. I know for a fact this is unlike him. He would never give me space, especially when I was not even asking for it.

I get in my car and follow him past seven lights, three stop signs, and all the way to the interstate, but it's as if he suddenly panics and speeds up significantly. Does he know I'm tailing him? I'm not sure if he spotted me, but he makes himself disappear and I can't keep up. Instead of trying to continue looking for him, I take the first exit I see and turn around, headed for his mother's house.

If he says he's going there, then that's where I'll be waiting. Let's see what he has to say after I talk to Alyssa and wait for him to get to her house. Let's see how long it fucking takes him.

Maybe I can talk some damn sense into him.

I cry the rest of the way to his house, the tears blurring the road. Quite frankly, I'm not sure how I haven't crashed. I'm not sure if I'm crying because deep down, I know he lied or because of the fiasco with my mother, but it doesn't matter. I wipe the tears from my face when I'm nearing the turn to get there, and I see mascara streaked on my hand. I use my sleeve to wipe my face and get rid of it, looking at myself several times in the rearview mirror.

I pull up to his house and park in the driveway, wanting him to know I'm here before he goes in the house. I want him to wonder what his mom and I have talked about while he's been gone and be fucking worried.

Maybe it's awful of me to want that for him, but I can't help myself. I need him to feel even a fraction of distress, as I've been distraught and worried over him for the past few months. It's never-ending now, especially since finding out about his bipolar disorder and the extent of his drug addiction.

I walk up to the door and ring the doorbell, shifting from foot to foot as I wait for Alyssa to get to the door. She opens it slowly, peeking her head out, and her surprise is evident in the way she looks around for her son, not knowing what to do with just me on her front porch. My stomach twists on itself as I get even more nervous, but I refuse to back down now.

"Alyssa, I'm not here for Zayne." I grimace, hoping she can see the pain in my eyes. I don't want to do this, but I have to. For him. *For us.* "May I come in?"

"Yes, of course. Please make yourself comfortable." She steps aside and motions toward the living room, the open-floor plan making it easier to see from the front door. "Would you like some coffee?"

"Yes, please, sugar is fine."

"Sit, please. I'll be right back."

I can hear dishes and spoons hitting the sink as she prepares my coffee, and my heart stutters in my chest for a second as I realize I don't even know why I'm here. I don't even know what the fuck to talk about.

Shit.

Alyssa comes back into the living room, holding a white ceramic mug and places it on the coffee table across from me. She sits a few feet away from me on the sectional couch, giving me some much-needed room, but still close enough that we don't have to speak loudly at each other.

"What brings you here today, Hallie?"

"I'd like to talk to you about Zayne. You weren't very clear at dinner a few months ago, but what you said seemed to upset him a lot. I would like for you to clarify and just tell me what you meant." I sound unhinged. I'm speaking one hundred miles per hour, but I'm sure she can understand it's taken a lot for me to actually talk to her.

"Hallie." Alyssa stops and closes her eyes, taking a deep breath as a tear escapes out of the corner of her left eye. She blinks them away as more threaten to spill out of her blue eyes. "I love my son more than anything, but when I look at you, I see a successful woman with a career, a good husband, and lots of kids. And Zayne... he's just going to drag you down, hold you back." She fidgets with her hands, twisting her fingers as she looks up from her lap and at me again. "He doesn't know how to hold on to anything good for him. He destroys things, it's what he's good at, and he's on drugs, Hallie." Her voice cracks as she says my name, and I can tell this was difficult for her to get out, no matter how easy she made it look during that dinner a few months ago.

"I know..." I whisper, the tears now falling from my eyes as I look at the ground, the walls, anywhere but at her. Shame burns its way into my very core, and I know she must be confused about why I'm with him, but how do I explain to her that I can't leave him? That he's more essential than oxygen, food, or even water?

"You do?" The confusion in her voice makes me look up at her, and she searches my eyes frantically. She doesn't expect me to be with him because I know the truth. Maybe leaving him is the healthy thing to do, but I just can't bring myself to.

"I do, but I can't leave him." I sniffle. "I know I sound stupid, but I love him." I cry harder, and she scoots closer to me on the couch.

"Oh, honey. You don't sound stupid." She wraps me up in a tight hug and rests her cheek on my head as I let myself be comforted by this woman who I thought hated me this entire time.

"I thought you hated me."

"Hallie, I don't hate you. I think he's not good for you, because he's not good for anyone, not even himself."

"Do you think I can help him get better?"

"No one can help him get better if he doesn't want to get better." Her eyes tell me a thousand things that her words do not, and I know I have to come to terms with that. I have to understand he's not mine to fix, no matter how beautifully broken he is in my eyes, he's not my project.

Just as I'm about to answer her though, Zayne walks in through the front door, stopping dead in his tracks as he looks from his mother to me and back to her. We're embracing on the couch and our cheeks are stained with mascara tear tracks.

His body is tense, preparing for an attack, and he looks like he might pounce at any moment. I can't tell what's going through his mind as he stands and stares; his silence is more disturbing than his outbursts.

He approaches slowly, carefully, as if he fears this interaction more than us, or maybe I'm just projecting and I'm the scared one. But now that I think of it, he probably expects us to corner and attack him and force him into rehab. He isn't too far off, I'm sure we could come up with some sort of intervention if we made an effort, but I don't want to spook him.

"What's going on here?"

"I thought you were here and decided I wanted to spend the day with you and your mom, but you didn't come here like you said you would." There, I said it, and my heart didn't stop.

I need a Xanax.

My heart is beating hard against my chest as he comes to a halt in front of me, his hand outstretched, waiting for me to take it, or worse, to deny him. I think if I denied him, he would lose his shit, however, so I grab his hand and let him pull me away from his mom, giving her one last apologetic glance as we stop in front of the door to the basement.

Knowing this could very well be the worst idea I've ever had.

CHAPTER 37

HALLIE

Zayne drags me by my hand down the stairs, and I struggle to keep up with him, trying my hardest not to trip and faceplant. He looks angry, yet I can't quite figure out why, especially considering he's the one who lied to me.

"What the fuck are you doing here, Hallie?"

"I didn't believe you. I wanted to see for myself if you were lying, and you clearly were. So how about you cut the shit and just tell me what you were actually doing after you left?"

"I was getting meth," he mutters under his breath, barely audible. I inhale a sharp breath and he just rakes both hands through his hair, as if he can't decide how to feel right now.

Well, that fucking makes two of us.

"You said you would stop doing this. How many times, Zayne?" I raise my voice, not giving a fuck if his mom hears me. I think she'd be on my side right now. "How many fucking times will you lie to my face before we're done?"

Zayne closes the distance between us and grips me by my throat, pushing me into the wall behind me and squeezing until my vision starts to fade to black at the corners. I feel my panties dampen from my arousal, and then I mentally slap myself for being so fucked up that I get turned on by this. Goddamnit my mind is a fucked up place to be.

"How do I fucking make this clear for you, Hallie? We will never, *ever*, be fucking done. Not in this fucking lifetime or the next, you got it?" He squeezes his fingers as he asks me the question, but I can't answer from the tight grip on my neck, so I tip my chin down in a nod in its place. He releases me slowly and takes a step back, looking me over with approval in his gaze. I cough until my chest aches from the force of it, bracing myself on the wall, and when I try to speak, I cough again.

"I don't want to witness you ruining your own life. I'm tired of watching it happen." My voice is hoarse, barely above a whisper.

"Then take a fucking nap, Hallie." I should probably be scared of him right now after what he just did to me, but instead, I feel relief that he won't let me leave him. "You're not going anywhere."

"I will leave if you don't stop this. I can't keep doing this with you."

"It's under control. I promise."

"Don't you dare fucking promise me anything!" My voice cracks as I close the distance between us and push against his chest. He doesn't budge, and that somehow makes me even fucking angrier. I beat my fists against him and lose my breath, sobs racking my body without my permission. I grip his shirt and pull him closer, burying my face in his neck, except I can't breathe from all the crying. So I resort to the only thing I know: violence.

I grab the back of his neck and get even closer, as close as two bodies can be with clothes on, and bite down on his neck until I taste blood. Zayne gasps, but he's not angry. I can feel his cock get hard against my stomach as I wrap my arms around him and lick his wound, loving the taste of his blood on my tongue.

He bends down a fraction and picks me up, gripping my ass,

and walks me to his bed, dropping me on it. He pulls his pants down as he watches me squirm, except I don't take anything off. I don't want to make this easy on him. I want him to work for it. I want him to show me he wants me.

I need him to fucking *destroy* me.

Zayne tears my shirt down the middle, not even bothering to take it off me, and then pulls my bra down to expose my breasts. He cups them both and kneads them, twisting my nipples before descending on them like a starved man. I grip his hair with my hands, and I yank, wanting to inflict pain, needing to.

I want him to lose control.

I crave it.

He groans against my right breast, and it reverberates through me. His licking and sucking slow down and his teeth clamp down on my nipple, making me cry out in pain as he lets go and licks it away. Fingers flick at the button of my jeans, and with one swift movement, they're undone and sliding down my legs.

Zayne wraps his arms around me and picks me up off the bed, my legs closing around his narrow waist. He walks us to the office, or gaming room is more like it, and drops down on the couch with me straddling him.

I lift off him and bring both hands to the side of his face, loving how the darkness embraces his features. He leans into my palm, nuzzling it, and butterflies explode in my stomach as his hard cock grazes against it.

I angle my face to kiss him, but instead I give him one long lick from his chin to his jaw, his muscles tightening under me. When I reach his ear, I take his lobe in my mouth and lightly suck, biting down as I let go of it. The sound he makes crashes through my body, and I work my way from his ear down to his neck with kisses, licks, and bites. His hands find my hips and he splays them wide as he holds me, and when I grab his cock his fingers tighten around me.

I push his cock to my entrance and lower myself on it, moaning at the fullness I feel when I settle myself. Rocking my hips slowly, I grab onto his shoulders and look into his eyes. We stare at each other while I go in circles, and I've never seen anything more erotic than this man's face when he's lost in pleasure. He tips his head back and groans, closing his eyes for a moment, but I slide my hands up to his neck and grip him, digging my nails in, demanding his attention.

Zayne's head snaps back to me and he grins, grabbing my hair tightly at the nape of my neck and holding on to it while I ride him. My pace increases as he begins to make those sweet sounds and I can feel myself getting closer to the edge, our moans now music to my ears.

With my hands still wrapped around his neck, I begin to squeeze, my grip matching my urgency. He keeps eye contact with me, but his eyes are now glazed over, and even in the darkness I see his neck beginning to turn red. "You better come soon, my love," I say as I tighten my grasp even more, my hands now aching in the process.

His eyes flash and he smiles widely, showing all his straight, white teeth. His smile drops when I lean in and lick his chin, my tongue darting up to his lips until they open on a silent gasp that he can't utter due to my assault on his neck. I take his bottom lip in my mouth and suck while I grind down harder on him, the friction of his pelvis against my clit pushing me off the edge.

His grip tightens on my hair as I begin to tremble and he knows my orgasm is crashing through me, the undertow dragging me in and spitting me back out. I moan into his mouth and bite his lip, my favorite thing to do. I know he fucking loves it, and it only makes me want to do it even more.

His body goes stiff underneath me, and he lets go of my hair to rake his fingernails down my back, digging them in as he gets closer to his climax and pushing his hips off the couch to meet me thrust for thrust as I change the rhythm. I let him slide me up and down on his cock, even though it hits my cervix painfully, and soon he's spilling inside of me.

"I need you to ruin my fucking life," I whisper in his ear, and

I feel my nipples getting hard again as his breath caresses the side of my face.

"It's a good thing that's all I know how to do."

I pull back and see the smile that lights up my entire world, and I know that he means every word. He can never hold anything good in his hands without demolishing it, but even now as he tells me these words, all I can think of is how grateful I am that my world is no longer shrouded in darkness.

I open my eyes and glance at the clock on the nightstand, which currently reads ten thirty in the morning. The room is freezing and pitch black since Zayne always takes everything to an extreme at this house, and I pull the covers even higher on my body until they're up to my neck. As I do, my hand brushes his arm and I pull back quickly as if I've been burned, because it feels like I have. His skin feels like it's on fire, or even possibly like he *is* fire.

"Zay…"

"Yes, baby?" He's having tremors, shaking slightly, but it's noticeable as he lies next to me in the bed.

"Are you okay?" I whisper, hearing the fear in my voice.

"I will be. I just need to use the bathroom."

About ten minutes go by before he makes it back to the bed, and he positions himself behind me to snuggle me. He's no longer hot or shaking, but I can't understand how the change came about. He didn't shower or do anything special.

My stomach drops at the realization.

Of course.

He's fucking high.

He can't even control himself long enough to do it after I leave. It's so bad now that he must do it all the time. He can't even wait to be alone. "Zayne, what did you do?"

"I did what needed to be done, baby."

I cry out and turn the other way, giving him my back, refusing to face him as I let myself break down all over again. I can't keep doing this. I can't take it anymore. I can't watch him die.

He soothes gentle circles on my back as I sob, and whispers words of reassurance that mean absolutely fucking nothing. I calm down long enough to ask, "How could you keep putting me through this?"

"This isn't about you, Hallie. I'm too far in, I don't think I could stop if I tried."

Realistically, I know he's right. But a part of me wants to be the center of his universe, the reason he gets clean. It's irrational, I am. "You would stop if you cared about me. Do you even love me at all?"

"Baby, you put the stars in my fucking sky." Zayne pulls me closer to him, my back to his chest. "You're everything to me."

"Then what the fuck are you doing, baby?"

A long sigh escapes him, "Surviving."

You're in too deep.

You keep dragging us against the current.

You keep pulling us under.

You're going to fucking drown us.

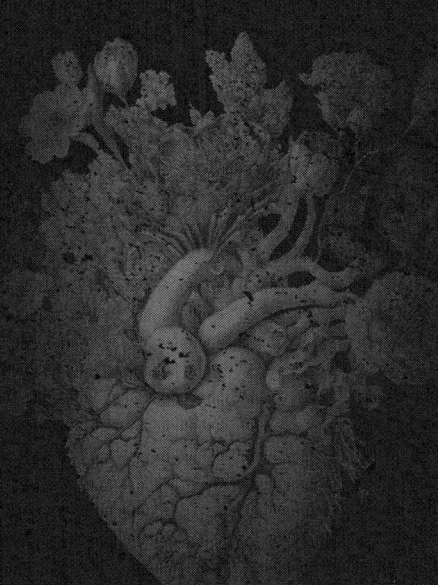

CHAPTER 38

HALLIE

I go home and think about how to get Zayne out of this mess. I'm supposed to start my residency in the next few weeks, which means I need my head in the game, especially at work. I can't be worrying about when he will be shooting up next.

I have everything planned out: my residency, working the night shift and saving up enough to move out and get my own place. The question is: how does he fit into this? He needs to give up the drugs. He needs to be a responsible adult.

Or I'm going to have to leave.

You won't.

I'm going to have to give him up.

He won't let you.

I'm going to have to be the sane one.

You're not.

I try to imagine my new reality, the one where I tell him to

I walk over to my nightstand, to the bottle of wine I keep there, and twist the cap off, ready to wash down the little blue pills in my hand. I know it'll be a little while before I feel the effects of the Xannies, so I grab a book from the bookshelf adjacent to my bed and lie down to read.

I end up spending the day in a drug-induced haze. Look at me, the pot calling the kettle black. Yeah, I see it too. I'm self-aware, but that doesn't mean shit at the moment. No amount of self-awareness will make me leave him, so instead I go back to my favorite cocktail.

Xanax and alcohol. Always. Forever. Back and forth. Hot and cold.

I've already had half a bottle of wine after the pills, so it's all downhill from here.

Literally.

I set the book down on the empty pillow next to me, my mind floating away from me, falling asleep against my will, as I try to think of all the times I should have left Zayne but couldn't. I still can't, and maybe that makes me weak. I know I'd written it before, even said it to his mother, but the weight hadn't indeed hit me until now...

What is love anyway? And if I feel it, how would I know? And does he even feel the same? Probably not, no matter how many times he says it to me.

My parents don't love me and have never wanted me. I should be used to it, the fact that no one chooses me, but instead I ask myself, why would he? Why would he, out of all people, choose me? If my own family can't even love me, what makes me special enough for him to love me?

The answer is nothing.

There's not one fucking thing special about me.

And no matter how many times he tells me I matter, I won't believe him.

Because no one's ever told the truth about it, and he belongs in the pile of liars.

The water has almost filled the tub halfway, but I don't want to stop it. I want it to overflow. I want it to ruin everything exactly the way he has ruined my life. But after today, I won't have to worry about my life anymore. Not after what I have planned.

I wish I could say it was a good run, but it's been fucking miserable. From the time I took my first breath, it's been an uphill battle. Fuck it, I don't want this anymore.

My tears are hotter than the water, but as I lower myself to submerge, the tears become the water, and I can't tell the difference anymore. I want to die, I decided that already, but all I can think about is wanting something, anything that will convince me to stay.

Yet I can't think of one damn thing.

I hold my breath and go under, and the ceiling looks a bit distorted from the bottom of the tub, but the blur does nothing to keep me from putting the pieces together. I've looked at this same image countless times, never being brave enough to go through with it, but this time I'm not looking to talk myself into it.

This time I want to talk myself out.

My lungs are burning, my chest is tight, and my vision frays at the edges, but not even a miracle will keep me underwater long enough to drown myself, so I go up.

My chest burns with the exertion as I suck in deep breaths, my body betraying me by letting out a sob. I grab the razor blade from the rug in front of the tub, the corner of it nicking my fingertip. I take a deep breath and set the sharp end against the skin on the inside of my forearm.

Horizontal or vertical?

Painful or quick?

I deserve to suffer.

Horizontal it is.

I dig the tip in, blood dripping from the tiny cut. I prepare to slice—

Knock, knock, knock.

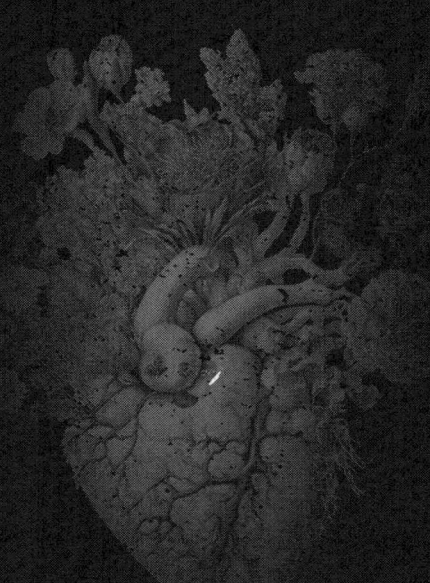

CHAPTER 39

HALLIE

My head is pounding to the beat of my heart, and as I squint my eyes tighter, I suddenly regret last night's activities. The high always comes with a crash. At least that's usually true for me, and as I think of the cost, I remember how hypocritical I felt as I guzzled a bottle of wine with a few pills.

Why do I even expect him to give up his vices when I can't give up my own?

I go to the kitchen and throw the pantry door open, slamming it against the wall from the force of my assault. Staring at rows upon rows of my own wine and liquor, I get a prickly sensation all over my body.

Shame.

I guess I'm just like my dad, too.

My mother would have a fucking field day at this revelation.

I take all the bottles to the sink and line them up on the counter, then begin to pour them out one by one, making sure to not leave even one behind. If I'm going to help Zayne get better, then I need to get better too. I think of my own stash in the little wooden box I keep in my dresser. I even think of my prescribed Xanax, which I'm clearly abusing, and I quietly grieve at letting them go. Shocking the hell out of myself, I go to my nightstand and take my pill bottle, walking to the bathroom as I open it. I take five pills out of it, which I save for a real emergency, and then dump the rest of the contents in the toilet.

Then, even more shocking…

I fucking flush.

I feel my chest constricting, my ears ringing, and my mouth dry. I let myself fall to the floor as the weight of what I just did fully settles on me. I have nothing to fall back on. No cushion. Nothing to soften the blows that life throws my way. I'm not ready, I'm not ready at all, but I decide I have no choice even as I feel the panic attack looming right around the corner.

Now it's Zayne's turn.

If I can make this sacrifice, then so can he.

It's time to get clean. It's time to have the life we talked about. It's time to have a life we enjoy living.

I don't realize I'm crying until I feel the tears rolling hotly down my neck and into the collar of my shirt. I'm not sure what's happening lately, but it's as if I'm constantly crying now. I haven't cried as much in my entire life as I have in the past few weeks. I don't even know why.

I grab my car keys from the dresser and head over to Zayne's place, hoping Alyssa is home and will help me raid his room and possibly the entire basement while he's not there. Today seems to be my lucky day, because Alyssa answers my knock as if she's been waiting for me the entire time. I explain to her that I want to look for his stash and get rid of it, and she looks concerned for my well-being, rightfully so, but then lets me in and I get to work.

Even *I'm* worried about my well-being if I'm being truthful. I know it doesn't take much for him to snap and lose his shit, but I've never been on the receiving end of that before. Not to a degree where he could truly hurt me. It's been directed at plenty of people on my account, but never because I was the source of his anger. Suddenly I wonder if maybe I just have a death wish. It wouldn't surprise me, truly. I'm as self-destructive as they come, but this is a new level for me.

I start at the kitchenette, tearing it apart until I'm sure he's hiding nothing in it. I destroy his bathroom, office, and bedroom and find fifteen baggies of meth hidden in different places. The air vent return is next, and I find six more baggies, but then I think to look in the pool table and there are even more. My hands shake as I try to think of any more places I might have missed, but there's no way to know for now.

I'm just stunned at the amount I uncovered in the first place. Understanding the extent of his addiction is a big pill to swallow and now that my own drugs are gone I wish I had never thought to do this. Because when he comes home and figures out I have flushed his entire stash, he's going to be fucking murderous.

I don't want to be here for it, but I can't back out at this point. Alyssa said he is on his way home and she will to talk to him first, but she wants me to stick around to take over before it gets too ugly. I believe I will see a new side to him tonight, and I don't feel ready.

I hide in the kitchen pantry when I hear him, which is somehow bigger than my bathroom at home, *fucking rich people*, and wait for Alyssa's cue to come out and drop the bomb on Zayne. She wants to talk to him first, and evidently I make stupid mistakes when I'm scared. Like right now.

I will my breathing to quiet even more so I can hear anything over the sound of my erratic heartbeat, but we don't seem to be on the same page. I have to strain to hear, but still don't hear anything even as I stay frozen and hold my breath.

Finally, as if on cue, I hear the front door slam shut and the house gets eerily quiet. Alyssa is in the kitchen waiting for Zayne, as she said she would be, and I hear the clattering of dishes as she puts them away.

"How was your day, honey?" Alyssa calls out to him. The suspense causes my arms to be covered in goosebumps, and I shiver in the cold pantry. Or maybe I just feel cold because I know I'm fucked.

"Fine. I just need to take a shower and then I'm going to Hallie's." I even parked my car around the back of the house on the land so he wouldn't know I was here. I guess we were successful at that, at least.

"We need to talk, it'll only be a minute."

"Fine." Zayne sounds annoyed, and like he's in a hurry. I bet he is. "Please make it quick. I need to use the bathroom." *I need to go shoot up*, I think for him.

"I think I've pretended long enough to not know the extent of your drug addiction, but it ends now," Alyssa tells him, her voice stern. "Zayne. Meth? Really? Why?"

If I could see Zayne's reaction right now, I know he would be frozen in place. He's either racking his brain trying to figure out how she found his stash or hating me for my betrayal. Probably both, but I only want what's best for him, so he can hate me all he wants.

"What the fuck are you even talking about?"

"Really, you're going to pretend you didn't have over 20 baggies of meth in the basement?"

"What did you *do*?" Zayne asks her quietly, his voice betraying the rage I'm sure he's feeling right now.

The silence that follows his question is deafening, but then he explodes, and like a fucking tornado, he destroys everything in his path. I hear as he sweeps everything off the kitchen island, glass and ceramic shattering on the floor. Alyssa screams, and I'm sure she wants me to stay in this damned pantry but I can't witness his loss of control from in here for one more second. I push the door open quietly and freeze at the commotion around me. He is literally destroying the house. Shards of glass are scattered on the floor and almost every surface of the kitchen island as well.

"Stop!" Alyssa says, her face turning a deep red color as her chest heaves with her screams. "I will call the fucking cops!"

"Then call them! I *dare* you! Fucking call them!" Zayne laughs, a deranged sound escaping his throat, and he spreads his arms wide, as if in surrender. He turns around, his body locking up as we make eye contact, and he lets his arms fall limp at his sides.

Surrender, I let my eyes tell him.

Never, he seems to tell me back.

I hate that it's come to this. I hate that I've gone behind his back and confided in his mother, seeking her help to get him under control. I hate that I've betrayed him.

As if on cue, the betrayal shines fresh in his dark green irises, and as he walks closer to me they light up as if on fire, flashing emerald now. "How *fucking* could you, Hallie? I trusted you."

"I—"

"How *could* you?!" he screams at the top of his lungs, spit flying out of his mouth as he gives into his anger, his pupils swallowing the forest in his eyes, turning them almost completely black.

I'm motionless as his rage spills over and he grabs me by my throat, slamming me against the pantry door that now closes behind me as my head crashes into it. Pain explodes in the back of my skull as I bounce from the door. I reach up to soothe it but come away with blood instead.

A lot of it.

I look down at the dark red, sticky liquid coating my fingertips and then look at Zayne, seeing his horrified expression as he quickly glances from my hand to my face and back as if he's confused.

"Oh fuck. Oh shit." His hands come to cup my face, turning my head to see the extent of the damage. "Hallie, baby. *Oh my God!*" His face is contorted, crumpled, and creased. He looks like he might throw up.

That makes two of us.

The air rushes out of my lungs as he falls to his knees and hugs my waist. "I didn't mean to. It was an accident. I swear I didn't mean to do it. I'm sorry. I'm so, *so* sorry!"

"Don't." I shove him away hard as I attempt to keep myself upright. "Do not fucking touch me, Zayne." He quickly removes his hands from me and falls back to the floor on his ass, pulling his knees to his chest and hiding his face from me.

"Alyssa, I don't feel so—" I can feel my blood rushing south, I don't know why, but it feels backward.

My head is spinning, and I see white spots in my vision as if the world is closing in on me, the dark edges growing black.

And then—just when I think I got lucky, it happens.

Everything goes dark.

The pain in my head is not unbearable, but it is distracting me. I vowed I wouldn't feel, think, or even be present. As if on cue, he pulls my hair harder, exposing my neck, and making me more vulnerable as he pounds into my mouth, my eyes watering from the force of it.

I suddenly miss the out-of-body experience. I miss not being fully present. I hate him more and more as the minutes tick by, and I feel physical relief when he finishes.

A reward.

I'm being rewarded.

"Where can I come?" he grunts, as if he ever gives me a choice, spilling into my mouth before he's done with the sentence.

I don't swallow it, though.

I never fucking will.

He hands me a napkin, and I spit it all out, every single drop.

And then, as quickly as he arrived, he turns on his heel and walks out, leaving me to my self-loathing and shame.

Leaving me to feel again.

Leaving me to wish I could die.

But I could never be that lucky.

God takes a morbid pleasure in my suffering.

Knock. Knock. Knock.

I narrow my eyes at the door opening, sudden panic seizing me, as if Michael is about to walk through it.

The doctor comes into the room wearing black scrubs and a white lab coat, his stethoscope around his neck. His eyes have pity in them, and I suddenly remember why I'm here. As if on cue, my head begins to pound a steady rhythm and I close my eyes, willing this all to be over.

Willing *myself* to be over.

Maybe if I die, I can finally know peace.

But the doctor—Dr. Cain—doesn't leave, in fact, he sits on a small black stool with wheels that he rolls around the room with until he's facing me. "How are you feeling, Ms. Cox?"

What a loaded fucking question. Do you mean is my heart shattered into a million pieces, or did my boyfriend almost kill me? Is my head hurting, or is my anxiety so crippling that it overshadows any other pain I could possibly feel? Do I need more pain pills, or would I rather take a Xanax right about now? Fuck if I know the answer to any of those questions.

"I'm in pain," I say instead, it seems to sum everything up.

"On a scale of 0-10, with 10 being the most pain you've ever been in, how would you rate your pain right now?" He asks me, the concern in his features making him look like a father.

But how do you even answer that question, what's the most painful thing I've ever experienced? Was it being forced to do anal? Was it my mouth getting fucked? Or is it truly just a gash on my head?

No, this isn't my worst pain.

"A six." That seems more reasonable than all the other pain I've endured.

"I would like to know what happened."

"I slipped and fell in the kitchen. I hit my head." Alyssa and I make eye contact, and I hold my breath as I wait for her to contradict me or even for the doctor to call me out, but neither of them says anything. I'm sure Alyssa probably expects me to tell on her son, possibly press charges against him, but I can't do that. I need him almost as much as he needs me.

So what if love hurts?

It's always hurt before.

"You have ten stitches on your head and a concussion. I will be discharging you with the understanding that you will be supervised tonight in case you need to come back. The nurse will review the discharge paperwork with you and educate you on what to watch for with this concussion and what to do for certain situations."

"Thank you, Dr. Cain."

The IV pump makes an obnoxious beeping that lets me know the bag needs to be replaced, but thankfully I'm leaving, so I turn off the pump instead and unhook the tubing from my IV catheter.

The nurse, wearing navy blue scrubs and her hair in a messy bun, comes into the room with a new roll of transparent tape and gauze, and I get ready knowing she's taking out my IV. She looks between me and the pump, telling me with her eyes that she's annoyed I touched it, but I ignore her.

She goes over discharge paperwork with me and stresses the importance of seeing my primary care provider within the week. I sign, and they take me to the car in a wheelchair. Once we get in the car and I look at the time, I startle as I read four in the morning. What the *actual* fuck.

I was in the emergency room all night, and as I stare out into the dark sky, I wonder if Brit is even home, or who will take care of me. What if I never wake up?

Stop the fucking drama.

I mentally slap myself for the millionth time this week, cringing from just thinking of how much it would hurt in real life, and that hurts like a bitch too. I imagine what I look like through Alyssa's eyes. She probably thinks I'm insane, but then again, seeing how Zayne just acted she probably thinks I'm the sanest person she's ever met, making me ponder about his dad. Is he crazy too? Is he deranged just like us?

I won't pretend I'm well.

But Zayne really took it to new fucking heights last night.

I don't even know how I'm supposed to act anymore, what I'm supposed to do, if I can stay with him. He said he was sorry, but is he genuinely sorry? Is this a habit of his? How do I know this won't happen again?

I can't actually know any of it for sure, and while it scares me shitless, I also feel a strange comfort. Knowing he will lose his shit again is much more comforting than wondering about it. At least I know what to expect, and there's beauty in that.

"Hallie, I know he lost control with you, but I just want you to know he really is sorry," Alyssa says as she puts her seatbelt on. "He always is. He doesn't mean to be so angry. He doesn't mean to be the way he is."

"I know," I whisper, my words too loud for my head, which currently feels like it's being split in half.

"I'm bringing you home with me. I'll take care of you until you're better. Zayne can go get your clothes from your place."

A twisted part of me feels a sliver of excitement at staying at his house with him for the foreseeable future, but then the rational part of me tries to burst that bubble quickly, and my joy dissipates as fast as it came. "What if he hurts me again?" I ask, twisting my fingers. Maybe I need an anxiety ring. Yeah, that's probably it. That'll solve all my problems.

"He won't. He will be too busy feeling guilty about what he just did to you and withdrawing from the meth. It's going to hit him any minute."

"You're going to have your hands full. Are you sure you can't drop me off at my house? I can figure it out."

"No. He did this to you." Alyssa shakes her head, tears in her eyes. It's probably so hard to witness your child doing this, going through this. "I'm making sure you're okay. I wouldn't be able to live with myself, otherwise."

I close my eyes and recline the seat further, resting on my side to avoid lying on the gash in the back of my head. I try to think of better times, happier times, lighter times. I can't think of any, though, and I know that this is the happiest I've ever been even as the black takes over.

My life has always been a series of monochrome moments, but he brought some color into my life for the first time ever—even some pinks have slipped in uninvited.

I'm not ready to give that happiness up yet.

I'm not ready to give *him* up yet.

Let's just hope the reward is worth all this pain.

CHAPTER 40

ZAYNE

The guilt has been consuming me all night since my mom took Hallie to the hospital. I have no fucking idea what came over me, but I really fucked up this time.

Fuck.

I *really* fucked up.

The horror on her face as she touched the back of her head and her hand came away covered in blood will forever be imprinted in my mind. I will never be able to unsee that, will never be able to forget it. I really hope she's okay, and I know she will probably never talk to me again now, however I will die in peace as long as she's alright.

It's been about twelve hours since I last slammed, and I already feel my hands slightly shaking. My body is entering the stages of withdrawal from the meth, and I don't feel ready to face it. I can't face this alone. I need her. I fucking need her, but I hurt her, because that's what I do. Just like I warned her.

Hurt me so fucking good, then.

That's what she told me, but it doesn't feel like she still wants me to. It feels like we're done. It feels like the end. I refuse, though. I literally won't live without her. I *won't* do it.

Chills skate down my spine and I wrap the covers tighter around my body, and for the first time in a very long time I have bumped up the temperature in the basement. My body shakes and my teeth chatter. I'm pretty sure I'm running a fever, but before I can think about taking anything, a wave of nausea crashes through me and I barely make it to the toilet before hurling.

What. The. Fuck.

I know this is about to get so much worse, and I have no hope about how detox will go, if I'll crack and call my dealer. One thing is for sure, though, I'm going to fucking try. I'm going to try to leave drugs behind. I'm going to try to be better for her.

I'll try and try and try, even if it's the last thing I ever do.

CHAPTER 41

HALLIE

Hating Zayne is something I never considered before, but as I lie here on the couch reliving last night, I think it's as close as I'll ever come to doing it. He hasn't come to check on me, not fucking once, and I've been back for three hours. It may be seven in the morning, but I haven't slept a fucking wink all night between the pain in my head and my anxiety.

Fuck me for flushing my Xanax. I could use one right about now.

Alyssa seems to be keeping up with my pain medication schedule, which is precisely what I need because there's no way I would be able to right now. I see her round the corner and she stops in front of the couch to watch me as I pretend to sleep.

Does she ever even sleep?

She must be superhuman.

"Hallie," her voice is soft, "it's time to take your medicine again."

I open my eyes slowly, as if I could even fool her, and she gives me a quick smile and an eye roll. I sit up slowly and she helps me, grabbing on to my arm as I lift up and keeping me steady as I sway on my feet. I wait a moment while I let my blood pressure adjust, and then walk with her to the kitchen as she holds my hand like she would a toddler.

"Do you want water or juice?"

"Water, please." *Zayne, please.* I want Zayne, even though I don't say it out loud. Instead, I press my lips into a tight line to keep the words in.

Alyssa gives me water and my pain medication and I swallow it down hastily, not drinking enough water and gagging on it. I gulp more water to help it go down, and she looks like she's about to say something about it but doesn't. She acts like a mom, at least what I imagine a mom would act like, but how the hell would I even know.

"Thank you. I'm just going to go back to the couch."

"Not so fast, little lady. I have breakfast for you. You have to eat something so you don't feel sick to your stomach after taking those narcotics. Although you're a nurse, so you know these things."

"Fine… I'll eat something," I reply, even though I'm not feeling hungry at all. Food won't make a difference, I already feel like throwing up even if it's for entirely different reasons.

She retrieves something from the fridge, and I see the most colorful yogurt parfait in a mason jar. It's strangely perfect. I feel warm all over, and I realize it's from how she's treating me. I can't be latching on to her. I can't like her. Her son almost killed me a few hours ago. I need to leave. I need to go.

I need to get the *fuck* out of here.

"It's okay, honey—"

The memory doesn't knock before it comes in unannounced.

"It's okay, honey. Shhhhhh. It's okay… it will get better in just a minute." He whispers in my ear, his breath sending spiders crawling down my back as the shiver rakes through my body.

Stop being so fucking weak.

"Hallie!" Alyssa doesn't quite shake me, but she's digging her fingers painfully into my arm. Then I finally realize I'm dry heaving on the ground, on my hands and knees.

My chest is tight and my ears are ringing, but I make myself take deep breaths. In and out, just like I have been told to do for the better part of eleven years, just like I learned before I used the pills as a crutch. It seems to make everything better for now—who fucking knew oxygen was this essential?

"I'm okay." I stand up slowly with her help and sit at the kitchen island, the yogurt parfait no longer appetizing, but I don't want to be rude to her. She's helping me, after all. "Just a bad memory. It happens a lot, I should be used to it anyway."

She looks like she wants to probe for more information. In fact, she looks like she's about to, but then we both hear a crashing sound coming from the basement and her eyes follow the trail of the intrusion as if she could see through the walls if she tried hard enough.

You're not trying hard enough.

"I should go check on him..." She trails off. "He's not okay, you know. He should be at the hospital right now. He looks like death. The withdrawals have been extremely difficult on his body, and I'm sure he's dehydrated. I will probably be taking him in later, so if you want to... you could see him before I take you home."

Home.

One word.

What is home?

Do I have one? Have I ever? Will I ever?

Why does it hurt so bad that I've overstayed my welcome?

"Check on him first, and then you can take me to him. I'd like to say goodbye." I clear my throat as the tears burn the back of my eyes, and something like pity, no, *understanding* shines in her eyes.

Alyssa disappears down the hallway and I get busy with my parfait, because I desperately need food in my stomach, and it's not going to eat itself. My car is still parked at the back of the property, and I wonder how I'm going to pick it up later, especially not being able to drive currently. I was told no driving until all dizziness and migraines go away, which could be a week or two.

About ten minutes later, she returns with a pained expression, but instead of asking her anything I just stand and follow her to see Zayne. She opens the basement door and I immediately gag, the smell of shit and throw-up overwhelming my senses. He undeniably needs a hospital. I breathe in through my mouth as we go down the stairs, and I hold on to the wall the entire way down, but Alyssa is in front of me just in case I decide to take a tumble.

We finally make it down the stairs and I see Zayne's crumpled form on the bathroom floor, the one not attached to his bedroom. He's breathing, but he's pale as a ghost and covered in sweat. His body shakes and he moans as if he's in pain. My heart *lurches* in my chest, fucking *aches*, fucking *breaks* for him.

But why?

His heart never broke for me.

Why am I still so weak?

I kneel by his side and brush a wet lock away from his face, his hair plastered to the tiles on the floor and his ears and cheeks. He looks miserable. He looks innocent. He looks evil.

My brain is at war with itself, it won't come to terms with what happened a few hours ago and the person I would give my life up for. How did we get here? I shouldn't have ever come over. I shouldn't have asked for help. I shouldn't have taken his stash. I have no one to blame for this but my damn self, as always. It's my fault, just like everything else has always been.

What a fucking disappointment.

"Goodbye, Zayne," I whisper, letting the tears fall in earnest now.

He doesn't open his eyes, doesn't react, doesn't even breathe.

I slowly rise, ready to end my humiliation, and he clamps his hand around my wrist. It's not painful, and I could pull away if I really wanted to, but I don't. His eyes open and I see the storm brewing in them, I see the green colliding with the blue and gray and it steals my breath away. He's so beautiful.

The storm turns into a hurricane as his eyes flick rapidly from side to side, searching my own. I don't give him anything, only returning a blank stare. I force myself to let him fucking suffer, if he's even capable of such a thing. But as I look at him on the bathroom floor lying in the fetal position, I tell myself this is enough pain.

It's not. It's not. It's not.

I'm in the eye of the storm now.

"You will never say goodbye. Never." He draws in a shaky breath, "Let's take a few days to calm down, and then we can talk." He shudders, his skin covered in goosebumps. "I'm so fucking sorry. I blacked out, I don't even know what happened. I just felt so angry and—I'm so, so sorry, Hallie."

I don't tell him I forgive him. I don't tell him anything at all.

I say nothing as he continues to stare at me, as he looks even more broken than before, as the tears run down both cheeks, mixing with his sweat. I say nothing when he lets go of my wrist and takes my hand, bringing it to his face to make my palm cup his cheek, his sobs echoing in the small powder room as his body shakes from the force of them. And then, I still say nothing as I force myself to get up and walk away from him, leaving him behind with a shattered heart as I make my way back up the stairs.

The funny thing about shattered hearts is how no one warns you about this being the outcome, because when it comes to love… no one comes out intact.

I let myself surrender to the pain, though, because as I said before, pain is temporary.

Right?

CHAPTER 42

HALLIE

It's been two weeks and not one word from Zayne, not a fucking peep. I hate to sound needy, but I was hoping for a better apology, a little begging, some groveling, but *nothing*.

Static.

Radio silence.

Alyssa brought my car back a few days after she dropped me back off at my apartment, not bothering to come in or say hello. It made me wonder if I did something wrong, although I know that's my abandonment issues and low self-esteem screaming in my ear.

Maybe I took it a bit far with the stash, but I feel like I did it in his best interest and because I care about him, possibly even love him. How did he repay me? By almost breaking my skull and gifting me a huge hospital bill.

One step forward, five steps back.

I stop by the flower shop near my home and buy Alyssa a beautiful arrangement I wish someone would gift me instead. The sunflowers, tulips, and other flowers I can't even pronounce the names of are neatly arranged in a glass vase, sitting on the passenger side of my car as I make my way to their home. I hope she's home, because I don't want to have to leave the flowers on the porch, or worse, talk to Zayne.

I park in the driveway and walk to the door, refusing to knock three times, ringing the doorbell instead. I hold my breath as I wait, until I can no longer hold my breath anymore. Just as I'm about to give up and put the flowers on the ground, the door opens.

"Hallie, please come in!" Alyssa throws her arms around me, wrapping me in a tight hug that makes me feel strangely safe.

Irrational.

I'm irrational.

Hugs aren't safe at all.

"Alyssa, that's not necessary at all. I just wanted to give you these flowers as a thank you for taking care of me and getting me home safely. Getting my car back to me was a great bonus, too." I tell her with a wink, and she laughs.

"I'm so glad you're doing better, but really I insist. Come in, please, and stay for dinner."

I'm caught between a rock and a hard place as I try to think of excuses to get me out of this, but my brain completely fails me and I just nod my head once and follow her into the house. It looks the same as it did when I was last here, minus the shattered glass on the countertops and the ground, and I'm not entirely sure why I expect it to look any different, but I do.

Maybe it's because I feel different, so I expect everything else to look that way too. Zayne refused to break up, but then he also didn't contact me for two weeks. Where the fuck do we even stand? How do you even bring that up?

"Is he home?" My voice is so soft it's almost a whisper, and I look down at my feet as I sit on the couch.

"He's in his room. He's doing better, although not emotionally. I think he said he would give you space until you were ready to talk, and if it's not right now, then let me know so I can tell him in advance. Since you being here might make him think you want to see him and not me." She smiles at me, but it doesn't reach her eyes. I know he's hurting, and at some level, even though she knows he fucked up, she must hurt for her son.

Hurt for him.

I wonder what it would feel like for a parent to hurt for me, because something hurt *me* so severely that their heart couldn't take it.

I guess I'll never know.

"It's okay. I can talk to him, it's been long enough," I reply, my face flushing under her scrutiny.

Alyssa and I eat dinner in silence, and Zayne doesn't ever come up to find out I'm here. Her pork chops and mashed potatoes with brown gravy are phenomenal, but I really love the air-fried baby carrots the most. They taste almost sweet, and I wonder if she'd give me the recipe.

Just as I shove the last bite of food in my mouth, I hear the basement door opening. My stomach tumbles, and I suddenly feel as if eating dinner was the worst idea I've ever had, though I don't let it show. I occupy myself by gazing out the dining room window, convincing my brain that the dark clouds are more important than him entering the room.

It's definitely going to rain soon.

Zayne clears his throat, and I turn around to look at him, making eye contact so intense that all the hairs on my arms stand up and my breath is shaky as I inhale. "Hi…" he croaks out, and I notice something akin to nerves in his voice, as if he's scared that I hate him and never want to talk to him again. I don't hate him, but I know I should.

Damn it, I should.

But I *can't*.

"Will you be joining us?" I ask him, refusing to look away. The forest green of his eyes turns to bright emerald as he takes me in, his gaze drifting down my body like a physical touch.

"I didn't know I was invited."

"You can sit if you'd like."

"I'm actually all done. I'll be in my room if you need me," Alyssa says, her voice neutral. She leaves the room, taking her half-eaten meal with her as Zayne continues to stare at me from the archway that leads into the dining room.

"I'd like to go for a walk," he begins, "Do you want to join me?"

"It's going to rain soon..."

"Hallie, are you scared of the rain?"

Yes. No. I don't know.

I'm scared of *you*.

I'm scared of everything.

I want to scream it, but I've already said that to him, so it seems pointless now. "I'll walk with you," I say, as we take the back door and step out onto the deck, his pool visible from here. "However, before I leave today, I need to know what's happening here between us." We continue to walk closer to the pool this time, and I can feel the beginning of a drizzle as the first drop falls on my cheek. I reach up to wipe it off, his eyes trailing the path of my finger, and he turns to face me.

"You're not leaving this house today." There's a finality in his tone that lights a fire low in my belly, and I'm ready to see where it leads.

Focus.

Don't stray from the course so early.

"Oh?" I breathe, ready for him to take over, control me, tell me what to do, make me do it. I need to feel it again. I miss the urgency, the burning, the fucking desperation he makes me feel. I miss *feeling*.

Make me feel.

Take me.

I need you to take it.

I tell him with my eyes, betraying my body and my brain. They'll never find out if I don't say it out loud. And Zayne understands, he *always* does.

He closes the distance between us, his black Converse meeting my gray Vans until he's almost stepping on my toes. I study them as if the black spot on my right shoe is more interesting than he is, but I can't even fool myself, so I know I'll never be able to fool him. He knows *all* of me.

Zayne grips my chin hard, drawing a whimper from my lips, and forces me to look up at him. I don't see the pain in his eyes. I don't even see regret. Instead all I see is hunger... desire. I know it's wrong, I know I should at least make him apologize, except right now I don't even want to. I don't want anything to ruin this moment.

His hand slides from my chin, up my jaw, and to the back of my neck where he tugs at the loose strands falling to my waist and forces my head back, his mouth crashing into mine in the same manner waves crash against the rocks.

Inevitable.

Zayne's tongue brushes against the seam of my mouth, as if expecting me to open for him, but I don't, I *won't*.

Chase me.

He yanks my hair harder and my mouth opens on a gasp, his tongue colliding with mine, swooping in and out of my mouth. I can't even breathe as he devours my lips in a way that makes him look starved, sucking on my bottom lip and then biting me hard until I taste blood in my mouth. *Yes.*

His free hand comes to my hip and pulls me closer, which I didn't realize was possible in the first place. I rest my hand on his abs and they jump, then I skate my hand all the way to his chest and grab onto his shirt, my nails digging softly into his skin.

I feel his chest flex underneath my fingers as he shifts his hand from my hip to my ass, squeezing me hard and making my head spin in circles. I buck my hips and try to rub against him, but instead of letting me, he just smiles against my lips. This is the best and worst kind of torture.

And I want more.

We keep fighting a war with our mouths, tongues colliding, teeth clashing, as we each battle for dominance. I moan into his mouth, the sound muffled as he pushes his tongue into mine, and his groan reverberates through my body, echoing until every single cell feels it.

"More," I whisper as I reach up to grab his hair, pulling hard as I fight against the urgency my body is feeling to let him take me right here, right fucking now. I don't even care if his mom watches at this point, I just want him, *need* him inside of me.

Zayne bends down a fraction and both his hands go to my ass, lifting me up to him. I circle my legs around his hips and lock my ankles, continuing to kiss him, holding his face between my hands. I realize it's almost sweet, but there's nothing sweet about us. We're only capable of wild, urgent, *desperate.*

I expect him to take us to a more secluded area, somewhere more private, especially as the rain falls harder. Instead, he kneels on the cool concrete and lies me down on my back, yanking my yellow sundress up to my waist and pulling my panties off in one swift movement as I reflexively help him by lifting my ass.

Spreading my legs for him, I relish in the power I have over him. He thinks he's always the one in control, or maybe he wants me to believe that, but I see him when I bring him to his knees, I see what I do to him as he comes undone for me every single fucking time, and it's more addicting than any drug I have ever tried.

He smiles down at me as he flicks the button of his jeans open and pulls them down with his underwear in one swoop, exposing his long, thick cock as the rain beats down on us, making his olive skin glisten against the soft glow of the moonlight in the dusk.

Zayne gets closer, his body now covering mine as he pushes into me with one thrust. He grabs my hips and yanks me closer, the concrete scraping my back, but I don't even care about the pain, I just want him. I wrap my legs around his waist to bring him even closer, until there's no space between us, just our bodies and souls colliding with each other, violent in their assault.

It's as if all time stands still, and I don't understand the significance of this moment until it's too late. Regretfully, I close my eyes for one brief moment as I enjoy the feel of him, and I wish I hadn't missed even one second of him, not even half of one second. I want to see all of him.

I feel the pressure building in my belly as I climb higher and higher toward my release, my feet dangling just over the edge. He reaches up to my chest, his finger splaying on it as he circles his hips faster, harder, but then his hand comes up to my neck and wraps around it. His fingers squeeze lightly at first, barely even there. He picks up his pace and his fingers start to tighten even more, until I can't breathe at all. It's not panic I feel however, it's a weird sense of peace.

I relax into his grip as I feel the orgasm within reach, and I reach down and grip his ass with both hands. I plant my heels on the ground and fuck him back, circling my hips, grinding my clit against him until my lungs are burning. My chest is on fucking fire as my vision goes black and stars explode behind my now-closed eyelids. I hear him groan in my ear as he spills into me, growing very still on top of me as I feel my body slipping, tumbling, falling.

"You're not fucking leaving me," He slaps me hard in the face to bring me back, the sting sharper as the rain coats my skin, but I open my eyes and look into his own, seeing me, seeing us, and never wanting it to end. "Not now, *not ever.*" I want to put this moment in a box and lock it up forever. I want to freeze time and stay here instead, but I know it's going to end soon, and I'd rather do it myself.

I reach up to kiss him, wrapping my legs tighter around him so he doesn't leave me yet. I can't bear it. "Why is it always so easy to fall back in step?" I whisper, looking up at the sky as the rain falls sideways, soaking us to the bone.

"Because we were made for each other." His eyes betray

everything, and for the first time maybe ever, he wears his feelings on his sleeve. It's beautiful. He is.

"But the stars didn't align for us, not even a little bit." The sadness in my voice almost makes me cringe, but I force myself to not take it back.

"No, but they will. I swear they fucking will."

And I don't even care that I know we're fucked up. I don't even care that we should count our losses and move on while we still can. I don't even care that I know how this ends.

He's my favorite sin, and I'm not quite ready to repent.

CHAPTER 43

HALLIE

The colors of the sunset explode over the sky as we cross the bridge onto the island. I fixate on the crimsons and oranges, marveling again at how my eyes are finally appreciating color for the first time in eleven years.

I know it's because Zayne is sitting next to me, one hand on the steering wheel and the other gripping my thigh. Life looks less black and white with him by my side, and I'm not sure how that makes me feel yet, but I decide to embrace it for now. Embrace the happiness, the sadness, the anger, the pain.

I feel it all.

Life never used to be a spectrum of emotions for me, I had turned that off long ago, but Zayne pulled me from the shallow to the deep end and then let me go. He doesn't understand that even though I know how to swim, I'm fucking terrified when I can't reach. I'm barely five feet tall. Which brings me back to now. I don't want to be swimming in the fucking deep end, I want to go back to shallow ground where I feel safe. I want to go back to not feeling anymore.

I remove his death grip from my thigh and slip my hand into his, enjoying how perfectly we fit. His hand wraps around mine, fingers interlaced, and I glance his way, getting a perfect view of his profile. Straight nose, strong jaw, full lips, long lashes.

Perfection.

We pull into a parking garage and he says this is his friend's family's condo, where we are supposed to be spending the weekend. There's a party happening here tonight, but I'm just glad to be near the ocean again. Zayne removes our suitcases from the trunk, glancing in my direction with a smile on his face, and I wonder what he's planning as he looks me over.

The elevators open up for us as soon as we push the button, and the silence is loud in the enclosed space. I feel him staring at my face as I keep looking forward, knowing he hates when I do that and hoping he will punish me for it.

"Naughty girl, you know exactly what you're doing right now," he says softly, as the elevator comes to a stop and we step out.

I don't reply. I simply trail after him as we pass rows and rows of doors. He seems to have been here before as he heads straight for the door he's looking for and unlocks it.

The condo is less spacious than I thought it would be, and I'm starting to wonder how many people are coming to this party. It's an open floor plan with the living room being the center of attention as soon as you open the door, along with one sofa and a loveseat arranged to be shaped like a 'L'. The coffee table is on a large rug that spans half the living room, and it's covered in palm trees. The decor is tropical and beachy—almost annoyingly, not my style at all.

I follow Zayne into one of the bedrooms. The walls are covered in wallpaper, an obnoxious black and white striped monstrosity of a pattern, though I force myself to keep a neutral face, since I don't know who owns this place. The queen bed is in the center of the room, the headboard a tufted cream. The one thing

I already love is the large window next to the bed. No blinds or curtains are blocking it, and you can see the expanse of the ocean from here. The beach is deserted and the waves make a path on the sand, further and further up as the tide comes in.

We get settled and move our luggage to one side of the room, the sun completely set now, as I sit on the bed to wait for Zayne to give me instructions. I don't know when the party is going to start, and quite frankly, after an eight-hour drive I do not feel like changing or getting ready. I decide I'll be staying as I am, not bothering with makeup or a fancy outfit.

I lay down in bed, and when my head hits the pillow, my eyes drift closed. I check my phone and realize an hour has passed. I'm pretty sure I napped the entire time I was supposed to be waiting, and I stir as I begin to hear the beginnings of party music in the background, as well as the loud voices of the people arriving. I scan the room and realize that Zayne is not here, he left me to take my nap alone.

Where the hell did he go?

I hope he at least is still here somewhere in this house, because I can't imagine making small talk with people I have never met before or even with ones I have. *I hate small talk so much.*

I open the door to the bedroom and slip into the hallway, noticing people piled up on the couches. As I get closer, I see about twenty others circling the kitchen island. Some people are opening containers of alcohol, others are throwing back shots, while some are smoking.

There's a huddle of people in the living room that I overlooked before. Aside from the ones piled up on the couches, there's others on the ground in front of them. As I step closer, I notice someone handing a lighter to Zayne and my heart stops along with my legs. My knees get weak and my body shakes with such force that I'm afraid I will fall to the floor, but I steady myself as I take deep breaths.

I walk quickly and glance over someone's shoulder to peer down at Zayne. His eyes are closed as if he's asleep, but no, his eyebrows are furrowed and the cute wrinkle between them is winking at me. I begin to relax until I see the smoke curling out of his mouth as his lips curve in a lazy smile. His friend, or whoever, nudges him and he opens his eyes. As they lock on mine, I feel something shift. I'm not sure what it is I just caught him doing, but he looks guilty, glancing down at his hands where he clutches—

A glass fucking pipe.

My stomach dips and I turn on my heel to run back to the bedroom, locking the door behind me to keep him out. Sadly though, he opens it with a spoon and locks it behind him.

A fucking spoon. Damn cheap locks.

For a luxury condo, they really should invest in better locks. What if I was running from a serial killer?

We stare at each other from across the room, the tension between us coiled to the point of snapping. Zayne rests his back against the door and I turn my attention back to looking out the window, but all I see is the glare and his reflection taunting my very existence. What the fuck do I even do now?

It's time for him to step the fuck up if he wants to make this work, or I'll have to make some difficult decisions that I'll need to stick to this time around. "Zayne..."

"Don't," he begs, and I turn around to face him to deliver the words that hurt me more than he can understand. "Don't fucking say it. Please."

"You need help."

"I'm fine. It's under control. This was just for fun, it won't happen again."

"That's what you always say. Now look at us." I chuckle, "Just fucking look at us. You need a rehab facility, and you need professional help. Your mom and I can't help you anymore."

Zayne looks flustered, his face flushed a deep red and his pupils so dilated I can see them from across the room. He looks at me, really looks, and shakes his head slowly. I can feel the beginnings of my heart splitting and I face away from him, convincing myself that he will concede if I beg enough.

"Hallie. I know you think I'm your project, but you can't fucking fix me. No one can. I'm not broken, and I don't want your fucking help."

I recoil as if he's slapped me, because it feels like he just did. He's bringing my deepest fears to the surface, and I feel raw and exposed. "Zayne, it's me or the drugs. Make your choice."

"This isn't fucking fair, Hallie." He's panting now, his chest moving rapidly as if he's having trouble breathing. "Please don't make me choose, you won't like the choice."

"So that's it then? Because you just chose." I dig my fingernails into my arm in the same way I did at the emergency department when he was manic, but this time I don't feel it. Nothing compares to the pain in my chest.

"I guess that's it."

I feel like I have whiplash, constantly being jostled by him until I don't understand what the fuck is happening, but this? This is the most straightforward he has ever been. There's not one doubt in my mind that meth is his number-one priority from right now until forever.

I'm *done*.

I glance over at our luggage in the corner of the room, between the wall and the dresser, and start gathering everything I see on the bed and in the bathroom. I head for my suitcase and drop it on the floor and start tossing all my belongings inside after getting it open. I zip it closed, struggling to breathe. Not sure if it's from anxiety or if the pain in my chest is a manifestation of the pain in my heart.

Zayne doesn't move, doesn't breathe, doesn't blink. He stares openly at me as I stand my suitcase up again and begin to roll it toward the door, but he's still blocking it. I try to go around him but he steps in front of me, and we dance around each other for a few seconds, forcing an exasperated sound out of me. "Get out of my way." I feel my patience slipping, I just want to get the fuck out of here so I can breathe again.

He didn't choose me. He didn't choose me. He didn't choose me.

"You're not fucking going anywhere." He narrows his eyes at me, and for a fraction of a second, I don't recognize him, this person he has become. These black eyes with barely any forest green visible do not belong to the same guy I shared my deepest, darkest secrets with.

"You made your choice." My voice cracks on the last word, and I curse myself for showing weakness. I want so badly to be strong, indifferent, uncaring, yet I can no longer achieve that around him.

I push him aside, barely, and he budges just a step with a look close to surprise crossing his face, but it only lasts a brief moment before a mask of indifference slips back over his features. It was, however, enough to walk around him. When I make it to the doorknob however, his hand meets my wrist in a tight grip and he twists it, until I hear a very loud pop. I breathe through the pain, the burn, the fucking agony, but I refuse to show him how much it hurts. He twists it harder though, and tears fill my eyes, though they don't spill.

Zayne lets my wrist go and I automatically cradle it to my chest, but then he quickly closes in on me, trapping me against the door. His breath is warm on my cheek and smells like mint and what he was smoking, but I don't flinch as he lightly drags his nose along my skin. Tears shine in his eyes now, a silent plea, but he doesn't speak. In fact, he says nothing at all.

Someone pushes the door open, bumping into us, and Zayne takes a few steps back, expecting me to do the same. I take my opportunity and quickly walk out of the room, expecting him to run after me, although he doesn't.

As I walk down the hall and into the kitchen, a guy standing by the sink looks in my direction. His beach blond hair looks almost green, and I almost want to tell him it's not his color, but as he looks down at my suitcase and raises an eyebrow, I ask him if he can give me a ride into town instead, just to a motel, and he indulges me. I'm not sure if he's drunk or high, and I probably should have asked him, but as I sit in his passenger seat I realize I don't care if I make it to the motel or if we flip off this bridge. I just want to get away from *him*. I want to hear myself again. My mind has been far too quiet under Zayne's dominance. But honestly, the only thing on my mind now is my painful wrist. It's as if the more miles I put between Zayne and me, the more my body wants to remind me he keeps hurting me.

I make it to the motel, and I'm slightly scared and concerned about my choices, but I check in and slip into the room alone. I set my suitcase on the floor next to the bed, unzipping it so I can find spare clothes. My phone vibrates with a text message from Zayne, only I decide to not open it—the previews on my notifications have been turned off for a while, so I can't see that either. Instead, I dial Brit's number and wait for her to pick up, but she never does. The phone just rings and rings and rings, then sends me to voicemail. Scrolling my contacts, I think about anyone in my life who would be willing to come get me eight hours away from our hometown, but not one fucking person comes to mind. Except for maybe one.

Courage is a funny emotion; it rises during the most uncertain times. I gather mine up and dial Daniel's number, and he picks up on the first ring. I take the phone away from my ear and set it on speaker, looking at my screen to find the time. Ten at night, so he should be in bed if he's the good boy I know he is.

"Hallie?" His voice is barely above a whisper, confusion laced in my name.

"Daniel, I need your help…"

"What's wrong?" His voice has lost the thickness of sleep and is now very alert, concerned, and something else I can't identify. "Where are you?"

"I'm right outside South Padre. I know that's far… but I left him, and I have no way home. I can't reach anyone and I need to get out of here. I need to leave, please, please, *please* help me," I beg him, and this time, the weakness in my voice doesn't bother me.

Watch me break a little.

Will you pick up my pieces?

"Text me the address, I'm on my way." I hear rustling in the background, probably him putting on some clothes. "And Hallie, don't let anyone in. Wait for me. I'll call you when I'm there, I won't knock."

I won't knock.

Does he know? Is it that obvious? Is my damage really there for everyone to see? "Thank you," I reply, letting the tears fall from my eyes and sniffling into the phone. "I'm leaving my phone on loud, but I know you have a long drive, so I'm going to try to get some rest. I can drive back so you can sleep in the car."

"That works. I'll see you soon."

"See you soon then." I put the phone down, my wrist throbbing to the rhythm of my heart. Seems like I need something for the pain, but I'm out of luck. I settle for the ice machine in the hallway, icing it for fifteen minutes before I decide to go to bed.

I turn off the lights and lie down, but sleep never finds me. I just toss and turn all night. My mind is running on overdrive and I'm unable to shut it down. I can't get it to turn off. I can't make it stop. What did Zayne do to me?

The hours pass very slowly, my life playing over and over on repeat, and I can't help but crave Xanax with every cell in my body. I try to close my eyes, but the memories come unbidden. I shake my head as if it will rid me of them, but my eyes keep growing more tired, and Daniel still hasn't texted me. I remember another day, another time, another nightmare...

"Daddy loves his little girl."

Toss.

His fingers dig into my hip and I flinch.

Turn.

My world goes black.

Toss.

I open my eyes, and there's blood running down my right leg, warm and sticky and dirty with him.

Turn.

I want to forget, forget, forget.

Toss.

I find the razor blade and return it to the inside of my thighs.
Turn.
I just want to die, die, die.

My phone rings, startling me enough to make all my thoughts vanish into thin air, and when I look at my screen, Daniel's name is on it. I take a deep breath and answer him.

"I'm here." His voice sounds tired, and rightfully so. He drove all night to get to me.

"I'll be right out," I reply, my body heavy and my wrist in pain.

I gather my belongings, use the bathroom, and brush my teeth, then head out to the parking lot. His black BMW is parked in the spot closest to the glass door and he looks handsome as the early morning sun kisses his skin. He looks like a golden god, a blue-eyed angel.

Daniel gets out of the car to grab my bags for me and then opens my door as well. I slip in and get comfortable, even though I intended to drive. He doesn't seem like he's going to let me though, and I could honestly use the nap.

But so could he.

Closing my eyes, I recline my seat and take a deep breath, hearing him get in the car a few seconds later. He doesn't say anything and I don't either. Instead, I let him drive me far, far away.

Away from all I've ever loved.

Away from myself.

Because every piece of me belongs to Zayne, and I left it all with him.

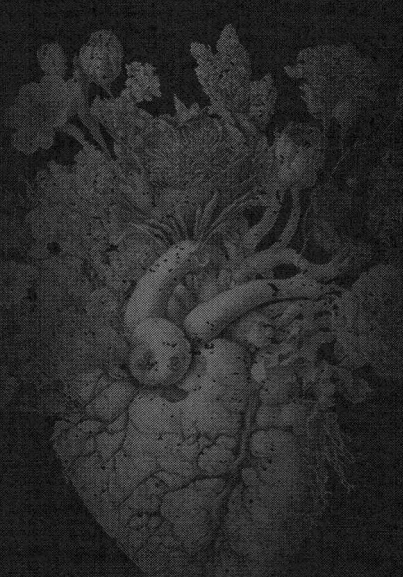

CHAPTER 44

ZAYNE

Hallie left me, and my world turned fucking black again. I stopped taking my meds and went back to the monster as if I had never left it, and the darkness? The darkness is tight on my heels, waiting for me to trip, and I just fucking might. Everything feels pointless now, I don't have the will to live anymore.

I'm tired of feeling miserable, unwanted, and out of control. I know it's my own damn fault. She left me for a reason, but I thought she'd be here forever, until the fucking end. Hallie made me empty promises and I just want to fill them back up, *I want her back.*

I didn't really mean I chose the meth over her, but I was high, and I only cared about that feeling then. Once I crashed, though… the force of what I did hit me so hard it knocked the breath out of my lungs. I didn't want her to fucking leave me, ever, but I can't seem to hold on to anything at all. One thing is certain though, she can't change me. She will never be able to. I'm too deep in the clutches of this addiction.

Addiction.

There, I said it. I want to accept the fact that I have a problem, I'm just not sure I'm mentally prepared to deal with it. I don't want to think of all the things I can do to fix myself, for I'm not even sure I want to do that either. I still debate if fixing me is enough to bring her back, but something tells me it's not. Coming out of this is an uphill battle, and now I'll forever be an addict. No matter how many rehabs I go to, meetings I attend, and milestones I accomplish, I'll always be this to everyone.

Broken.

Damaged.

A fucking junkie.

I drive to the party in a haze from the meth and the heartbreak, and I'm not really sure which one is gripping me harder. It's as if they're battling for dominance as I struggle to... *live.*

The lights are all turned on outside, and there are so many people hanging out in front of the house that not even a patch of grass is visible. I park across the street and walk into the house, the smell of sweat, sex, and drugs in the air. I have one goal tonight: to get so drunk and so high that she ceases to exist.

Life, however, has different plans. I'm not sure if there's a magnetism that keeps pulling us toward each other. If it's our souls seeking each other out, or if the universe just likes to fucking mock me, but as I see Hallie sitting on Daniel's lap, I decide it must be the universe.

Mocking me.

Laughing at me.

Pointing at me.

Snap out of it.

Hallie is drinking from a solo cup as Daniel watches her every move, and she gets even cozier on his lap as the drink starts mixing in her blood, relaxing her visibly. It's subtle. Probably no one else would even notice; he definitely wouldn't. But me?

I know every single fucking part of her darkness, and I don't run from it. I want to hide *in* it, embrace it.

She just won't let me anymore.

I go around the couch and stay out of sight, coming up behind them and crouching to their level so only they can hear me as I get close to where their faces almost touch each other, cheek to cheek.

"I told you next time he touched you, I would fucking kill him. Do you not take me seriously, Hallie?"

I see her stiffen, and I feel oddly satisfied, proud, and somehow the opposite at the same time. I want it to be *me*. I want her to want *me*.

"Zayne, please don't make this harder than it needs to be. I can leave quietly, and we can forget we ever saw each other."

Forget? "It's that easy? You just forget?" I laugh, an ugly sound even to my own ears, and I know there's no humor in it. "You can pretend all you want, but I know better. I know you cry yourself to sleep every night. You're probably popping those pills again, but you can lie to him," I point at Daniel, "just not me. Because even if you want to hide from me, you can't. Your darkness fucking loves me, and I can wait this out."

"You're going to be waiting forever."

"Hallie, please talk to me, alone." It sounds like I'm begging. She probably thinks I'm pathetic, and maybe I am, but I can't let us end this way. "Just for a minute, please, give me the chance to explain myself. I want you back. I never wanted you to leave."

"There's nothing to explain. You said everything that needed to be said last time, and I don't mean to hurt you when I say this, but I will never get back together with you. I will not continue to do this to myself. You chose the drugs, so embrace them. Take them all if you want. You lost me."

The knife twists in my chest, and I'm out of breath, the pain so agonizing I almost drop to my knees. It's as if my chest is caving in, and it's an agony I've never felt full force before now. I don't need to feel them to know there are tears on my face, and as I reach out to wipe them away, I see a flicker of emotion in her eyes.

There she is.

My Hallie.

However, it doesn't last long, and she doesn't wait for a response, leaving me behind and heading out of the party.

To wherever this *stranger* goes now.

With him.

Not me.

Never me anymore.

I'm just not sure I can keep doing this.

I'm not sure I can find the will to live.

I don't know how long it takes me to get home, but sometime later, I stumble down the basement stairs, not even bothering to be quiet since my mom isn't home. I just want to go to sleep. I want to forget her, I want to pretend she never happened. In a moment of weakness, I go to my bed and smell my pillows, looking for traces of her. Looking for breadcrumbs that will ease the ache in my chest.

I inhale deeply and she's still *here*. She never left. I'll have to deal with what I have for now until I can get her back. Her words echo in my brain, in my ears, in my body.

I will never get back together with you.

You lost me.

You lost me.

You lost me.

I shake my head, trying to rid myself of the memory, but it's pointless. I'll never forget. She doesn't want me, and I'm not good enough for her, so it makes this choice even easier. I need to let Hallie finally be free of me, and I know I'm not strong enough for that. There's only one way out of this relationship. I've been afraid of the darkness for so long but giving in now sounds more appealing than ever.

Is this where you wanted me?

Is this the weakness you were waiting for?

I'm here, come fucking take me.

The darkness whispers back, and I know what I have to do.

My mom is on a flight home, so I know she won't be able to get here on time or even listen to the voicemail. I tell her goodbye and that I love her. I tell her it's not her fault and she is wonderful. I tell her everything she should hear but I haven't cared enough to say.

But I save my tears for Hallie.

I dial her number, knowing she will reject the call. It goes to voicemail on the first ring, and I do my best not to break down before talking.

"Hallie, it's me. I just wanted to say I love you, and I know that's random, but I know I didn't say it enough. I love you so much, and I hope you're okay. I wanted to tell you goodbye and say it's not your fault, so please don't feel guilty. Don't hate me, either. I hope you remember only our best times. Goodbye, Hals." I turn off my phone so I don't lose my courage if she calls, I know she will only do it out of pity, because she's a good person. Even after everything, I know she doesn't want this for me.

I grab my rig and go to bed, wanting to smell her one last time. I put the powder on the spoon, double if not more than the amount I usually take, and add water, then cook it and drop a cotton ball in it. I draw up the monster into the syringe and find my tourniquet, quickly wrapping it tightly around my arm, and then I line up the needle to the first vein that's accessible.

I won't be picky now, not when it's over.

I inhale deeply, feeling the tears prick my eyes and blinking them back, and I remind myself that I don't have time to be weak. I'm on a mission, and I need to finish.

I slam.

I smell the pillows, inhaling deeply as if I can memorize her even in death. I would drag her to my grave with me if she were here. I would never let her go. My body gets that familiar sensation I now know so well, but it's magnified, multiplied.

I feel... *euphoric.*

Like I've never felt before.

The rush is too strong. My heart is beating out of my chest and I'm sweating and I want to throw up. I know how this ends.

And I *feel* it.

The boat is sinking, and I'm running out of time.

And now I know.

I feel it in my bones.

I'm about to drown.

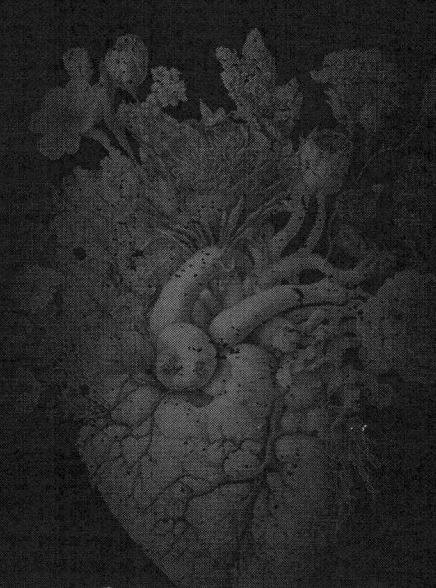

CHAPTER 45

HALLIE

Growing up, I always noticed the sun, but now there's no warmth. All the colors dimmed again, as if they only presented themselves for a short time again to mock me. It's almost as if the colors and the short-lived happiness blended together and permeated my barriers.

Osmosis.

I know it's all connected, connected to him. He's not in my life anymore, and the light has vanished again, my world black and white in the same way it used to be just mere months ago. Somehow it feels like a lifetime, the months that have passed, and some silly part of myself feels as if I'm different now.

Pathetic.

I'm crying in my bed as Brit walks Daniel out, and I feel guilty that he had to witness my mental breakdown. I feel awful he knows how much I care about Zayne, because even after all of it, I know he wants a chance with me, and I don't mind putting him on the back burner. I know it sounds fucked up, but solitude and I will never be together.

If Zayne and I are done, I have to find someone else.

My phone vibrates on my nightstand, and when I flip it over, I see a new voicemail from him. I know I shouldn't be surprised but seeing his name on my screen is still like the first time, and it makes my stomach flip.

I decide to play the voicemail, and I'm not sure if it's the overly quiet background, the way his voice cracks on every other word, or even the way he's clearly crying, but all the hairs on my arms stand on end. This doesn't feel like a regular goodbye. This feels like something is horribly wrong.

I jump off the bed and begin to put my shoes on, and Brit comes in at the same time as I stand up to get my keys from the dresser, ready to go. She narrows her eyes at me and puts her hands over her hips, blocking my doorway so I can't get out. Unfortunately for her, I don't have time or patience left for her shit. "Move, Brit. I love you, but fucking move," I say, pushing her softly to get through.

"He called you, didn't he?" She moves out of the way for me, spinning on her heel to follow me out of my room.

"He's in trouble, I need to—"

"He's *always* going to be in trouble, Hallie. He's a drug addict," she says softly, and for just one moment it makes me want to hit her.

"He needs me, Brit. I need to go to him, so please move aside." My voice shakes, maybe from the anger or the fact that I'm falling apart. But it doesn't matter, I just need to fucking go to him.

"You need to let him go if you want to find yourself again."

"I don't know who I am without him anymore."

I run out of the apartment and speed the entire way to his house, not bothering to close my doors or even take my keys out of the ignition when I arrive. I don't knock, I just open the front door and run to the basement door, pushing it open so quickly it slams against the wall. I flip the light on and run down the basement stairs. It's quiet and cold and feels empty, but I know it's not.

I know he's here.

I get to his bedroom door and it's wide open, but his room is dark, the lights off. I flip them on and he's on his side, face on a pillow. As I come around to look at him, I gasp. I can't hold it in.

There's vomit on the pillow and the side of his face. His lips are blue, actually more than just his lips, his face is blue. I snap out of it and grab him by his shoulders, but he's dead weight and it's fucking difficult to put him on the floor by myself. His limbs awkwardly dangle from the bed and hit the ground hard, yet I still manage to get him on his back.

I slap his face, then check his pulse and feel nothing at all.

I dial 911 and set it on speakerphone while I begin chest compressions like his life depends on it, because it most definitely does; I can feel his ribs cracking underneath my hands. I give the most basic information and relay that this is clearly a drug overdose.

"Zayne! How dare you? How fucking dare you?!" I scream until my lungs burn and my voice is hoarse. "Do not fucking leave me!" The tears fall from my eyes and onto his bare chest, making my hands slippery on him, but I can't stop. I pause to check his pulse—

Still nothing.

I wipe frantically at his chest to get the moisture off, then I interlace my fingers and put all my weight into the next round of compressions. More ribs give way with sickening crunches, but I barely have a grasp on reality.

His skin is still warm.

He can't be gone.

He *can't* fucking *leave* me.

How fucking *dare* he?

Voices bring me back to the present, and I put even more effort into my compressions, afraid I'm not doing enough, afraid I'll never be enough and he will die because of it.

Please don't die. Please don't die. *Please* don't die.

Two paramedics go down the steps with a board, and another hauls something in his hands. "We have him from here, ma'am," the shorter man says, and he kneels on the ground next to me, ready to take over my compressions. But I don't stop, can't stop. I don't want to let him go—

"We need to take over so we can get him to a hospital before it's too late."

Before it's too late.

It's not too late.

Or is it?

I nod because I don't think I can speak, and he takes over, beating on Zayne's chest with much more strength than I could ever muster.

"Do you know how much he took?"

"No, I just found him like this." My voice cracks, and all semblance of control is lost. "Please, please save him. *Please* don't let him die!" I sob again and I have snot running down my face, but I don't fucking care. If he dies, nothing will ever matter again.

Don't die on me, please, baby.

Please don't leave me.

I can't live without you.

I watch them put him on the board as sobs take over my body again, the paramedics carrying the dead weight with ease. I'm unable to breathe, and I feel a panic attack waking up in my chest. It rouses slowly, but it's clear that it's strong as my hands begin to shake, and I start hyperventilating.

Two paramedics strap him in, then carry him up the stairs, and as soon as they make it to the top, they put him on a stretcher while a third person straddles Zayne and begins chest compressions again.

I get on my hands and knees and gasp for air, but it doesn't work. Instead, I sit down and put my head between my knees, gulping air down, even though it feels as if I will throw up any moment. My heart beats so fast it feels like it's speeding out of me, and I will it to pump the fucking brakes.

Once it settles, I look for his phone on the bed and find it turned off. Turning it on, I run back up the stairs to get back in my car.

I watch the paramedics disappear.

I watch them take him away from me.

Away.

Just like he was before.

But different.

This isn't a choice.

I didn't want this.

I just want him to live.

The ICU is cold, dark and gloomy. The lights in the rooms dimmed or completely turned off. The eerie quiet is broken by the constant sounds of the monitors, a language only the nurses know by heart. The glass doors give you insight into the ruination of each patient, while at the same time you have no fucking clue what could be wrong watching from the sidelines.

That's Zayne.

He's intubated, sedated, and with tubes attached all over his body, including a new permacath that graces his neck for the CRRT machine filtering his blood, saving his kidneys and his life. At first glance, though, you would never know this happened from a methamphetamine overdose. You would probably think he had some sort of accident, or maybe has a chronic condition.

Live.

Live for me.

I called Alyssa on the way to the hospital, and it was, without a doubt, the most difficult phone call I've ever made. I reached her when she was just turning on her phone and walking out of the plane, and she had yet to listen to his voicemail.

It's been five days since his overdose and she just now left the hospital, so I came to sit with him to keep him company. I know we aren't together anymore, but the thought of him being alone during this time makes a new panic attack bubble up.

The sliding glass doors open as the doctor and nurse stand in front of them, and I hold my breath as they come into the room. They look over at Zayne and then at me as if trying to figure out if I'm allowed information. I clear my throat and pull out my phone, ready to call Alyssa if they need her.

"Good morning, Ms. Cox." The doctor looks down at his tablet, his white hair shining silver against the monitor lights. "Will his mother be in today?"

"Good morning. I'm really not sure, but I can call her if you need me to?"

"Yes, please. We do have some news."

I call Alyssa, and she answers on the second ring. I explain that they have news and she says she can't come in due to work but that I can put her on speakerphone, and she consents to me being present in the room for the news. The doctor agrees and pulls up a stool to sit across from me while the nurse flushes lines and changes bags.

"His hemoglobin and red blood cells came back low, so we will administer blood products today. His kidney function is slightly better but still not where we want it to be. His creatinine is still very elevated, so we will be continuing his dialysis treatments via CRRT machine." The doctor pauses, and my hands begin to shake. This is the part where he tell us bad news, I can just feel it.

"Lastly, after getting his MRI results back, he had three strokes in the occipital part of his brain and is experiencing some swelling. Once we wake him up, we will be able to determine the extent of the damage, and as the swelling goes down we will have a more accurate picture of how he's been affected. We know that he's detoxing right now, which we are helping him with, and if we wake him up it will slow down his healing. We will keep him sedated and paralyzed until we feel comfortable that he won't rapidly decline. Please let me know if you have any questions."

The next ten minutes are spent with Alyssa asking questions

and the doctor rattling off responses that I can't even hear over the roaring of the blood in my ears.

Stroke.

Strokes.

Three.

Baby, what did you *do*?

The tears fall from my eyes unbidden, but I don't stop them or cover them. I just let myself grieve as the doctors explain he's still not in the safe zone. The next few days will be absolutely critical between the swelling of his brain and his acute kidney injury. I wonder if he feels his body detoxing or if they really have it under control for him. If the sedation is working enough that he doesn't realize what's happening, the extent of this damage, or if he will hate me for saving him.

I couldn't let you go.

But I also can't stay.

Please forgive me.

I move to the recliner, getting ready to go to sleep. I haven't been on my phone lately, I canceled all my shifts at the hospital, and I'm not on speaking terms with Brit. She just keeps hitting too close to home at the moment; I know she means well and she loves me, but I can't just abandon him.

I close my eyes and take deep breaths, count to ten, imagine sheep, butterflies, rainbows—all the things that will never be part of my life, until I fall into a deep slumber.

"I'm sorry I've been such a bad dad, and I hope you don't keep your kids from me in the future." Michael looks remorseful for once, and I don't know how to respond. I just look at my shoes and pick at my nails, hoping he's done, hoping he'll never talk about it again.

I clear my throat and look around, hoping my mom stays inside the house and hears him so I don't have to tell her eventually. As if reading my mind, Michael keeps talking.

"You can tell your mom, you know? I understand if you do. I won't be upset."

My blood runs hot and then cold and then freezes.

"I won't be." And for a brief moment, he really does look apologetic, guilty, and possibly remorseful, but then again, he has so many masks it's hard to tell which one is real and which is not.

But telling my mom?
Shouldn't she already know?
Wouldn't she see the connections?
Didn't she permit him by now?
She has to know that something is wrong.
She has to know what he has been doing all these nights for the past year.

Tainting me.
Smudging me.
Infecting me.
Ruining me.
Destroying me.

I shift in my sleep, hearing the nurse come in to turn off the noise from the IV pump, but once she leaves sleep welcomes me back again.

"Mommy, I need to talk to you ..."
"Okay, what is it?"
"It's about Michael. I know you won't like it, but I need to tell you something."
"I know you don't like him, but—"
"He raped me."
The silence is heavy, stifling, suffocating.
"Raped you? What did he do?"
"A lot. He made me, uh, suck his—"
"That's enough." She holds her hand up, seemingly done with me, but then she asks, "How many times?"

And I want to scream that it wasn't all he did. I want to scream that he did it so many times I lost count. I want to scream that he ruined my fucking life.

But I don't.
"Once?"

I don't know why I say it. I don't know why I protect him. I don't know why I am the way that I am.

What use is coming clean if I still have dirt on me?

I know what she'll say, though. I know I'm just a whore to her, she's said it many times. If I tell her how many times it's been, she won't hold it against him, she'll hold it against me.

So really, this isn't me protecting him, this is me protecting me.

The door interrupts our conversation and my mom runs to it, opening it wide and throwing punch after punch at Michael, all landing on his face. She keeps hitting and kicking and punching and pulling hair, until all we see is a heap of tangled limbs, and he still hasn't fought back.

"Babe, what's wrong? Why are you acting like this?" However, I don't miss the look he gives me from across the room, and when my mom glances back, she tells us all to go to our rooms.

The next day my mother gets us all in the car, Michael missing work for us to head into town to an unfamiliar place. We stop in front of what looks like a house, but upon closer inspection, it's a place of business for the occult.

We enter, a bell chiming above our heads, and a lady comes to greet us from the back of the shop. My mother tells her we need a reading about my past, and she retreats with the odd lady, whispering behind my back.

After shuffling, the lady sets some cards on the table, and my mom sits to the side, preoccupied with her hands. She places five cards on the table, but I'm spaced out, so I don't even hear her. I do understand she's explaining something to my mother, but I can't understand the point of this.

Why are we here?

Then clear as day, the lady says, "It never happened. Your husband didn't do that to her. Your house is haunted and she probably imagined it, or the ghosts made her see it."

My stomach drops.

The ghosts made me see what?

We exit the establishment, and my mom stops short before getting to the car. She turns to me and looks at my splotchy face and tear-stained cheeks, but her gaze has no sympathy. "At least you know it wasn't real. You imagined the whole thing. It's okay though, now we have our answers."

"I didn't imagine anything, Mom! It happened!"

"Liar. Don't fucking lie to my face."

I dip my chin in submission and walk away, opening the car door as well as the door to all my new insecurities and doubts.

She thinks I'm a liar, so I am.

She thinks I'm crazy, so I am.

She thinks I imagined it, so I did.

But how do you imagine an entire year of your life?

Did I imagine it?

Did I? Did I? Did I?

The nurse is nudging me, and when I look outside, it's still dark, and another nurse is waiting with her by the bed. "I'm so sorry to wake you, but I need to turn on the light and didn't want to startle you. We have to change his dressing for the permacath."

I see them put on a mask and then their sterile gloves, and I realize she's teaching the other nurse how to perform this skill. I watch in awe from a distance, but it makes me sad to think this will be me soon, learning how to do it all.

Not because I don't want to, but because my future no longer includes *him*. That's why I don't care about it anymore. I wish I could say I thought Zayne and I would be together forever, but that would be a lie.

I just wanted a little more time to sit in my *suffering*.

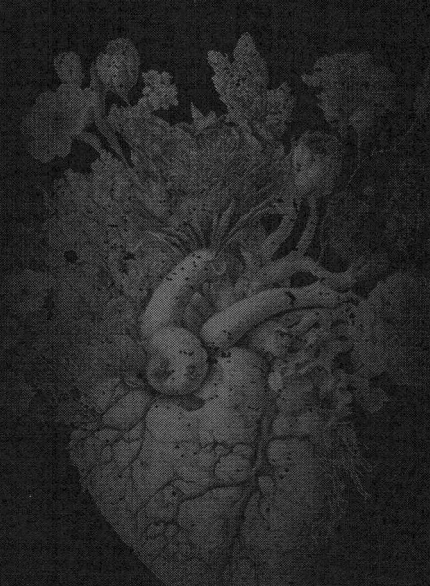

CHAPTER 46

HALLIE

It's been a few days since I came to visit, and instead, I have been staying holed up in my room with no desire to get out of bed. I'm not eating or showering, and honestly, I forgot to brush my teeth for a few days. It's not because I'm forcing myself to stop doing these things, it's because I don't even think of them anymore, so I just… don't do them.

However, today is a day where I'm forced to do it all, because Zayne is getting extubated. They finally believe he's well enough to try to pull back on some of the interventions, and I want to be there for that.

I get dressed in jeans and a sweatshirt because it's cold in the hospital, along with my favorite pair of gray Vans. I put my hair up into a bun and don't bother with makeup, not because I don't care, but because I'll probably cry it all off and look insane when this is done.

The drive to the hospital is peaceful despite my nerves, and

I play "I'll Look After You" by The Fray and remember the good times with Zayne; there were a lot of good times.

When I arrive at the hospital and go to his room, the nurse informs me that they have already been tapering the sedative and paralytic since the last shift, and he should be awake soon. Once he wakes, they will try to remove the tube and then see how he tolerates it.

A few hours later, Zayne does wake, clearly disoriented, as he looks around the room in a daze. Then, he makes contact with the tube and tries to pull it out. I stop him and call for the nurse on the call light.

She pages the doctor and sometime later, they are all in here, ready to take it out. Once they do, Zayne coughs a few times and clears his throat, but it sounds hoarse. He looks around, shaking his head, and he tries to speak and fails.

"Zayne, take some deep breaths. Everything is okay." He obliges, and the monitor goes from desaturation to 94% oxygenation about thirty seconds later.

"H—" The words are not coming out, his voice is so hoarse, though I can see his lips form my name. "I can't see you." It comes out as a harsh whisper, and tears begin to fall from his eyes, the deepest green I've ever witnessed.

The doctor quickly comes to his side and begins to shine a penlight in Zayne's eyes, telling him to look up and down and to the side. They tell him they will be doing more scans and running more tests on him, and they will figure out the extent of the damage as well as devise a rehabilitation plan. According to the nurse, the neurologist on board will be coming to see him later today, and I relax knowing that he will be able to give us more answers.

Everyone exits the room, and Zayne lets his head fall back onto the pillow with a soft thud. I look at him, *really* look at him, and see the circles under his eyes, his hair sticking to his face, and I know exactly how I'll be spending my time.

I gather all the supplies for a bed bath, having done my fair share of those, and he seems grateful when I'm done, sighing contentedly and smiling as he settles back in bed. I help him brush his teeth, help him eat his dinner since he can't see it, and even cut his nails for him.

When I'm done, he pats the bed, signaling for me to sit next to him. He makes some room, and I sit on the edge of his bed, but he weakly attempts to pull me in so I end up lying next to him.

"I love you," he struggles to say, and I'm sure his throat is very sore, which is contributing to his hoarseness. Nevertheless, this was an arrow to the heart. I should've known he would say this after all I had done for him in the past few hours, days, and weeks.

"I love you, too." My voice cracks, and I hate how pathetic I sound, but I know he needs to hear it too, needs to hear it before I walk away for good.

"Stay." He takes a deep breath and closes his eyes, one tear making its way out of the corner of his eye. He's so beautiful. "Don't leave me." His words are barely a whisper, yet it feels like he's screaming them at me.

I shake my head, then remember he can't see me. "I can't stay. We're too damaged. We only hurt each other."

He feels for me until his hand is on my face and pulls me in, giving me one soft kiss and hugging me to his chest. I'm trying not to get tangled in wires, and it's difficult when it's all that exists in this room, but I give him the best hug I can manage and hope I can survive with half my heart beating in my chest.

Zayne's shoulders shake with the intensity of his sobs, and my tears also begin to fall. I kiss him again, our tongues tangling as we hold each other's faces, never wanting to let go. I kiss the corner of his mouth, his cheeks, his eyes, his forehead. I tell him I'm sorry, I tell him I love him, I tell him I'll see him again.

But none of it eases the pain.

None of it makes me believe a word I say.

"I love you, Zayne. Maybe one day the stars will align for us, after all. Take care of yourself, please. Look for me when you're better, truly better. Look for me when you can choose me."

He closes his eyes and then opens them back up, and the last time I look at him is with tears in his forest green eyes, but this time shards of blue cut through, reserved just for me. I realize that maybe there's always blue in his eyes when he cries and I won't get to find out, which I will always regret.

"Don't leave me, Hallie, please, baby." His voice is stronger with his pleas, and it almost makes me falter.

I wish I could say I didn't leave.

But he doesn't understand that staying isn't in my DNA.

And leaving—

Leaving is who I am, that much I know.

Maybe it's self-preservation.

Maybe I'm just a fucking masochist.

The razor blade slices horizontally through the skin on both my wrists and I flinch from the pain when I put my arms under the hot water. The cuts are deep, and I see the tub quickly filling with red, knowing it's just a matter of time before I fade away but also knowing it would have been a quicker death had I done it vertically.

Is this a cry for help?

But who would even fucking listen?

No one, that's who.

Maybe I want it to be slow.

The door is unlocked, not that it matters right now because no one is home, and I don't expect them to be for quite some time.

I'm starting to feel heavy and cold, even though the running water should be hot. I try to move my arms and can't, but my eyelids open, thankfully, and now the entire tub is red.

I smile and close my eyes; I don't feel the pain anymore.

My breaths become shallow and all I hear over the water are my short gasps, too loud in my own ears. I want to turn them off, they're distracting me.

I'm finally getting what I want.

Peace.

Light.
Freedom.
I'm tired, and it feels like I'm beginning to fall asleep but then I hear—
Voices.
Banging.
Screaming.
Crying.
All from my brothers.
Someone grabs me.
I open my eyes and see my mom trying to get me out of the water, not one tear on her face. She really just doesn't care at all, I'm nothing to her.
The water is off.
"She's so fucking dramatic!"
It's over.
The only thing I've ever wanted . . .
They take it away.
Just like everything else.

The boxes are put together, and I start packing all my belongings, tossing shoes, shirts, and pants all into one box, as if my OCD won't make me take it all back out. Sometimes I enjoy testing my limits, even when they end with anxiety. I want to see how far I can take it and how much it controls me.

I know I only have so long before Zayne gets out of the hospital, so I have to act fast. I applied for a residency position three hours away and found an apartment, which Brit applied for after telling me she wanted to come with me. She insisted on paying rent for now, since her family would be the ones paying for it anyway. She also applied for the same hospital, which means we will be doing residency together.

I would love to say I'm excited, but quite honestly, I don't feel anything. Nothing at all. This is the hardest thing I've ever done, but I've been telling myself that I wanted something different for my life. I wanted healthy, I wanted strong, I wanted stability. Zayne can't give me any of that.

I remind myself to learn when to give up. I say this to myself often: if something isn't working, then learn to give up. Learn to walk away. You don't always have to stick it out.

Learn to give up.

Learn to choose yourself over anyone that isn't serving your best interests.

I never learn my lessons, though, so I know I won't follow my own advice.

Brit hands me the last of the items in my closet, and I tape the box closed. I look around and everything is empty, just the way I am. I fall to my bed and cry, my body shaking as I let the sobs take over, not caring at all that she sees me break this way. She's seen worse. This doesn't scare her. She's damaged, too. Nonetheless, I'm not damaged, not anymore. Now I'm just fucking shattered beyond repair.

Brit comes around the boxes and sits on the bed next to me, stroking my hair with tenderness as she shushes me. "It's okay to not be okay, Hallie. Let the darkness consume you, only then can you recognize the light." I cry harder, which I didn't know was possible, and bury my face in the mattress, refusing to breathe, feel, and be. "Remember: every struggle makes you stronger, and so far, you're the strongest person I know," Brittany says, rubbing my back. "I love you."

I don't reply, I don't say anything at all, but she doesn't take it personally. There's not really anything to say, I just let myself feel. I am often in the depths of my misery, but nothing has ever compared to this moment. No pain has ever matched the gaping hole I have in my chest, and as it stands, I don't think anything ever will. But we gather everything we own, including our courage, and leave everything and everyone else behind.

The same way they've always done to *me*.

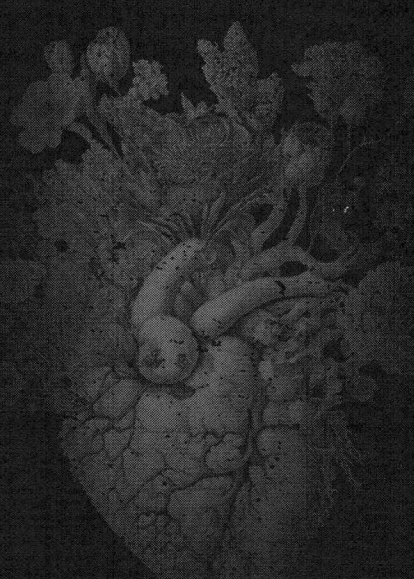

CHAPTER 47

ZAYNE

For two months, I've been trying to reach Hallie, and for two months, she has rejected my calls. I'm not sure if she listens to my voicemails or reads my text messages, but I fucking miss her. I can't sleep, I can't eat, I can barely even breathe. I crave her as much as I crave meth in my veins, and I can't have either of them.

I spent one month rehabilitating for my strokes after my ICU stay, and then I spent one month rehabilitating for meth after that. I've been doing everything I can to stay off drugs, and my mother has been supportive of it. Although she's not stupid, she knows I can only be strong for so long, especially with school starting right around the corner. She recognizes that if something is wrong with my life, I'll fall back in the trap, and everything is wrong with my life right now. I can't blame her for being scared, I can't even blame her for her lack of trust in me, but I'm trying.

Fuck, I'm trying.

I know I have to want it for myself, and I want to say I do, but Hallie is the priority. I want to be sober for her, not for me. I want to be the man she needs. I'd do anything to get her back.

Anything.

She's the only person on this planet who truly knows me and still accepts me.

It's why I went to rehab, and it's why I've been working on recovering from my strokes. Even my vision is improving, having come back gradually over the last few months. I still can't see perfectly, but I can see, which is a relief and more than I can ask for after doing what I did. I still can't deny though, that it was the scariest moment of my life, even more than death, waking up blind, knowing I might never be able to see her face again.

The most beautiful sight in the world.

My mother is driving me to Hallie's apartment since I convinced her I needed to apologize in person and tell her I love her. She agreed under the condition that I accept Hallie's decision, whatever it may be, and of course I told her yes. Only I didn't mean it, not one fucking bit.

I'd rather die than not be with her.

Clearly.

My mother drops me off by the door and then goes to park to wait for me, expecting this to take a while. I knock on the door, bracing myself, taking deep breaths and thinking of everything I rehearsed in the car. All the different ways I'm sorry, all the reasons I love her, all the promises to change.

I didn't, however, expect to be greeted by a stranger.

"Is Hallie home?" I ask the girl, trying to look around her to peek into the apartment. I'll be damned if she's going to hide from me.

"Hallie? There's no Hallie here, love. I live here now."

My chest tightens, my ears ring, and I can't fucking breathe at all. I drop to my knees, hands getting cut by the rocks and something that looks like crushed glass under me. I don't feel it though, the only pain I feel is in my heart.

My mom must have been paying attention, and I see her getting out of the car and walking my way. The girl at the door looks scared, but then offers to help me stand. I decline. After a minute I stand up slowly, brushing off the dirt from my hands, careful to pick out the glass that is stuck under my skin instead of pushing it in further.

"She doesn't live here anymore, Mom. Where the fuck could she be?" I ask, turning to face her, the blue of her eyes looking almost transparent in the sunlight.

"Oh baby, let's go back to the car…" She looks between me and the car, as if hoping I'd teleport to it or something.

"I don't want to go to the fucking car! I want to know where she is!" I can feel myself beginning to hyperventilate, and my mom starts rubbing my back, but I brush her off.

"Let's go home and figure this out," my mom whisper-shouts, and I'm sure she's embarrassed I'm causing a scene. Nothing new there.

She grabs my hand and steers me back to the passenger side door while I cry again, and a look of pity crosses her features; but instead of making me mad like it would have a few months ago, I feel grateful that she even gives a damn about me.

She might be the only one at this point.

Somehow I know I won't be finding out where Hallie is, not if she doesn't want me to, and that makes me so fucking angry, I can't help the scream trying to make its way up my throat.

I get in the car, slamming the door as hard as I can, then bury my face in my hands and let all the rage out, the scream only muffled slightly by my palms over my mouth. I cry and shake and scream until my voice is hoarse, and my mother just calmly sits next to me, probably checking the weather on her phone. It's disturbing how normal my mental breakdowns seem to her now, and I suddenly regret my moment of weakness.

"Let's go home, Mom. I need to make some calls." And just like that, she pulls out of the parking lot and heads home, not once looking in my direction. Not that she'd see me anyway. Not really.

The only one who's ever seen me is Hallie.

My days and nights all bleed into one, and I spend most of my time in my bed surrounded by the darkness. I have no intentions of getting up, no plans to get through it. The pain is overwhelming, my chest feels like someone tore through it to rip my heart out, and I just want to forget.

Forget she ever existed.

Forget she doesn't want me.

Forget I don't matter.

Unfortunately, my mother doesn't make that easy for me; she comes in every day to check in on me and force me out of my room for a predetermined amount of time. If I don't do it, she threatens to admit me.

I get out of my bed and go to the bathroom, taking a shower with the hottest water my skin can manage without burning off. I'm sore from lying in bed all day, every day, and I still can't get Hallie out of my mind. I refuse to go back to the monster, though. I know it will be hard to stay clean, but I have to find her. I have to get Hallie back.

I pack my bags and head up the basement stairs, taking them two at a time in a rush to leave my house. My mother intercepts me, but I brush past her and run to my car, slamming the door and locking them before I put my seatbelt on. She comes to scream at my window and hits it, but I reverse out of the driveway and leave.

I know where she is.

I know *exactly* where she is.

And nothing will stop me from getting back to her.

CHAPTER 48

HALLIE

The day is dark and gloomy, the storm clouds gathering in the sky, ready to pour out their fury in the form of precipitation. It's perfect for me; the day matches my mood and makes me think of him all over again. Must be fucking nice to have an outlet, to be able to let all those *feelings* out.

I curse at the sky as I get ready for work, the only respite in my shitty life. Who knew I would crave work so I don't have to think about everything else happening to me?

Ever since I left him, there's no brightness left in my world. I don't even feel hunger anymore. I don't feel happiness. I don't feel fear. Instead, I feel nothing except sadness and anger. If I'm being honest, I can't decide if it's too much or not enough. I want to drown in the nothingness. At the same time, I want the searing pain to stop my breath. I just want everything to stop.

I put on my compression socks and then slip on my scrubs,

the material rubbing against the fresh cuts on the inside of my thighs, the only pain I want to feel at this point.

The universe keeps trying to beat me into submission, but I won't let it; I know I'm fucking resilient. I know I'll turn it all off again, eventually, it's just a matter of time. Feeling doesn't come easy for me, and I know that, but you know what does? Dissociation, and I know I'll get back to that ultimately.

The sexual abuse, my relationship with my family, foster care, and even Zayne have taught me some meaningful lessons. You can go through hardships in life, and you can get beat down, but you can also get back up.

I'll fucking crawl if I have to, but I know I'm going to make it. I'm still in control.

Even through the ten pounds I've lost, the bags under my eyes, and my oversleeping, I refuse to show it to the world. I refuse to show my pain. No one around me understands why I'm not myself anymore, and I know that it's because no one has lived through what I have. Sometimes the trauma is too much, and sometimes life takes things and doesn't give them back. Every time I leave Zayne behind he keeps a part of me with him, and all my parts are starting to run out. I come and go, and I leave my hopes, my dreams, my very breaths in his grasp, and he holds on tightly to all of it.

I'm sorry I've neglected myself.

But this time of my life has been the most I've ever *felt*.

As I think of all the ways I've fucked up my life and everything I'll do to fix it, I finish getting ready for work and drive to the hospital. My residency finally started, and I'm sitting in a classroom for eight hours a few times per week to do pointless tasks that make me feel like I'm back in school again, but I endure it because this is good for me, and I need to keep a tight grip on the few things that are.

All the residents sit at the round tables, watching a PowerPoint presentation shared on a projector. We are discussing strokes—of course—which immediately makes me think of Zayne. The acronym FAST is mentioned repeatedly: facial drooping, arm weakness, speech difficulty, and time.

The professor announces that we have an assignment due in a few hours and we need to partner up. The guy sitting next to me turns my way, flashing me a white smile that makes my insides just a tad bit warmer. His blond hair is short, catching the lights of the projector, and I notice it somehow still manages to be curly at the top. His blue eyes crinkle at the corners of his smile, and I can't help but to just smile back.

"I'm Damien Carlisle," he whispers, and his eyes dance over my face as I keep my smile in place. "Do you want to be my partner for today's assignment?"

"Hallie Cox. Sure, but you're pulling the weight today."

He chuckles and shakes his head. "Only this once."

The rest of the day goes by in a blur, between smiles and chuckles and blond curls catching the lights. His smell is stuck in my nostrils as I make my way out of the education room; coconut and sea salt, and I love the way I can't shake it off.

Maybe this is what I need, to press the reset button.

My very own version of a clean slate.

"We should hang out some time," he says as he slowly looks at me with approval in his eyes. "Let me see your phone."

I hand it over, not caring about how easily I've given in. I want to move on. I need to, and he's the perfect escape from Zayne. Damien puts his number in my phone, and I text him immediately telling him it's me after leaving the conference room, only he doesn't reply yet.

I walk alone toward the parking lot, my steps not as heavy as they were this morning, and for the first time in a very long time, I feel something akin to hope blossom in my chest. Surely I can forget *him*, erase him, pretend he never existed.

My car is still a few rows away in the very full parking lot, and my visibility is already affected due to my height, or lack thereof, so I pull my keys out and begin to press my lock button to locate my car by the beeping. I hear the sound getting closer, and I walk faster, watching my feet so I don't step in puddles from the rain that's been falling all day. It looks like the clouds are finally clearing up, and I think of how badly I want to see the colors of the sunset bleed all over the sky again. Will I be able to appreciate it now? Will the colors still look dull? Will I still be indifferent?

I look up from the gravel road and come to an abrupt halt a few feet away from my vehicle. There, sitting on the hood of my car, is Zayne. He smiles at me softly, clutching his leather jacket with both hands. His onyx hair is wet from the rain and his eyes are the deepest green I've ever seen.

Conflicting thoughts race through my mind, and my heart squeezes in my chest, struggling to beat regularly as I falter. How did he get here? Does he want me? Why did he come? *Why didn't he come sooner?*

"I choose you."

I breathe in deeply, filling my lungs until it's impossible to fill them anymore. I fight the tears, but they fall from my eyes as I shake my head, trying to clear them. He's not supposed to be here. I ran away, I left him behind.

I left you.

But even as I remember all our faults, all our lies, all our weaknesses…even as I see our demise in slow motion, I stop in front of him and grab his face in my hands, kissing him in a way I never have before, with tenderness and *love*, and I can't help the thought that crosses my mind:

Home is not a place but a person.

And it's always been him.

And it always will be.

I'm home now.

WHAT'S NEXT?

Thank you from the bottom of my heart for reading Shattered Hearts! Please don't forget to review if you enjoyed the book. Reviews are so important to indie authors like me. I am forever grateful for your support!

If you'd like to be part of the community and talk about the series, join the Facebook Group, Ruby's Darklings.

Book 2 of The Broken Series, *Battered Souls*, is expected to release in December 2022. Dive back in for some more Hallie and Zayne, along with a third main character. After this, you can expect Book 3, *Tattered Bodies*, to release in the spring of 2023.

Stalk me:
My website is authorshaeruby.com
Sign up for my newsletter at authorshaeruby.com/newsletter
Follow me on Facebook at Facebook.com/authorshaeruby
Join my Reader Group at Facebook.com/groups/rubysdarkling

AFTERWORD

As someone who has struggled with mental illness since my teenage years, this book was hard to write. However, the story needed to be told. I wanted to shed some light on the realities of living with mental illness, as well as being around other people who also have it. I hope I did it justice, as I used a lot of my personal experiences with Bipolar 1 Disorder, anxiety, sexual abuse, and PTSD to bring the characters to life. My hope is to bring awareness and help even if it's just one person to seek help. When you're feeling hopeless, like you can't do this anymore, and you want to give up, remember that you *can* do this. There's no shame in seeking help, the suicide hotline is there for when you need it. Don't write the period to your sentence, write a semicolon instead. You *do* matter, and I believe in you so much.

So much love for you,
Shae Ruby

ACKNOWLEDGMENTS

Shattered Hearts has been a difficult journey full of ups and downs, a manic episode, and a depressive one too. It was also simultaneously the easiest thing I've ever done. Writing this story felt so personal to me and bringing to life damaged characters that are so near and dear to my heart further solidified the need to bring awareness to these topics. I know it's hard to talk about it, but it needed to be said. This story is not for everyone, and if you can't relate to Hallie and Zayne, then I'm so happy for you. But for those of you who can relate, just know that I see you, I'm right there with you. Writing this book could have been a lonely journey, but I surrounded myself with the best, most supportive people. Even then, it was frustrating and draining.

To my readers, thank you for being here and reading a little piece of my heart and soul. I poured so much into this story, and I really hope you can see that. This is all for you. To my husband, Conner, even from thousands of miles away you still found a way to support me. Thank you from the bottom of my heart for always believing in me. I love you. To my mother, thank you for being part of this journey and supporting me. It means more than you will ever know. I love you.

To my best friends, Michayla, Kim, Aliveah. Thank you for being here when I needed you. The amount of meltdowns, crying, happiness, complaining, and frustration that you put up with is out of this world, and all my gratitude goes out to you all on a silver platter. I love you so much.

To my amazing alpha and beta readers Michayla, Sarah, Kim, Carissa, Aliveah, Brooke, and Lori. I literally couldn't have done it without all your help. You went above and beyond, and I appreciate every single one of you for taking the time to hop on this journey with me. I love all of you, thank you so much again, and

Taylor from Taylored Text LLC, for the work she put into it. Thank you for loving the story and being a friend through it all.

To the editor of this edition, Angie from Lunar Rose Editing Services, thank you so much for all your hard work with re-editing this book. I know it was a lot, and I appreciate you more than you know for fitting me in at such last minute. You're amazing!

Quirky Circe, your talent always blows me away! I am absolutely in love with the covers for this series! I can't believe that I get to work with you! Thank you so much for everything you do.

Hype Girls PA Services, I can't thank you enough for how you have set me up for success. Without you, none of this would've been possible. People are discovering this book thanks to you and your hard work, and I am forever grateful. Riley, you're the best! I can't thank you enough for your help! You're amazing and I love you!

Lastly, I want to thank a very important part of this journey: my Instagram and TikTok community. Your support means more than you know!

XOXO,
Shae Ruby

Printed in Great Britain
by Amazon